Dedication

To Joan,
*for your humor, love,
companionship, and your
creative spirit;
I'm glad you're my daughter.
To my mother,
whose listening ear has brought a
balm to my soul and clarity to my
thoughts.
To abused women everywhere,
may God give you courage and strength
to use the pain, devastation and terror
you suffer,
to point you toward a path
and a home where there is safety
and peace.*

Acknowledgements

Many people have had a hand in the writing of this book. Without their gracious help this story would never have been written. To begin with, Professors David Hamilton and Pat Stevens encouraged me to write and assured me I had talent. Professor Susan Kratz helped me get the story started and off the ground. The staff at the Domestic Violence Intervention Program in Iowa City, especially Sue Sass and Alda, spent hours helping me understand how abusers use various tactics to control their partners, the effects of that control, and that it is all part of "Domestic Violence." Larry, (I omitted the last names of Larry and Alda for their protection) my co-facilitator at the Batterer's Education Program, provided on-the-job training in using the Duluth curriculum, and Julie Schultz and Lori Traeger were wonderful in their advice about the difficult cases. In the process, all three added to my understanding of domestic violence and what it takes to motivate men to reconsider their behavior choices. Caring Mennonite pastors in the Kalona area, Jay Miiller (yes, double-i is the correct spelling), Elmer Miller, and John King, provided supportive counseling to a handful of hurting wives and grappled for ways to hold abusive husbands accountable and to influence them to stop abusing and controlling their wives. Daring men and women wrote and published books about domestic violence and control tactics (page 247) when society still blamed abused women and asked, "Why doesn't she leave?"

My sisters, Judy Halteman and Jean Zook, my sister-in-law, Sharon Helmuth, and my mother, Martha Helmuth, listened to me talk ad nauseam about the pain and damage that has been forced on wives and children in the name of husband headship and submission. At times they agreed and at other times debated with me, thereby encouraging me to question, rethink, and clarify my conclusions.

Dale Helmuth, my brother, supplied how-to details that are specific to the setting of this story, which is the farm where we grew up. Paul and Curtis Helmuth and Jacob and Esther Yoder, provided farming information and history specific to this area and this farm. Dick Snakenburg got down to the nitty-gritty details of crop and hog farming operations and the amount of land and finances needed to succeed. He discussed with me what to call the all-in-one hog building/corn-crib/granary. In a day of specialized feeder-pig and finishing sheds, readers may not know what "hog stable"—the term we'd used for that building as I was growing up—meant. My brother, Dale, reminded me the Pennsylvania Dutch term the Amish and Mennonites in this area used for that type of building was "saa shtall", which translates literally to "sows' stall," or to "hog stable" in the general sense. I chose to keep the term we grew up with, since it is commonly used in the Kalona area. Joe Stoddard and Brad Miller graciously helped me understand enough about the woes, repairs, and bodywork of tractors to be able to weave them into a story. My mother, Martha Helmuth, (who deserves to be credited more than twice) answered questions on a variety of topics about our farm, farm living, and the community. Blanche Miller added quilting details I had forgotten. My sister, Jewel Zook, in spite of her heavy responsibilities in home-schooling and caring for her husband and eight children, took the time to discuss quilting and what on earth to call the covered-bridge-like alleyway that is a unique feature of our haymow, which our grandpa, John I. Helmuth, designed and built. Larry Zook, my brother-in-law, supplied a description of a tree remover at work that was so specific I could visualize it. Dean, (sorry, I didn't get his last name) at the Hills Bank, explained the requirements and process for securing a farm loan.

Margaret Horn, with whom I met regularly to read and critique our writing, (check out her novel, *You Know I Don't Love You*) encouraged me, gave me the incentive to keep writing, and helped me round out my story. Steve Warner, Darcy Thomas, Julia Kramer, Ruth Schlabach, and my daughter, Joan Delight Gordon, read and critiqued the story to make it fit for you, the reader.

To all these and to those I didn't mention by name, to my family and friends who encouraged and supported me in this endeavor, who urged me on, asking if the book was published yet, to you the reader, who do me the honor of reading this work, and to God, the great "I Am," who made the writing of this novel possible and brought it together, I offer my deepest gratitude.

Be ye therefore followers of God as dear children:
And walk in love, as Christ also hath loved us, and hath given
himself for us an offering and a sacrifice to God for a
sweetsmelling savour...
Submitting yourselves one to another in the fear of
God.
Wives, submit yourselves unto your own husbands, as
unto the Lord. For the husband is the head of the wife, even as
Christ is the head of the church: and he is the saviour of the
body. Therefore as the church is subject unto Christ, so let the
wives be to their own husbands in everything.
Husbands, love your wives, even as Christ also loved
the church, and gave himself for it; that he might sanctify and
cleanse it with the washing of water by the word. That he might
present it to himself a glorious church, not having spot or
wrinkle, or any such thing; but that it should be holy and
without blemish. So ought men to love their wives as their own
bodies. He that loveth his wife loveth himself. For no man ever
yet hated his own flesh; but nourisheth and cherisheth it, even
as the Lord the church: For we are members of his body, of his
flesh, and of his bones. For this cause shall a man leave his
father and mother, and shall be joined unto his wife, and they
two shall be one flesh.
This is a great mystery: but I speak concerning Christ
and the church. Nevertheless let every one of you in particular
so love his wife even as himself; and the wife see that she
reverence her husband.

-Ephesians 5, verses 1-2 and 21-33

Chapter 1

The windshield wipers swayed to and fro, whisking away huge, downy-soft flakes of snow before they melted. Cocooned in her snow-covered car, Yvette Miller forged a path through the trackless sea of pristine white, scarcely hearing the muted purr of the engine as she focused on discerning where the sides of the road ended and the ditches began. She loved the muffled stillness, the sense of being insulated in a sheltering curtain of fluffy white flakes.

She turned onto Stringtown Road, where the snowplow had passed both ways. As she braked at Stringtown Grocery, her car slid past three cars parked at odd angles. She parked between a car and the lone horse and buggy.

Inside, she waited for her eyes to adjust. *They should light the lanterns. I can barely see.* She turned toward the first aisle, but three people crowded in the baking supplies section, so she surveyed the homemade pies, angel food cakes, cinnamon rolls, and cookies at the end of the row while she waited for them to move on. She gazed at the pies. *If I could buy one pie, just this once.*

"Come on, Evelyn," a man's low impatient voice came from halfway down the second aisle. "It's time to go; we don't need that stuff."

Yvette looked up. The middle-aged man took a bag of something white from the woman and put it on the shelf. She didn't know them, and if the woman's low cut shirt was anything to go by, they weren't Mennonite.

"Yes, we do," the woman grabbed the bag off the shelf. "What's the rush? Our appointment isn't until nine-thirty. I don't want to twiddle my thumbs for half an hour. Why don't you go in the cooler and get some cheese?"

"No! We have to go *now*. You can shop for groceries tomorrow."

"Stop it, Bob!" she hissed. "Sit in the car if you can't be civil."

"We'll be late for..." his words faded as they moved down the aisle.

The man's voice reminded Yvette of her husband's. Guiltily, she turned her back on the pies and considered the jars of homemade strawberry, blueberry, and peach jam in the next row.

"...not very nice to his wife." It was the faintest of whispers from just around the corner, but she could hear the words distinctly.

"If she'd respect his wishes," a louder voice whispered back, "he wouldn't talk to her that way. She brought it on herself and embarrassed herself in front of..." the voice faded as Yvette escaped back to the first row.

What if you honor your husband's wishes and he gripes anyway? And what if he chews you out for buying instead of baking the pie he wants?

She picked up a pie to check the price in the dim lighting, remembering the first—and last—time she'd bought an apple pie fifteen years ago. Luke, her husband, had refused to eat it, saying she obviously didn't think he was worth her time and effort to bake his favorite foods with her own hands.

"Don't be ridiculous," she had retorted. "I earned the money and then bought the pie for you. Doesn't that prove I think you're worth it?"

He had raged at her then, storming about the house, kicking chairs, slamming doors, and knocking a vase of red carnations onto the floor while he accused her of wasting his money and forcing him to eat *store-bought* apple pie.

She'd been shocked at his display of temper. Her father hadn't resorted to rages, and nothing in their dating days had hinted Luke was prone to such behavior. Exhausted and eight months pregnant with their firstborn, she'd told him she'd bake the next pie. When that hadn't soothed him, she'd done her best to evaporate into her chair. But that hadn't calmed him, either.

"No," she whispered, "I won't give him an excuse to throw a temper tantrum. I'll find another way to cut corners. Oh, God, please help me."

"May I help you?" a cultured voice from behind her inquired.

Startled, Yvette glanced over her shoulder. "Delores!" she spun around and shook her friend's arm, laughing, and making Delores's large hoop earrings sway. "You had me confused for a second. At least you didn't fake a Dutch accent so you'd sound like a store clerk. I'd have been *really* bewildered."

"Next time I'll ask in Pennsylvania Dutch," Delores grinned, her blue eyes dancing, "I used to speak it with my grandma all the time."

"Mom and I speak it, too, if we don't want the children to understand and Luke isn't around. He gets offended if I talk Dutch in front of him. Says it's rude to use a *mangled dialect* in front of people who don't understand it."

"He has a way with words," Delores turned toward the pie display. "I better get home so Steve can take a break. Are you going to buy a pie?"

"No, I'll bake several; we're almost out. I can mix pie dough and prepare the apples and filling while my Valentine cookie dough is chilling."

"Luke still expects dessert with every meal but breakfast? I don't know how you do it. Tell Luke you have to stop burning the candle at both ends. You look tired. Let me buy you a pie so you can sleep."

"Thanks, Delores," embarrassed, Yvette looked away and watched a mother and her two girls, all in veilings and long dresses, leave the store. "I wish I could, but Luke never has liked other women's pies." On the spur of the moment she couldn't think of a more understated, yet plausible reason.

Delores frowned and ran a hand through her short blonde hair. "When Steve took me out for our anniversary, we saw Luke and his friend eating lobster. Luke had an apple turnover for dessert. Isn't apple pie the same thing?"

Yvette evaded the issue. "Alex must have taken Luke out. They go out several times a month except when Alex's tax season is in full swing."

"Luke must have taken Alex out this time; Luke paid for it."

"Yeah," Yvette shrugged, trying to appear unconcerned so Delores wouldn't guess Luke's spending bothered her, "they like to treat each other."

"So give yourself a break; let me treat you."

Yvette stepped forward to get a cart and avoid her friend's gaze. If only she could accept without provoking Luke. Could she transfer it to her own pie pans? No, her pans were too big; he'd see the pie didn't fit the pan. But refusing her friend's offer seemed rude. "Could I take a rain check?"

"Of course. How about homemade chocolate chip cookies? Or does Luke object to buying cookies, too? If you put them in the cookie jar, he won't see anything unusual. I'll put them in your car so you can claim innocence."

"Thanks, Delores," Yvette wiped away a tear.

"You're welcome. Could I—could I say something as a friend?"

"Sure," Yvette watched her select three packages of cookies.

"Forgive me if I'm speaking out of turn," Delores lowered her voice and put the packages in her basket. "No Bible passages talk only of the wife's part. What would Ephesians Five mean *without* those three submission verses?"

Yvette thought for a minute. "It would sound like the husband is to love his wife so much he'll sacrifice his own desires for her sake."

"Exactly. What if it meant the husband should get what he wants?"

"There wouldn't be verses about husbands loving self-sacrificially." Her eyes widened. "Wow! Luke acts like those verses don't exist! He's *way* off, isn't he? Oops," she clapped a hand over her mouth, "I shouldn't malign my husband like that."

"Why not?" Delores met her friend's eyes. "You aren't gossiping or slandering. We're discussing what is true and right. Keeping silent would only hide the truth and allow wrong—even evil—to have its way."

"Please, don't tell anyone about this." Yvette's brow furrowed as she chewed a fingernail. "Luke would be so embarrassed and blame me."

"Of course I won't. It's up to you to decide when you're ready to talk about it. But if I figured it out, it's possible others can, too."

"I know. And thanks for the insight on submission. I'll study that passage more. Maybe that's exactly what I need to motivate Luke to cherish me. It feels wrong when Luke demands his way, but he says *God* decreed the husband is to be in charge and he's obeying what God says."

Delores shook her head. "You've been doing your part in submitting *and* his part in self-sacrificing. No wonder you're worn out; God never intended you to carry a double load. Your body is the *temple of the Holy Spirit*, and you're supposed to take care of *your* body, too."

After Delores had gone, Yvette started down the first row. She selected clear plastic bags of whole wheat flour and brown rice flour, placed them in her cart and read the labels on the shelves one more time to make sure she hadn't forgotten anything. Doughnut mix, cake mix, gluten. Gluten! What an inspired idea for Valentine's Day! If she baked bread maybe *that* would inspire Luke to cherish her. Hadn't he complained last week she never baked bread anymore? Maybe Valentine's Day would be special if the aroma of fresh-baked bread greeted him as he walked in the door. She'd serve sloppy Joes on homemade bread for supper, and wouldn't decorate with valentines, since he didn't like them. *"Oh, thank-you God for answering my prayer for help!"*

Excited about her plans, she strolled down the aisle with a light step and imagined what the day would be like. When Luke came in with a bouquet of red roses he'd exclaim about the aroma of homemade bread and apple pie, and he'd sit down to chat with her and the children. She'd slice warm bread and serve it with thawed strawberry jam. Luke would ask about their day and they'd laugh and talk with him because they sensed he had changed.

She stopped to put pint tubs of spaghetti sauce mix and sloppy Joe mix in her cart, and moved up the next aisle. Surely, if she got it right this time, her dream would come true. If she created a fulfilling Valentine's Day with Luke and the children, she'd have clues how to develop a loving, close-knit family.

Then she remembered Delores's point and stopped by the homemade noodles. Had she been *too* submissive? If she yielded less would Luke cherish her more? She frowned. According to Luke, she wasn't submissive enough. He'd told her over and over if she'd just do what he said, life wouldn't be so frustrating. Baffled, she shrugged and pushed her cart to the checkout.

Chapter 2

"**H**ow come the dishes aren't washed?" Luke pulled on the dark brown towel, turning it on its roller until he found a dry spot. Picking up a comb from the corner shelf above the rectangular cast iron sink, he looked into the mirror and saw his glower had drawn his dark bushy eyebrows together in the center, making one solid black brow. He studied his irritated expression, noting how his brows shadowed his eyes and made them look mean. Below his mustache, his full lips were pressed in a tight, thin line. *Good,* he ran the comb through his short, wavy, dark brown hair, *she'll see I'm a man to be reckoned with.*

He replaced the comb and strode into the kitchen. "Aren't you going to answer? I *said* how come the dishes aren't washed?" he stopped to survey the dishes stacked beside the sink, the cookie cutter and flour on the pastry board, and a dozen heart-shaped cookies on waxed paper.

"Don't start this again," Yvette hurried to the microwave, took a soup plate of chili out, and set it on the table, her dark brown pony-tail bobbing with every move. "Can't we be free of your griping for *one* day? Be reasonable. I want to finish baking before chore time."

"And *I* hate seeing a mess while I eat," he sat at the table. "You have *no* respect for me in my *own* house."

"Shall I move them to *your* floor? I know!" she brightened her eyes, feigning excitement at having found the perfect solution. "*You* can wash *your* dishes before you eat. I'll fill *your* sink for you," she turned on the faucet.

"Don't be an idiot; I have to fix the tractor. Get me a spoon. I can't eat without a spoon."

She rushed to get him a glass of filtered water, a soup spoon and saltine crackers, then turned off the spigot.

"I wish you'd honor my wishes instead of making a big deal of Valentine's Day," he crushed a handful of crackers between his palms and dropped them into his bowl. "You're supposed to bake pie; there's only one piece left.

13

Jesus said, 'If you love me keep My commandments,'" he stirred the crackers into his soup. "Obviously, you're lacking in love."

"I don't refuse your requests," she rolled out a ball of cookie dough. "In fact, I'm scrambling to bake bread and pie as you requested. On top of that, I milked the cows at five this morning, just as you expected, made breakfast, got the children off to school, made the beds, and put the clutter away before I started baking. And tonight I'll chore again. All day I'll expend energy to do as you've requested. If the chores are to be my first priority and meals with pie my second, the dishes will have to wait."

"It doesn't take all day to make a pie," he hated how lame that sounded, so he sampled her delicious chili to appear the victor. "What is this!" he yelped. "You didn't put chili powder in it. This is *beanless beef soup*, not chili."

"It has chili in it." Appearing unruffled, she put down her rolling pin and got chili powder for him. "The children don't like hot spices."

"They'd like it if you'd make it right," he sprinkled chili powder on his soup until it was coated. "Aren't you going to eat?" he frowned.

"I want to cut these before the bread dough rises. There goes the timer." He watched as she silenced the buzzer, took a sheet of cookies from the oven, and scooped up and transferred each heart-shaped cookie to the table.

"If you hadn't baked those sugar cookies you'd have plenty of time for washing dishes," he stirred his chili, suspecting he'd made it too spicy.

"The cookies are for the children," she peeled an unbaked valentine cookie from waxed paper and moved it onto the cookie sheet. "I enjoy doing things for them and sharing a special treat with them. Why don't you try it? They're important, too. Anyway, I don't expect you to keep your shop in perfect order; I think you could be as gracious to me."

"That's different. The shop is a workroom, not a commons area."

"The kitchen is a workroom, too. Stop demanding the impossible."

"It's not impossible. All I ask is a clean kitchen and decent food."

"If that's *all* you want, I assume you'll chore tonight?"

He glanced up in time to see her suck in her cheeks to stop her grin, but she couldn't erase the sparkle from her eyes. *Won't she ever cut the comedy routine?* "Of course not," he shoveled a bite into his mouth and blinked rapidly to make his eyes stop watering until he could wash it down.

"Then you expect much more than a clean kitchen and decent food. You expect the perfect superwoman. Well, I'm not; get used to it." She went into the washroom. Apparently she hadn't noticed his watering eyes.

"Where are you going?" he asked, then gulped half his glass of water.

"To get the eggs," she thrust her arms into the sleeves of her jacket.

"Come on, Yvette. You can do that after I go back out to work."

She didn't reply and went out the door into the entrance that also led to the cellar. Sighing, he sat back and listened to her boots tapping as she went down the cement basement steps to get an egg bucket. Suddenly aware of heat and an aroma coming from the oven, he opened the door to check. Two apple pies with fancy swirls cut in their upper crusts bubbled on the top rack. *So she did bake pie and I've been an idiot again. Well, it's not my fault. She could have told me.* When he heard her footsteps cresting the stairs, he tried again.

"Yvette," he called, "I'll stop griping. You can come back now." He heard the outer door squeak. "What about the pies?" he yelled. The door banged shut. "Me and my big mouth. Now I have to eat alone and hope she'll remember the pies. At least this way I can add milk or Yvette's decent chili to my bowl instead of enduring this spicy stuff."

~   ~   ~

Straightening his aching shoulders in the shop that afternoon, Luke stopped to check his watch. Three o'clock. The shop was chilly since he hadn't replenished the wood in the old pot-bellied stove. He'd break early and go to Kalona to pick up roses for his wife. Wishing he'd never have to repair a tractor again, he wiped his tools and put them in their drawers in his red tool chest. He detested fixing tractors even though he'd become proficient at it in his dad's mechanic shop. He wanted to *drive* tractors, not fix them. But his father-in-law had taught him he'd have fewer break downs during the busy seasons if he maintained his machinery in the slack winter months. Besides, if he wanted to buy a five-hundred-acre spread some day, he had to make sacrifices and repair his machinery rather than replace it with expensive newer models. This year he had decided to overhaul his aging 830 Case tractor, the machine he used for mid-sized jobs like hauling manure and bringing in hay.

Finished with the tools, he exited the shop as a black, horse-drawn buggy clopped and rumbled past on the black-top road. Although he couldn't see which of his Amish neighbors was peeking out the tiny window, he paused to wave, then closed the shop door and strode toward the milk house to wash up.

He wondered if Amish men bought flowers for their wives. With their drab black trousers and suspenders and their scruffy beards, they'd look absurd carrying flowers to their buggies, he decided. *At least I buy my wife flowers once a year, although what she wants with a silly bunch of flowers is beyond me. But Grandpa told me it's very important if I want a happy wife.*

As he smeared degreaser on his arms, he remembered Valentine's Day seventeen years ago. He had given Yvette a dozen white roses before they went to a gospel concert in Cedar Rapids. On the way home, he parked overlooking the Iowa River, and they gazed at the moon and it's reflection on the water. He hadn't planned to propose, but he'd felt so close to her at that moment it felt right. Back at her house, their house now, she'd served him apple pie topped with homemade vanilla ice cream. Bringing himself back to the present, he rinsed the goop off with the spray nozzle and wiped his arms on his denim pants so he wouldn't get chilled in the forty-degree weather.

When he returned from town with a dozen red roses, he entered by the front door, and stepped into the blue-painted dining room. He paused to savor the plush light-blue carpet he'd insisted on. The blue-flowered tablecloth, which matched the curtains Yvette had sewn, was free of clutter just as he liked it, and so were the built-in china hutch and work counter which ran the length of the wall on opposite sides of the room. He heard voices in the kitchen and as he headed that direction, he caught a whiff of homemade bread. Holding the roses behind his back, he peered around the refrigerator to watch his family.

His three children munched on milk and cookies at the green, built-in table. At the stove, his wife stirred food in the frying pan, the swell of her trim hips, contrasted by her tiny waist, drew his attention in spite of her bulky, wine-colored sweatpants. He let his gaze travel up her torso and fasten onto her short, bouncing pony tail. She looked twenty-five he observed with satisfaction.

Surveying the room, he noted rows of red-iced heart-shaped cookies on the green counter nearest him, more cookies cooled in no particular order on the slide-out cutting board, and five loaves of bread cooled on dish towels on the counter. He looked for the apple pies he'd seen at noon, but they were out of sight, while baking utensils had been added to the stack of dirty dishes on the counter. Luke sighed and shook his head. Once again she'd ignored his wishes.

"Greg, that is Tanya's cookie," Yvette reminded their eldest son, as his hand started edging toward his sister's cookie. "Three cookies are your limit."

"Aw, come on," his dark bushy brows, which so resembled Luke's, drew together in a scowl. "I'm almost sixteen. I deserve an extra cookie."

"Stop whining," Kyle said, his mouth full. "Be glad you get three."

"Yeah," Tanya piped up, "my friend, Sally, only gets one cookie when she comes home from school, and Jill gets two."

"Shut up, Twerp," Greg retorted. "You are only *six*, so one cookie should be enough. *Men,* like me, need more cookies than dorky little kids."

"Greg," Yvette warned. "I will not tolerate that kind of talk."

"Sorry," Greg leaned sideways and grabbed for Tanya's second cookie. Tanya snatched it off the table before he could, and he toppled her glass, spilling milk across the table. Kyle, who sat across from Tanya, shoved his chair back and jumped up. His chair smacked into Yvette, who bumped against the stove.

"Greg," Luke marveled at Yvette's calmness, "refill Tanya's glass, then clean up the mess. After that, change your clothes and start the chores."

"But Mom," Greg argued, "you said I could relax for half an hour."

"You just forfeited that privilege. Go, refill Tanya's glass."

"Aw—" his full lips curled into a pout.

"Greg, do as your mother tells you," Luke stepped around the corner. Shushing Tanya before she said more than "Dad's got—" he kissed Yvette on the mouth, then stepped back. "Will you be my Valentine?" he brought the red bouquet from behind his back and affected a courtly bow.

"Dad's being silly," Tanya giggled.

Luke noted with amusement that Greg, who had risen from his chair at Luke's command, stood and stared at his parents' exchange, while Kyle, pink-faced, averted his eyes and backed against the full-length cabinets in the corner.

Yvette took the bouquet and curtsied. "Of course, milord," she murmured with eyes downcast. "Thank you for the roses."

Luke swept her stiff body into a bear hug, ending the charade. Her head barely reached his shoulder and she felt small and fragile in his arms.

"Kyle," Yvette turned to the stove and Luke let her go, "would you get the large clear vase out of the bottom of the china cupboard?"

"Sure, Mom," he squeezed past his parents and collided with Greg, who was slimmer and a head shorter than his younger brother. Luke saw Greg glance up as he leaned back to shove Kyle out of his way, but when he saw Luke watching, he switched to pretending to steady Kyle. "Sorry, Bro," he mumbled.

Luke snickered at Greg's clumsy cover-up and snagged a cookie off the cutting board. "These cookies smell scrumptious."

Turning as he munched his cookie, he saw Tanya's gaze flick from one person to the other as if looking for more entertainment. Then she looked at her empty glass which lay as it had fallen. "Greg, get me more milk."

"I will," he flared with a side-long glance at his parents. "Let me clean this mess first." He started sopping up the milk on the table.

"Mom said to fill my glass *first*," Tanya insisted.

"Oh, all right!" Greg spat as he snatched up the glass. He jerked open the refrigerator and filled the glass, then stomped to the table and plunked the glass in front of Tanya, sloshing milk on the side. "Are you satisfied now?"

"Thank-you, Greg," Tanya drummed her heels on her chair and dipped her cookie in the milk. Greg scowled as he sopped up the mess. Luke could tell from his furtive glances he wanted to leave the rest. But with both his parents watching, he had to repeatedly rinse and wring out the wash cloth until he had wiped up the whole mess from the table, chair, and floor. Throwing the soggy rag toward the sink where it splatted against the window, he stalked to the stairs.

Luke wanted to snap at Greg for ruining the mood, but restrained himself lest he ruin it even more. Not sure what to do, he watched Yvette stir the ground beef with one hand and hold the roses with the other.

"Change into your chore clothes, Kyle," she said when Kyle returned with the vase, "then you can relax for half an hour."

As she snipped the rose stems, Luke turned to stir the ground beef. "Sloppy Joes," he breathed in the rising steam, "yum." He watched with pride as Yvette arranged his roses, her fingers lingering on each velvety one.

"Do you want supper now or after chores?" Yvette positioned the ferns in the vase. "I planned to keep supper warm in the crock pot until the chores are done. But if you want to eat now..." she brought the bouquet to her face.

"Cut me two slices of homemade bread and we'll eat supper later," he blew on a spoonful of the ground beef in its sauce, then sampled it. *Delicious; she added brown sugar. I married a superb cook.* "Is that okay?"

"Sure," she blinked.

He resented her obvious surprise. Couldn't she tell he was trying to be agreeable? For goodness sake, he wasn't *that* self-centered.

Grabbing two more cookies, he walked into the dining room to find the mail. Not seeing any, he called, "Yvette, where's the mail?"

"I didn't have time to bring it in. Could you get it?"

"She never gets it right," he grumbled to himself as he crossed the L-shaped porch. "If it's not dirty dishes or choring late, it's mail still in the box. If she'd just do what she's told, I wouldn't have to try so hard to be pleasant. When will she ever—yuck!" he wrinkled his nose, lifted his work shoe out of the mud he had stepped in, and backed onto the porch.

Disgusted, he surveyed the lawn. A large area of firm-looking mud blocked his path to the mailbox. He'd have to go to the end of the porch where the grass was thicker, or use the driveway. He chose the thicker grass and wiped his shoe as he went. "This is the last straw!" he snarled as he charged toward the house, mail in hand. "I won't put up with such a mess."

"Yvette," Luke strode across the dining room carpet. Irritated that she didn't answer, he clomped into the kitchen where he found her sitting, resting her head in the crook of her elbow on the table.

"Get off your lazy behind and get to work!" he slapped the mail on the kitchen table beside her ear. "The place is a pigsty and you're taking a nap!"

She jumped to her feet and rushed to the stove.

"I take a trip to Kalona to get you roses, and I find the counters full of dirty dishes and no mail! I have to get the mail myself, and find our yard is full of *mud!* I've had it with you! This is *not* housekeeping by any stretch of the imagination!" he flung out a hand indicating the unwashed dishes. "I don't know of another woman who lets the dishes stack up like that, or lets the yard turn to mud. You are *incompetent* and the *poorest* excuse of a wife I have *ever* seen!"

"Calm down, Luke," Yvette scraped the Sloppy Joe filling into the crock pot. "There is no need to get so irate. The—"

"I *won't* calm down! Your laziness is inexcusable! None of the neighbors have muddy yards, why should I put up with it?"

"Their husbands don't order them to tie a dog to the tree until he scratches all the grass off the lawn and their wives don't milk cows."

"That has nothing to do with it. Stop lazing around on your fat fanny. I refuse to be a laughingstock because of you. It's one thing to have a messy *house*, but it's *intolerable* when it extends to the *yard* where everyone can see."

"I have a trim fanny," eyes laughing at him, she wiggled her rear. "And how can you be a laughingstock when the hedge hides the yard?"

"People can see behind the hedge. I *won't* put up with this. Clean the kitchen and fix the yard. Do you hear?"

"I seeded the yard last year, but it didn't take. Shall I seed it again?"

He caught a hint of timidity in her voice and it angered him. The first year of their marriage she'd pretended she didn't know how to make him happy and had consulted him about everything. He'd put up with it for months, then told her he wouldn't tolerate her nonsense; she was to make her own decisions and take the consequences for them. "Don't try that 'little-ignorant-girl' stuff on me again!" he shouted. "I don't care what you do to the lawn. Just *fix* it." He sorted through the envelopes as if their interaction was over.

Luke saw her glance at him as she padded stocking-footed past him. She motioned to the loaves of bread. "I fixed the bread and jam you wanted," her voice sounded flat. "As for the yard, I can't get to it for a few weeks."

"Why not?" he opened his pocket knife as he turned to look at her.

"I have to do the taxes first," she straightened the dishtowels on the three-pronged rack in the corner

"What!" his heart started to race, and he clenched the knife in his fist. "They should have been done weeks ago! Alex wants them by the first of *February*. Next you'll have us paying late fees. You're so irresponsible! I don't know why I *ever* married you."

"I've wondered that, myself," she gibed, making him want to hit her. "Anyhow, Alex wants the taxes by the first of *March*. That gives me two weeks—plenty of time to get them done."

"He wants them done by *February*," he slit open an envelope.

"I've been compiling our taxes for fifteen years, and he always says the first of March is soon enough. It seems to me, I'd be the one to know."

Startled that she would insist she was right after he yelled at her, he glanced up and saw her standing erect in the doorway, her hands on her hips. "Well, la de dah," he rolled his eyes, "you got *something* right."

19

~   ~   ~

That evening after supper, Luke sprawled on the couch, forcing the boys to take the recliner and stuffed chair.

"How was school?" Luke asked during a commercial break.

"Okay," Kyle said. "I got five valentines."

"Kid stuff," Greg scoffed. "Girls pay attention to your car and clothes. When will you buy me a car, Dad? I'll be sixteen in September."

"I'm not buying a car for you to wreck."

"Ryan's folks got him a car."

Luke snorted, "That's a trash-heap, not a car. If Steve Webster wants to drop money in a bottomless hole, that's his choice; I'm not that stupid. Yvette," he bellowed, "are you coming?"

"She had a *big* stack of dishes to wash," Kyle said.

Luke sat up to look into the dining room, and saw Tanya playing with Barbie dolls at the table. "Tanya, where's Mom?"

"She's putting the chickens to bed."

"Why not call it *roosting the hens*?" Kyle mused. "After all, she's chasing a few stragglers into the roost section so they don't poop in the feeders and nests all night. I think it's—"

"Yvette," Luke interrupted when he saw the washroom door open, "come here." He could see her take off her boots and coat. Stocking-footed, she crossed the plush blue carpet and came to the double-wide living room door.

"Yes?" she leaned against the doorjamb.

"Come on," Luke invited, "watch this show with us."

"Not tonight. I better start on the taxes."

"The taxes can wait. You're my valentine. I purposely sat on the couch and saved this spot for you," Luke patted the seat. "Come sit."

"No," she pushed herself off the doorjamb. "*Responsibility* calls."

"Look, I'm sorry I said you're irresponsible. I didn't mean it. Come here; you have the responsibility to spend time with me, too."

"So," she tilted her head, "I have two jobs to choose from. I choose..." she pursed her lips "...the taxes. Tanya can keep me company."

"Yvette," he despised himself for the begging he heard in his voice, "I brought you flowers and apologized; what more do you want?"

She walked away without answering and he sighed.

"Well, Dad," Greg smirked, "you'll have to grovel a day or two."

"Mind your own business," Luke glared until Greg looked away. It rankled that Greg was right. He'd compliment her cooking and rent family movies tomorrow. Maybe she'd come around without too much groveling on his part. After all, he'd apologized already.

20

Chapter 3

Yvette sat on the front porch swing with a pad and pencil, and buttoned her red sweater against the breeze. Sunny and pleasant, the day felt warm for mid-March. The snow had melted except where it had been shoveled into piles. Tired, she laid the notepad and pencil beside her, and closed her eyes. *Surely I can relax a few minutes.* She concentrated on relaxing her shoulders, her jaw, her forehead, and her stomach. It took her a moment to realize her nausea and headache had eased. *Strange. Can tension make a person feel sick?*

Why were her muscles so tense? Things were going great ever since the Valentine's Day fiasco. She'd cried herself to sleep that night and woke up an hour before the alarm sounded the next morning. She had considered her options and decided the only one she hadn't tried was to stop reasoning away Luke's irrationalities and just *do* as he asked. So she'd tried her best to keep the house clean, the children well behaved without reprimanding them in front of Luke, and to keep the dishes hidden or washed. She'd taken all the tax papers to her cold workroom upstairs, so she could leave them out until she finished.

Her muscles tensed. She concentrated on relaxing them again, then resumed her reverie. Her hard work had paid off. Luke had been friendly since his lame apology on Valentine's Day. One night he had invited her and the children to watch wholesome movies he'd rented. He'd put his arm around her and she'd snuggled with him on the couch. Kyle had popped corn, then sat cross legged on the floor. Tanya had snuggled with her mother, and played with her Barbie dolls. Greg claimed disinterest and read a sports magazine. Halfway through, Yvette had caught him engrossed in the movie. She'd nudged Luke, nodded toward Greg, and they'd snickered. Yvette grinned at the memory.

During those family times, she'd felt more relaxed with Luke than she had been for ages. After years of trying, she had *finally* discovered how to keep him happy. From now on she'd remedy *all* his complaints, even the nonsensical ones. She'd keep things in perfect order no matter what messy project she was doing. With Luke happy now, maybe Greg would become caring, too.

Her muscles tensed again and she sighed in frustration. Were her efforts to avoid Luke's reproofs and earn his love causing her muscles to tense up like this? Surely not. Yet every time she thought about working hard to keep him happy she tensed up and got that sick feeling again. What was going on?

Keeping her eyes closed, she pushed on the porch floor with her foot, setting the swing in motion. A tractor started at the hog stable. Her lids sprang open and she jerked erect. Luke would be upset to see her napping when the lawn was still muddy. Snatching up her pencil and notepad, she stopped the swing and returned to the task at hand. The tractor starting up probably meant the boys were going to grind and mix feed, but it reminded her Luke was around somewhere. She didn't want to give him reason to accuse her of being lazy.

She contemplated the far corner of the yard where the thick grass was a soggy green-brown, then drew a rectangle on her notepad. Rising wearily, she circled the muddy area, moved next to the hedge, and spotted Luke striding to the house. He saw her in the yard and veered toward her, skirting the mud.

"You look busy," he peered over her shoulder.

"I'm trying to decide what to do with the lawn," She glanced back at him. "Would you care if I made the muddy area into a flower garden?"

"As long as we can go straight to the mailbox without getting muddy or wet, I don't care. You'll have to maintain it, so suit yourself. Landscaping isn't my area of expertise, anyway, so I'll defer to your judgment on such matters," he put an arm around her shoulders. "How was the trip to town?"

"Fine. Tanya and I told knock-knock jokes on the way."

"How much money did you have left this time?"

"Forty dollars. Thirty for the kids and ten for me."

"When will you spend your quarter and what are you going to buy?"

"I don't know," she shrugged, "there's no hurry. It took four years to save five hundred dollars. Maybe I'll buy perennials for the front yard."

He let go her shoulders and went to lean against the nearest crimson maple tree. "Did you see or talk to anyone in town?"

"I talked to Margie Bender," she hugged her notepad to her chest. "She asked me if I was going to piece a quilt top for the Mennonite Relief Sale again this year. I said I could if the weather won't let me work on the yard."

"That's the way to do it," he nodded, "leave her hanging."

"I didn't intend to make her job more difficult than it already is."

"Margie thrives on problems," he snorted. "She invents them."

"Don't be like that, Luke," Yvette picked up a stick, puzzled at his attitude. "Margie does a great job as president of the quilting committee."

"Sure. That's why she asked the church for more funds."

"Because of her, the sewing circle did *twelve more* quilts this year than the year before. She shouldn't have to pay for them out of her own pocket."

"Of course not. Let her spend wildly and send the church the tab."

"Making quilts for needy people is *not* 'spending wildly.' I don't see why you disparage someone as decent and talented as Margie."

"I'm not disparaging her. I'm stating things as they are. Margie is a spender. She's probably embezzling funds for her own use."

"What a *rotten* thing to say, Luke. Why do you choose to be nasty? Don't you have work to do?"

"There's no need to be touchy," he slid his hands into his jeans pockets. "I think Margie is a trouble-maker. *You're* the one who's nasty." He sauntered toward the west end of the porch.

Bewildered, Yvette watched him go. Had she been the nasty one? She didn't think so, but now she couldn't remember how the conversation had turned ugly. She didn't have time to mull it over because Tanya, who had been riding bike in the circle drive beyond the hedge, rode around the end of the hedge and up the walk, dropped her bike and hurried over.

"Stay out of the mud!" Yvette reminded before Tanya stepped into the muddy area. Tanya changed direction and continued up the walk and onto the blue porch that formed an L around the square, white, two-story farmhouse, then circled on the thick grass to her mother.

"What's that?" she reached for the notepad.

"It's a map," Yvette let her take it, suppressing a smile, knowing her six-year-old wouldn't be able to make heads nor tails of it.

"A map of what?" She caught her lower lip in her teeth, drawing Yvette's attention to the distinctive double peaks on her thin upper lip, a trait she'd inherited from Yvette and Yvette's mother, Clara.

"Our yard. See," Yvette squatted down to Tanya's level, "here's our big house," she pointed to it on the map, "and Grandma's smaller house. These five circles in a row are the trees, and the rectangles are our L-shaped hedge. This curved line is the arbor where we go through the hedge to get the mail."

"Why are you making a map?" Tanya let go of the notepad.

Yvette glanced into Tanya's dark blue eyes and wondered what quirk had assigned blue eyes to her dark-brown-haired daughter, from a brown-haired, brown-eyed family. "I'm drawing a plan so the yard will be useful and pretty."

"Oh," Tanya wrinkled her snub nose. "I'm going to ride my bike."

Yvette rose. "Wait, Tanya; I need your help. If this whole yard was a playroom, what would you want in it?"

Tanya's blue eyes perked up. "I'd want a tower with a window so I can be Rapunzel and let down my hair." She pulled her chest-length hair as far down as she could, tilting her head back for maximum length.

Yvette turned away to hide her smile. "Who will be your prince?"

"Kyle," she skip-danced around her mother. "He's kind and can sing. And he's the best brother." She stopped skipping to look up at Yvette. "I wouldn't want Greg; he's mean. Is it okay to not choose Greg?"

"Certainly. She ruffled Tanya's dark curls. "I hope you never choose a mean prince. But a tower room is a great idea. It could be part of Cinderella's palace, too, and the rest of the yard could be a ballroom. What if we put a room and your window at the corner of the hedge far enough away from Grandma's house you don't have to worry about being quiet when she's sleeping?"

Tanya considered the location, and then nodded, bouncing her brown curls. "Don't forget the Rapunzel window," she skipped to her future castle.

"A window," Yvette mused. "I'll figure out how to do that and check with Grandma to make sure this is okay with her. Why don't you ride your bike, and I'll work on this map and figure out how to do the tower room? Okay?"

"Okay, Mom," arms outstretched like an airplane, she ran and made a buzzing noise, then banked her plane as she veered around the muddy patch.

Yvette continued planning, then went to her mom's house. Raising her hand to knock, she hesitated. Could she talk to her mom without Luke finding out and getting upset? If he found out she'd gone to her mother's, he'd accuse her of disrespecting his feelings. On the other hand, she needed feedback, and Luke wasn't likely to come in the house for awhile. She'd risk it.

She knocked, opened the door a crack in order to hear her mother's "Come in," then stepped into the small house. Window-boxes filled with a profusion of dark red geraniums on top of low bookshelves lined two sides of the sunny room. Against the third wall stood a walnut-stained, oak china hutch, with its matching table and chairs in the center of the room. Yvette's favorite was the knotty pine, cathedral ceiling with its two skylights. Someday she'd live in this house and this would be her favorite room.

Clara appeared in the living room doorway wearing a soft pink dress that she used to wear to church. "Well, come in!" she enveloped her daughter in a long hug. "It's been ages since you've been over here alone. Where's Luke?"

Yvette pulled out a chair and sank into it. "I don't know where he is, but I figured if he wants me to take care of the muddy yard, he shouldn't get upset when I ask for your input. I've missed you, Mom."

"I've missed you, too. After Luke let you visit Ben and me every day at the hospital last fall when Ben was sick, I thought he had dropped that once-a-month rule. But when the funeral was over, I lost you as well as Ben."

24

"I'm sorry, Mom. Luke got really nasty after that."

"I know he did; it wasn't your fault. Luke hung around your house all fall and winter—or at least the days I was home—and glared every time you and I met in the garden or I went to your house to get eggs or milk. "

Seeing Clara's nervous glance at the window, Yvette said, "Luke talked to me in the yard a few minutes ago, so we should be safe this time. I still miss Dad so much, and I can rarely talk to anybody about it. I tried sharing my grief with Luke, but he told me to get over it and move on."

"You and Ben were so close, I wondered how you could laugh and joke when you and Luke came over for your once-a-month visit."

"I had to fake it with Luke around. Could I have reprints of Dad from family get-togethers and our growing up years? I have professional ones of you and him, but he's usually half-hidden behind someone in my snapshots."

"He never was one to be in the limelight." Clara placed a stack of photo albums on the table in front of Yvette and sat at the head of the table.

"Thanks," Yvette started turning pages. "I didn't dare ask to see these when Luke was along. How are you doing? Has your grief subsided?"

"It's not as intense as it was those first months. Sometimes I think I see his tall frame, but it turns out to be Kyle or Luke. Then it hits me all over again. I call my friends or your sisters sometimes, and that helps. Besides, my mid-wifery and mother's helper work supplies me with lots of hugs."

"Here's one of Dad cuddling Tanya when she was two weeks old."

"She reminded him of you. Spending time with her was like reliving your growing up years. I think he was more her father than Luke is."

"I'm glad she had Dad."

"I'd guess that's why she comes over so much. She pours over those photo albums like you are. She and I have grown closer since Ben passed on."

"You've been a balm to her heart," Yvette put a hand on her mother's age-spotted one. "I've been hurting so much, I forgot to help the children deal with their loss. It's time we put together a memorial of their grandpa."

"Better not let Luke see it."

"Actually, he's been nicer this past month. I made a major effort to keep the house as he likes it so he won't get upset, and it's been working. It was my fault he got upset. I lets things slide too much."

"I don't believe it was your fault, Yvette. No matter when I go to your house to get eggs, it's never messy. Sometimes you're baking pies or canning, and have a few dishes on the counter, but otherwise it's spotless."

"He doesn't like dishes on the counter, not even when I'm baking or canning. So I cleaned out the big corner cupboard to hide the dirty dishes when I'm too busy to wash them. Now he doesn't have any reason to complain."

"That sounds extreme to me. It's demeaning to you—and to Luke, too. What could be more perfect than a mess on the counter that results in the smell of pies in the oven and a tasty dessert for supper? If you play superwoman and hide the realities of life from Luke, you'll end up with trouble down the road."

"This month I put out extra effort to keep things as Luke likes them and it has paid off. Now he's warm and loving like a husband should be."

"Are you sure it's because you've perfected your housekeeping?"

"Come to think of it," Yvette picked a speck of lint off the table, "he *did* tell me I'm the nasty one today, and it had nothing to do with the house." She recounted the conversation. "Was I the nasty one?"

"Absolutely not. Luke was slandering Margie's character."

"He keeps saying, 'If you'd just do what I tell you.' But I was and he still got nasty. If submission isn't the issue, what is?"

"Who knows? Ben—your dad—wasn't that way. I notice Luke is driving you harder and harder. You look tired. How much sleep do you get?"

"Usually five or six hours a night."

"He won't be happy when you fall asleep at the wheel or get sick."

"I know, I know, but you aren't the one who has to live with being yelled at or put down if you don't do things just right."

Clara sighed. "I don't think losing sleep and running yourself ragged to keep everything perfect for Luke is going to work in the long run."

"Oh, Mom, if you knew how badly I want our marriage to succeed. When I'm not griped at all the time and the children can talk to Luke, I feel we have a reasonably good marriage. But if doing everything he wants isn't what creates a good and peaceful marriage, what is?"

"You can't *make* Luke be decent, but you don't have to wear yourself out to appease him, either. When I see you pushing yourself to the limit, I remember how tense and self-critical I feel when I drive myself that hard. Is it real peace when you sacrifice your dignity to gain peace with Luke?"

Yvette tried to think that through a minute, then shook her head. "I don't know. I'm so tired I lose my train of thought." She wasn't going to tell her mom about her tension and sick stomach, or her mom would really worry.

"You should be in bed."

"I couldn't sleep; Luke could come in and scare me out of my wits. But I didn't come to talk about Luke," she placed her map on the table. "What do you think of this? We can consider it our memorial of Dad."

"What is it?" As Clara bent to look at the notepad, Yvette noted the few dark strands in her mother's white, page-boy styled hair. Were they fewer than six months ago? She hated to see signs of aging on her mother. She had just lost her dad and couldn't bear the thought of losing her mother, too.

"It's a map of the yard. Luke asked me to fix that spot the dog ruined. I wish he'd let Greg get another dog; Greg took Duke's death pretty hard and has been meaner ever since. Anyway, I've been drawing a plan to turn the front yard into a flower garden and patio. I'll take the patio all the way up to your house if I can afford it, since there's a sparse spot under the trees by your house, too. But I want to make sure you like the plans."

"You're the owner. You can do what you want."

"I know, Mom, but I don't operate that way. You live here, too, and it's as much your place as it is mine. Our agreement was that you could live here rent free. It was *not* that I could change anything I want and if you hate it that's just tough. Besides," she flashed a saucy grin, "you've become artistic in your *old age* and might give me some ideas to perfect the plans."

"I've always been artistic," Clara retorted.

"Yeah, *old-fogey* art," Yvette grinned, remembering how she used to tease her mother by calling her an old fogey. "Your taste has improved."

"No, yours just matured," Clara's hazel eyes twinkled.

"What do you think of putting a rock-wall-garden here?" Yvette indicated the rectangle she had drawn on the map. "The rock-garden would form one side of a room and the L in the hedge would form two other sides."

"That's a good idea; it may satisfy Tanya's yen for playing in the timber. You could plant low shrubs on the fourth side to enclose the area."

"Do you know where I'd find inexpensive shrubs and flagstones?"

"Last week Doris Yoder, one of my pregnant clients, said her husband has flagstones to get rid of at a place he contracted to demolish." Clara shook her head, "It's so amazing how God times things perfectly."

"It sure is. If I can get them cheap, maybe Luke won't gripe at me or accuse me of spending too much money. The plants and lawn furniture will cost enough. I can't think how to make the window Tanya wants."

"Get Kyle to help you. He's creative; it'll turn out stunning. He helped Ben design this curved sidewalk when the sun room was added on."

"Good idea," Yvette checked her watch. "Oh my, it's chore time and I haven't started supper." She rose and rushed to the door. "Oh, Mom," she paused to call over her shoulder, "would you call about the flagstones?"

Yvette hurried home and into the kitchen, nearly colliding with Luke.

"What's the rush? Where's the fire?" he held her upper arms.

"It's chore time and I didn't start supper," she took half a step back, but waited for him to let her go. She didn't want to seem insubordinate, or whatever it was that angered him with little provocation. She took another tiny step back as he loosened his grip. When he released her, she opened the refrigerator.

"You work too hard," from behind he put his arms about her waist. "I never see you relax. Why don't we eat out tonight and give you a break?"

"That's so expensive, and I'd rather spend the money elsewhere—I want something tangible to show for it."

"Let's celebrate," he nibbled her neck. "We endured my folks for New Year's and the taxes are done. The children all like Mexican; it'll be my treat."

"I hadn't decided what to cook, yet," she leaned away from his mouth.

"So relax with me," he pulled her back and shut the refrigerator.

She complied, feeling awkward and without choice. Something didn't feel right, but it felt good to be held and released from work.

On the couch, Luke pulled her close and picked up the remote. He flipped through the channels and chose a wine-making show.

"Is there anything we can relate to?" Yvette leaned her head on his shoulder. "We don't drink wine or beer and neither does anyone I know."

"This will round out your education."

Yvette glanced at the clock. Four forty. She tried to focus on the TV. One man tasted the wine and explained how this wine differed from the other. She shifted her shoulders and crossed her ankles. Luke held her tighter.

She sighed and glanced at the clock again. Four forty-two. She tried to nestle into a more comfortable position, but Luke held her too tight.

"Hold still," he gripped her arm.

At that moment the vague feeling that something was wrong hardened into conviction. She knew she didn't dare cross him or he would get upset. She searched for a solution to the situation. If she had a book, or her knitting, or could work on her plans for the patio she wouldn't feel so trapped. She didn't dare get something to do; she might upset him. She'd close her eyes and relax. Maybe she'd sleep. She closed her lids. Ah, that felt good.

Luke jostled her. "Are you going to sleep?" he removed his arm. "I thought we'd do quality time together like we heard in the sermon, but you're spacing me off." He sighed, "I can't make our marriage work by myself."

Yvette glanced at the clock and scrambled to her feet. Four forty-five. "I was spacing the *show* off, Luke. I asked you to change the channel."

"Of *course*, it's *my* fault. Okay, I have broad shoulders. I can take it. Of course, *every* time we sit down to watch TV it has to be a show of *your* choice." He clicked off the TV. "Well, the mood is ruined now." Shoulders slumped, he got up from the couch.

Confused, Yvette watched him leave the room. Was she required to *watch every* show he chose? *He* had picked the movies this past month. She rubbed her eyes as if to clear them. Was he still planning on going out for supper? Or had the mood been ruined for that, too?

Chapter 4

"**W**ell," Yvette sighed as she and Kyle continued on to Iowa City after dropping Tanya off at her friend, Jill's, house, "now we'll rescue the flagstones if they're still there. Luke said if I wait a week so he can haul home the seed corn and beans he ordered, he'd let me use the pickup every day for two weeks. He brought home bags of hog, chicken, and cow food supplement to last several weeks, too. I cooked all week and put cakes, cookies, pies, pizza, potatoes and ham, chili, lasagna, and casseroles in the freezer."

"So that's why there are several kinds of cookies in the cupboard."

"You weren't supposed to find those. They have to last a month so I can devote my time to creating our patio before gardening season starts."

"I'll help as much as I can. Anything to get away from Greg."

Not Greg again! I wish I knew how to stop his bullying. Yvette slowed for a curve, "I appreciate your offer, but I only expect help on Saturdays."

"I'm glad I got to help today. I was waiting to talk to you privately."

She smiled at him. "It's been awhile since we've had a heart to heart."

They passed through the square-framed truss bridge over Old Man's Creek. "The water is high," Kyle pointed. "We haven't even had the spring rains yet. Looks like we're in for some flooding."

They made small talk until they entered Iowa City. "What were you waiting to talk about with me?" Yvette prompted.

"Greg. Can I hit him? He makes fun of me and calls me names, and teases Tanya until she cries. I think I hate him."

"I'm sorry he's a pain when I'm not around. Here's the street, and this is the house." Yvette turned into the drive. "It looks too nice to demolish."

"Grandma said the woman who lived here died recently and the University of Iowa bought the house so they can tear down this whole row of houses and put up a big building. That's why we get free flagstones."

"That's sad. Come on," she got out of the truck. "Let's investigate. It feels eerie, like she'll come out and ask why we're here."

They rounded the back of the garage, and stepped onto a patio of irregular flagstones interrupted with small mulched gardens. Bare-branched trees and shrubs grew in the mulched areas and shrubs lined two fence rows.

"Wow!" Kyle stared in awe. "What a huge patio and garden."

"It is beautiful. If we lay the flagstones in the order she has them, it won't be so hard to fit them together in our yard. We may as well take all the flagstones; what we don't take will probably wind up in the landfill. Let's start on the far side, so we can walk on flagstones instead of mud."

They worked in silence until they found a workable pattern. Lift a stone, scrape the mud off, fit the stone like a puzzle on the patio until they had a pickup-bed layer, then load them onto the pickup in the order they had been.

"What about Greg?" Kyle knelt on the patio and scraped mud off a stone. "I've ignored him and told him to stop it, but he does it all the more,"

"He needs teaching on what it takes to be a strong, respectable man." She sighed, "I've hoped and prayed my boys wouldn't stoop to bullying."

"Could you talk to him?" Yvette heard the hope mingled with despair in his voice, and ached for him.

"I could. But if he suspects you told on him, he would harass you even more. I'll wait for the right opening so he doesn't connect it with you."

"Knowing you plan to talk to him will make it easier to take."

"I could tell him what qualities I respect and admire in men and talk of contributing to society. He has to stop thinking of masculinity as being more powerful or dominant than others. Do you think that will work?"

"How will contributing to society help him stop picking on me?"

"If he uses his strength to build people up, he's likely to be pleased with himself and won't need to put you down to make himself look better."

"But what about Dad? He farms and helps people after a disaster, and still is nasty at home. Why does *he* keep putting us down?"

"Are you telling me Dad puts you down?" she stalled for time.

"He does it in front of Greg. He tells me to stop being a chicken. Last summer when we were practicing pitch and catch, he barreled the ball real hard and fast at my head and called me a wimp when I ducked and didn't try to catch it. Then he went on and on about me being *mama's boy*."

"That was last year. Isn't he nicer now?"

"No," he looked disgusted. "Yesterday he came up in the haymow and saw me rolling a bale of hay end over end. He said only *women* roll bales. *Men* carry them. He made me carry it to the hay rack. The twine hurt my hands even though I had gloves on, and the hay scratched my legs through my jeans."

"I carry bales and I'm no man! It's *character* that makes us respectable men or women. Making a difference takes courage, perseverance, kindness, and so on. When a man builds others up, society says, "*That* is a *man!*""

"Mom? Am I—" Kyle paused, then started again, his eyes downcast. "Do I act like a man? Do you admire and respect me?"

"Most certainly. I was so proud of you when you used your creativity to help Tanya stop being afraid of spiders last year. It takes a *man* or a *woman* to care how others feel. Tanya turns to you because you're the *man* in her life."

"But I'm not a respected basketball player like Greg. My friends and I are nobodies. Kids in school like the boys who play sports."

"And Greg is no good at art. If all men played ball, who would build or farm or prepare tax forms? You don't have to be good at sports. Simply use your talents in a responsible way like you are right now."

"But what shall I do about Greg?"

"Try acting like you don't care, or laugh it off as if what he said was a joke. Tell Tanya how you're going to handle him, though, so she won't think you betrayed her. Let's role-play so you'll be prepared to deal with him. I'll be Greg." They role-played as they worked until they had a load of flagstones.

As they started for home, Kyle asked, "What was going on between you and Dad last night when we went out for supper? You were quiet and Dad talked a blue streak. You moved away from him when he put his arm around you. Was he nasty to you?"

"I don't know. Something didn't feel right and I felt uncomfortable and trapped. I haven't figured out why. Maybe it's just me."

"No, Dad acted weird. He knows we don't like beans, but he ordered beans for us, anyway, and glared at Greg when he said he hated beans. You ate with your left hand, since Tanya was holding your right hand under the table."

"And you were doing bird imitations," Yvette kept her face straight.

"What! I was not!"

"Yes you were. You were watching us all like a hawk," she teased.

Kyle grinned sheepishly. "Well, everyone was acting weird. Maybe we should role-play how to deal with Dad. So why we did we go out to eat if Dad was being nasty again? "

"I didn't dare refuse. He thinks I'm supposed to do everything he wants, even though it feels all wrong to me."

"Just like going out for supper felt all wrong," Kyle observed. "I felt like I do when Greg makes fun of me or calls me names."

"You felt intimidated and humiliated?" A chill ran up her spine. No wonder she felt confused. Had Luke invited them out to degrade them? Were Mom and Delores right and her lack of submission was *not* the problem?

After turning in their drive, Yvette backed the pickup toward the house at the end of the hedge. They unloaded flagstones, fitting each layer in the order it had been. The family car was not in the garage, and Yvette assumed Luke and Greg had gone to Kalona for lunch or parts. Feeling free from censure and Luke's demands, Yvette and Kyle warmed up cream of mushroom soup, refilled their thermos with hot chocolate, and left for another load before chore time.

During the next trip, Kyle told what was happening in his life: kids in school, his drawings and how the kids liked them, and the story he was writing. Yvette listened and asked questions for clarification. As the day wore on they got sillier. Yvette taught Kyle silly songs she had learned in school. By the time they finished unloading, they were making up words to songs and giggling.

"Where on earth have you been?" Luke glowered as they stepped into the house. "You didn't leave us anything to eat."

"Oh," with an effort, Yvette wiped her smile off but couldn't drop her flippant tone, "we figured you went to Kalona and were fending for yourselves."

"You know better than that."

"Which part?" Yvette batted her lashes, aware of Kyle's eyes on her. "That you went to Kalona or that you were fending for yourselves?"

"You are supposed to prepare meals for us."

"You can feed yourselves; you aren't helpless. Kyle and I are going outside. When we come in, I expect you to act like a husband who is glad to see his family. Come, Kyle." She took his arm and propelled him out the door.

They stood on the porch. "I'm sorry about that," Yvette said.

"*Dad* should be the one apologizing. He's such a *jerk*."

"He's your dad; be respectful. Let's go in, and see what happens." Yvette opened the door and they went in acting as if they hadn't just been in the house. "Hi, Luke," Yvette saw him gazing into the refrigerator and went past him to the washroom. Kyle withdrew to the bathroom. "What would you like for supper?" she dried her face. "Beanless chili or spaghetti and meatballs?"

"Spaghetti," Luke grunted.

"How's the tractor coming?" she set a bag of cookies on the table.

"It's not. They have to order the part I need." He took the pitcher of milk to the table, got a clear glass out of the cupboard and sat down.

Kyle came out and helped himself to two cookies. "Isn't there anything else to work on while you wait?"

"What is this?" Luke frowned. "Twenty questions?"

"We're saying we love you," Yvette put an arm about Luke's shoulders and brushed her lips across his temple, "and we're glad to be home."

Luke slid his arm around her waist and rubbed his bristled chin on her palm. "Sorry I was a grump. Forgive me?" He pulled her onto his lap.

32

Chapter 5

Cradling a mug of hot coffee, Luke perched on the end of a saw horse in the shop. He'd finally finished putting the engine together, but he still had to start it to make sure he'd done it right, and who knew how long the final repairs would take. Someday, when he owned five hundred acres, he'd never fix another tractor. He dug into a tin of homemade peanut butter cookies he'd snitched from the house, and bit off half of one. At least Yvette had been submissive lately. The trouble was, something felt wrong, but he couldn't put a finger on it. He frowned and tried to focus on where that feeling of unease came from. It was something about Yvette and her demeanor. She was doing what he said, but she behaved as if she was doing what *she wanted*. He couldn't be sure he was in charge or if that was what she wanted to do anyway.

Shucks! Now he'd have to get up earlier and go out to find what they'd done wrong. He'd have to sacrifice precious hours when he should be painting the tractor. If he didn't get it done soon, the tractor wouldn't be ready to haul manure when the ground conditions were right. Being late with hauling manure would make him late for planting, which would reduce his yield and give the neighbors reason to look down on him. But he had to get the manure out, since the manure pit and the lagoon were full and this would be the last chance to empty them until May or June when they put the first cutting of hay in the barn. He'd have to disinfect the brood-sow shed to prepare for the baby piglets, too, and then vaccinate the piglets after they were born and clip their teeth and tails.

Get the wife to help. He sipped his coffee and weighed the thought. Which was more important: fixing the yard or easing his work load? If he didn't want a muddy yard, he'd have to let her finish the job. Meanwhile, he'd enjoy their nights. But he couldn't let her get too close or he'd be mush in her hands.

He went in for breakfast and afterward retreated to the shop to get away from Kyle's and Tanya's jokes and laughter. It wasn't fair he had to bear the responsibility of keeping everyone in line. These last weeks of sleeping in or working on the tractor rather than checking everyone's work had lifted a heavy weight off his shoulders. Now he'd have to make the rounds again.

Greg came out as his mother and siblings left to get flagstones. "They're nuts," Greg confided as he threw the bolt and opened the double doors. "Kyle used to be fun to tease, but now he makes me feel like a heel." He sprang up on the tractor and turned the key, while Luke stood on the side and listened to the engine grind and finally start. Luke watched as Greg drove the tractor around the circle drive, brought it back and parked.

"It doesn't have any pep and it smokes," Greg reported.

Luke patted the hood. "It's hot, too. I'll check the timing," he opened the inspection hole and made adjustments. When Greg took it for another trial run, the engine responded with vigor. Luke gave the thumbs up signal.

"I finished this one quicker than I expected," Luke said after Greg dismounted. "If the painting goes well, I'll be ahead of schedule. Here, I'll show you how to run the sander. I want all the rust sanded off."

He demonstrated, then handed the sander to Greg and watched to make sure he got the idea. Satisfied, he stepped back and got his tools out of the chest.

Greg stopped the sander. "Why you don't take this tractor to the professionals for overhauling and painting, anyway? For that matter, why don't you get a newer and bigger tractor? We have the money."

"And what should I do while I pay someone to do the work?" Luke challenged. *Be careful, Luke, don't stifle his independent thinking.* "We might have extra money on hand, but I don't want to squander it. Sooner or later there will be repairs or an opportunity to buy land."

"Why do we work all the time? Other farmers relax in the winter."

Luke dusted the hood of the tractor with his hand. "But they are at the mercy of market prices when they only do crop farming, and can take a big hit some years. Personally, I like your grandpa Ben's thinking. Yeah, we have more work because of our multiple commodities, but we have minimal financial difficulty, too. When the milk prices are down, hogs and eggs are usually up, and vice versa. Work is a big part of life. The secret is to enjoy it."

"Yeah right. Like you enjoy farming."

"I jumped at the chance to farm," Luke leaned on the beige tractor hood. "When I worked at my dad's mechanic shop, I decided I wanted to be a farmer. Marrying your mom gave me that chance and I wouldn't trade it for anything. I was hoping you'd want to take over the farm."

"Never," Greg sat on the stool. "I plan to play in the NBA."

"Don't let playing with the varsity go to your head. Professional ball is a full time job; to make the team you'd have to practice every spare minute."

"I need practice shooting under pressure; *you* should play with me."

"Get Kyle to play with you; basketball season is over."

Greg snorted. "He's a klutz. I need to play with the guys at the gym to stay competitive. If I don't succeed it will be because *you* held me back."

"They play during chore time; you took off enough during basketball season. If you can't succeed in spite of your responsibilities," Luke stood up straight and pointed at his son, "it will be because of your *own* lack of drive and determination. I will *not* have you shifting your share of the chores onto the rest of the family. You will hold up your end around here. Is that understood?"

Greg scowled and turned the sander on, then got up and kicked the stool into place before stepping on it and applying the sander to the hood.

Luke watched him to make sure he wasn't taking his temper out on the tractor, then went to take the fenders off. He loosened the bolts and laid the fenders on a plastic sheet on the cement floor, then inspected Greg's work. Greg turned off the sander and waited for his father's verdict. Luke ran his hand over the metal and sighted down both sides, looking for waves or specks of rust.

"Looks good. You got all the rust off, but there's a slight indentation here," he pointed to the spot. "If you sand around it, it'll be less noticeable."

"You do it," Greg thrust the sander at Luke. "I'll make it worse."

Luke finished the job, then moved to the other side of the tractor. "I'd like to finish sanding and priming today. We should haul manure this week; the spring rains won't hold off much longer."

"Use the 1070," Greg moved his stool to sand the other side.

"That's too much power for hauling manure. Wastes fuel and money. The 300 is too small, so I don't want to use it, either."

"The manure pit is full; I can't scrape down the sheds."

"Scrape toward the pit and make a pile in front of the pit door."

~   ~   ~

By the time Yvette, Kyle and Tanya came home, the hood and both fenders had been sanded, and Luke had masked the areas he didn't want painted.

Greg looked out the window. "They're laughing and carrying on, and Tanya's unloading flagstones, too. They look too heavy for her."

Luke went to the other window to watch. "She's carrying the smaller ones. Kyle is a mamma's boy," he frowned. "Do you see it?"

"Yeah. He acts like Mom. They laugh at the same stuff."

"I'll put a stop to that. He can help me today while you help Mom."

"I don't want to be a mamma's boy. I'd rather haul manure."

Luke pondered that. "You're probably right. She has all of April to finish the project. But I don't have enough work for both of you in here. You can clean out the brood sow shed and the chicken house."

"I'm not going to muck them out by myself," Greg glared at his dad. "Why don't you hire someone to put double doors on those buildings so we can get the skid loader in there instead of mucking them out by hand?"

"Widening the doors will ruin the buildings. Use the 300 to pull the manure spreader to the door. Kyle can help muck out part of the time."

"Why don't you have *him* load the manure?"

"You said you'd rather do that than help Mom, so I'll hold you to it. Kyle needs to be around me more if he's going to stop acting sissified."

When they sat down for the noon meal, Luke informed the family of the change of plans, talking as if he needed Kyle's help as well as Greg's, and leaving out that he could be finished with all his responsibilities in ample time without their help. He saw Yvette and Kyle exchange glances.

"You'll have to milk without me, then," Yvette reached for the salt on the stove. "I doubt I'll be back before you're done milking."

Is this a power play? Luke stared at her. *It is.* "I expect you back before chore time," he speared a piece of cooked carrot.

"When you take my helper, I can't," she mashed her potato. "I need to finish my work and I won't waste our resources on half a load."

Luke glared at her, considering his options as he chewed on a bite of pork roast. She was right about not getting half a load. If he ordered her to stay home, he'd look stupid since *he* had told her to fix the lawn *now*. Furthermore, he could end up with consequences he didn't want, like not having use of the pickup when he needed it. Lacking a way to win the impasse, he changed the issue. "How long are we to keep fending for ourselves? You're just trying to get even with me for telling you to do the job in the first place, aren't you?"

"Luke Miller," she stared at him, exasperated. "Do you mean to tell me you've been married to me for sixteen years and still don't know I don't operate or even *think* that way? Don't try to pin *your* sins onto me. Anyway," she ended on a flippant note, "I didn't know I was so important."

"Isn't there any way to speed things up?" he frowned, abashed by her reprimand, but not willing to drop the offensive.

"If I had more help instead of less, we could get two more loads today."

Luke considered this while chewing the last bits of pork off the bone. The only item that needed immediate attention was mucking out the brood-sow shed. He could prep the fenders during chore time and paint on Monday. The little wife would get her way this time, but he'd win by having her at home.

"I like that idea," he said, "we'll all go."

"Dad," Greg nudged his leg under the table, "What about—"

"Not this time." Luke noted the confusion on Greg's face; he'd explain later. Hopefully, giving in to Yvette wouldn't cause Greg to think him a wimp.

Chapter 6

As she packed a lunch for Delores and herself, Yvette marveled at how fast the work had progressed with Luke and Greg helping on Saturday. Luke didn't remind Yvette of his expectations and Greg hadn't picked on Kyle or on Tanya, who played with Barbie dolls. Due to the extra help, Yvette finished removing the flagstones two days sooner than she'd calculated. Yesterday she dug bulbs and stored them in bags in the basement until she could plant them.

Finished packing lunches, she drove toward Iowa City, stopping to pick up Delores, who brought out stacks of greenhouse planters of various sizes.

"Without your earrings, you could pass for a man with your short hair, brown overalls, and work boots," Yvette laughed as Delores climbed in the cab. "Did you have a hard time persuading Steve to let you come?"

"No. For me it's the other way. Steve keeps urging me to take time off to take care of myself. His mom had some emotional crisis because of overwork or stress, and he wants to make sure that doesn't happen to me."

"And you do what he says?" Yvette slowed for a tight curve.

"Steve isn't my boss. We discuss our concerns and dream up solutions we both like. Apparently, that's not how Luke operates?"

"No, it isn't. I can't imagine Luke caring what I want or need."

"I was disturbed by our talk at Stringtown. I hadn't realized Luke was *that* difficult. I should have caught on earlier. I had thought you're fortunate to have him. He's good at everything, and your folks would've had to sell the farm outside the family if you hadn't married him."

"I would have farmed it myself if I hadn't married Luke. Dad was disappointed when he ended up with four girls and no boys, but he was thrilled when I enjoyed farming and started buying him out. I thought you knew that."

"Since we never talked about it, I assumed," Delores repositioned a thermos at her feet. "What is that saying? I made us a donkey's relatives."

Yvette grinned at the play on the word. "It's a natural assumption. Women don't usually farm. In this case, my folks and I had already started the process of transferring the farm to me when Luke came along. I had the cow herd over half paid for and was doing three-quarters of the farming. If anything happened to Luke, I'd keep on farming. I love our place, and don't want to sell it—ever. Besides, it's an inheritance to pass on to my children, like my parents passed it on to me, and Dad's parents passed it on to him."

"What if none of your children want to farm?"

"I'd rent it out and live in the grandpa house until I die. What about your place? Do any of your children want to take on the greenhouse?"

"I don't think any of our five know what they want to do yet. Ryan's sixteen and into cars. Heather's thirteen and into volleyball. Michael, Jason, and Jill haven't developed any sustained interests yet. They all help in the greenhouse, and we've been encouraging them to develop their God-given talents and interests. If no one wants the greenhouse, that's okay."

"I wish Luke could do that. Kyle draws every chance he gets and is in the choir at school, but Luke taunts him for not being manly."

"Luke does that?" Delores widened her eyes. "When we were at your house, he proudly showed us Kyle's drawings."

"Not when Kyle was around to hear it."

"That's sad. I bet it puts you in a difficult position."

"I've decided to do what is right for Kyle. We sing together and I keep a variety of art supplies on hand. Luke scolds me, but I don't feel right urging Kyle to be what he's not. Do you think I'm doing the wrong thing?"

"You're in a hard spot when Luke disparages your opinion and Kyle's talents. I suspect he is abusing you and the children."

"What do you mean?" Yvette absently noted half a dozen brown horses in the field they were passing; their heads hanging low, their haunches turned toward the north wind, and their tails blowing between their legs.

"Taunting Kyle, degrading you and ordering you about is abuse."

"I thought—I thought it's not called abuse unless he hits me. I try to do what he wants, so he hasn't been as critical and blaming lately."

"When one partner continually criticizes, blames, accuses, and puts his spouse down, it's verbal and emotional abuse."

"Kyle pointed out Luke humiliated us a in a subtle way, too." As Yvette slowed for the stop sign, she told what happened at the restaurant.

"That's abuse. You felt confused because he *treated* you to a meal and *controlled* what you could eat and talk about at the same time."

"That's what he did with that wine documentary, too," Yvette told what happened and the disagreement about Margie as well. "I couldn't make sense of his behavior; he seemed loving otherwise. I thought our marriage had turned the corner because I submitted and didn't leave dirty dishes on the counter."

"Luke's behavior has nothing to do with what *you* do, Yvette. The discord in your marriage is *entirely* from him. Because he wants to control you, he *devises* situations he can use to meet his goal. If he can't find anything to complain about, he changes the rules or finds another way to humiliate you."

"Are you sure?" Yvette frowned, waiting at the stop sign for a string of cars to pass. "How do you know that?"

"My sister, Joyce, is married to an abuser. We used to be close before she married Eric, but now she only calls if she won't arouse his suspicions. I called the Domestic Violence Intervention Program in Iowa City to find out what to do. They sent me a packet and a list of books to read. Last fall I took their training course so I can help Joyce and other abused women."

"That's why you looked at me so funny at Stringtown and offered cookies instead of pie. You knew Luke—" Yvette fumbled for words as she turned onto Highway One.

"I had known Luke wanted pie twice a day. When I found out he made *you* bake it, I guessed those weren't the only ridiculous rules he had for you."

"What can I do, Delores? All these years I've tried to be what he wants so we have a loving marriage, but I only succeed temporarily."

"That's because he keeps changing the rules," Delores twisted to reach her woven yellow bag. "Did he expect pie every day when you first married?"

"No," Yvette sighed, "back then he wanted me to submit anytime he wanted sex. When I gave in, we had peace for awhile. Then he asked me to always serve dessert for supper. Later, he wanted pie—especially apple pie. Then he got mad if I made any of the cream pies. He wanted fruit pies."

"And from there he escalated it to pie twice a day," Delores opened the yellow bag and took out two plastic-wrapped, iced cinnamon rolls, "it has to be made by you, and now you can't have dirty dishes on the counter."

"What can I do?" Yvette wailed. "Over and over again I'd think his expectations were stupid, so I wouldn't comply. But he'd insist I *have* to submit, so I'd tell myself to stop being bull-headed. After I gave in, we'd have peace for awhile, so I thought it was my fault. But it's been so *hard* to do what I think is ridiculous. And since I refused in the first place it's humiliating, too."

"He *makes* it humiliating so he feels more powerful. When you distance yourself from him because you feel bad, he acts lover-like to convince you he's a good guy," she peeled the wrapper back and held the half-exposed cinnamon roll out for Yvette. "Have one. I bought these at Stringtown yesterday."

"Thanks," Yvette took it and savored a bite before continuing. "But what can I do to make him stop demanding such ridiculous stuff?"

"You can't *make* him do anything, but you *can* take steps that will discourage his controlling and abusive ways," Delores peeled back the wrap on her own roll and licked her fingers. "Unfortunately, Luke's interpretation of submission may be so engrained in you, *you'll* feel you're doing wrong. The basic idea is to stop the payoff he gets. Find a way to reverse the consequences so they fall on *him* instead of on you."

Yvette tucked a bite of roll in her cheek. "How do I do that?"

"For instance, what are the consequences of baking apple pie?"

"A mess in the kitchen, tiredness, and less time for other things."

"Ah, all of them provide excuses to yell at you, and he made it worse by choosing the most time-consuming pies as his favorites," Delores tore off a section of her roll. "To redirect the consequences to him you could tell him if he wants pie he has to buy it," she popped the piece in her mouth.

"I'd be spared the mess and could use the time for bookkeeping. Or I could bake pie for him, and refuse to do other things he wants so I'd have more time with the children. He'd get terribly upset."

"It sounds like he's using fits of rage to control you. Instead of letting his temper work for him, you can sidestep so the consequences fall on him. Tell him when he uses anger to control you, he'll sleep on the couch."

"I can't enforce that," Yvette braked for a semi coming off the interstate, "there's no lock on the door. But I could be sexually unavailable." She wanted to tell Delores about last week when she'd been so tired she'd turned Luke down and cried uncontrollably, but couldn't. Not yet. It was too personal, too embarrassing. "Are you saying I should stop submitting?"

"Not exactly," Delores stopped to lick her fingers. "Your focus should be to do what is right in *God's* eyes. I think you need to reexamine the Bible and decide if *you* think Luke's interpretation is the correct one."

Yvette pulled up behind a car in the left turn lane. "I know Luke acts as if the part about husbands loving and sacrificing for their wives isn't there. But whether he does his part or not, I'm *still* supposed to submit to him."

"That's what he wants you to believe. In Malachi it says God hates a man covering himself with violence toward his wife. The danger in accepting Luke's view is he has taken it out of context. The context of Ephesians Four and Five is for Christians to be compassionate and gentle with each other, to build one other up, to put off the old sinful self and become like Christ. When Luke humiliates you and demands service, he throws out the part about husbands loving and sacrificing for their wives, and throws out the rest of Ephesians and many other passages besides."

"I never thought of it in that way, but I feel it on a gut level," the left arrow turned green, and Yvette eased the pickup onto Sunset Street.

"Luke keeps you focused on your so-called imperfections so you don't notice his glaring faults," Delores took a swig from the red half-gallon water jug. "He's insisting a husband has the license to lord it over his wife, to sin without consequences, to pile rules and responsibilities on his wife, and to dole out dire penalties if she fails to perform as he decrees. Do you recall anything in scripture which suggests that is what Paul had in mind?"

"Absolutely *not!* If that was what Paul meant, he would have said," Yvette cleared her throat and began in a ponderous preacher voice: "'Husbands, lord it over your wives just as Christ lords it over the church and demands obedience. For the husband deserves to have his wife give up her life for him, as the church did for Christ.'"

Delores stared at her friend. "Good grief! That's heresy!"

"Don't look at me as if I believe it. *Luke* acts as if *he* believes it."

"That's what's wrong with his belief! The Christian couple is a symbol of Christ and the Church. A husband who demands his wife act out his own role of symbolizing Christ's self-sacrifice turns the symbolism into heresy. The Church did *not* die for Christ. To say that the Church did—even through symbolism—is like saying Christ needed redemption. Wait till I tell Steve this. He'll have a *fit.*"

"What do you mean, *he'll have a fit?*" Yvette frowned as she tried to picture Steve storming about because she'd uttered sacrilege.

"He'll be distressed our churches don't teach against husband dictatorships, when doctrinal symbolism is involved. And you are right. If he meant to say the husband was to be in authority over his wife, Paul would have said so. Paul uses the words 'authority' and 'lord it over' and 'rule' elsewhere, and would have used them in Ephesians Five if that was what he meant. The words he chose point to an equal relationship."

"This is so frustrating," Yvette sighed. "One side of me knows you're right and I can't keep submitting like I have been, but the other side doesn't see any way to *stop* submitting and still be scripturally correct."

"There are other passages that indicate submission isn't always the way to go. In Proverbs, men with Luke's behavior are labeled fools who must be dealt with differently. Consider the account of Abigail, who *didn't* submit to her husband's rude order to not feed David and his men. Her non-submission was rewarded although her husband got very angry. Or Queen Jezebel, who did a type of submission by arranging the murder of the man who refused to sell his vineyard to Jezebel's husband. She was condemned for it."

"I didn't think of those examples." Yvette stopped for a red light, "But every time I stand up for myself, Luke insists I must submit *in everything.*"

"Isn't it odd his *everything* doesn't include offering to chore or wash the dishes, and urging you to take time for your development? According to the directive to husbands, *that* was what Paul had in mind. You're to submit to his *cherishing* of you, not his misuse of you. First John says *We love Him because He first loved us.* Our submission to Christ comes as a *response* to His loving self-sacrifice for us, *not* from a *demand* that we obey Him although He's been nasty to us. And *that's* what Christian marriage should be like."

"So you're saying when I submit to Luke's nasty demands, we are symbolizing the church submitting to the devil?"

"Exactly. Luke's selfish and abusive behavior is wrong. Although there's a verse where slaves are told to obey their harsh masters, there's not a single scripture where wives are told obey their harsh husbands. As Christians, we are to submit to one another, but Luke is using false doctrine to coerce you to submit to his sinful behavior. There is no way that can be biblical."

"You're right. Paul tells husbands to *not* be harsh to their wives."

"You got it. And he tells Peter to not yield to the wrong doctrine of false teachers—not even for a minute. Luke is distorting the *gospel* when he tries to convince you you're sinning or aren't saved if you don't obey him."

"His gospel would be 'Believe in the Lord Jesus Christ and obey your husband's every whim, and you shall be saved,'" Yvette snickered.

"You're good at those sacrilegious paraphrases," Delores grinned.

"Luke keeps me confused," Yvette stopped the pickup in the street and backed into the drive. "And I haven't heard a single preacher say wives aren't supposed to do certain things for their husbands; they emphasize submission. One said, '*Submit, but don't be a doormat,*' but to me it translated into '*Be a doormat, but don't be a doormat,*' and didn't make sense."

"That was because Luke forced his definition of submission on you." Delores opened the pickup door letting in cold air. "Are you ready to work?"

They got hand shovels from the pickup bed, rounded the garage, and surveyed the backyard. The earth was packed but dry where the patio had been. The five trees had piles of dirt and trenches around them where Yvette dug for bulbs, while the beds around the bushes hadn't been touched.

"You've been working hard," Delores observed. "How many of these bushes are you planning to get?"

"I should have twelve to sixteen, maybe more, to create screened off areas and give an illusion of privacy." Yvette turned her back to the wind, put her hood up and tied it. "I'm tired of digging; the cold wind makes it worse."

"Don't give up yet. Why don't we get the small stuff in one area, and ask Steve if he'll bring the tree digger to get the bushes and trees? Since you promised us half, that's the least we can do."

After Delores called Steve on her cell phone, the women dug up bulbs, ferns, hostas, and peonies that had started to emerge, and roots of perennials they couldn't identify. They giggled as they planned a prank-filled party for their daughters, who shared the same birthday. By lunch time, they'd prepared half the yard for the tree digger. Pleased with their progress, they got in the pickup and ran the heater to warm up while they ate.

"Oh, it feels good to sit down," Delores leaned her shoulders back against the seat and arched her stomach out to stretch her back muscles.

"How are your hands holding out?" Yvette tipped the thermos and poured steaming cream of chicken soup into Delores's bowl. "Mine held up surprisingly well since I've been wearing thick gloves, but they weren't doing so well a couple of days ago when I had on thin gardening gloves."

Delores cradled the bowl in her hands. "The warmth feels good." She inspected her thumbs and palms. "No blisters; I varied how I dug."

"I've been wondering," Yvette poured soup for herself and screwed the lid closed, "where do I start changing how I respond to Luke?"

Delores didn't answer right away. She took two crackers, placed them at the edge of her bowl, blew on a spoonful of soup, then took a bite. "The soup is delicious and warms me up inside; thank-you very much."

Yvette held out a sandwich bag. "Have some baby carrots."

Delores took a few and paused before taking a bite. "I think I'd make small changes at first. You want to do what's right, not act like a rebel. Look at *your* needs and the children's needs and start there. First, you need more sleep so you don't ruin your health and you'll be more available to the children. You may want to consider areas where you could save time, like baking cake instead of pie or not serving dessert at all some days."

"Then dirty dishes wouldn't be an issue. The mess could easily be cleaned up before Luke comes in." Yvette crunched down on a carrot.

"And that could have a snowball effect and free up time elsewhere."

"If I do bookwork during the day, I'd get to sleep earlier at night. Luke will stomp around the house and accuse me of not submitting, though."

"Call his bluff before his control escalates further."

"I'm glad you gave me another angle to consider at Stringtown. It kept me from assuming I was at fault when Luke accused me last week."

"What happened last week?" Delores reached for a slice of cheese.

Yvette hesitated, then decided Delores would understand. She told how she had turned Luke down, bit his tongue when he thrust it in her mouth, and ended up crying. "The more I tried to stop crying, the faster the tears came. That day I came smack up against the truth. No matter how much I yield, I can never satisfy Luke. Submitting won't sway him to be a loving husband. All my efforts to build a loving marriage are futile. A decent marriage will always be out of my reach. I had no strength to try harder, and Luke still demanded more," Yvette took her last bite of soup and put the bowl in her picnic basket.

"How awful!" Delores squeezed Yvette's hand. "Luke's conduct is despicable. But there's a positive side now that you know you aren't at fault."

"Oh, yeah?" Yvette hugged her solar plexus. "What?"

"Since you know you can't win by obeying Luke, you have nothing to lose if you try a different approach."

"You're absolutely right. I *have* nothing to lose. Either way, Luke will accuse me of not submitting. I may as well get creative." She felt hope bubble up and clasped her hands to contain herself. "This is so exciting! If I change my response to Luke, maybe he'll grow to love and value me. I'm so excited I can't sit still. Are you ready to start digging again?"

The women got out of the pickup and braced themselves against the wind as they pulled on their gardening gloves and knelt to continue digging. After a long silence, Delores scrambled to her feet. "I hear Steve's truck."

They opened the gate as Steve brought the flatbed truck, towing a trailer with a skid-loader on it, to a halt in the street. He jumped down from the truck, crossed the ditch in one stride, and joined the women at the gate.

"Hi, Yvette," Steve spared her a nod before turning to Delores. Yvette caught his look of *I'm so glad to see you* as his eyes met his wife's, and felt a pang of regret that she never saw that look in Luke's eyes.

"How's it going?" his tone was friendly and caring. Although nearly as tall as Luke, he didn't tower critically over them, as Luke did, and Yvette sensed whatever they did was acceptable to him. She relaxed.

Delores returned his look and turned to point out where he could start digging. Yvette watched them. *That* was what she wanted her marriage to be like. The contrast between the reality of her life with Luke compared to what could be, swept over her, engulfing her with pain. With an effort she brought herself back to the job at hand.

Steve drove the skid loader, with a cone-shaped digger mounted on its front, into the back yard. Yvette watched as he lowered the square steel frame around the first bush. The blades sliced at an angle into the ground, then hefted the bush up and deposited it into a nursery pot. Fascinated, she watched two more bushes leave the ground, then went back to her digging.

With the silence ended by the loud brum of the tree remover, the women worked without talking, except for yelling instructions. Yvette kept seeing the tender expressions on the faces of her friends, and mulled over her talk with Delores. Her life with Luke was a bleak existence at best, and at worst a terrorist dictatorship. She wanted to cry, but could not in front of her friends.

Chapter 7

On Sunday morning, after sending the boys in to shower, Yvette lingered in the barn with a newborn calf. She took a deep breath, taking in the scents of hay and cow dung muted with straw, luxuriating in the sliver of time that had become a favorite—likely because she didn't have to cook breakfast.

Years ago, when the boys were small and her dad had helped her milk cows, Luke insisted she cook eggs on Sunday morning, and they sit as a family around the breakfast table before going to church. She'd reasoned it would save time if everyone ate cereal at their convenience, but Luke stood firm.

While Luke watched TV in the living room the next Sunday, she'd hurriedly dressed the boys and fixed bowls of cereal for them, then showered and dressed for church. By the time she finished, it was past time to leave and Luke grabbed a bagel to eat on the way. Furious, he'd insisted she cook breakfast *first* the next Sunday. She complied, but didn't have time to shower before dressing for church. As they climbed in the car, Luke had sniffed and said, "You smell like a cow. You aren't going to church like that."

"Yes I am. When you pile work on me, you'll endure my cow perfume during church." Immediately after the service, he'd herded the family to the car instead of talking to his buddies. After that, he ate cereal on Sunday mornings.

Yvette grinned as she picked up the gallon-sized galvanized bucket, dipped two fingers into the tepid milk and offered them to the big-boned, lanky, black and white bawling calf. *Delores was right. When Luke paid the consequences, he dropped his unreasonable orders. I'll look for more ways to make the consequences for his rules fall on him instead of on me and the children.*

The calf turned away, bawling through the slats of the wooden stall door, forcing her to focus on the task at hand. From the lot outside, his mother answered and kept lowing. Yvette held him against the wall so he couldn't turn away, dipped her fingers again, and stuck them into his mouth when he bawled.

"You want Mama," she crooned. "Here's her first milk—it's colostrum—special made so you don't get sick. Come now, suck it off my fingers."

He kept bawling and struggled to get away from her.

"Come on, Buster, I don't have all day," she backed him in the corner, set the bucket down, dipped again and wiped the milk on his tongue and the roof of his mouth, but he resisted and nearly knocked her over. "I can't let you run with your mama; you'll get wild and unmanageable. Come on, suck. Your mouth is dry; I don't think you had anything at all this morning."

When he kept bawling and didn't suckle her fingers, she retreated to the calf-sized hay rack and feed trough in his pen and sat on the narrow wooden trough to recover her strength and consider her options. If she gave up now he'd have to wait until noon when they came home from church. That would be too long for a newborn to go without sustenance. How could she get him to suck?

For that matter, as Delores had said, how could one make *anyone* do what he didn't want to do? After reading the books and packet Delores had loaned her—the books that described Luke and their marriage so well she'd hated to stop reading and read late into the night—she realized he didn't *want* a harmonious relationship. According to the books and Luke's arguments, he wanted to be her *master*, not her companion. And he never felt like a winner unless he made her the loser. Yet, she had thought when he talked of having a good marriage, he meant peace and happiness for *both* of them, not just for him.

She shook her head. Intellectually, she knew Luke had been misusing her, but in her heart she couldn't accept that he had been *creating* conflict. The idea felt too foreign, too bizarre. Surely there was another explanation.

She drew her knees to her chest, bracing her feet against the trough ledge as she recalled the past few days. Her course of action had seemed clear when she talked with Delores, but the next day she'd awakened confused. What if Delores was wrong and God held her, Yvette, accountable for not submitting? What if her refusal to submit caused their marriage to fail? The community would look down on her as insubordinate, flighty, and selfish. The children would suffer from his constant griping. So she'd kept the house perfect, chored on time morning and evening, and satisfied Luke in bed.

The confusion stayed with her and spilled over into her work. She'd dithered for hours over the sequence of the various pieces of blue fabric for the Mennonite Relief Sale dahlia quilt. She settled on a sequence that made it look like a shadowed and highlighted flower. On Saturday she'd vacillated on the placement of the bushes, perennials and bulbs for the patio. She finally decided to trust her instincts and plant the bulbs while she had Kyle's and Tanya's help.

Luke had come out to the front yard and chewed her out in front of the children for suggesting he and the boys help salvage flagstones. "The ground is perfect for hauling manure," he'd said, "but the tractor isn't ready. If you'd stop lazing around and waiting for help, I could get *my* work done on time. But now the hood isn't painted and rain is in the forecast. I'll be late with planting, and it's all because of *you*. From here on, you are *not* to ask me for help. When I say I need both boys to help me, you are not to challenge me. Is that clear?"

"Loud and clear," kneeling next to a hole Kyle dug, she'd dumped in a scoop of bone meal and stirred it into the loose soil in the bottom of the hole, then glanced at the children to see how Luke's griping affected them. Tanya glanced from the hole before her knees to Luke and back again. Kyle focused on the hole and she couldn't detect any expression on his face. "Why blame me? You had a week to paint it since you and the boys helped get flagstones."

"I had forgotten the manure spreader had to be fixed and a board on the fence needed to be replaced or the calves would get out and we'd waste time chasing them in," he braced his hand against the porch pillar.

"It didn't take all week to fix the fence and the spreader," she placed a bulb in the loosened soil and motioned to Tanya and Kyle to do the same. "Did you forget you went to Iowa City and spent half a day with Alex? And Monday you took all afternoon in Kalona to get a part for the manure spreader. Were you waiting for the part to come in the mail or something?"

"Very funny. Winter is supposed to be a time of rest and relaxation for a farmer," he shifted his feet, "but I overhauled the tractor instead. A man's gotta go out with the boys and take days off now and then."

"But you must feel guilty you took time off. Otherwise you wouldn't come out here to blame me. Think how far ahead you'd be if you hadn't taken time to come out here and gripe. In fact, if you paint it now, you could be in the fields by next Friday. Doesn't it take a week for the paint to cure?"

"Not for newer paints. It takes two or three days—four maximum."

"So paint it today, and it'll be ready by Tuesday or Wednesday."

"Of course, you're too *stupid* to get it," he sauntered to the edge of the hole and kicked a mound of loose dirt in it. "If you hadn't insisted I help you, I'd be hauling manure right now. That *one day* put me *way* behind."

"Haul manure with the hood off," she brushed the excess dirt aside.

"That's stupid. Dirt will get in the engine."

"You won't stir up much dust," Yvette placed the twelfth bulb in the hole, then pushed a pile of loose dirt on top. Tanya rushed to help crumble dirt onto the bulbs. "You can clean off specks of manure that blow that far forward. Kyle, could you dig a hole where Tanya was kneeling?" Kyle moved to comply.

"Just great; fried manure on my new engine."

"You could stop and wipe the tractor off when the wind blows a few splatters on it," she grinned as she visualized Luke stopping to wipe specks of smelly fermented manure off the tractor. "On second thought, you could *lease* a tractor and put this one in a museum so it won't get dirty."

"Very funny. I prefer my idea of leaving the hood off the tractor."

"Your idea?" she snorted.

"Of *course* it was my idea. *Your* idea was to *lease* a tractor."

He'd followed her suggestion and hauled manure with the hoodless tractor that afternoon, while she'd finished cutting pieces for the blue quilt. As she cut out quilt pieces, her confusion over her marriage had dissipated, only to intrude again when she surfaced to cook or chore. She resented the intrusion of chores, preferring to create. She'd felt as if she'd met a complex and exciting, but lovable person—herself—with whom she couldn't spend enough time. That night while Luke used her body, she'd retreated into the joy of planning her next creation, even as she moved to hurry him to completion. She felt obsessed with creating beauty. Nothing mattered as long as she could create.

Yvette dropped one leg over the trough's shallow lip, and the bawling calf shied away, reminding her she hadn't fed him. Now that she'd rested, she'd see if she had the strength to get him started by pouring milk down his throat. She fought to pin the struggling calf against the wall, back him into the corner, and hold his nose up while she tipped the bucket and poured milk into his mouth. When he swallowed, she poured again and stuck her fingers in his mouth. This time he suckled them. She lowered his mouth into the milk while he sucked her fingers, and with sporadic bucks at the bucket, he drank all of it.

~   ~   ~

On the way home from church, Greg drove and Luke chose the front passenger seat, as usual. "Where'd you go after church?" Luke looked over his shoulder. "I waited for you outside the women's bathroom."

"You were talking when I came out," Yvette noted how bony his nose looked in profile. "I talked to Margie about the quilt top I'm piecing."

"You ought to make one for *our* bed," he grumped.

"I don't want to. You'd find something to criticize about it."

"What is it with you? You haven't been yourself lately."

She studied the greenhouse they were passing and noted Delores and Steve's competition had a long table of flowers outside. *Probably pansies and the like.* "Well, I'm sure this is me," she faced forward.

"Good; I volunteered for the Georgia tornado cleanup crew."

"Not again! You don't have to drop your responsibilities and go help *every* time there's a tornado somewhere in the United States."

"I don't go every time. And even if I did, why not? I know what to do and how to get it done."

"What about your family? Don't our needs count for anything?"

"Can I go, too?" Greg asked as he drove past the Amish Sunday School house where long lines of black buggies were parked side by side, brown horses waited at the hitching rail, and groups of boys stood in circles, hunching their white-shirted, dark-suspendered shoulders against the cold and clenching their fists in their pants pockets as they watched them turn the corner and drive past.

"No," Luke said, "you have to go to school."

"Don't be ridiculous, Luke," Yvette said. "You can't go either. The sows are due to farrow any day. You can't afford to go now."

"They asked me to direct a work crew, so I'm going. You can handle the farrowing house. I cleaned and disinfected it, and the calf stable is cleaned out. I'll do the brooder house and manure pits when I get back."

"Shifting your work onto me is despicable, Luke," she glared at his profile. "Last year I had to plant corn and beans besides planting the garden, and now you make me take care of pigs. I haven't dealt with sows and piglets for years. My time is full with my own responsibilities; I don't need yours, too."

"This will be a refresher course for you. After all, when I die you'll need to know how to do my chores if you keep the farm. Anyhow, the people in Georgia have to change their plans, so you can change yours."

"I do not appreciate you leaving me in the lurch like this without even consulting me. Maybe I'll take *your* sows to market instead of caring for them, like Sam Zook did when his brother dumped the job on him."

"If you do," he roared, thumping the dash with his palm, "you'll be one sorry woman. I will not tolerate you undermining me like that."

"Stop yelling," Yvette glanced at Tanya beside her, catching her wide-eyed stare fixed on Luke as if she couldn't look away, and beyond Tanya, Kyle's face turned to the window. "You're scaring the children."

"It's time they toughen up; you've been too soft on them."

"They *need* softness with you about; they do poorly in a war zone."

"*You're* the one who makes it a war zone. If you'd just get behind me and *support* me in my decisions, things would be just great around here."

"I fail to see how things will be just great with us doing *your* work as well as our own. When are you leaving and coming back?"

He flicked her a glance. "We leave at six tomorrow morning and get back late Saturday night on the twelfth of April."

"Two whole weeks! That's *not* okay with me! Why don't I go somewhere for two weeks and expect you to be responsible for my chores?"

"You can talk and threaten all you want; it isn't going to change my mind. God has given me the gift of administration and expects me to use it."

No one spoke as Greg turned in their drive and parked. The children spilled out the doors and hurried into the house ahead of Luke and Yvette.

"I want my bags packed today," Luke said as they walked toward the house. When she didn't respond he snapped, "Did you hear me?"

"I heard you," she tried to sound calm in spite of the lurching in her midsection. *I refuse to do one iota of extra work just to calm Luke's temper.*

"Well, when are you going to pack for me?" he demanded.

"I'm not," she said without heat as they entered the house.

"What do you mean, you're not? I told you to pack my bags! *Jezebel!* What a conniving woman! You do anything to get your way."

Yvette didn't respond. *Sticking up for my principles could hardly be called conniving. If I keep yielding to Luke's increasingly ridiculous demands to avoid his rage or in the name of submission, how many wrong things will I do in the process? Might I someday conspire to kill a man like Queen Jezebel did?*

~ ~ ~

Yvette woke the boys at five the next morning, an hour before Luke planned to leave for Georgia. As she crouched in front of the hearth stove fanning a tiny flame, Luke, bleary-eyed and in his navy bathrobe, stomped into the dining room, making the dishes in the china cupboard rattle. Yvette tensed.

"I want breakfast before I go," he said.

"I'm putting coffee on and making peanut butter and honey on toast for the boys and myself anyway," she forced a friendly tone as she pushed the stove door shut and rose. "I'll put bread in the toaster for you."

"I want two eggs," he said. She could feel him staring at her, but she refused to look at him. She wouldn't be intimidated by him this time.

"Help yourself," she headed to the kitchen, detouring through the washroom so she wouldn't pass near him. "I'd like to chore on time."

Luke snorted. "That's an excuse. You don't *ever* chore on time." As she rushed through the washroom, she saw he'd moved to the kitchen and she'd have to go by him after all. His glaring eyes threatened a blow up. "I'd think you'd want to cook eggs, bacon, and hash browns—the works—before I leave."

"I can't stop you from going," she hurried past him and got the can of coffee, "but I won't support your inconsiderate behavior to your family."

"What a bunch of feminist drivel!" he trailed her to the counter. "It's *your duty* to support me whether you agree with me or not. If anything happens to me, you'll be sorry you didn't act like a Christian wife should."

"Possibly," she shrugged, dumping the coffee filter with its used grounds into the waste basket. "And if any of us get hurt, you'll be sorry you insisted on leaving us in the lurch—especially if it's by one of the brood sows."

"Okay, you said your piece," he crossed his arms over his chest and planted himself between her and the coffee pot. "Now cook my breakfast."

"Not now," she crossed to the sink and rinsed the filter basket.

He blocked her as she turned toward the coffee maker, glaring and thrusting his face, nose to nose, in front of hers. "What did you say?"

She recoiled and her heart skipped a beat then galloped wildly. He stepped forward, closing the gap between them, and she forced herself to stand still and erect. She glimpsed the spoke-like ridges in his dark brown irises before her gaze dropped to his wide muscular chest. She wanted to run, to give in—anything to stop this horrid tension, to slow her pounding heart—but remembered her talk with Delores and made herself keep her voice even and calm as she rephrased her answer. "I said *no.*"

She changed direction to step around his bulk.

He blocked her again, his arms still across his chest.

"Stop it, Luke," she felt panic rising from the pit of her stomach and took a deep breath to tamp it down. "This filter basket is dripping and leaving a mess on the floor," she cupped a hand under the basket to catch the drips. "If you don't let me pass, I won't make coffee, either."

He straightened and stared down at her.

She stared back.

"What a *rebel*! God will punish you for your rebellion like he punished Miriam for rebelling against Moses." He stomped to the refrigerator and yanked open the door, snatched the milk pitcher and plunked it on the table.

Stomach clenching, Yvette busied herself at the coffee maker, keeping Luke in her peripheral vision while she took out a fresh filter and dumped in scoops of coffee which she forgot to count. Luke charged toward her and her insides jumped, then stampeded as he stormed by, knocking her shoulder and causing her to spill water. Her hand shook as she filled the coffee maker reservoir, spilling more water. She steadied the pitcher with her other hand.

Luke jerked pans and lids out of the cupboard, crashing them in rapid succession onto the counter until he pulled out a non-stick pan, then slammed the cupboard door and dropped the pan on the stove with a clatter.

Feigning absorption in wiping up the spill, Yvette waited for him to move from the range so she wouldn't have to pass him to get to the toaster. When he stomped to the refrigerator, she scurried into the corner, keeping tabs on him as she fumbled to get four slices of bread out of the bag and into the toaster. As she pushed both levers down, he marched to the stove and smashed two eggs onto the counter, making a yolky, egg-shelly mess.

"Now look what you made me do!" he shouted, slinging the egg mess from his hand. "If you'd made my breakfast, this wouldn't have happened. *You* can clean up the mess, you good-for-nothing insubordinate *rebel*!"

In the silence that followed, she heard the stair door creak and realized someone—hopefully the boys and not Tanya—had come down. Her insides churning, she wanted to rush to cook his breakfast to put an end to this awful ordeal, but if she gave in to his bullying now, he'd do even worse later.

She put on a calm front and spoke in a quiet but firm tone. "You can yell and scream all you want, Luke, but I'm done giving in to your bullying. This atmosphere you created is not fit for children or wife. So *stop* it."

"*I* didn't create this atmosphere," he snarled, "*you* did. No self-respecting husband would tolerate his wife refusing to cook his breakfast." He stalked to the refrigerator, while Yvette made herself stay in the corner until the toast popped up. "You are asking for trouble."

"You plan to banish me like Queen Vashti?" she forced a humorous tone. "Oops, it's not your kingdom; you'll have to exile yourself."

The toast popped up at the same time Luke returned to the range with two more eggs. Her hands shook as she edged past him with three hot slices of toast, her eyes watching his arms and heels. Once out of the corner, she sighed with relief and hurried to get the peanut butter and honey mix out of the refrigerator and spread them on the toast before it cooled.

Usually the boys came to the kitchen to eat, but this time she took the open-faced sandwiches to them. She stopped short at the threshold of the dining room. They weren't huddled around the warming hearth stove. *Oh, God, please don't let Tanya be the one who came down and heard Luke's fit.* She rushed to the living room. *It would be bad enough if Greg and Kyle heard it, but if Tanya did—* She broke off her prayer as she stepped into the living room and saw Greg in the dark far corner pulling a shirt over his head and Kyle buckling his belt.

"Do you want me to bring your coffee in, too?" she whispered, taking a bite of her toast. It felt dry and sticky and the sweetness of the honey turned her stomach. She swallowed several times before it went down.

The boys exchanged glances. "I don't want anything," Kyle said.

"Me neither," Greg took the slices intended for Kyle and himself and put the faces together. We'll get milk from the bulk tank. Let's get out of here."

Yvette folded her bread and tiptoed after them to the washroom, glimpsing Luke sitting at the kitchen table, wolfing down his breakfast. They put their sandwiches on the window sill while they yanked on coats and boots.

When Luke's chair scraped back, her stomach lurched and she saw the boys jerk and exchange glances. Luke approached the washroom doorway and pinned them with his stare. Their movements slowed as they faced him. "This must be a record," he drawled, his eyes studying each one in turn. "It's only ten after five and you're ready to go out the door. You think I don't know you ignore what *I* say and usually go out at five-*thirty*. You're hurting yourselves with your lack of respect for me. If you'd get out to the barn at five, the cows would give more milk and you'd have money to burn."

Yvette wanted to tell him if they made more money, he'd lay claim to it, but his manner warned her to say nothing so she kept quiet.

"Too chicken to say anything, huh?" Luke sneered. "Well, that's a first." He turned and stalked into the dining room.

Yvette heard the rattle of windows with every step he took and jumped when he appeared at the other door to the washroom.

"I'm going to take your tools," Luke jerked open the tool drawer, "so mine don't get stolen." Yvette and the boys watched helplessly as he selected both hammers, her entire sets of socket wrenches and red-handled screwdrivers, her needle nose pliers and two pairs of regular red-handled pliers, and her pipe wrench, and tossed them onto the built-in worktable.

Greg started forward. Yvette grabbed his coat and pulled him back.

"Where's the vice-grip?" Luke pawed the contents of the drawer back and forth so fast he likely couldn't see it if it was there. He yanked the drawer out so it fell on the floor and spilled half its dusty nuts, bolts, washers, screws, nails, and odds and ends onto the light blue carpet. He kicked the drawer then yanked open the next one. "What's the vice-grip doing in this drawer?" he glared at her. "This isn't where it belongs. You were hiding it from me."

"Not particularly," she stared back. "The other drawer was full."

"So toss out the nuts, bolts and screws. Of course, you're too *stupid* to reach such an *obvious* conclusion."

"I use those, too, so it's *not* an obvious conclusion. Unlike you, I can't go to town every time I need a washer." She winced as soon as the words left her mouth. Now she was in for it.

He glowered at her. "So *this* is what you've come to," he spoke in a soft but deadly tone. "*This* is the attitude you're teaching my boys. You should be *ashamed* of yourself. *You* are responsible for wrecking our home. *God* holds *you* accountable. I'll deal with you when I get back." He stomped to the bedroom, leaving the mess on the floor.

"Come on," Greg nudged Kyle's shoulder, "let's get out of here."

With coats open, they dashed out the door. Yvette tied her kerchief behind her head, then grabbed their sandwiches and rushed outside.

They started choring in tense silence, waiting, Yvette thought, for another ugly scene. With Luke being so mad, they didn't know what to expect. He could come in the barn and chew them out even more.

As soon as Greg, who was in the feedway, finished dumping grain into the wooden feedboxes, Yvette grasped a two-foot piece of rubber hose and pushed the door open to let in the first bunch of crowding, black and white, Holstein cows. When eight cows had rushed in, she pulled the door shut on the neck of the ninth determined cow, and hit her nose with the hose to make her step back. Seeing that Kyle was rushing from cow to cow, fastening the box-stall chains about their necks, Yvette started washing teats.

Although it was windy and below freezing, Yvette left the top half of the Dutch doors open so they could see when Luke left. Every time they heard a vehicle, they stood up to see if it was Luke. Finally, when they heard a vehicle and stood up to look, Yvette saw Luke whizzing past in the dark blue family car.

As a balloon soars and swirls when the neck is released, so the tension in the barn crew sent them hurrying to gather at the door of the cow stable, all talking at once. Yvette noticed Kyle's shoulders had dropped, the lines on Greg's forehead and the tension around his mouth had vanished.

"What are *we* supposed to drive?" Greg protested. "He won't like us driving the pickup all over the place for two weeks."

"Why does he get like that?" Kyle asked. "I'm never going to be like him when I get married and have kids."

"Do you think Tanya slept through all that?" Yvette babbled. "I should check on her and make sure she's okay. I hope he didn't wake her up."

"I thought he was going to explode," Kyle released a noisy breath.

"It's not fair," Greg spat. "He won't let me play basketball with the guys, but he can go for two weeks at a time. Why can he leave whenever he wants to and make us do *his* chores? Now we won't have time for any fun."

"If you pitch in," Yvette said, "I'll *schedule* time for fun while Dad's gone." *Maybe Luke's absence will give me a chance to talk with Greg, especially now that basketball season is over..*

"It's not going to work, Mom," Kyle said. "We still go to school and there's not much time for fun after we do *our own* chores."

"Come on," she coaxed. "Let's have a *good* time while he's gone."

"He's a *jerk*," Greg slapped the barn wall for emphasis.

"Don't Greg," Yvette said. "He *is* your dad. Let's turn this batch of cows out. I'll help start the next batch, and then check on Tanya."

"You better go now, Mom," Kyle urged. "Greg and I can manage."

Yvette rushed to check on the girl and found her huddled on her bed, crying, with blankets in disarray around her and one over her head.

"What's wrong, Honey?" Yvette soothed, hugging her daughter through the bedding, and clearing the blanket from her face.

"I'm s-scared," Tanya snuffled. "I heard that b-banging around, and was a-afraid he would come up and-and..." she stopped.

"He's gone now," Yvette caressed Tanya's back as a wave of helpless rage swept through her. How could he traumatize his daughter like this?

"I w-want to be in the barn with y-you," she sucked in a shaky breath.

"Okay. How about if you sit on the shelf in the cow stable? We'll take a pillow and blanket with us, and if you want to lie down or snooze, you can."

"Ok-ay," she sniffled and crawled out of the covers, shivering.

"Oh, God," Yvette whispered, "please help us."

~   ~   ~

They got in from chores later than usual, and Yvette asked Greg to pack the lunches while Kyle showered and changed and she prepared breakfast. Greg complied, but Tanya refused to dress herself for school, getting underfoot as she hugged her special baby blanket to her chest and hung around Yvette.

"Can we take pie to school?" Greg set a stack of plates on the table.

"Sure. I was planning to bake more today anyway. How about pumpkin pie for a change? That doesn't take as long to prepare as apple pie."

"Yes!" he crowed. "Pumpkin! Dad's stupid for not liking it."

"Don't call your dad stupid, Greg. Tanya," exasperated, she hugged the girl and nudged her onto a chair, "please sit in this chair so I can move without stepping on you. And please don't cry," she added when Tanya's lower lip begin to quiver. "I'll be with you as soon as I finish making breakfast." She selected a pan Luke had left on the counter and got eggs from the refrigerator. "This morning was rough, but Dad's gone now. His actions were unacceptable, and none of us will ever act like that, will we, Greg?"

Greg shrugged and spun each white, burgundy rimmed plate to its place on the table.

When Kyle came downstairs, Yvette asked him to watch the eggs so she could help Tanya dress for school.

"I don't want to go to school," Tanya crossed her arms over her chest.

"You have to go to school," Yvette ushered her upstairs and to her room, wishing she had time to hold Tanya before the bus came. "I know Dad scared you this morning, but he's far away by now, and you don't need to be scared. School will help you think about other things."

"But Mom," Tanya wailed, her voice muffled as Yvette pulled the girl's nightgown over her head, "the teacher will get mad at me."

"I'll send her a note saying you're upset. Here, put this shirt on."

"I don't want that Bert and Ernie shirt; it's babyish. I want the red one," from the bottom of the pile Tanya pulled a soft shirt she never wore, jumbling the rest of the shirts in the process.

"Whatever for? I thought you don't like that one."

"It's your color, Mom. It'll be like having a hug from you all day."

"Oh, Sweetie," Yvette blinked back tears and hugged her. Tanya wouldn't dress herself, but cooperated when Yvette dressed her. She refused to eat breakfast, and hung back when Kyle announced the bus was at Lester's.

"Jill will be at school," Yvette gave her a note for the teacher.

"Come on, Butterfly," Kyle said, "you can sit with me on the bus."

Taking his outstretched hand, she ran with him to the bus.

Yvette sighed as the bus drove out of sight. If only Tanya wouldn't be so fear-prone. Luke's absence didn't seem to comfort her at all. It was as if his behavior reminded Tanya that the world was full of shouting, angry monsters.

Returning to the kitchen, Yvette cleaned up Luke's slimy egg mess, praying for him so her anger wouldn't boil over, then piled the dishes on the counter and started cutting pie dough. She'd bake pumpkin, pecan, banana cream, and peanut butter pies, her children's favorites, and she'd bake and freeze two apple pies for Luke so she wouldn't have to bake next week, too.

By the time the bus dropped off the children, she had baked eleven pies—almost twice as many as she could make when she had to peel apples for seven pies and top them with crust—had a dozen popovers in the oven, and a pot of creamy tapioca filling on the stove.

"How was your day?" she asked as the children rushed to the kitchen, dumping their lunch-boxes on the counter and shrugging backpacks on the floor.

"What's for snack?" Greg asked.

"Popovers!" Tanya peeked into the oven. "Can I help fill them?"

"Where's the banana cream pie?" Kyle peered into the refrigerator.

"Each of you gets *one* pie this week," Yvette said. "You can choose when and where to eat it. But that's all you get until next week."

When Yvette took the popovers out of the oven, everybody scrambled to fill them and wolf them down, then went to relax and dress for chores. Tired and achy from being on her feet all day, Yvette lay down on the couch and closed her eyes. *Oh, that hurts and soothes at the same time.* She dozed off.

Something jerked her awake and she bolted upright. It was Tanya, pressing a kiss on Yvette's cheek. "Oh, it's you," Yvette smiled. "I thought—"

"You thought I was Dad," Tanya finished for her. "I'm sorry, Mom. I didn't mean to scare you, but I couldn't stay quiet anymore. It's five o'clock. The boys went out already. Kyle said to let you sleep."

"What sweethearts you children are," Yvette rose wearily and headed for the washroom. "Do you want to come out to the barn tonight?"

"Yeah, but I have to go to the bathroom, first."

Tying her red kerchief behind her head, Yvette heard Tanya call, "Mom! There's a bug in the bathtub!"

"Stomp on it," Yvette said. Knowing how her daughter hated bugs, she went to investigate. She stifled a chuckle when she saw Tanya standing on the toilet lid while hanging onto the shower curtain and leaning forward to peer into the tub. "What are you doing? Don't tear the shower curtain."

"I'm afraid the bug will crawl up the curtain and get out of the tub."

"It's just a spider; it won't hurt you." Yvette put an arm around her. "Why don't you hop down and dress for the barn? I'll deal with the spider."

"Get the spider first," Tanya insisted.

"Let me get past you to get a square of toilet paper." Tanya complied, standing up tall and moving her hands to the top of the shower curtain, allowing her mother to duck under her arms. Yvette tore off a square of tissue and squished the spider with it. "Shall I flush it down the toilet?"

"No!" she shuddered. "It will crawl up when I'm going to the bathroom. Put it in the stove." Tanya jumped down from the commode and followed Yvette to make sure she disposed of the spider properly.

Yvette tossed the tissue into the hearth stove. They watched the paper flare into flame, then disintegrate and become a part of the hot coals."

"What was that?" Yvette and Tanya started when Kyle spoke.

"Kyle! Were you trying to sneak up on us?" Yvette closed the stove door and shook her head. Lately, every time she looked at Kyle, she marveled at his resemblance to Luke's dad, August Miller. For years Kyle had been the family misfit, but since his growth spurt, he walked with a long stride, talked with a deepening bass, and smiled an embarrassed half-smile, like August.

"Kyle!" Tanya ran to take his hand. "I saw a spider. Mom squished it and put it in the stove."

"You didn't scream, did you, Butterfly?" Kyle ruffled Tanya's curls. "I thought you quit being afraid of bugs."

"I did, but that one scared me."

"Would you like to study an ant farm with me again to help you not be so afraid of bugs? I think Mike still has the one I showed you last fall."

"Okaay, but it won't help."

"It did before," Kyle hugged his sister's slim shoulders. "We can go to the library and get books about bugs and read *Charlotte's Web* again."

Tanya had hated the bug picture books, Yvette remembered, and even though she had loved Charlotte, the spider, she had not gotten over her fear of spiders that summer. Yvette had often found her cowering in the stuffed chair in the living room, especially when Luke ranted and raved throughout the house.

The thought brought Yvette up short. Was Luke's nasty behavior the reason for Tanta's excessive fears? Last summer the tractor had broken down and needed repair after repair and Luke had scolded his family for one thing after the other. Yvette had neglected the house and spent time with her dad in the hospital. Tanya's fear of creepy crawlies hadn't dissipated until she started first grade, roughly the same time Luke stopped ranting and started combining.

Thinking of last fall reminded Yvette of her dad's death and the harrowing weeks that followed when Luke was sick with the flu. Tears had often clouded her vision as she combined beans during the day and into the night. Mornings and evenings she'd milked, cooked for the family, tended Luke, and thrown loads of laundry in the wash machine and dryer, but the laundry piled up, anyway. But the worst was the grief she couldn't allow herself the luxury to share with anyone. Then Luke had recovered and forbidden her to "go crying to her mother." Tears welled in her eyes. She turned to the hearth stove so the children wouldn't see them and get upset or worried.

"I see it's chore time," she moved toward the washroom, stopping to put the nuts, bolts, nails, and screws into the drawer Luke had dumped.

"Dad makes me so mad," Kyle knelt and helped pick up items. "We shouldn't have to clean up his mess."

"I don't want to see it for two weeks. Tell you what, dump it on the floor when he comes home; we'll leave it there until he picks it up. If we let the consequences fall on him, he'll think twice before he acts like this again. But we'll all have to step over the mess if he refuses to clean it up," she fitted the drawer in its slot, glanced up, and noticed Kyle held one arm against his midriff. "What's wrong with your arm, Kyle?"

He rose. "I got a paper cut on my finger when I went to check which cows are due to dry up. I came in to get a bandage."

"Take the whole box to the barn; I keep forgetting."

~   ~   ~

That night after chores, they invited Grandma over for supper and games. As everyone worked to clear the table and wash the dishes, Yvette saw Greg corner Kyle first and later Tanya, taunting and calling them names.

"Greg," Yvette glared at him, "be respectful, or you will write an essay about the costs and benefits of belittling your brother and sister." Since he hated writing essays, he chose to behave the rest of the evening. Even when Tanya got upset that no one else voted to play *Chutes and Ladders*, Yvette noted Greg didn't tease her, but agreed she could team up with Grandma to play *Racko.*

As they played the last round of *Racko*, Yvette compared the relaxed mood of the evening with the atmosphere when Luke had been present. They had constantly glanced at Luke, not sure when he'd make a cutting comment, not sure if it was safe to voice an opinion or suggestion. He had chosen every video they had seen and the games they played. Even though Luke had seemed warmer, she hadn't dared reprimand Greg in front of Luke, since he often ordered her to leave Greg alone, and Greg continued to harass his siblings. Compared to how she felt now, she hadn't been relaxed at all then.

Chapter 8

By Friday, the sows still had not begun to farrow, leaving Yvette free to quilt. After the children boarded the school bus, she left the dishes on the counter, phoned her mother from her workroom, and invited her over to talk and quilt. She hadn't been quilting long when she heard her mother's knock on the door. She ran downstairs to meet her and escort her upstairs.

"You're keeping the house spotless even though Luke isn't here to fuss at you," Clara observed.

"Let's not talk about the house," Yvette said. "What I'd like to hear is what life was like as you were growing up. I know you grew up on a farm in Lancaster County, Pennsylvania, and that you met Dad at Bible School, but I meet your family so rarely, I know very little about them."

"They shunned me when I left the Amish a year before Ben and I met. After that they thought I didn't do anything right. Oh, my!" as they entered Yvette's room. "You changed the storage room into a workroom."

"You haven't seen it before? Oh, I suppose not, with Luke making us keep our distance. I've had this as my workroom for a number of years. Luke made such a fuss if I left my projects out and the room you used as a sewing room was too small for my various projects."

"Isn't it cold in the winter and hot in the summer?"

"That's what fans and heaters are for."

"The sloping ceiling scarcely allows room to roll the quilt."

"It's a tight fit, but I'd rather deal with that than with Luke's griping. I've been thinking about decorating in here. Do you think it's selfish to beautify a place just for me rather than spend time and money on the family?"

"*You* are part of the family, too. Luke and each of the children have a room to retreat to and express personal tastes. It seems to me it would be an uphill battle to renew your spirit in this ugly room. If I were you, I'd hang pretty curtains in the window and lay a rug over the ripped gray linoleum. This red dahlia quilt brightens it up; I hope it's for you and not the Relief Sale."

"I planned it for this room," Yvette pulled a folding chair to the quilt and sat down. "I pieced a full-sized blue dahlia spread for the Relief Sale. I'll give it to Margie on Sunday so the church women can quilt it."

"Did you quilt the parts that are rolled up?"

"I started quilting this yesterday; I'm not that speedy. I'll never forget the first Lone Star quilt I did. I started on the outside and by the time I got to the center of the star it puckered up and wouldn't lie flat."

"You did a good job with this one; the center lies flat and the colors line up without clashing. That can be so hard to do with reds."

"I'm thinking of bringing my red accents in our bedroom up here. Luke doesn't like them anyway. But I'm concerned the bedroom will be unbearable to me if I take my accents out. I avoid going in there as it is," she started quilting where she left off. "But I'm afraid seeing the accents up here will remind me of the day I brought them home and ruin any sense of solace."

Clara sat at the quilt and pulled her ladder-back chair forward until her stomach touched the rolled up quilt on the frame. "What happened?"

"We were about to make love when Luke looked toward the dresser and saw the translucent red vase the day I bought it. He stopped everything and kept looking at it," Yvette twisted the thimble on her finger round and round and stared blankly at it. "'Why'd you get that ugly thing?' he asked with such a look of disdain on his face. It felt like he was saying *I* was ugly and loathsome. I felt so exposed, so—so despised. I wanted to disappear into a hole, to jump off the bed and out of his sight, but knew he'd get mad if I did. So I reached over and grabbed the first thing I could find to cover myself. It turned out to be that horrid itchy blue wool blanket Luke had on his side of the bed. You know how sensitive my skin is where wool is concerned," she made herself look at her mother. "But I kept that blanket on. I felt I could endure that better than having him see my body. Then he started touching me and said 'You buy such tasteless junk; I ought to hire a decorator so the house looks decent for once and we can get rid of your gaudy trash,'" she stopped to swallow the lump in her throat. "Every time that incident comes to mind, I feel like trash all over again."

Clara reached over and squeezed her hands. "I didn't realize he'd spoil your pleasure in the items you enjoy, and at such a vulnerable moment, too. Is his love-making—if you can call it that—always so cold?"

"What do you mean?"

"Doesn't he pleasure you at all?" Clara selected a needle.

"Pleasure?" Yvette resumed quilting. "As far as I'm concerned, the sooner he finishes his business, the better. Oh, I make sure *he* has a good time."

Clara shook her head. "No wonder Luke doesn't want you to talk to me. He's been cheating you in the bedroom and in every other area and doesn't want me to find out. I'm surprised he didn't make sure I had other commitments before he left, like he usually does. I used to ponder why he'd ask Ben and me to help you while he's gone, but when we had prior commitments he'd go anyway. I was free to help twice, but he stayed home both times. Then I figured out he was making sure we were too busy to talk with you while he was gone."

"It makes sense, considering Luke makes sure he's present when we get together. He must have assumed you'd be busy this time."

"Well, we're on to him now," Clara threaded her needle. "I hear him yell at you, but I had no idea he carried his hostility to the bedroom."

Yvette swallowed twice to get rid of the lump in her throat. "Christian radio keeps reminding me, 'For better or for worse, marriage is for keeps,' so I try to make our marriage work and to not think about the hurtful things he does. I considered getting rid of the vase, but it warms that cold and sterile bedroom."

"Then buy pretty things especially for your workroom."

"I have money saved for that kind of thing; why not? You'll have to see my room after I've decorated it." *What if Luke looks at my room when it's decorated? He won't say anything nice. Why do people choose to be so critical? Mom's family, for instance.* "I don't get it," Yvette frowned. "Why do your bothers and sisters criticize you? Didn't they leave the Amish, too?"

"Yes, but I was the *first* to leave and joined the *liberal* Mennonites. I stopped wearing a veiling, cut my hair and wore pants. The rest joined the Beachy-Amish or the Conservative Mennonites. Ruby, who is closest to my age, isn't as critical toward me, but she's often too busy to write."

"Why did you leave, anyway?" Yvette drove the needle up and down through the quilt with her thimble. "You never told me that."

"I didn't approve of the practices of the Pennsylvania Amish. Like *bundling*, for instance. When a couple courted, they'd sleep in the same bed fully clothed. I didn't want to do that, but it was expected. And the youth drank, partied, and acted wild. I didn't think those things pleased God."

"Did you live at home after you stopped being Amish?"

"No, I lived with our Mennonite neighbors. I had been invited to their oldest girl's wedding, and was impressed how the young people studied and lived according to the Bible, not by the letter of church laws."

"You passed the importance of living according to the Bible on to me. Sometimes I want to forget about submitting and tell Luke a thing or two. I talked with Delores, and she said I should *not* submit to wrong doctrine and that Luke is throwing out Ephesians Four and Five except those three verses about wives submitting. Is she right? Have I been doing wrong all this time?"

"I think she's right, but I wouldn't say you've been doing wrong. Usually wives yield to their husbands and it turns out fine because the husbands yield to their wives, too. When you have a husband like Luke, it can take a while to see the pattern and figure out what to do about it."

"Delores says I should follow my gut instinct more," with a razorblade Yvette sliced her thread level with the quilt, making all trace of the tail of thread disappear under the quilt's top layer, "and if I feel something isn't right, to stand up to Luke. Most of the time it's no big deal when he goes on a tornado cleanup crew, but this time he left us with a major project, and it *is* a big deal. So I protested about his trip to Georgia, but he wouldn't change his plans. All I could do was refuse to pack his bags or cook his breakfast, and I even feel guilty about that. You taught me to live according to the Bible, Mom, yet now you tell me to not submit to my husband. Isn't that inconsistent?"

"I don't think so. The Bible tells us to obey our government, too, but the apostles refused to stop preaching the gospel. They said, 'We ought to obey God rather than men.' Luke insists on harming you with ridiculous demands, too much work and continual criticism. That is unscriptural. The Bible says Luke is to care for his body and also nourish yours like he does his own. Instead, he's been oppressive, and that's wrong."

"It's hard to stand up to Luke and live with his cutting words and his stomping and slamming things around. I never know what hurtful thing he'll do or say next. On top of that, I'm not convinced God will consider me blameless if I don't submit to Luke."

"I've been reading up on the subject and don't think submission is the issue," Clara stuck her needle in the quilt and held Yvette's eyes when she looked up. "Again and again when you are totally submitting to him, he adds a whopper to his demands or cuts you down out of the blue over a minor detail. I think the real issue is domination. He wants to assert *power over* you. He's *lording it over you*, which Jesus taught the disciples *not* to do, and he has nearly convinced you the submission rule overrides all other Christian doctrine."

"You have a point. I focus so hard on submission, I don't step back and look at other Christian principles."

"In essence," Clara shifted closer to the edge and resumed quilting, "He's misusing scripture to bully, enslave, and degrade you. The Apostle Paul says, 'God bought you with a price, don't become a slave of men.'"

"So I better figure out how to balance other Christian principles with submission. Those two Christian books Delores loaned me should help."

"This is the perfect time to read and catch up on sleep. Take it easy while Luke's gone. You haven't had a break all winter and the gardening season is almost here. If you want, I'll come over and help a few days."

"I'd like to catch up with *you* more than with work or sleep. It's my chance to spend time with you every day and I want to take advantage of it."

Clara selected a pink spool from the thread box. "I'd like that, too."

~   ~   ~

On Monday morning, Yvette stayed asleep until the alarm sounded. For months she'd kept waking an hour or more before the alarm bleeped and couldn't go back to sleep. Now she dozed in bed a few minutes and luxuriated in the release from inner tension as the comments she'd heard yesterday at church, when she took the quilt top to Margie, replayed in her head.

"Look!" a woman had exclaimed. "It looks like a real, blue flower."

"It's beautiful," another breathed. "I like the feather plumes you marked for the border. It'll bring top price. I wish I could afford it."

"How do you do it, Yvette?" Margie said. "Every year you bring one that's prettier than last year's, and every year your quilt gets the highest bid."

Yvette had blushed. She had little experience with compliments.

She got out of bed, called the boys, and called the time and temperature phone line as she habitually did. When she heard it was thirty-two degrees and freezing rain was expected, she turned on the pole light and peered outside. They'd had snow during the night and ice on top of that. Ice-encased trees bowed low under the weight. The driveway, yard, and sidewalks resembled a lake of shimmering white ice. *Oh, no! That looks like trouble. Hey, maybe today I'll get a chance to set Greg straight about submission and manliness.*

She turned from the window as the boys arrived downstairs, Greg appearing bright-eyed as usual, and Kyle groggy. "Look outside. It's a winter wonderland. The forecast is for freezing rain, and bad weather means they'll cancel school and the sows will likely have their pigs."

"Can I go back to bed?" Kyle stumbled into Greg.

Greg snorted. "Yeah, at midnight."

"Hopefully, it won't take that long," Yvette turned up the thermostat. "But the way the tree limbs are weighted down, I'm surprised the electricity is still on. Maybe if we work fast, we won't have to milk any cows by hand. I'll put wood in the hearth stove *after* we come in from the barn."

"Race you to the barn," Kyle sprinted for the stairs.

"Kyle," Yvette called after him, "your laundry is on the couch." She waited until he changed direction, then continued, "After you get dressed, Kyle, would you go to the farrowing house and turn on the electric heater and put the sows in farrowing crates? Take a bag of deicer with you and make a path as you go. Greg, could you spread deicer on Grandma's sidewalk and bring up the lanterns from the basement, just in case the electricity goes off? I'll make sure the flashlights work and fix a snack to take to the barn."

After an hour of washing udders, transferring milkers, letting cows out and in, and chaining and unchaining them, all the while focusing on keeping all four milkers running without leaving them on any cow too long, Greg called from the feedway, "Look out the south door. It's awesome."

Yvette finished washing her cow's teats, listening to the airy noise of the milker as Kyle attached the last two teatcups to his cow, then unbent and rushed to the door, two steps behind Kyle. Kyle swung open the upper Dutch door and they gazed out in wonder. Morning sunlight spilled over the earth, causing the sagging power lines to sparkle, the fences lining the roads to glitter, the fields to shimmer a dazzling crystalline white, and the neighbor's timber to resemble a glistening fairyland.

"Wow!" Kyle breathed.

"It's beautiful," Yvette said. "But the way those power lines sag, the electricity could be cut off anytime, and we'd have to finish by hand."

They scurried back to efficient milking. After another half hour, they all breathed a sigh of relief as Yvette took the milker off the last cow. They had made it. Hopefully, the power would stay on all day this time.

Minutes later the lights went out and the milking motor shut off at the beginning of the wash cycle. Yvette looked out the milk-house window. Gray clouds blocked the sun and brought a freezing drizzle. *Oh, God, where's my chance to talk with Greg?* "Let's go in for breakfast," she said. "Thankfully, our cook stove uses gas, and the hearth stove burns wood. "

Letting Tanya sleep in, she outlined the plans for the day over eggs, toast and bacon. They'd pump water by hand and carry it to the hogs, sows, cows, calves, heifers, steers and chickens. Since Kyle had reported the sows were restless, they'd check the farrowing house every hour or two until the sows started to give birth. Then she'd stay out there in case of complications.

After breakfast, Yvette saw her chance. "How about warming up around the wood stove and reading the Bible before we go out? We haven't done that since last time Luke was gone, and I forgot last week."

"I miss our family Bible reading times," Kyle got his Bible and pulled a chair to the stove. "They make me feel cozy and start me thinking."

She looked at Greg. He said nothing, but got a chair and his Bible.

They took turns reading Ephesians Four and Five aloud.

"What do you think this passage means?" Yvette asked.

"The husband is to be in charge," Greg zeroed in on the second half of Chapter Five, "and the wife is supposed to do what he says."

"Look again," Yvette urged. "Read what is written to husbands. That will be your part. Where does it say the husband is to be in charge?"

Greg scanned the page. "Verse twenty-three. The husband is the *head* of the wife. That means he's to be in charge of his wife like Christ is in charge of the church and a physical head is in charge of a body."

"Study verses twenty-one and thirty-three, the beginning and end of that marital section," Yvette said. "How do those verses sum it up, Kyle?"

"The first one says submit to each other," Kyle shifted in his chair, "and the last one says a husband is to love his wife as he loves himself, and the wife is to reverence her husband. Do we *have* to talk about *this*? We won't get married for a long time."

"Now is when you are forming attitudes about marriage. You need to know what God says, so your marriage has a chance to succeed. What do you think submitting to each other means, Kyle?"

He shrugged. "Giving in to the other person, I guess."

"It's talking about *wives* submitting," Greg thumped his stocking-clad foot on the floor. "Verse twenty-two states that clearly."

"So you think he's just talking to wives in verse one?" Yvette pressed. "Are only women to be followers of God and live a life of love? Jesus gave Himself for us, and only wives are supposed to copy Him, right Greg?"

"Well, no," he muttered, looking for verses to defend his view. "It says wives are to submit to their husbands in *everything*."

"So it does. But if the Apostle Paul meant that husbands were to be in absolute charge, wouldn't he have said, 'Husbands, *rule* your wives'?"

"Maybe," Greg defied, stony faced.

"Are you saying the husband is *not* to be in charge, Mom?"

"Look closer, Kyle. Does loving your wife as you love yourself sound like being an authority over her? Does giving yourself for her give the impression of being her boss?"

"No, "Kyle frowned. "This is confusing, Mom. Dad says—"

"But look at what *The Bible* says," Yvette interrupted.

"It sounds like the husband is supposed to love his wife so much he will die for her," Kyle's frown deepened. "That's what Jesus did."

"Was dying the only thing Jesus did for us? Greg, what do you think?" she noted his resentful expression.

"He healed and taught the crowds," Greg tossed his Bible on the table then leaned back, "but husbands can't heal their wives."

"Not the way Jesus did, but their behavior can have a healing effect. Encouragement or comfort are more healing than put-downs or criticism. He can serve her by giving his time and attention like Jesus did. Easing her workload will keep her from getting over-stressed or sick."

"Dad doesn't help you," Kyle blurted out, "and you aren't sick."

"No, but I often hurt and am tense on the inside."

"From the put-downs," Kyle nodded. "Me, too."

"Delores says some women get sick when they're constantly griped at by their husbands. We all feel better when people are kind and thoughtful. The same is true of husband and wife. Marriage isn't about the husband making rules and bossing his wife. It's about him serving her self-sacrificially."

"I don't know," Kyle shook his head. "I mean, life would be better if Dad was kind to us, but if I ever get married, I couldn't be self-sacrificial."

"You don't think you could be like Steve Webster?"

"Well, maybe."

"There's another side, too. Do you think this means the wife should selfishly get her way all the time?"

"No. She's supposed to submit to her husband."

"So step back and tell me what the marriage looks like."

Kyle thought for a minute. "They both care about each other and try to do what the other one wants."

"Exactly. I couldn't have said it better. Now let's pray."

After they prayed, Greg chose to feed the chickens and gather the eggs, and Kyle opted to take the kerosene heater to the brood-sow shed. That left pumping water and carrying it to the livestock. Yvette picked up two five-gallon buckets and headed for the hand pump. She grasped the pump handle, and drew in a deep breath as she gazed at the white barn. With all the snow and ice on the ground, the trek to the barn looked endless. Her shoulders slumped. Why had they built it so far from the house? And why had she let Luke sell the windmill? *I can't pump and carry enough water for all the animals. But I have to, even if it takes all day.* Squaring her shoulders, she began to pump.

She was almost to the barn with her second load, when she heard Kyle say something from the farrowing house. She stopped so she could hear him. "Come out here," he rushed toward her on the half melted path and pulled up the hood of his sweatshirt for protection from the freezing drizzle. "A sow started having pigs," he slipped to a halt in front of her.

She set the heavy buckets down. "I should go out right away, but the watering tank is empty. Hear the cows bawling? They probably finished eating hay and are thirsty. If we don't get water to them, they won't produce milk. Would you pump water for the cows so I can go the farrowing house? It would go faster if we had a fifty gallon drum on the skid-loader bucket."

"There's an empty big blue one behind the machine shed."

"Great. You'll need the short hose to siphon the water out of the drum. I'll send Greg to help pump."

"There goes our fun for the day. I'll empty these buckets for you."

"Is the farrowing house warm enough? It should be at least seventy to seventy-five degrees in there for the wet newborn piglets."

"I don't know."

"Never mind. I'll get a thermometer. Where's Greg?"

"Gathering the eggs. There he goes to the house."

Yvette turned. Bare-headed in spite of the freezing rain, Greg carried a yellow, covered-wire egg bucket full of brown eggs. "Always has to be macho," she shook her head. *Lord God, I need time alone with Greg.*

She shuffled as fast as she dared to get the thermometer from her work-room. As she reached her room, stocking-footed and in her chore coat, Tanya came out of her room, tousle-haired, sleepy-eyed, and clutching a purple teddy bear to her pink Barbie nightgown. Yvette stopped to hug her.

"I'm so tired," Tanya pillowed her head on her mother's bosom.

"Wait; my coat's dirty," she shed her coat and hugged the girl a long moment. "I need the thermometer," she eased out of Tanya's embrace. "The sows are having pigs, and I h—"

"Can I watch?" Tanya interrupted, her face now animated. "Please?"

"Sure, after you get dressed, eat breakfast, and comb your hair," Yvette snatched the thermometer off it's nail and rushed to the door. "Can you do that by yourself? I have to take care of the animals right away."

"Mom!" Tanya chided, "I can dress myself and get cereal."

"Don't forget to put on boots and mittens," Yvette rushed down the stairs. *A week ago, when Luke was such a brute, I had to dress you.*

In the kitchen, Greg stood hunched over the counter, sneaking an iced cinnamon roll. Yvette frowned, "We have loads of work to do, and you're in the kitchen stuffing your face. Put half of that back, then help Kyle pump water for the cattle. We'll stop for a break later. It sounds like Kyle has the loader by the pump now, and I don't want him to do the pumping by himself."

"Then you help him," Greg mumbled, his mouth full.

"I have to go to the farrowing house. A sow started having pigs. You can drive the loader to the watering tank if you want."

"Okay, okay," he waved her away. "Let me eat in peace."

Outside, the freezing rain changed to huge, wet flakes of snow, adding a thin layer of snow over the ice. Despite the deicer, the path was hazardous. Yvette slid her feet in short shuffling steps, not daring to lift a foot off the ground. The brood sow shed was cold and the birthing proceeding normally, so she shuffled to the house to get matches, and then back to the farrowing house. She lit the kerosene heater and placed it in the aisle, behind the farrowing sow.

Tanya came out and they watched a wet, shivering, newborn piglet stagger to its feet, and turn away from its mother to nuzzle one of the vertical metal bars of the farrowing crate. Yvette nudged it around its mother's hind legs and to the sow's nipples. The piglet latched on and began to suckle. Bored with waiting for another birth, Tanya wandered from sow to sow and discovered a sow giving birth at the far end. Yvette moved the heater behind that sow.

The boys came in and Yvette rushed to meet them at the door. "Quick shut the door," she whispered. "It's only sixty degrees in here, and the piglets are shivering. The kerosene heater can't keep up. I need to get towels to dry the pigs; could you boys stand watch? Remember to keep your voices quiet."

"When do we get our break?" Greg hissed. "I thought you said if we pitched in we'd have fun while Dad's gone."

"Wow, you must think I'm powerful! Maybe if I snap my fingers the electricity will come on and the snow and freezing rain will stop. I'm doing the best I can, Greg; please don't complain. I'll bring out cinnamon rolls and hot chocolate. If one of you brings two bales of straw out here we can sit down."

In the house she put milk on the stove, added chocolate, put the rolls in the oven to warm up, then hunted for her most ragged towels. When everything was ready, she put the rolls, cups, and thermoses of hot chocolate in a bucket, stuffed the towels on top, then shuffled to the farrowing house.

As she stopped to open the door, she overheard the boys talking.

"...inclined to think Mom is right," she heard Kyle say. "If Dad did like she pointed out, we'd all be happier. Would you want your daughter to be afraid of you like Tanya is of Dad?"

She paused, her gloved hand on the latch, large flakes of snow falling on her lashes and blurring her vision.

"No, but I'd like to have things my way, like Dad does. I don't want to get married if I always have to give up what I want. That doesn't sound fair."

"The way Dad treats Mom isn't fair. If he'd try to please her like she tries to please him, *that* would be fair. He should discuss and decide stuff *with* her. Why don't you try bossing Kathy around?"

"Kathy's not my wife."

"But it's dishonest to be sweet to her now so you can boss her after she marries you. If you don't plan to treat your wife right, you shouldn't marry at all. And if you want to marry, you better practice being nice to your family."

"That's easy for you to say," Greg sneered, "*you* are Mom's pet."

"I am *not!*"

Yvette lifted the latch, which produced immediate silence, and opened the door. "Sshh," she said. "Don't rile the sows into getting up. When they lie down again, they'll end up crushing or smothering their piglets."

"Sorry, Mom," Kyle shifted his feet, "I forgot."

"Two more sows started having babies," Tanya murmured.

"I'm glad I brought towels," Yvette sat on the wooden three-foot-high gate, swung her legs over, and dropped to the other side. Help yourselves to the eats, but don't take more than your fair share."

After they'd eaten, Yvette checked the thermometer. "Sixty-three. We gained only three degrees. Come. Let me show you how to lift the pigs by their head and neck when you dry them, so they won't squeal and upset the mothers."

"I know how," Greg said. "I've done it many times with Dad."

"Good. Then I'll check on Grandma. Kyle, would you please fill all the water tanks and pans? It won't be such a big chore if we keep after them."

At her mother's, Clara invited her inside. "How are things going? Nobody answered when I phoned, so I figured you're all outside."

Yvette told her about their day.

"Do you need my help? I'm still sleepy since I assisted at a birthing till two this morning, and it took an hour to drive home on the snowy roads, but I think I can stay awake," Clara rubbed her eyes. "The baby was two weeks early."

"We should have a handle on things. We'll call if we need help."

"I called around and the whole neighborhood is without power. Lester reported it, so hopefully the power will come on before chore time."

"I hope, too. Do you need water or anything? I'll spread more deicer so you can come over tonight. There's no point in you staying here alone."

They spent most of the day in the farrowing house, drying off the newborns, clearing their airways and helping them find a teat. While Greg took his turn hauling water to the various animals, Kyle heated mushroom soup for lunch, poured it into thermoses and carried it to the farrowing house.

"Remember our conversation when we dug up flagstones, Mom?" Kyle kept his voice at a murmur as he handed Tanya a bowl of soup. "The one about feeling closer to each other during difficult situations?"

"Yes," she placed the piglet she'd rubbed dry in front of the heater.

"Well, this is one of those times. Dad's gone, the sows are giving birth, we have an ice storm to deal with and no electricity, and I feel cozy inside. This is almost fun. Do you know what I mean?"

Yvette opened her mouth to say, *If your dad knew how much fun we're having, he'd never have gone to Georgia,* but stopped herself before she voiced the thought to the children. Stalling for time, she sat on the bale beside Kyle and poured herself a bowl of soup as she considered how to reply. "Don't you want crackers, Tanya? There are some in that bucket."

Tanya shook her head and drank the soup from her bowl.

"I know what you mean, Kyle. Something about the quiet atmosphere, the specialness of seeing piglets being born, the crystallized world outside, our working together—you're right, it does feel cozy."

The power came on at four-thirty. "Hallelujah!" Kyle blew out a breath in relief. "No more pumping water, and we'll have time for games tonight."

Yvette dug three grease crayons from the cabinet at the entrance and handed one to each son. "I think the sows are done giving birth, let's number them and let them out for feed and water while we milk." They wrote large red numbers on the back of each sow so she'd return to her corresponding crate, then one by one opened the door to each crate, and urged each sow to back out.

When they finished milking, and went to let the sows back in with their piglets, a few of the sows wanted to go in the wrong crates. One sow got indignant when Yvette and the boys redirected her to her own crate. "Bring the extra gate over here, Greg," Yvette held the crate's door protectively in front of her as the sow came at her, woofing angrily, her sides heaving, her nose pushing at the metal door which was inches from Yvette's leg. "Hurry!" Greg rushed over with a four-foot rough-wooden panel and guided the snarling sow into her crate.

With a sigh of relief, Yvette closed the crate door behind the sow and fastened it. "We should have numbered the sows last week and let them in and out of their crates so they know where home is, but I forgot that step."

After they had finished the chores, they went in for supper with Clara. "I wish we could go ice skating," Greg said as he cut the pecan pie into eighths. "Dad didn't let us go all winter and now the ice on the ponds is too thin."

"What a perfect way to end the day," Yvette grinned at Clara. "Hurry, Kyle, help put supper on the table. We'll go ice skating tonight."

"We can't go anywhere," Greg scoffed. "The roads are ice."

"Exactly. The Lord gave us ice, so we'll skate on the road."

After supper they dressed for winter fun and Clara went to her house to put on additional layers so she could watch from the porch swing. Yvette dug out various sizes of ice skates, and none but Luke's fit Kyle's big feet.

"Won't Dad get upset?" Kyle pulled on the left skate.

"Not if you take good care of them," Yvette said as she laced Tanya's skates. "Greg, the skates you have on were my dad's."

"Who wore my skates?" Tanya stuck her other skate out.

"All of us girls did. They said I could have them since their families moved south or west, where the ponds don't freeze."

"I wish Dad would let us visit them," Kyle said.

"You'll have to write letters or e-mail them like I do," Yvette said.

Yvette spent the evening teaching her children skating techniques and games. They took an old chair and a sled out to sit on if anyone got tired or fell down, and Tanya discovered she had more confidence if she pushed the chair ahead of her. Clara watched awhile, then went to her house. An hour after bed time, they returned to the house, tired but exhilarated.

Chapter 9

After breakfast the next day, it was Greg's turn to choose which chore he'd prefer. To Yvette's surprise, he chose to clean and grade the eggs after gathering them, leaving Yvette and Kyle to work in the farrowing house. Tanya watched from behind the gate at the entrance as they let the sows out of the crates and chased them outside at the other end of the farrowing house. As soon as Kyle latched the door behind them, she climbed over the gate and joined Kyle and Yvette in the aisle between the two rows of farrowing crates. Yvette hefted a board off the top of a crate and fitted the board's end between two vertical rods in the low fence of the piglets' creeping area, making the board stand on edge.

"What's the board for?" Tanya frowned.

"To keep the treated piglets apart from the untreated ones," Yvette reached over the partition and picked up a sleeping piglet by its head and neck. It let out a squelched scream.

Tanya tilted her head to the side as she watched her mother clip the pig's teeth. "Why do you cut their teeth?"

"To keep them alive," Yvette held the pig out to Kyle so he could vaccinate it. "Before we clipped their teeth and tails, the pigs bit and chewed on each other's tails and ears, and some of them bled to death. Sometimes we had hogs that were nearly ready for market die from loss of blood."

"Does it hurt the pigs?"

"Probably. But not as much as being chewed on would hurt," she clipped the piglet's tail. "When they are little, they don't bleed much. See?" she showed the remaining stub to Tanya, then put it back in its straw-bedded pen on the other side of the separating board. It grunted and ran to the far end.

"I'll get the next one," Tanya leaned into the pen and picked up a piglet. It screamed, causing a sow to woof and snuffle in alarm outside the door.

"Let me pick them up, Tanya," Yvette grasped the wriggling piglet by its head and neck, which reduced its shrieks to a toneless, nearly silent wail. "I have to pick them up a certain way so they can't squeal real loud and upset their mothers. I don't want any of the sows to attack us when we let them in. Thank-you for offering to help, though. I appreciate your helpful attitude. Yours, too, Kyle. I think Greg is starting to follow your example."

"Don't get your hopes up," Kyle filled the syringe. "He shapes up every time Dad goes on a trip, but he'll be a jerk again when Dad comes back."

"If we help him see being considerate benefits him more than being a bully does, maybe he'll stay decent."

"I wouldn't count on it."

By noon they finished treating the piglets and let the sows in. This time none of them got woofy. Clara came over for dinner and helped wash dishes before they played table games. She paired up with Tanya to play *Dutch Blitz*, and they got five hundred points first.

"That wasn't fair," Greg sorted cards into four decks: red buggies, blue plows, green pumps, and yellow barrels. "No one else had partners."

"It's not fair if Tanya plays without help," Yvette said.

"Yeah," Kyle gathered his cards from everyone's piles. "Anyway, there are only decks for four, so somebody had to double up or sit out."

"It still wasn't fair. Grandma's faster than Mom; she should have had her own deck. Tanya should have paired with Kyle."

"That's enough, Greg," Yvette turned to hide her grin. Clara would have been much faster without Tanya to slow her down, but she couldn't say that in front of Tanya. "Don't spoil our fun with your complaining."

After supper Kyle played games with Tanya so Yvette could rebound for Greg in the barn. Greg rolled one of the barn's huge double doors back on its track, charged into the driveway where his grandpa had mounted a hoop, and went for a lay-up.

"*Somebody* moved the tractor out and swept the floor," Yvette teased as she pulled the double door closed. "Getting ready to put up hay?"

"What's that?" Greg cradled the ball and pointed at a white spot on the cement floor.

"It looks like pigeon poop. It's too big for sparrows."

"It can't be. Dad and I fixed the windows, and Kyle and I sold every pigeon in the mow."

"Look up past the hay fork. There's one perched on the pulley at the very peak. Either you didn't get them all, or a window is broken."

"That buzzard!" Greg flung his bill cap on the floor at the sidelines.

"I believe it's a pigeon," Yvette snickered.

Greg shot her a dark look. "It's not funny. I hate climbing up there to fix a window."

"A pigeon in the barn isn't *that* terrible. Come on; shoot baskets." Yvette kept count and rebounded while Greg shot 50 free-throws and 50 from all over the court except from the sides where the overhanging lofts interfered.

"Why'd they have to make those overhangs anyway?" Greg plopped down on a bale of hay at the foot of the ladder to the mow. "I need to practice from the sides, too."

"Because this is a barn made for housing animals and storing hay. It didn't occur to your great-grandpa to make this area into a gym when he built it. Are you done practicing already?"

"Yeah, it's boring when there's not enough variety."

"I have an idea how to make this week more fun," excitement buzzed through her. "Let's make a maze of tunnels in the haymow and throw a birthday party for Tanya and Jill Saturday before Dad comes back. The kids missed two days of school, and a birthday party would help make up some of the social time they lost. The rest of the week's supposed to be warmer, so the ice and snow will be gone and it shouldn't be too cold for a haymow party."

Greg eyed the half-full mow, then climbed the ladder.

As they worked together, Yvette listened to Greg's ideas when they differed, then asked him to listen to hers, and led him into finding solutions they both liked. When they finished, Yvette sat on a bale of hay in the walk area. Greg did likewise and chewed on a stalk of alfalfa.

Yvette drew in a deep breath. *Here's my chance. Oh, God, please put Your words in my mouth.* "Umm, the hay smells good." She pulled a piece of alfalfa out of her bale. "Do you think we made the tunnels secure enough so no one will fall through if they walk on top?"

"They're just lightweight kids," he ran his hand through his hair.

"Are all the hay holes blocked so no one will fall from the haymow?"

"The only ones not blocked are where we drop hay into the rack, and the one that goes down to the driveway. There's no way to block those, since they're the whole length of the mow and go up to the rafters."

"I'll need you and Kyle to help keep the children out of those areas. The girls' friends are decent, but who knows how they'll behave when they're all together. One of my cousins fell out of the haymow into the cattle shed once. She had a concussion and broke her leg. I'm glad we're doing this, though. Most of the children don't live on farms, and this will be an experience they'll never forget. I used to love making hay tunnels and burrowing through them."

"Yeah, I should have a slumber party out here for my birthday."

"You want to get poked by hay stems all night?"

73

"We'd be in sleeping bags."

"It's not the sleeping part I'm concerned about. How will your friends behave when they have others to egg them on? They could set the barn on fire."

"My friends aren't idiots."

"But with all those hormones clouding their judgment, who knows what damage they'd do. By the way, did you enjoy doing this with me?"

"I guess so."

"Did you feel stupid, or did you feel your opinion mattered to me?"

"That's a dumb question," he snickered. "What are you getting at?"

"Just that when people respect each other, they have a good time. If I had bossed you around, or put you down, would you have enjoyed making this maze for Tanya and her friends?"

"Of course not."

"The behaviors you choose now will shape you into the kind of man you will be when you are married. Do you want your family to enjoy being with you because you are kind and respectful? Or do you want them to feel afraid and avoid you because they think you'll get mad?"

"I don't know," he chewed on the stalk of hay.

"Bullying may *seem* to get you respect, but underneath your family will resent and distrust you. But, when your wife and children win, so will you."

"Are you done now?"

"One more thing," she hoped he'd look at her, but he kept staring at the hay-strewn floor. "Do you remember the passage where Jesus told his disciples the Gentiles lord it over others, but the disciples are not to be that way?"

"Yeah. So?"

"Would Jesus approve of husbands lording it over their wives?"

"Probably not."

"You have the potential to become a caring person, Greg. A strong man who battles for others in nonviolent ways. I can see you championing the homeless or the abused. That is the type of manliness Jesus endorsed. As a husband you can champion your wife and children, and provide resources to develop their talents."

"Aren't moms supposed to do that?" he met her eyes.

"Sure. But what if I encouraged your skill at basketball, but Dad said you couldn't have a basketball and hoop at home, or couldn't be on the team?"

"I couldn't practice enough to get really good at it. He won't let me play with the guys as it is, and it's boring to shoot hoops alone."

"Exactly," she stood up. "People often won't develop their talents if they get criticism and road blocks instead of support. Do you want to be a good influence or cause resentment?"

"I get your point, Mom. Let's go in. I'm cold."

~   ~   ~

Luke drove the van across the swollen Mississippi River from Illinois into Iowa. Rain had slowed their progress the last two days in Georgia, and they had decided to leave earlier than planned. Impatient to be home, Luke had exceeded the speed limit and refused to allow anyone else to drive. He wanted to get into the fields. But mostly he yearned for his wife. He imagined her surprise when he got home, her welcoming arms. Convinced she'd be hungry for him, too, he envisioned her leading him into their bedroom with the beautiful red accents he'd disparaged so she wouldn't get proud. He'd give her the red, tulip-shaped lamp he bought for her, and she'd be so pleased she wouldn't know how to respond. He'd set the lamp on the dresser and take her in his arms. He nearly groaned just thinking of the pleasure of it.

"Let's stop at a lock and dam," George, who was in the passenger seat and the owner of the van, suggested, interrupting Luke's train of thought. "I need a break to stretch my legs. We don't get to see the Mississippi every day, and it's spectacular when the water is high like this."

"I'd rather keep going," Luke said. "We'll be home in two hours."

"My legs are cramping," George protested. "I need a break."

"We'll take a vote," Luke said, assuming the rest of the men would side with him. "All in favor of stopping raise your right hand." He looked in the rear view mirror and counted raised hands. They all wanted to stop.

Out-voted, he turned the black van toward Lock and Dam Nineteen.

~   ~   ~

Kyle and Greg went out to the barn to place treasure-hunt notes for the children. Greg said little, but thought a lot. He hadn't expected two weeks of cooperating and acting respectful to be so much fun. The three evenings they'd cleared the tree limbs and sticks that had fallen during the ice storm had been the most surprising. They'd started out setting aside the longer limbs to build a fort and throwing the remaining branches on a pile for a future bonfire, and ended up talking about anything and everything. A warmth had started to creep around his heart, one that frightened him even while it satisfied a hunger he hadn't known he had. *So this is what Kyle and Tanya shared with Mom all along.* It tantalized and drew him, and he wanted more, much more. Yet he hated the wanting. If he let himself crave such a feminine emotion, how could he be a man? He'd make a sniveling beggar of himself and always be at the mercy of those who provided the warmth. *Maybe I can demand it.*

As they surfaced from placing the treasure notes in the tunnels, Kyle watched the changing expressions on his brother's face: bemusement, longing, a firming of the jaw that suggested determination. He waited until Greg came out of his reverie, lifted his blue bill cap, ran his hand through his hair, then re-placed the cap on his head.

"Got it figured out?" Kyle eased down onto a bale of hay.

"What?" With a nasty expression, Greg opened his mouth to say more, then shut it. He sank onto the opposite bale, took his cap off and fingered it, turning it round and round. "My thoughts are private."

That's a switch. Maybe he'll become my friend. "I'm here if you want to talk," Kyle changed the subject. "Dad's scheduled to come home tonight."

"Yeah." Greg popped the sizing buttons on the back of his cap.

"Sure was an interesting and fun couple of weeks. With the ice and snow all melted and the mess cleared away, it's hard to believe we had a storm five days ago. I liked it better with Dad gone. We had to work harder, but life was more enjoyable. I even like you better. Dad's a bad influence on you."

Greg refastened the buttons. "He thinks you're around Mom too much. He'll probably make you work with him so you can learn how to be a man."

"I'd rather be around Steve," Kyle turned lengthwise on the bale and hugged his knees. "Remember the day we were at the greenhouse and he con-sulted Delores before he told the workers what to do? Dad would never do that. He would have embarrassed himself by telling them to do something they'd already done. According to what Mom showed us in the Bible, Steve is doing it right, and I admire him for that. Do you think he'd hire me this summer?"

"I always thought Steve was a wimp."

"Steve is strong and manly. He's unselfish and considerate of others, so his family *likes* to be around him. Dad's the wimp."

"How so?" Greg ambled to the alley-way and leaned on the end stud.

"He's not man enough to realize others are important, too. He belittles people so he'll *look* bigger, but looking bigger doesn't actually *make* him bigger. We all respect him less because of how he treats us. Don't you ever watch Mom and Dad? Mom tries not to show it, but she hurts because of Dad."

"Dad says it's her own fault," Greg straightened to his full height. "If she would just do what he says, he wouldn't get on her case."

"She almost never does anything wrong. Come on, Greg, you gotta admit he's nitpicking or he gets mad at her *because* she does what he says. Like when she didn't have as much money for him as he expected."

"That was because she spent too much on groceries."

"It was because he wanted *all* the gas money, even though she'd filled the tank for him. When I shop with her, she shops as if we're poor because Dad gripes at her, and keeps saying he doesn't get enough money. You're the math whiz; look at the budget. Dad gets four times more spending money than all the rest of us put together, and he tries to make Mom give him our tiny share, too."

"Are you sure?" Greg frowned. "Mom's the one who budgets and writes checks. If she needed more money, she could help herself."

"Not without a blowup from Dad," Kyle stood up. "Dad keeps an iron fist on her spending, and it isn't because we're poor."

"If you say so," Greg shrugged.

~   ~   ~

At one-thirty Yvette and Delores surveyed the dining room one last time. Multitudes of pink and purple twisted streamers Yvette had bought at a garage sale draped from the ceiling-fan-light to the outer corners of the ceiling, and a bouquet of big round balloons punctuated the center. Delores and Jill had arrived at ten, and the four had decorated the chocolate cupcakes Delores baked.

"I hope this will be the best party ever," Yvette finished taping the pink and purple gift wrap on the last small party gift.

Delores twisted a streamer one more turn. "All the parties after this will seem like duds."

"This may be the only chance we have to put on a good party. I want Tanya to have at least *one* memorable birthday."

"I think you'll get your wish. If it flops it won't be your fault."

"Thanks, Delores. Let's put these cupcakes in their hiding places and check that the notes are where they belong."

In the hayloft, the women deposited the treasure and crawled through the tunnels. "It's perfect," Delores's eyes sparkled as she exited a tunnel. "Those cracks between the bales let in enough light so they won't be scared and can find and read the treasure notes. Here, let me pick the hay out of your hair."

"We better go in," Yvette brushed hay off Delores' jacket. "I don't want the girls to come and investigate. That would spoil the surprise."

After the chattering and giggling party guests arrived and deposited their gifts on the table, Kyle shushed them. "I have something to show you in the barn. But you have to promise to follow our directions and behave your-selves. We don't want anyone to get hurt."

The guests, six girls and four boys, promised.

"You too, Tanya and Jill," Delores prompted.

"I'll behave," Tanya bounced up and down and fluttered her hands. "Are you going to show them the baby calves?"

"Wait and see," Yvette flashed her I've-got-a-secret grin.

They trooped to the barn and climbed the ladder to the hayloft. Kyle took pictures of the group and Greg handed out numbered treasure notes to half the children and told them to select a partner. Delores reminded them to explore *all* of the tunnels before they started searching.

The women and boys sat down on bales of hay to wait and exchanged glances and grins at the prank they'd planned. One of the tunnels was tall and wide, lined with plywood, had boards stored on the floor, and obviously led to the walk-through area. Each of the hay tunnels either formed a circle that turned back on itself, or led to a dead end. The wide wooden tunnel had a surprise opening into a short hay tunnel where the women had stashed six containers that held two chocolate cupcakes apiece. Muffled giggles, squeals and whispers floated out. "Do you think we made it too hard?" Yvette asked.

Delores shook her head. "It's easy if they follow directions, and they'll do better in school for having had this fun lesson."

"But will they consider that wooden walled area a tunnel?" Yvette frowned. "You could call this roofed alley between the mows a tunnel, too."

"They were told to explore *all* the tunnels; that includes *both* wooden tunnels," Delores whispered back. "You have a weird haymow. I've been in a few, but none was L-shaped or had that covered-bridge effect."

"It *is* a unique barn; my grandpa built a mow above the extra shed. Without this covered alley, we couldn't get to the east mow when the barn is full, unless we go downstairs and climb a different ladder."

Finally, after half an hour of crawling in the tunnels, a pair of girls with hay in their hair and clothes, came out. "We looked and looked, and we can't find the treasure," Janet, the taller one, complained.

"Did you follow all the directions?" Delores asked.

"Yes."

"Apparently you missed some. What directions did you follow?"

"We went down the steps in the tunnel, and up the steps, and turned right, then the tunnel ended. See," she showed Delores the note, while Kyle took a picture, "that's what the note says, and we didn't find any treasure."

"Where did the tunnel end?" Yvette asked.

"In a wooden walk-way where some boards are stored."

"And what were the directions Delores gave before you started?"

"I know," her partner, Danae, spoke up. "Explore all the tunnels."

"Did you check all of them?" Kyle asked.

"I don't know."

"You better go back and check," Greg advised.

The girls went back into a hay tunnel, and wisps of their murmured conversations reached the ears of the waiting adults. Five minutes later they heard a whoop, and shortly Janet and Danae came out of the wooden tunnel, each grasping one end of the treasure container.

"Can we open it now?" Janet asked.

"Does the number match the number on your treasure notes?" Yvette checked the numbers they showed her. "Okay, you can open it."

"That wasn't fair," Danae took a bite of chocolate cupcake, her mouth edged with white icing. "That space really isn't a tunnel."

"Why?" Delores asked as Jill and Tanya emerged with their find.

"It's not a *hay* tunnel."

"That was fun!" Adam stepped out of the tunnel with his partner, Joe. Two more pairs clambered out behind them. "Can we play in there again?"

The last pair came out of the tunnel and opened their treasure. "The frosting is smeared all over the lid," Stacey complained.

"We'll exchange those for cupcakes in the house," Yvette soothed.

When they returned to the house, Yvette directed a boiled-egg-on-the-spoon relay in the living room, then headed for the kitchen. Someone burst in the front door and collided with her as she walked by. It was Luke.

"What are you doing here?" she blurted, embarrassed when she realized the children and Delores had stopped their activity to watch.

"I live here," he hugged her and showered her face with kisses. "I came home early to see my darling wife. What are these kids doing here?"

"You guys can go back to playing your game," Yvette reminded, amused as the shamefaced group sprang into action.

"It's Tanya's birthday," she ducked out of his arms and rushed to the kitchen, conscious of Luke following her. "Jill and Tanya are having a combined birthday party and invited ten guests. What brings you home so early?" She took a half gallon of ice cream out of the freezer, and brought it to the table. "I didn't expect you until ten o'clock tonight."

"I thought we *agreed* Tanya wasn't going to have a birthday party this year." He took a cupcake with a pink rose in the center, peeled back the paper and took a bite. "Yum, chocolate. Where'd you get that light, creamy icing?"

She opened the end of the box. "I said I was too busy to host a birthday party. But the ice storm changed everything, and the children were cooped up for two days earlier this week."

"What ice storm?"

She hesitated while she searched for a serving spoon, looking for a way to avoid divulging any details. Telling him would tarnish the specialness of the bond she had shared with the children while he was away, and give him opportunity to criticize all the fun they'd had. She decided to give him the briefest of information. "We had an ice storm. As you can see, it melted away."

"What did you do while I was gone?"

"Oh, I don't know..." she glanced around as if she was too busy and distracted for this conversation. "...chores and some quilting, I guess."

"It doesn't look like you made any progress in the front yard."

"No, I didn't," she dug the spoon into the ice cream and deposited a medium-sized slab on the top paper plate.

"Wanna play in the sack with me?" he reached for another cupcake.

"Those are for the children," Yvette ignored his sexual overture. When his hand stayed poised over the cupcakes, she added, "If you have another, there won't be enough to go around."

He counted them. "You have fifteen cupcakes and only ten guests."

"Ten plus the two girls is twelve. Add Greg and Kyle, that's fourteen. Add Delores and myself, that's sixteen.

"Oh. But you and Delores aren't children."

"Delores is a guest, and Greg and Kyle helped with the party. You already ate one, so I'll have to go without."

"Then I better eat another one, too," he grinned and picked up a rose-topped cupcake, "so there won't be hard feelings."

"Delores and Jill brought these, and we all decorated them together. The girls and Delores will be very disappointed if you do anything to ruin their party. If you finish dishing up the ice cream, and pour punch into those picnic cups, I can repair and decorate those two cupcakes that got smeared."

"What's in it for me?" he teased, raising his eyebrows suggestively.

"How about two very happy and non-disappointed birthday girls?"

"You aren't any fun," he put the cupcake back on the table.

When the guests had gone, and Delores and Jill had taken their leave, Tanya hugged her mother. "That was the best party ever, Mom. The treasure hunt in the tunnels in the haymow was the best part."

"Better than the gifts?" Yvette pulled back in surprise.

"Everybody does that. The treasure hunt was," she paused, hunting for the right word, "*special*. Can I have a tunnel party in the haymow next year?"

"We'll see. A lot can happen in a year."

~   ~   ~

That night, Yvette dreaded going to bed with her husband.

"Why are you wearing that *nun* outfit?" Luke gibed as Yvette came into the bedroom dressed in a flannel, blue-flowered nightgown. He lay shirtless on his side of the bed with his arms behind his head and the blankets bunched at his waist. "It's buttoned up to your chin. Is that supposed to turn me on?"

"If it's buttoned to my chin," she lowered her chin to the top of her nightgown, "I must be a bizarre looking woman."

"You know what I meant," he ignored her humor. "I thought you would dress in something sexy, or in your birthday suit."

"I don't feel like being sexy."

"I'll fix that." He turned on his side facing her, his elbow making an indentation in his pillow as he propped his jaw on his palm and watched her.

Lifting the edge of the comforter, she paused and looked at her husband. She noted his tousled hair still damp from a shower, his dark brown eyes eager, expectant, and something she couldn't define. The sight of his chest hair reminded her of the first days of their marriage when she'd reached to feel the dark mass, and he'd barked at her to keep her hands off.

And like a key in the lock, it clicked. Just as he had decided how much she could talk with her mother, he had also decided what she would do in the bedroom. Most of what he initiated was repulsive or embarrassing to her and left her feeling disconnected, while he denied her the little intimacies that would have brought her pleasure or a sense of closeness. The look in his eye was that of a predator who planned to take, control, and possibly destroy.

Her doubt and confusion vanished. No longer would she conform to her husband's law that no matter how he manipulated, used, humiliated, and mistreated her, he was still a good man, but if she refused to comply with his whims she was a wicked and detestable woman, deserving of contempt and punishment. If turning him down made her less than perfect, so be it.

The irony of the contrast between Luke's definition of her behavior versus his, compared to the truth, swept over her, and she snickered as she got into bed and pulled the covers to her neck. All these years she'd focused on her own behavior and had tried to be *perfect*, while Luke made no attempt to be faultless and repeatedly chose the most selfish and sinful behaviors.

"Why are you giggling, and why did you look at me like that?" Luke's eyes narrowed and his brows drew together.

"Did I giggle? I'm sorry. I was..." she tittered again, "...thinking."

"Stop thinking," he growled.

"You want a *yes woman*?" she struggled to stop snickering.

"Of course not."

"That's good, because your *yes woman* just flew out the window," she fluttered her hand up toward the window. "She's never coming back."

"Fine. Now get over here."

"No, thank-you. I'd rather go to sleep."

"Okay, if you want to play hard to get," he sat up, placed his pillow next to hers, and began to scoot sideways toward her, "I'll move your way."

"I said, *no*."

He stopped short. "What do you mean, '*no*?' You are my *wife* and I expect sex from you. I've gone without for two whole weeks; you owe me."

"I don't want a fault-finding, demanding stranger to make so-called love to me," she turned her back and scooted to the edge of the bed.

"That is the most ridiculous thing I ever heard of. Can you imagine Val allowing his wife to turn him down?"

"I have no idea what goes on between Val and Annette in the bedroom. Now I'd like to sleep. I'm very tired." She turned off her bedside lamp.

"So what am I supposed to do?"

"Sleep."

After a long silence, she heard him plop his pillow down on his side of the bed, snap off his own lamp, and flop down with a sigh.

During the night Yvette awakened from a sound sleep. Disoriented, she struggled through the fog of sleep to discover what had roused her. Feeling hot, she moved to flip back the comforter, but couldn't lift her arm. Wide awake in a flash, she realized Luke's shoulder pinned hers down, his arm imprisoned her waist, and his deep breathing indicated he was asleep.

Disgusted at him for ignoring her refusal, it was the last straw. She would not put up with his disrespect another minute. Knowing she was too pinned down to move him off her, she pondered how to get away from him without waking him and causing a ruckus. She decided to slide from under him by moving her feet to the floor. At least he didn't have a leg thrown across her, too. She kicked the covers back and twisted her torso to put her feet on the floor. The weight of her lower body gave her the leverage she needed to slide from under his shoulder and off the bed. His arm went with her and his hand flopped over the edge of the bed, waking him as she slipped to the floor.

"What?" he jerked awake with a snort.

"SShhh," she whispered, "go back to sleep."

"Uh," he grunted and resumed his even breathing.

She padded out of the room, stocking-footed, and climbed the stairs to her sanctuary. She had to move the stacks of papers from her bed and get a blanket out of the cupboard in Tanya's room. Lacking a bedside lamp, she snapped off the light and felt her way around the quilt-in-frame to her bed.

She lay down and pulled the blankets to her chin, tense with listening, half expecting Luke to discover her missing and start stomping and roaring his displeasure. All was quiet except for once when she heard the bed creak as one of the boys turned over in his sleep. She wished she had brought the digital alarm clock up so she could tell time in the dark. But if Luke woke in the night, its absence could warn him she wasn't in bed. She'd likely wake and turn off the alarm before it beeped. After a long time she turned on her side and slept.

Chapter 10

Greg screamed, but no sound came out. In a fascination of horror he watched Dad, his face livid with rage, tower over Mom with his hands on her chest as he backed her against the floor-to-ceiling corner cupboard in the kitchen. Greg tried to run to protect her, but his feet wouldn't move. He fought through the paralysis, and just as Dad's hands circled Mom's neck, he broke through and jerked forward. But his parents had vanished.

Disoriented, item by item he tried to make sense of what had happened. Ahead of him, he could make out the dark outline of his chest of drawers with his basketball lamp on top. His face and chest were hot and sweating, but when he sat up a shiver ran up his back as the cool air touched him. It must have been a dream. He lay back down, going over the dream in his mind. It had been so real, like a silent movie. He shuddered, wondering what it meant.

Then he heard it, the faint chattering of his windows, the thud of footsteps downstairs that made the walls and floors quiver with each step. He heard his dad's voice bellow, "Yvette! Yvette! *Where are you?*" He threw back the covers and rushed to kneel over the floor register to hear better. Quietly pulling up the black rectangular metal grid, he lay on his stomach and peered down into the living room. When the shuddering of the walls stopped, and a fainter "Yvette!" floated to his ears, Greg guessed his dad had gone to the kitchen. Then the rattling resumed, and Greg could hear footsteps thudding through the dining room toward the stairs.

Nervous and afraid, he replaced the grid, frantic when it didn't fit in place on the first try. He scrambled, shivering, back into bed, yanking the blankets off his bare feet in his haste to cover himself. The heavy tread on the stairs had the same menacing quality the man in his dream had when backing his mom against the cupboard. He lay rigid in his bed, too scared to adjust the blankets even though his feet were freezing.

"Yvette!" The call wasn't that of an indignant calf bawling for its mother, as the previous ones had been. It was of an enraged bull.

He heard his mom's hissed, "Sshh, you'll wake the children," and his dad's loud swearing, "What are you doing up here? Get back in my bed where you belong!" Galvanized into action, Greg threw back the covers and raced to the hall. He had never before heard his father swear.

"What happened to your no swearing rule, Luke Zachary Miller?" Greg saw his mom standing in her flannel nightgown outside her lighted workroom. His dad stood on the landing, looking up at his wife through the balustrade. Greg could see the side and back of his dad's dark head and bare shoulders, and his hand gripping a baluster.

"It's *my* house," Luke growled. "I'll swear and wake the kids if I please. It's your fault. If you'd be in our bed, I wouldn't have any reason to swear." His Dad's manner reminded Greg of his dad's behavior in his dream. Greg edged closer to his mom, pressing his back against the wall to evade his dad's peripheral vision. Yvette glanced at her son, then moved a step down the hall. When Luke responded by shifting to his left, turning his back fully to Greg, Greg relaxed his indrawn stomach and took a deep breath.

"Luke," Yvette glanced at her watch, "it's four o'clock in the morning. Go back to bed. We can talk about this in private after chores."

"We'll discuss this *now*! Get down here!"

"I want to sleep without someone waking me, so I'm sleeping up here. There's no point in discussing it. My mind is made up."

"What's wrong, Dad?" Kyle spoke from behind Greg and Greg started. He hadn't noticed Kyle coming out of his room. "Is there a fire?"

Luke turned and glanced at the boys, then spat at Yvette, "See what you did? You woke the whole house! You don't consider anyone but *yourself*. You're just a self-centered *shrew!*" He pivoted toward his sons. "There's no fire, boys," a smile tugged at the corners of his mouth. "I was worried about Mom." Confused, Greg wondered if he had heard those savage words, or if he had imagined them.

"As you can see," Kyle said, "she's okay. Mom, Tanya's crying."

"We'll talk at noon then," Luke turned and stalked down the stairs.

Greg saw his mom's mouth open and shut as she watched his dad go down the stairs. She shrugged. "Thanks, boys," she smiled at them. "You behaved like *real men* tonight. Go to bed, now. I'll reassure Tanya."

~   ~   ~

Two weeks later, Yvette crouched next to Audrey, the second cow to develop a case of mastitis since Luke returned from Georgia, and slid her thumb and finger down the cow's teat to force the stringy clumps of milk out. It massed in the bottom of the bucket like a mound of cottage cheese. The cow lifted her hoof, and Yvette leaned hard against her flank to prevent a kick.

"Come on, now. I know it hurts, but I'm being as gentle as I can. If you'd sleep in the clean free-stall instead of in the manure, you wouldn't get infected and I wouldn't have to scrub the filth off your udder or treat you."

"This is the third time she's had mastitis this year," Kyle watched her insert an antibiotic, prepackaged in a syringe with a blunt-nosed needle, up the cow's teat. "It's a shame to throw her milk away."

"It's not her fault. If Greg would scrape down the cow lot every night, she wouldn't find manure to lie in. You better get ready for school. I'll come in as soon as I'm finished with Audrey and wash the equipment later."

"Why don't you let up on yourself now that Dad stopped griping?"

"I want to finish the patio and my quilt before gardening season starts." *He doesn't need to know my nervous stomach has been waking me early every morning, making sleep impossible. If Luke would go away I could relax again.*

"Take a break. We can work on the patio all summer."

"That sounds tempting," she unchained Audrey, who backed out and made a beeline for the door. "Actually," she hung the chain on its nail, "I'll get a break when I help Delores in the greenhouse today. It was a relief to go to Iowa City last week. Did you see the supplies I bought to beautify my room?" she shut the door after the cow and went with Kyle to the house.

"I saw you had a pile of stuff on the floor."

"Yeah, I couldn't stand Dad's carping anymore, so I dumped them in my room and escaped to the brooder house so he couldn't find me."

"That was smart. He acted gentleman-like and lovey-dovey after that."

"He invited me out for supper tonight."

~ ~ ~

Yvette stepped into the greenhouse and inhaled. As always, something about the scent of foliage, the huge light-filled space, and the rows of long tables covered with flats of flowering and lush green plants, soothed her spirit.

She found Delores, wearing huge rainbow-colored hoop earrings, perched on a high swivel chair at a work bench, transplanting a solid mass of lush marigold seedlings from one flat to multitudes of flats of four-packs.

"Happy birthday," Delores waved a dirt-soiled hand. "Have a seat."

"Thank-you," Yvette stood on tiptoe to scoot onto the chair. "I'm impressed you remembered my birthday. Want help with these marigolds?"

"Sure," Delores poked a hole in the dirt with the eraser end of a pencil, then inserted the roots of a seedling. "Here's a clump of seedlings," she broke off a section of dirt, roots and marigolds and put it on a saucer in front of Yvette, "and here's a flat of four-packs filled with dirt."

"What a welcome change," Yvette pulled a seedling from the clump.

"You're the change I need; talk to me. What's going on between you and Luke? I saw your face when George bragged on Luke after church. 'Luke's so diplomatic,'" Delores mimicked. "'He organized and motivated the crews so well, the cleanup and reconstruction just *flew*.'" She cleared her throat and reverted to her normal tone. "You looked like you were trying not to gag."

"What do you expect? He dropped his diplomacy after he got back." Yvette told about Luke's first night home. "Those weeks with him gone were so calm, so fun, so—" she sighed. "It's how a kid feels when the bully doesn't come to school. No one criticized me or got mad if I sat down to relax. I couldn't go back to the way things were, I just couldn't."

"Have you slept with him since that first night?"

"No," Yvette shook her head, "I told him I'd think about it. Then after the children left for school on Monday and I went into our bedroom to change clothes, Luke came in with the notion that since I was undressed, I was his for the taking. He overrode my protests and pushed me down on the bed. I made myself stop struggling and go limp like a rag doll. He swore and got off me then, but chewed me out and blocked me from getting my clothes. He was scary. Until recently, he's always had a no-swearing rule. I didn't want a repeat of that episode, so I moved my things to my workroom and put a lock on the door. I got the boys to move my dresser up when they came home from school."

"And Luke had a royal conniption?"

"He sure did. But I didn't budge. I started buying things for my workroom. I bought fabric to make curtains and a beautiful red lamp that's shaped like a delicate tulip. Someday, I plan to paint the room and stencil a border of roses. But what about you? Do you have your own special place?"

"Steve and I dream of hiring a professional to paint a mural of the Swiss Alps on one wall of our bedroom so we can imagine we're on a romantic holiday. Of course, we can't afford the mural or the holiday."

"Kyle is an artist. He's not a professional—yet, but he would do a good job. How about hiring him to do a mural for you? He'd be so proud if he could show Luke his art brings in money."

"Great idea, Yvette! I didn't think of Kyle. What a perfect solution! Steve will be absolutely thrilled; we've dreamed of this for so long. Speaking of solutions, I found information for your submission question. This concerns the meaning of *head* as a metaphor for Christ and husbands. Traditionally, *head* is thought to mean authority because that's what it means in most languages. But *Beyond Sex Roles*, a theological book I've been reading, says the Greek word for *head* in Ephesians Five is referring to life-giving and nurturing, and suggests we use the term *servant-provider* instead of *head*. I think that makes perfect sense.

Jesus served people and sacrificed Himself to give us life. And now He provides for our nourishment and growth. Husbands are to copy His headship of giving life and providing growth through sacrificial serving and nurturing, *not* through *taking* advantage, ordering, or making rules."

"That matches other Biblical passages, yet it's opposite of what Luke's been insisting on all these years. It describes how Steve treats you, doesn't it?"

"Yes, Steve is life-giving. He encourages me to pursue my interests and makes sure time and money are available for my growth. As a result, I'm healthy and more *me*, not just a woman who meets the family's needs."

Yvette drew in a deep breath and blew it out. "So when the husband is abusive and controlling, he's not being the 'head of his wife'?"

"Exactly. Instead of nourishing her to fullness of life, he's destroying her. His toxic behavior harms his wife's physical, emotional, and spiritual health, and according to First Peter, his prayers are hindered."

A tear trickled down Yvette's cheek and she brushed it away. "That explains why I'm so tired and tense and have trouble sleeping."

"It's normal for abused women to feel tense and super alert all the time. They constantly have to gauge how safe they are. Our bodies aren't meant to handle chronic stress like that; it brings illness."

"Clarifying the definition of *head* adds more weight to the don't-submit-to-abuse side. If Luke's headship is not life-giving as a servant-provider, then I can't possibly submit to him as the church does to Christ."

"Exactly. I'm relieved you see it clearly now. But I warn you, life could get rough. As you stand firm, Luke could take a look at himself and stop trying to control you or he could fight harder to force you to submit."

"Things are much better now. He badgered me for two days about my supposed marital duties. But when I wouldn't back down he quit it. He helps me with the dishes after supper, and suggested the boys wash dishes three nights a week. That's a switch for him; he used to say dishes are women's work. He stopped pestering me for sex, and tonight he's taking me out to eat."

"He's likely trying to get what he wants."

Yvette filled her flat with dirt, then returned to her chair and resumed transplanting. "Perhaps. But shouldn't I give him the benefit of the doubt?"

"Actually, when abusive men put on charm, that's abuse, too."

"What?" Yvette stopped transplanting and turned to study Delores's face to be sure she wasn't teasing. "You can't be serious."

"I'm not joking. As long as Luke believes he's entitled to get his way, his nice behavior is just another tactic to get what he wants. I've concluded the nice phases are the nastiest of all, because the abuser deceives his wife into believing he won't abuse her anymore, so she trusts him again."

"What if Luke really *did* change this time?"

"I hope he will be loving from here on out, but I doubt it."

~   ~   ~

After chores, Yvette and Luke dressed to go out for supper. Greg went to a friend's house for the night and Kyle stayed home with Tanya. Yvette didn't know what to expect from Luke. Would he control what she could eat?

"You're wearing red again," he said as she came down from upstairs. "I can see why you like that dress; you look beautiful in it. And your hair is gorgeous when it's loose like that and curled under."

"Thank-you," she flushed, remembering the last time she wore the dress to church he'd said the wide neckline that flaunted her collar bones and the ruffled hem that stopped just above her knee on one side and dipped below her calf on the other made her look like a whore. To avoid another put-down, she never wore it again—until now—although it was one of her favorites. Tonight she'd taken a chance, hoping he wouldn't disparage her if she wore it to eat out.

"I want to apologize," Luke began after they ordered their pizza. "I've been a real schmuck to you all our married lives, and especially recently. I'm very sorry. I know an apology doesn't make up for what I've done. I was a jerk to go to Georgia and leave you to handle the sows. Kyle told me how you dealt with a power outage during that ice storm. He told me a few home truths, and I'm ashamed of myself. Then to top it all off, I came home and tried to force you. I can't believe I could stoop so low. Can you forgive me?"

"Of course I forgive you, Luke," Yvette squeezed his hand.

"Thank-you," he clasped her hand between his. "I don't deserve you. It tears me up that you've been in pain because of my self-centeredness. *That* is going to change. From now on I am committed to making sure *you* are happy. I've tried so hard to ensure I'm not hen-pecked like my dad, I've become an insensitive idiot. I don't want to *ever* be like that again."

"Your parents have a great marriage! They respect each other."

"I don't see it that way. I saw Dad's frustration when he had to consult Mom about everything. I decided my marriage would not be like that."

"Your dad consulted your mom because he *valued* her opinion. If he was frustrated, it was about the situation. He once told me his dad was king at his house, and that he, your dad that is, vowed he'd *always* make sure he and his wife were of one mind before taking action. I assumed you'd be like him."

Looking confused, Luke shook his head. "And I always thought—"

"But why? Where did you get the idea your dad was unhappy?"

"From Grandpa. When I was a kid, and Dad discussed family plans with Mom, Grandpa commented to me, *What a sissy! When is he going to take his God-given role?* Once when Dad and Mom were arguing, he told Dad to

88

stand up and be a man. Later he told me Dad would never be happy until he took charge. That made a big impression on me. I thought Grandpa was right."

"I had no idea. I just..." she blinked back the tears, "...hurt."

"That's going to change," he caressed her hand. "I love you, Yvette, and am committed to never hurt you again. What changes do I need to make?"

Something feels wrong. Yvette tugged to free her hand.

Luke tightened his grip. "Please, tell me. I won't get mad."

Yvette searched his eyes, and the memory of what Delores had said came flooding back. *The nice phases are the nastiest of all, because he deceives her into believing he won't abuse her anymore, so she trusts him again.* Ah, that was why she felt uncomfortable. But Luke seemed sincere; she'd chance it.

She took a deep breath and relaxed the hand Luke held. "Recently, I've become aware of how good I feel when I'm creative. Kyle feels the same way. He needs you to," she hesitated, wondering if she was saying too much, "to be supportive of his God-given talents, including art and music."

"I want to do as you ask, but I can't change my mind in an instant. I don't think dabbling with paints will make him a decent income."

"He could be the next great painter, Luke," a shiver ran down her spine at the thought. "One whose work touches people and brings them to God. Think of Thomas Kinkade's work. What if he had not been allowed to paint?"

"You make a good point. But I don't want to confuse Kyle by supporting his art today and changing my mind later. It's an expensive hobby."

"Not anymore than it is for you to eat out every week," Yvette leaned forward until she came against the table. As long as he was listening, she'd fight for everything she could get for their children. "You get more spending money than the rest of us combined; why not spend some of it on the kids?"

"Touché. I *have* been self-centered, haven't I? It's no wonder you don't want to sleep with me. I'm willing to change if you'll give me a chance."

"I'll give you a chance, but right now I need space to heal." His forlorn look tugged at her, but she couldn't bear to allow him intimacies so soon after he'd tried to force her. *He has to reap what he sowed, so he won't try it again.*

~   ~   ~

After eating, they headed home. "I wonder, have you truly forgiven me?" Luke took his eyes off the road and looked at her.

"According to my definition of forgiveness, I have. But—you won't like this part—forgiveness doesn't mean I trust you as if you never hurt me."

"Then you haven't forgiven me."

"Trust takes time to develop. I'd be a fool to trust you when you've repeatedly shown me you're untrustworthy. But I'm giving you the chance to show you will respect me and never put me down."

"That's not biblical. The father *completely* forgave his prodigal son and restored him to the family without the son having to prove anything."

"Maybe. We don't know if the father *trusted* his son enough to make him an accountant of the business. Please don't expect me to pretend I can trust you completely, and don't ruin my birthday."

"Your-your birthday?" Luke sputtered. "Oh, no, I totally forgot. Oh, I know. I can give you the gift I bought in Georgia. It's your favorite color."

When they got home, Kyle and Tanya were already in their beds. Luke retrieved the lamp, unwrapped and in it's box, and presented it to Yvette.

"Oh, my," she said, startled. It was identical to the one she had purchased for her room upstairs. Not wanting to ruin Luke's pleasure, she decided not to mention she had its twin. "This is exquisite, and definitely my color." She touched a red glass petal. "Thank-you Luke. Where shall I display it?"

"I thought you'd want it on your night stand in the bedroom."

"But the lamp that's there matches yours." Yvette frowned.

"Those are garage sale lamps. We can replace them."

Yvette kept silent. Should she look for another lamp for upstairs and put that one in Luke's bedroom? She shrugged, took the new lamp to Luke's bedroom, and placed it on the night stand next to the brown one.

Luke watched her from the doorway. "Are you going to sleep in here tonight?" She thought he seemed unsure of himself.

"I'm not ready for that yet." She hated how hard it was to tell him no, and she hated to hurt him, but she couldn't sleep with him. Anyway, if she relented this soon, he'd learn he could get by with anything if he sweet-talked her. "How about if I make hot chocolate and we snuggle on the couch? No TV or romantic music, no petting or necking. Let's just enjoy being together."

"I can try, but it's tough to be close and not wish for more."

"You're so one-dimensional," she rolled her eyes. "Forget it; I'll go up to bed. I need to catch up on sleep anyway."

"Don't go," he grabbed her hand. "I'll behave; I promise."

"I'd hate to make things *hard* for you," she headed for the kitchen. "By the way," she grinned at him over her shoulder, "the pun was intended."

"You're not playing fair," he caught up with her in the kitchen.

"Usually you're the one who doesn't play fair. Isn't it my turn?"

"Maybe so. But I don't have to like it," he sat down to wait for his hot chocolate.

Chapter 11

Yvette firmed the soil around the scented heliotrope in the wooden half-barrel next to the porch, then sank onto the porch and surveyed her handiwork. A profusion of burgundy geranium vines cascaded down the irregularly stacked flagstones of the rock wall garden, and clematis vines climbed halfway up each side of the heavy wires she and Kyle had fashioned into arches on top of the wall to create the window for Tanya. Adding the barrel of purple heliotrope expanded the patio onto the porch with it's hanging baskets of fuchsia.

Inhaling the sweet scent of heliotrope, she sighed with contentment. Her efforts had finally paid off and their marriage had turned the corner. For the past month, Luke had prepared the fields for spring planting and came in long after she had gone upstairs to bed. But on Sunday afternoons, they cuddled in Luke's bed and made love. Instead of demanding repulsive sex, Luke caressed her and allowed her to touch him. In all their years of marriage, she'd never experienced such satisfying lovemaking.

"The patio looks marvelous," her mother spoke from her front door. "Your dad grew those varieties of blue and deep blue Delphinium, and those red Sweet Williams, too. They were his favorites. It's a perfect memorial."

Yvette looked up. "It did turn out well if I say so myself. Can you think of anything Luke could criticize—besides Dad's favorite flowers, I mean? I made the clean and direct path to the mailbox, and got solid wood lawn and lounge chairs instead of the flimsy aluminum ones he hates. I used the largest flagstones for the rock wall so it will be solid and safe for children to crawl on."

"There's not a thing he could complain about. You put in everything he wanted, and he's not likely to recognize Dad's flowers after all these years."

"I keep reminding myself to stop thinking he'll criticize me. He's not like that anymore. I'll share my miniature Garden of Eden with him tomorrow. I can imagine us soaking up the atmosphere under the Crimson Maple trees."

"It's an idyllic place, Yvette. Luke should be pleased. Here comes the bus. I better finish my work so I can talk with Tanya when she comes over."

The school bus dropped the children off, and they dashed through the rose arbor. "Wow," Kyle stopped short, "you made the rock wall into a garden. I never saw ivy bloom like that. What are they?"

"Geraniums. Aren't they beautiful?"

"You made steps to my window and left a spot for me to climb through it," Tanya squealed as she shrugged off her backpack and raced to the arch.

Yvette watched her climb the wall and sit in her window. "It'll be even better when the clematis vines cover the arch." She turned to Kyle and Greg. "Did you boys see what I bought for you? One of those chaise lounges is for you Greg, and—"

"You got the park benches I wanted," Kyle whooped. "They have fancy scrollwork for the legs *and* the armrests. Oh, thank you, thank you, Mom. Can I get my water colors out now?"

"Change your clothes first."

"Ahhh," Greg eased himself down on a lounge chair, "just what I need after a long day at school. Can you bring our snack out here, Mom? I can lie back and look into the trees for hours without ants crawling on me."

"You can have your break out here, but don't dally," excitement started bubbling in her belly. "Remember, Dad's taking us to the Mennonite Relief Sale for supper tonight, and we want to get there before they stop serving."

"Can we have homemade pie and ice cream, too?" Greg asked.

"You just want a chance to talk to Kathy again," Kyle teased. "What if she's not serving in that building this year?"

"That's enough teasing, Kyle," Yvette said. "Greg's been decent to you and doesn't deserve to be picked on." She went in to get their milk and cookies. The excitement expanded upward and outward, filling her very being till she wanted to dance for joy. Something very good was about to happen. She didn't know what could be better than she already had with Luke, but her heart sang with expectation.

After chores, they made it to the Relief Sale in time to eat the pork supper, but were the last ones through the line. Yvette waited for Luke to make a cutting comment, then chided herself as she remembered he had changed.

"I should have come in from the field earlier to help you chore," he said with a wry, lopsided grin. "I'm not used to considering my family, I guess."

Yvette's stomach muscles relaxed. She hadn't realized she'd tensed up. "Apology accepted," she smiled over her shoulder at Luke as she followed their children into the building. The people behind the serving table with its steaming roasters served them at once. Only a few patrons sat at the long rows of white-paper-covered tables. Yvette selected a table furthest from the clean up crew, who rolled up soiled white paper, and stacked folding chairs.

After supper, Yvette, Luke and Tanya walked from booth to booth, Tanya holding hands with either parent. Luke bought strawberry pie, rhubarb pie, cheese curds, homemade noodles, and a print of a girl holding a kitten.

"We should buy cookies," Yvette said.

"Let me buy them for you. What kind do you want?"

"I won't know until I see what kind they have. Look at Tanya," she gestured with her chin toward their daughter. "She's been watching that woman decorate cakes for ten minutes. Just wait; she'll want you to buy one."

"Would I be out of line to buy a cake *and* cookies?"

"It's going for a good cause and will cut my work load. While you're at it, buy several more pies, too."

They took their purchases to the car and met Greg and Kyle returning from the general auction barn. The boys offered to keep an eye on Tanya in the children's activity barn, while Luke and Yvette went to see the quilts. Luke took Yvette's hand as they strolled toward the quilt barn. Yvette looked down at their joined hands then up at Luke. He smiled at her and squeezed her hand. She couldn't stop a smile in response and sighed in satisfaction.

Hand in hand they shuffled through the sawdust, studying the quilts strung in rows in the quilt barn, then returned to join the crowd at the blue dahlia quilt Yvette had pieced.

"I want this blue one," Yvette heard a blond teenager say.

"I can't afford it," the white-haired woman with her replied, "It'll be the most expensive one here."

"You always say that, Grandma," the girl pouted as the pair walked away. "You always make me settle for ugly stuff."

"She knows how to pick 'em," a man in the crowd chuckled.

"That woman's right," Luke whispered in her ear. "Yours will be the most expensive one, and it's worth every inflated cent it will bring in."

"Come on," she tugged on his hand. "Red's prettier."

"Your quilt is the prettiest one I've ever seen."

They rounded up the children and went to the homemade pie and ice-cream building with its yellow anti-bug lighting, where each selected a piece of pie, and Kathy, Greg's crush, added scoops of ice cream.

~ ~ ~

The next morning during chores Yvette imagined Luke's expression when she showed him her patio creation. He'd look awed, then he'd snuggle with her on a park bench. After a few dreamy minutes he'd say, "Wait till Alex sees this." She smiled at the thought and pondered when would be the best time to show it to him. Not before breakfast; he'd be too hungry to enjoy it. But after breakfast he'd be ready to sit and relax a few minutes, and they could look forward to an evening under the trees after supper.

When Yvette came in after morning chores, Luke, dressed in town clothes, was combing his hair at the washroom sink.

"You're going to town?" she blurted, trying to sound surprised rather than dismayed as she unknotted her kerchief. There went her plan to show him the patio after breakfast. "I thought you wanted to get ready to cut hay."

"I'll do that Monday. I'm going to the auction to buy your quilt."

"You want something that expensive on your bed?" out of habit she kept her voice expressionless and her face toward the coat hooks so he wouldn't see her frown or hear how much it mattered to her.

"That's *our* bed," Luke swatted her behind.

"That's strange," she hung her wraparound chore apron, furrowed her brow in feigned confusion, and fought to keep her lips from curving upward. "I thought this is *your* house and *your* furniture."

"You know what I meant," he grinned and moved to swat her again.

She sidestepped into the coats, covering her behind with her hands. "If it's my bed, too, I should have a say what goes on it, shouldn't I?"

"You have a right to voice your opinion," he returned his comb to its place on the corner shelf, "but it's my job to make the final decision."

"Do you think I'll *want* to sleep with you when you're dictatorial? Where's the loving self-sacrifice you're commanded to exercise?"

"I'm sorry you don't like my decisions, but you'll have to put up with them. In this case, that quilt belongs here and I'm going to buy it."

She knew from the finality in his tone he expected her to be quiet and accept his decision, but the sick feeling in her stomach urged her to reason with him. She hesitated, then decided she couldn't let dread of his temper keep her from speaking up. Maybe if she presented good reasons and an alternative, he'd reconsider. "I'd rather you didn't buy that quilt. We didn't budget for it—especially not at inflated relief sale prices—and it'll cut a hole in our savings. Please, let that one go and I'll make another one at a fraction of the cost."

"No, after this the quilts you piece will bring us money. I want *that* one, and I want exclusive rights to that blue flower design. Then everyone will know I have the prettiest bed in the state of Iowa, maybe in the whole world."

"You're crazy," she circled her pointing finger around her ear.

"Want to come with me?" he stepped aside as she neared the sink.

"Sure," she dumped cloudy water from the basin and turned on the spigot to refill it, "but the children and I are going to Mechanicsville to get the chicks we ordered. I haven't spent much time with the children lately, and two

94

hours on the road will help remedy that. You could take us out for the pancake breakfast at the Relief Sale, though."

"Why not?" with one big hand he grasped the doorframe next to his head. "The money will help starving people in Ethiopia or displaced people in Iraq. We'll take two vehicles, eat breakfast together and go to the quilt auction, then you and the children can go to Mechanicsville, while I hang around at the sale. Your quilt is eighth on the list, so you won't have to be at the auction very long. What do you think?"

"It sounds workable, but let me check with the children, first."

"Come on, Yvette," he sighed. "Can't you *ever* make plans without asking permission from the kids? *We're* the adults here."

"That's true, but since we already had plans, I need to consider their feelings. I'd want the same courtesy if I were in their shoes."

"Maybe so, but waiting around for your answer gets old very fast."

"And being pressed to make spur-of-the-moment decisions without consulting the others involved gets old for me," she turned off the faucet. "Please, Luke, don't do this. I thought you were going to stop that junk."

"You're right, and I apologize. In my eagerness to spend time with you, I forgot to wait patiently. Please remind me again if I forget; I don't want you to consent to things if you aren't comfortable with them."

"Apology accepted," she picked up the bar of soap and began to lather her hands and arms. "I'm guessing the boys will go for the pancake breakfast, but Tanya won't be interested unless she knows Kyle is going."

"You should put a stop to that. She shouldn't hang around Kyle all the time; he'll never learn to be a man as long as he's playing nursemaid."

"Give them time," she bent over the sink and splashed water on her face. "Keep doing your part, and they'll stop it. They're more relaxed since you stopped being harsh and critical, but I expect they'll always be extra close."

"You're saying it's *my* fault he's a sissy?"

Seeing his feet change from a relaxed stance to a battle-ready one, she rushed to defuse his anger. "I'm saying that's how they learned to cope with the stresses you brought into their lives," she ran fresh water, squeezed her eyes shut, and rinsed her face and arms. "What's going on with you today, anyway? If you're going to be like this, I don't want to go anywhere with you. You aren't going to change back into the old Luke, are you?"

"Of course not. I'm just grouchy because I'm hungry."

"Don't take it out on us; we don't deserve it," she felt for the towel. "There's food in the kitchen; make a piece of toast to tide you over."

"That's a good idea," Luke sauntered to the kitchen.

As Yvette showered and dressed, she recalled their conversation. Had Luke changed? He still brushed off her input, and got mad when she said Kyle's behavior was caused by Luke's critical ways. But he'd only done that this morning, probably because he was hungry. She'd give him the benefit of the doubt, since he'd quit it then. Anyway, the children had cheered when she'd suggested going to the pancake breakfast.

That brought to mind her plans for showing Luke the patio. He'd seen it during stages of construction, but she guessed he hadn't seen it finished. Surely, she wouldn't have to wait 'til tomorrow to show it to him.

As she went downstairs, she met Greg dashing up the stairs, a towel around his waist and his wet hair tousled. Kyle and Tanya sat on the built-in worktable, dressed and drumming catchy rhythms against the cupboard doors with their heels. A horn sounded. Yvette looked out the window and saw Luke sitting in the car at the end of the walk.

"Kyle," Yvette paused at the table, "please tell him to go without us if he can't be patient. He can buy tickets; we'll come later in the pickup."

The rhythm stopped. "You tell him. He'll chew me out."

"Okay then, you and Tanya can fill the jug with ice water and bag up cookies and carrots to eat on our trip to Mechanicsville." She dashed to the car, opened the passenger door and bent down to look inside. "Stop leaning on the horn, Luke. Kyle refused to come out and talk to you. If you're in that big of a hurry, why don't you pitch in and help? Or go and buy tickets for us?"

"Yes, Boss," he honked the horn again.

"I mean it, Luke. If you don't quit the attitude, you'll eat pancakes by yourself. I won't put up with that kind of behavior anymore."

"Come on, Yvette, I'm spoofing you. Can't you take a joke?"

"Behavior that drives your wife and children away is no joke."

"Okay, I'll cut the act. I'm sorry; I got carried away. I'll be on my best behavior for the rest of the day. Deal?" he held out his hand.

"No," she snapped. "Be on your best behavior the rest of your *life*."

"You drive a hard bargain. What's in it for me?" he winked at her.

She felt like grinding her teeth but controlled herself. "How about the satisfaction of doing what's right and enjoying better relationships?"

"Ah, you're no fun."

"Enjoyment and satisfaction go deeper than fun, Luke. Don't our cozy times satisfy you? Do you *need* to keep us on edge for you to be happy?"

"Why not?" he smirked. "Doesn't it bring out the best in you all?"

"No, it's destructive. Tanya gets more scared of spiders and social situations, Greg gets disrespectful and nasty, and Kyle carries responsibilities that are too grown up for him. *You* are supposed to be the grownup, not Kyle."

"I *am* the grownup."

"Then stop acting like a spoiled child."

"I was just having fun."

"It's not fun when it hurts others, Luke. It's *abuse*." She had resisted calling it abuse to his face, and now watched him warily.

"Okay, okay, you made your point." He inched the car forward until she closed the door and stepped back, then he hit the gas, making the tires spit gravel as he peeled out the drive.

Yvette and the children followed fifteen minutes later in the red extended-cab pickup. They met Luke at the ticket kiosk, and got in the breakfast line. Luke held her chair for her when they took their plates to the table, and acted the gentleman throughout breakfast. Yvette didn't relax until they joined the queue filing into the open-sided auction building and Luke maintained his good behavior. After Yvette led the way into a row of chairs and sat down, Tanya tugged on Kyle's hand and pulled him past Greg and their parents to sit on Yvette's other side. Yvette caught Luke's eye and cocked her head toward Tanya and Kyle in a *what did I tell you?* manner.

"That's uncalled for," Luke frowned. "I didn't do a thing to her."

"She caught your attitude," Yvette whispered.

"You could teach her to toughen up."

"Shift responsibility onto her so you can keep being a jerk?"

"Sshh. The auctioneer is getting ready to start."

She quieted but tuned out the auctioneer's jokes and the crowd's laughter. What could she do to convince Luke to not revert to his abusive ways? In the past she'd ignored his obnoxious comments and that hadn't stopped him. Today she'd asked him to stop it, and he'd only stopped temporarily. She needed a plan. Apparently, neither ignoring his behavior nor requesting change had worked for any length of time. But refusing to sleep with him and moving out of his bedroom *had* been effective for over a month. She'd give him one more chance. If he acted up again, she'd refuse to sit with him or talk to him, and she definitely wouldn't get into bed with him.

That decided, she watched Kyle and Tanya at her left play tic-tac-toe on a napkin, then leaned forward to see what Greg was doing. He was looking at someone on the bleachers to the right. She followed his gaze and recognized Kathy, Greg's crush, who was sitting with her mother watching the auctioneers and the bid-takers as they worked the crowd.

"What number are we on?" Yvette whispered to Luke.

"They finished number six," he pointed at his quilt auction guide where he'd recorded the final bid next to each of the first six quilts listed.

"You aren't actually planning to buy that quilt, are you?" she absently studied the yellow crib quilt on the display board.

"Of course I am. That's why we're here."

"Please reconsider. I can make you a *king-sized* quilt that will reach the floor. This one is for a full to queen-sized bed."

"I don't want to wait and I don't want anyone else to have it. Besides, blue will go with the rug and we can toss that rose-colored spread."

"What's your bidding limit?" A couple meandered into the row ahead of them and sat in the seats in front of Luke and Greg.

"You don't get it, do you?" he whispered directly into her ear. "I *will* buy that quilt even if it takes all the money I have in savings."

"It's *my* savings, too," she muttered. "I have some say in this."

"I heard you. But I'm the head of the house and what I say goes."

"Don't get mad at me when there's not enough money in the bank."

"Hush," Luke wrote the bid on the auction guide, "my quilt's next."

On the stage, the auctioneer took off the microphone and handed it to Bruce, the next auctioneer. An elderly husband and wife, whose names she couldn't recall at the moment, opened up the Giant Dahlia Quilt Yvette had pieced and laid it flat on a huge, slanting, cloth-covered display board.

"That is *so* pretty," Yvette heard someone behind her breathe.

A woman stated the name and size of the quilt, that Yvette Miller had pieced it and the women's sewing circle had quilted it, then a flurry of bidding started. In seconds the bidding reached fifteen hundred dollars and everyone but Luke and another bidder—a man on the bleachers—had dropped out.

Yvette looked at the man high up on the bleachers again. She couldn't tell who he was; the daylight behind him made him into a silhouette. He nodded at her. She nodded back and turned her attention to Bruce, the auctioneer.

Hearing eighteen repeated over the speaker system and seeing Bruce look at Silhouette Man, Yvette realized Luke had just bid seventeen hundred dollars, and her heart began to pound hard and fast. Taking a few deep breaths, she tried to slow it down, but it kept racing and pounding. She saw Silhouette Man hesitate, then nod. Bruce turned to Luke. Without hesitation Luke nodded at the auctioneer's repeated nineteen. Yvette put a hand on Luke's forearm. "Please, Luke, it's not worth that much. Let him have it."

Silhouette Man nodded at two thousand, and the auctioneer focused on Luke. "Don't listen to her," Bruce bantered into the microphone. "She'll tell you she can make another one, but she'll never get around to it."

The crowd laughed.

"Twenty-one, twenty-one," Bruce rattled on, and Luke nodded.

Heart pounding, Yvette held her breath and watched Silhouette Man.

Silhouette Man shook his head, and the auctioneer repeated twenty-two several times before calling "Sold! To—" Luke held up his card, "—to number two hundred forty-four."

The crowd clapped.

"Thanks to all the bidders, especially the runner-up," Bruce said.

Yvette tuned out the noise around her. Twenty-one hundred dollars for her quilt! How on earth would she account for that in the budget?

"Mom," Kyle's hand on her arm brought her back to her surroundings, "can we go now? Tanya's tired of looking at quilts."

"Certainly," Yvette collected her things. "I'll write out a check for the quilt and get the receipt, Luke." She doubted he would wait for the receipt. At the cashier's trailer, the children waited outside while she wrote a check from their joint account and asked for the receipt. At the next building, an attendant brought them a black garbage bag fastened with a tag labeled *two forty-four.*

"Are you sure that's our quilt?" Greg hefted the bag as if testing its weight. "It looks too small. He looked in the bag. "Was the back navy blue?"

Yvette flipped a corner of the quilt. "That's the one."

"Let's go," Kyle knocked on the table, "Tanya wants to see the chicks."

Greg drove to the hatchery, and they discussed the auction and how exciting it was when Luke bid on the quilt. Kyle thought he could never bid for anything, and Greg said bidding was easy as long as you had the money to pay for it. Tanya said she wanted the doll blanket they put on the board after Dad bid on the big quilt, and Yvette promised to help her make her own.

After they returned home and deposited the fuzzy yellow balls in the brooder house, Tanya wanted to show the chicks to Jill, so Yvette invited Delores and Jill over. Delores accepted, but only for an hour, since it was a busy Saturday at the greenhouse. After showing them the chicks, Yvette led them between the two houses so they would be surrounded by the vegetation and flagstones when they walked onto the patio.

"What a paradise!" Delores exclaimed as Yvette stepped out of the way so she could see the place. "This is awesome."

"Do you think Luke will like it?" Yvette barely noticed when the girls ran to play McDonalds under the arch.

"He'd be crazy not to," Delores stepped into the first bush-lined room. I like the way you used the bushes and flowers to make secluded areas. The ambiance of this place makes me want to sit down and relax on one of those park benches. This wall is stunning. The flowers look delicate against the contrasting rocks." She moved into the open area under the crimson maple and sank onto a wooden lawn chair. "We should hire you to design our place. It would encourage customers to be creative, which would boost sales."

"I'd love to, but I don't know when I'd find the time. This farm keeps me busy. By the way, Luke apologized, believe it or not, and has been behaving more like Steve. Our marriage is much better. Thank-you so much."

"It's an answer to prayer. I'll keep praying his change is permanent." She glanced at her watch. "That hour went fast. Come on, Jill, let's go home."

~   ~   ~

Mid-afternoon, while the boys ground and mixed feed for the hogs and Tanya was at Grandma's house, Yvette came up from the basement with a pack of T-bone steaks in time to see Luke walk in, take the quilt off the dining room table, and strut to the bedroom sporting a self-satisfied smile. She dropped her package on the kitchen counter, followed him into the bedroom, and helped him spread the quilt on the bed and plump up the pillows on top.

"Now it's truly *our* bed," Luke rounded the bed, put his arms around her and toppled them onto the bed. Yvette squealed and they tussled until Luke allowed her to straddle him and pin his arms above his head.

"You got me," he teased. "Am I a keeper or will you toss me out?"

Yvette tilted her head to one side. "Yeah, I'll keep you."

"Does that mean you'll move into our bedroom again?"

"I like the way it is. You're more romantic when I sleep upstairs, we're *both* in the mood when we make love, and I get a full night's sleep every night. Besides, now the clutter in my bedroom won't annoy you."

"*I* don't like it," his smile vanished. "Doesn't that count?"

"Of course. But the new us is still too new. If I move down here now, we'll go back to the way we were, and I don't want that."

He flipped her to the side and shot off the bed. "I do all this for you and this is the thanks I get?" he glared down at her.

"Luke, stop it!" she scooted away from him, frightened by his sudden change of mood. "You didn't do this for me. I didn't *want* this quilt. Let's build a friendship first. Please? I don't want to dread being near you again." She held her breath and waited for his reaction.

"You're right," he sat on the bed. "I won't pressure you, okay?"

She let out her breath and nodded.

"Come here," he beckoned. She snuggled into his warm embrace.

"I have something to show you," she said at length. A feeling of foreboding came over her. She paused, wishing she could take her words back. But she'd opened her mouth and he'd get upset if she uninvited him. She took a deep, fortifying breath. "Come on. It's outside." She led him to her patio.

From the porch, he surveyed the yard in silence.

"What do you think?" she wanted to bob up and down like Tanya.

"It's," he paused as if searching for the right word, "different."

"Is that good, bad, or so-so?" she covered her mouth to contain herself.

"There are too many bushes."

"You think so?" she turned her face away so he wouldn't see the hurt in her eyes. She could tell he wasn't teasing. "I thought Tanya and her friends would love having their own play area. And after they grow up, we can put in a hot tub or a picnic table."

"There are too many flowers, and—and it's gaudy. People driving past can look through the rose arbor and see those blue and red flowers your dad used to like so much." He pointed at the rock-wall-garden, "But that rock pile over there is especially gaudy."

"No, it's not," she blinked back tears. "Flowers are never gaudy."

"They are when you make a show place with them. Front yards should be where kids play tag and football, not where they neck behind the bushes."

"Delores loves it, and the children had fun playing on the stone wall. The bushes create the illusion of privacy, but they aren't so thick we can't keep tabs on the children. What's with you, anyway? You told me to fix the yard. I did and the result is beautiful. Why can't you say so?"

"*I* think it's tasteless. What's that wire on those ugly rocks?"

"They aren't ugly. It's an arched trellis, designed so the children can pretend to serve in a restaurant, play Rapunzel, or whatever they want."

"It's tacky. You asked what I thought, and I'm giving you my honest opinion. There's no reason to be argumentative. The whole thing should go to the landfill. If you had consulted me before you went to all that bother, we wouldn't have this mess. I expected you to sow grass seed."

"I *asked* for your input, and you yelled at me to just fix it and later said as long as there's a direct path to the mailbox, you didn't care what I did."

"It never occurred to me you would cover the *whole* front yard with rocks and put bushes and a wall in the middle of the yard."

Yvette thought she heard a hint of smugness in his tone, but dismissed it as improbable. "I designed the yard to be a place of beauty and fun," she snapped. "The placement of the bushes and wall is aesthetically pleasing."

"You don't have to be argumentative all the time. You created a gaudy showplace. Now all you can do is accept it and get over it."

"But I worked *so hard* to please the whole family!"

"I'm sorry you worked so hard for nothing," he laid his arm across her shoulders. She dislodged his arm by bending to pick up a twig. "*I'll* scoop it up with the skid loader and haul it to the dump so you don't wear yourself out. You won't want this embarrassing eyesore when friends come to visit. In the meantime, the hedge will hide it from those just passing by."

101

"If you say so," Yvette blinked back tears and hurried into the house and upstairs to her room, before she allowed herself to cry.

Once she started crying, she couldn't stop. She loved the patio, had loved every minute of designing and creating it, and dreamt of idyllic hours there with Luke and the children. But he despised it. It was as if he despised a part of her. She had put her heart and soul into creating a place Luke would enjoy, but had failed to gratify him. All her efforts were for nothing if Luke hated it. Huddled on the gray broken-old-linoleum floor, she wept quietly, sopping up tears and blowing her nose with tissue after tissue.

Why could she piece beautiful quilts, but end up with a gaudy patio that embarrassed her husband? Had she gotten too cocky, too sure of her artistic ability? She visualized the patio, the delicate burgundy flowers against the contrasting backdrop of hard, sand-colored flagstones. She still thought her creation was beautiful. Was something wrong with her perception of beauty? Maybe she should limit her focus to decorating this room and piecing quilts.

After she cried herself out, she blew her nose and rose to prepare supper before chores. As her hand touched the old-fashioned, wrought iron latch on her door, a thought flashed through her head. Her mom, her children and Delores had *loved* the patio. Maybe *Luke* had the poor taste.

She entered the kitchen and caught Luke whistling as he took the box of vanilla ice cream out of the freezer. He started, but kept whistling.

He's cheerful, as if our conflict didn't pain him at all. "Where are the children?" she washed her hands. "It's time for their snack, too."

"You aren't going to serve them ice cream, are you?" he dropped a heaping serving-spoonful of ice cream on top of the wedge of apple pie already on his burgundy-rimmed plate. "Ice cream is expensive."

"So why are you eating it?" she got four spoons from the drawer.

"I want to. And don't tell me I can't have ice cream," he dug out another whopping spoonful and smothered the mound with chocolate syrup.

"I wouldn't dream of it. Where are the children?"

He closed the box. "The boys are teaching Tanya how to play ball in the back yard. They couldn't play in the front yard," he added pointedly.

"The tree limbs have been in the way for years," she slid open the window above the sink. "Come in for ice cream and pie," she yelled, and watched the children drop their bat, ball, and gloves and come running for the unusual before-chores snack.

Chapter 12

The next morning, Luke woke to somebody shaking him. "Time to get up." *What in the earth? Oh, Kyle.* He peered through the semi-darkness at his digital alarm clock. Seven-thirty.

"I'm too tired," Luke groaned. He rolled onto his stomach, hugging Yvette's pillow to his chest. "I'm gonna stay in bed till noon."

"But it's Sunday," Kyle argued. "You have to get up for church."

"I didn't get to bed 'til three. Go to church without me." He heard the door close, and opened an eye to verify the tranquil darkness. He slept.

The house was quiet when Luke woke at ten. He faintly recalled Kyle coming in to wake him, and the memory of the day before flooded back. He plumped the pillows under his head and stretched in satisfaction.

Even though he'd studied the progress of the patio every day while Yvette and the boys were milking, when she showed it to him and he heard the pride in her voice, he'd thought he couldn't breathe. Debilitating fear had squeezed his chest. In that moment, he'd felt desolate and alone. It was as if her physical body stood beside him, but she had become a stranger and her spirit was disappearing into the flagstones, bushes and flowers she'd artfully arranged. He *hated* feeling so scared. His reaction had been instinctive. He'd swung blindly to alleviate his pain, and scored. When Yvette hurried away—in tears, he guessed—he'd gone to the living room to watch TV, but hadn't been able to focus on the program because of the satisfaction bubbling up in him.

Unable to sit still, he'd gone to the bedroom to gloat over the quilt he'd defied Yvette and their budget to buy. Never again would he debase himself by kowtowing to Yvette. A wide segment of the community had seen him bid on Yvette's quilt. Word would get around how he valued his wife's creations and gave generously to charity, and no one would have a negative thing to say about him. He'd be highly respected in the community.

What pleased him most, was that she'd believed him and didn't have a clue the patio was inviting, restful, and lovely. At last he'd convinced her to doubt her artistic ability, and that gave him the advantage he needed. He'd haul her creation to the dump and never let her retreat into her artistic world again.

Elated, he'd wanted to celebrate, and had helped himself to ice cream and pie. When she'd seen him, he'd concealed his nervousness, afraid she'd see through him and escape into her own world. Her pink, puffy eyes told him she had, indeed, been crying. He squelched a pang of guilt and focused on his pleasure in being the man of the house. The kids' presence had added to his elation, because he knew his family had no idea he was celebrating under their noses. At bedtime, he'd been too keyed up to sleep, so he watched TV until he went to bed at three o'clock in the morning.

He took his time showering, then went to the kitchen for coffee and cinnamon rolls. He couldn't recall ever feeling so masculine, so capable of achieving anything he chose. *This* was what had eluded him all these years. Now that he had experienced wholeness, he wasn't about to give it up.

The children acted shy toward him when they came home from church, and that pleased him. He ruled this farm, and was accountable to no one. The sooner they accepted that, the better. "Yvette, bring my dinner to the living room," he grabbed a handful of chocolate chip cookies and headed for the couch. He exulted in Yvette's and the children's stares of disbelief, hoping they'd protest so he could display his power again. But they said nothing.

Yvette brought him an enormous glass of water and a serving platter piled high: four pieces of barbecued chicken, a heap of mashed potatoes with gravy, a few peas and carrots, and lettuce salad smothered in French dressing.

When he had stuffed himself, he took his plate to the kitchen so he could see his family's distress. They had finished eating, except for Yvette who had half a wedge of whipped-cream-topped strawberry pie on her plate. The empty pie tin sat in the middle of the table.

Flabbergasted, he stood staring, while Yvette savored two more bites. He roused himself out of his stupor and took his plate to the counter while he formulated what to say. Hoping to proceed to lovemaking that afternoon, he couldn't afford to alienate his wife, yet he had to confront her.

He leaned against the counter and stared at Greg, who pushed his chair back and mumbled, "I think I'll play on the computer," as he ducked out of the kitchen. Tanya scurried from the room, but Kyle cast a questioning glance at his mom and hesitated before he rose and cleared the plates off the table. Finally, with a backward glance, Kyle left the kitchen.

Luke approached the end of the table. "Why didn't you serve me pie?" he put on his hurt-little-boy voice. He knew very well why.

"House rules," Yvette waved a dismissive hand. Her next bite left a smear of whipped-topping at the corner of her mouth. "Those who leave the table get no dessert," she said, her mouth full. "Anyway, you had cookies."

"But you know how much I like pie, especially *strawberry* pie. Did you save any for me?"

"No, unless you want the last bite on my plate."

"Forget it," he grunted. "I'm stuffed. Are you going to cuddle with me? It'll take me a couple of hours to digest that scrumptious dinner and get in the mood for some hanky panky."

"What about the children?"

"They can play outside. It's a balmy spring day."

"Don't act stupid. You know what I mean."

"I know," he refrained from rolling his eyes, "you don't want them to hear the bed creak and guess what we're doing. As if it matters."

"Believe me, it does. They're home today, so it won't work."

"Tell them to go out and wade in the creek. That will take several hours, and the water level should be low enough."

"If they like the idea, I'll cuddle with you after the dishes are done."

Luke went to the living room and planned how he would handle love-making this time. First, he'd snuggle with her until she seemed relaxed. Next he'd kiss her until she clearly wanted more. Then he'd skip all the rest of the foolishness and go directly to intercourse. Just the thought excited him, and he clicked on the TV to take his mind off his desires.

After the children had gone to the creek and Yvette finished the dishes, he and Yvette made love. Everything went according to plan until he tried to skip the fondling. Yvette protested and rolled away from him. When she sat on the edge of the bed and started getting up, he hauled her back into his arms and pretended a driving passion that demanded to be sated at once without caressing her at all. She seemed unsure what to do, then gave as he persisted in feigning feverish desperation. He climaxed, intensifying his sense of supreme masculine power, waited to see the disappointment or distress on her face, then apologized for losing control.

Afterward, bubbling with elation, he went to the living room to watch TV. Soon he'd regain control of their marriage. This week, he'd go to her room and make love on her bed. If that didn't motivate her to move back to his bed, he'd visit her every night until she gave in.

He made popcorn and sat down to watch a comedy and plan his next move while Yvette and the children played table games. He'd wait until she went up to bed, then he'd follow her. Since they'd already made love, he'd get her used to the idea of having him in her room and on her bed.

After the children went to bed, Yvette woke him when she perched on the arm of the brown stuffed rocker in the living room. "I considered what you said about the patio," she said.

This sounds promising. "What can I say? When I'm right, I'm right."

"Not this time. Mom, Delores, Jill, Tanya, Kyle, Greg and I all like the patio and think it's beautiful. But you claim your single dissenting vote is the right one. Something stinks, and you need to re-examine your taste."

Feeling like he'd been caught with his pants down, he groped for a way to handle this snag. Coming up empty, he stalled for time. "You're starting an argument so you can have the last word," he eased into a reclining position on the couch and arranged the toss pillow under his head. He tried to appear in control and unconcerned. "Well, I'm not falling for that trick. As I said, it's a matter of taste, and I can't change my taste."

"Hog poop. Sloppy, smelly, hog poop. I don't believe you, Luke, and I don't believe your apology this afternoon. Your rotten, power-trip game-playing is destroying our marriage."

Luke scrambled to regain his advantage, and fought the urge to bolt up-right. "I don't like being falsely accused of dishonesty and game-playing," he met her eyes and put on an expression of injured dignity.

"Spare me the theatrics," she leaned forward. "And keep your equipment off the patio. If you hate it so much, you can use the backyard."

"You can't stop me from scooping it up."

"You're right, I can't stop you. But if you do, I will tell everyone I know, and the whole community will think you are a monstrous jerk."

"Let's not resort to threats," Luke backpedaled. "Let's invite guests for dinner and get their opinion of your patio. I bet they will agree with me."

"Who would we invite?"

He liked her suspicion; it meant he had the upper hand. "How about Alex and Janet? They've never been to the Mennonite Relief Sale, so they won't automatically say, *It's so beautiful!*" he effected a falsetto imitation.

"And if they like it?"

"Then I'll let it stay."

"You'll let it stay anyway. But sure, let's have the Hamilton's over. Janet and I have a lot in common. They have one daughter, right?"

Just to show Yvette he was boss, Luke made himself lie on the couch an additional fifteen minutes, then took his time getting to the phone. Making sure Yvette could hear his end of the conversation, he invited their guests, choosing a date in the beginning of June. Hanging up the phone, he mumbled an excuse about checking the pigs, then went to the shop to call Alex again and ask him to say the patio was tacky and tasteless.

"What if I don't think it is?" Alex asked.

"You owe me one for covering for you last week. Will you do it?"

"Sure. I hope you're not asking me to make a fool of myself."

That night Luke decided to delay his visit to Yvette's bed until he could be sure of success.

~   ~   ~

While Yvette cooked in the kitchen, Luke reclined in the living room, preferring to leave the TV off while he waited for the Hamiltons to arrive for Sunday dinner. He relived the events of two weeks ago and savored the elation he'd felt then and the excitement he felt now. Showdown day had arrived, and he would be the victor. After today, she'd have to believe he'd been honest about his taste, and by extension about his loss of control in the bedroom, and Yvette would stop avoiding him as she had been these past two weeks.

He hadn't noticed she was avoiding him, until she bought a cooler and packed lunches for him to carry to the fields while he planted corn and beans. Other years he had looked forward to seeing her park her bicycle in the lane and start across the field on foot, his dinner in a bucket. He'd stop the tractor and wait for her, then pretend impatience so she wouldn't guess how important he felt when she brought him dinner. Now that he carried a cooler, there were no delays or visits over dinner. Except for Sundays, he only saw her at breakfast.

Even then, he wasn't sure she was avoiding him until he found her door locked when he went to her room to carry out his plan to make love in her bed after he came in from planting at one o'clock in the morning. Rather than make a fuss, he'd decided to act as if he hadn't a clue she'd put a lock on her door. Demanding that she open her door to him would be foolish, unless he planned to follow through with kicking it in if she refused.

When the Hamiltons arrived and Luke saw Yvette hurry from the kitchen, Luke joined her at the front door to greet their guests.

"Where's your daughter?" Yvette asked after they'd greeted Janet and Alex and ushered them inside. "I thought I saw her when you arrived."

"Jody is looking at your patio," Janet chuckled. "She's nuts about flower gardens and has been begging to make a show piece of our yard. After seeing yours, I'm inclined to let her. Yours isn't tacky or ostentatious at all."

She put the kibosh to my plans. Luke glanced at Alex and shrugged.

"Mom!" Jody slammed through the door. "You should look at their patio. It's gorgeous! It's what I was talking about. Come on," she tugged on her mother's arm, "you've got to see it."

"Jody, say hello to your hosts," Janet turned the girl around.

"Oh, hi," Jody said. "Can we eat on the patio? It's utterly divine. Where are your kids? I thought you said they had kids, Mom."

"Kyle went to check the chicks," Yvette replied, "Greg went to gather the eggs, and Tanya is in the kitchen arranging the vegetable platter. Would you like to meet her while your mom and I dish out the food?"

"That sounds like a great idea," Janet glanced at her husband. "Come Jody, we'll let the men visit while we meet the family."

The men went into the living room and looked out onto the patio.

"Do you still expect me to say the patio is awful?" Alex asked.

"There's no point," Luke's shoulders slumped. "After Janet's and Jody's enthusiastic comments, Yvette would discount your dissenting opinion, no matter how convincing you are. This is so embarrassing I can't even look at my wife. I know she's thinking *I told you so*."

"She created an ideal hideout for you, why disparage it?"

"I don't want her to get a big head," Luke produced the first plausible excuse he could think of. "I want her to stay *my wife*, not get lofty ideas. I had her persuaded to let me scoop it up and take it to the dump."

"I wouldn't go that far. You can enjoy it when she's too busy to notice. I should have told you Jody loves flowers and gardening."

"Can you still say something negative about it? Maybe that it'll be a lot of work to keep up, or something like that?"

"She could take that as a compliment. I can say *you* did a good job, and *you* are a gifted artist. That will keep her from getting a big head."

"I'll never live this one down," Luke groaned.

"You don't have to. When you're about to lose a fight, remind her how often she gets her way—like when you let her keep the patio. Add how she owes you, how expensive it was, and anything else you can think of."

"Great idea," Luke slapped his friend on the back. "You're saving me from eating an enormous piece of humble pie."

After their guests had gone, Yvette went upstairs, taking Tanya with her. The boys went outside, and Luke drifted into the living room, wishing he had a place of his own to think and putter without interruption. He was tired of the TV. Drawn to the windows, he looked out on the patio.

Alex had repeatedly complimented him for the exceptional job he had done and said he could make a fortune at landscaping.

At one point Janet said, "I thought this was Yvette's handiwork."

"She just helped," Alex had fabricated before his hosts could speak.

Luke had expected Yvette to be upset at the turn of events, but she'd appeared fascinated with Alex's references to Luke's creative work. Or maybe she was amused. No, that wasn't it, either. He wasn't good at reading Yvette's expressions. Hopefully, she wasn't enthralled with Alex.

Chapter 13

Luke wiped the dripping sweat off his brow with the back of his hand to avoid leaving a streak of grease. The day was hot and muggy, typical for July. He wished he could be in the air-conditioned house, but he had to prepare the combine to harvest oats and soybeans. At least the machine shed provided a cooler place to work. With his blue cotton shirt soaked with sweat, and his jeans sticking to his thighs and hampering every move, he eased himself down on a low stool and stretched his legs in front of him. A faint gust of a breeze brought a fleeting moment of relief, then the oppressive heat bore down on him again.

His thoughts automatically returned to his wife. He still had not found a way to manage her. His failure mocked him as he greased the combine, as he drove the tractor cutting swathes of hay, as he ate supper or as he watched TV. No matter what he did, his failure intruded into his thoughts, stealing his sense of manly strength and competence

Burning with rage, he carped at everything, but nothing worked. When he cut her down to size so she'd submit to him, she told him to please quit it and left the room if he didn't comply. One time while she cooked dinner, he kept telling her she was a lousy cook. She calmly turned off the burners, set the pans aside, got in the car with Tanya and drove away while he ordered her back in the house. After that he kept his mouth shut while she cooked so he wouldn't go hungry, but the restriction infuriated him, as did her nonchalance about keeping a spotless house. She'd left the dishes undone one night, and when he told her to get up and wash them, she refused. That set a precedent which she repeated often. His fury at his helplessness rose in proportion to her calm demeanor.

Instead of appeasing him, she and the children often picnicked on the patio before meal time, leaving him to eat alone. Instead of sitting with him in church, Yvette and the children sat with friends or with the choir. Yvette visited the women's Sunday School class and refused to return to the class he preferred.

And after he chewed out her and the children on the way to church three Sundays in a row, they refused to ride with him anywhere.

Although he had been stymied so far, he refused to admit defeat. He *would* find a way to assert his leadership, to be a *man* again. Perhaps he'd do what Grandpa had done—take charge of the finances and leave the wife so little money she'd stay at home. Come to think of it, Grandma hadn't had a driver's license. He'd hide the keys so Yvette could only drive if he permitted, and he'd take over the bookkeeping. That would shift responsibility onto his shoulders, but would also make their marriage the way God had intended.

Relieved at having found the solution, he looked out the open door and noted the brown-green grass. Listening to the birds twittering in the trees, he heard a jenny wren. Then he heard the lowing of cattle that had irritated his senses most of the day. At first he had assumed it was a cow bawling for her calf and ignored it, then he had been so deep in thought he had tuned it out. Now he realized they must be out of food or water.

He struggled to his feet and strode out to investigate. From the gate he could see cows milling around, bawling. Some nosed the concrete floor around the hay ring, while others stuck their heads into the ring, stretching to reach the few tufts of hay in the center. Their shoulders pushed the ring a few inches, one cow pushing it forward, another pushing it to the side.

Luke gritted his teeth. "Looks like Greg didn't feed the cows and *I'll* have to feed them." *Is Greg copying his mom? Last week he told me I'm petty, ridiculous, and stupid. It's his mother's fault. That shrew! She's teaching him to thumb his nose at me. She'll pay for this!* He strode to the machine shed, swung up on the mid-sized 830 with its rear-mounted forklift, and buzzed to the big round bales behind the hog stable. Backing the tractor to a bale, he stabbed the fork into it, hoisted it up, then buzzed past the machine shed and parked close to the house to tell Yvette to help.

"Yvette," he called as he clumped into the cool, air-conditioned house. He found her sitting on a chair in the middle of the kitchen cutting up green, yellow-transparent apples and singing along with a gospel tape. He snapped off the tape. "Come out right away and watch the cows while I unload hay. The boys didn't feed them before they left to catch chickens this morning, and you let Tanya go to Jill's house, so you're the only one left to help."

Yvette kept her eyes on the apple in her hand as she cut it into quarters. "I have a batch of boiling apples nearly ready for the strainer, plus two canners of jars close to boiling. I can't leave in the middle like this. Can't you drive through and shut the gate after yourself?" She dropped the quartered apple into the dish pan that was nearly full of cut up apples, took another apple from the dishpan of whole, green apples on her lap, and looked up at him. "Greg does."

"Getting on and off the tractor takes too long. And if cows get out we'd waste time chasing them in. Just turn the burners off and come out."

"I daren't turn the burners off," with a deft twist of her wrists she cut out the butt end of an apple. "The jars might not seal, or the sauce will get too brown. I'll come out as soon as the two canners are done."

"How long will that be?"

"Maybe half an hour, but I can't be sure."

"Just leave it on and come out then," he motioned toward the door, hoping if he acted urgent enough she'd comply without thinking it through.

"I have to see when they start boiling so I can time them. You like your applesauce just right, you know," she grinned at him.

He almost grinned back, then stopped himself. If she thought she could use laughter to charm him into forgetting why he came in, she had misjudged him. "I didn't ask if it fits with your plans. I said come help me."

"Be reasonable, Luke. I don't want to make the mistake I did two years ago. You and Greg wouldn't eat that batch. Kyle, Tanya and I ate some of it, and the rest had to be thrown out, since we aren't the big applesauce eaters."

"I *am* reasonable and you're making it up to get out of helping me."

"Don't you remember all the dark brown applesauce you said was too gross to eat?" She tilted her head to one side. "You told me to throw it out, that such *crap* was not to be served at your table. Remember?"

"No," he lied. He did remember, but if he admitted it to her, he'd have no chance of getting her to cooperate. If he could shift the blame for *something* onto her, he'd win this argument. "You're just trying to *rule the roost.*"

"You can think that if you like. It's your privilege."

"I know what's wrong with you. You got *women's lib* ideas from your *friend* Delores. She should be disciplined for teaching heresy. Some friend. You shouldn't consider someone who sows discord in our marriage a friend. All she does is stir up trouble. I said come help me and the *Bible* says you are to *submit* to me as if I am Jesus, Himself. Now come on!"

"Jesus would be considerate. Lester opens the g—"

"Don't compare me to the neighbors! Of course he's not going to drag someone all the way down the road to watch the gate for him! Look at me when I'm talking to you! Put that stupid apple down!"

She looked up and stopped cutting, but didn't put it down.

"The Bible doesn't say to submit to your husband if you agree with him," he pointed at her, "it says to submit to your husband in *everything*—as to the *Lord.* If you don't submit to the Lord, that's *rebellion*," he lowered his voice on the last word, moved closer, and put a hand on her shoulder as he locked eyes with her. "And rebellion is as the sin of *witchcraft*," he spoke slowly so she'd have time to apply it to herself. "If you don't submit, you're the same as practicing witchcraft which *God* condemned with the *death penalty* in the Old Testament. That's a very *serious* offense." He softened his voice, "I wouldn't want you to go to Hell for refusing to submit."

"Your theology is wrong, Luke," she set her dishpan on a nearby chair dislodging his hand from her shoulder, and went to the stove. "We're to submit to each other." He hated her mild, unperturbed tone; its contrast to his made him sound like a loser. "I have to do what *I* believe." She lifted the lid on the kettle and stirred with a large stainless steel spoon. "I almost forgot the apples. Fortunately, they aren't scorched. If you want help," she put down the spoon and turned to look at him, "*ask*. Don't order me around."

"How *dare* you tell me what to do? You'll pay for your defiance. You're a self-centered *feminist*!" He spat the last word.

"Now you know." She turned the cassette player on again.

"Forget it then. I don't want help from a pig-headed *egomaniac* anyway." He charged out the door and slammed it after him, muttering, "That obstinate woman. She thinks she has to rule the roost. I don't know why I married her. Now what am I to do? Wait until she comes to help?" He strode to his Case tractor, which he had left idling in the driveway. One hand on the steering wheel, he mounted the tractor, and sat undecided. To unload without Yvette's help felt too humiliating, but to wait for her help was mortifying, too. If Yvette had obeyed him he wouldn't be in this predicament. *Blast that woman!* He'd demonstrate his authority. When she came to watch the gate, he'd keep her waiting while he did something trivial like trim weeds. She'd be annoyed and he'd win after all. Perfect! He smiled as he shut off the tractor and jumped down. The instant his shoes hit the gravel he heard the cattle lowing.

"Drat," he muttered. "There goes my plan; I have no choice." He heaved himself up on the tractor and turned the key. It wouldn't be so bad if he didn't have to go through two gates. He drove to the first gate, vaulted to the ground, opened the gate, mounted the tractor again, drove through, stopped and dismounted to close that gate and open the next one. The calves stared at him, but didn't venture close. When he opened the second gate, several cows headed for the opening. He waved his arms vigorously, and they backed off enough for him to drive through. As he jumped down to close the gate a dozen cows crowded around the bale of hay, tearing bites out of it and butting each other.

"Get out of here!" he waved his arms vigorously and kicked the belly of the nearest cow with his steel-toed shoe. She grabbed one more bite and leapt away, strewing wisps of hay as she went. One by one the other cows started and jumped back when the cow blocking him from view moved away and they saw him so close. Concerned they'd tear the bale apart, scatter the hay and trample it, he swung aboard the tractor and maneuvered it through the herd as fast as he dared, taking care to not injure a cow while he backed the tractor to the red bale ring. Hurriedly, he jumped off the tractor and shoed the cows away before he tipped the ring on its side, hopped on the tractor, backed and lowered the bale into its spot and eased forward so the bale would stay in place as he withdrew the fork, then jumped off the tractor again to drop the hay ring over the bale.

He drove away from the herd crowding around the bale of hay, opened, drove through, and shut the two gates without any cattle attempting to get out, parked the tractor in front of the machine shed, and sat thinking.

Yvette had won—again. He'd known he could do it without help, but he hated the hassle. Even worse, he hated the humiliation. He was a respected man in the community, but any time he and his wife disagreed she was always right. Something was wrong with that. He had to get her to do what he said and be sexually available to him again. He had to get his self-respect back before people realized he couldn't manage his own household.

As he returned to prepping the combine, he heard a vehicle drive in. He went to the machine shed door to see, but didn't recognize the dark green sport utility vehicle that had stopped under the maple tree in front of the house.

A tall man got out and tugged up his dress pants.

"Alex, old buddy!" Luke called out and strode to meet his friend. "What brings you away from your air-conditioned office in the middle of a hot afternoon?" He wiped his hands on his jeans before pumping Alex's hand.

"I needed to get away from the office and into fresh country air." He sniffed. "No hay cut? I'm disappointed."

"Did you come to help put hay in the barn in that white shirt?"

"Actually, I came to sit under the shade trees on your patio and shoot the breeze. My staff told me I'm stressed out and ordered me to take a break."

"You're welcome to sit on the patio *I* made anytime. Oh, come see the canoe I bought," Luke led his friend into the back of the machine shed where his sky blue canoe lay on it's side.

"When did you buy this beaut?" Alex ran a hand over the blue paint.

"I bought her two weeks ago and took her out, but it's a hassle to fasten her onto the pickup without buying a topper, first. Want to take her along when you and I go camping this fall? If you want to do it again this year, that is?"

"Of course, I do. We've been going on a yearly camping trip since third grade, why stop now? Especially when you bought a canoe." Alex started toward the door. "It's hot in here. Let's go to the patio; it'll be cooler there."

The men crossed the driveway, bantering as they went. Rounding the hedge that was covered with hot pink blossoms, they stepped onto the patio. "It's prettier than I remembered," Alex inhaled, "and the flowers smell sweet."

113

"How're Janet and the kid doing?" Luke changed the subject.

"Oh *Janet* is doing fine, just *fine*."

Luke caught the sarcastic edge in Alex's tone. "Come and sit down," he motioned toward the three wooden lawn chairs Yvette had purchased, stained, and finished. Alex chose the chaise lounge with arms, and Luke settled for the armless lounge chair. "Ahh, that's better," Luke positioned the recliner way back, hoping to impress Alex with how relaxed a man could be on his own patio. But Alex didn't seem to notice.

"You look tense," Luke hid his disappointment. "What's up?"

"I'm fed up with her," Alex smacked the armrest. "She's been argumentative for months, and now she claims *I'm* abusive."

"You're kidding! I thought she's the ideal wife. Your house is always clean and in order. You never said anything about this before."

"I thought she'd get over it, but she's getting worse." Alex paused to swallow. "She's on anti-depressants and seeing a shrink. She says the house isn't important, and I can warm up my own food when I get home late. She went out and got a job as a *secretary*. I told her she can pay half the bills if she gets a job. She insists she'll only pay 'a *percentage* of the bills,'" he mimicked in a sarcastic falsetto. "She won't listen to a thing I say."

"You have to *show* women who's boss. Keep the car keys, so she can't go to work or anywhere without your permission."

"That may work in the country or in small town Kalona, but not in Iowa City. My wife would take the bus or a taxi, or even ride her bicycle."

"Then don't let her have so much money."

"How am I supposed to do that? She inherited seventy-five thousand dollars and won't use it for our living expenses."

"Oh, that's right; her mom died and left Janet everything. Sorry, I forgot. She has you over a barrel. No wonder you're mad. I'm furious, too," Luke slammed his shoe on the end of his lounge chair for emphasis. "Women have become self-centered. They call it *feminism*. Life has become a living hell for us; it's no wonder men are violent. I'd like to pound sense into women's heads.

"I'd like to pound sense into *Janet's* head. We had a row this morning. She registered to go back to school without asking me first and I nearly slugged her. I think she's getting ready to leave me."

"You have to keep her home. There has to be a way for both of us to succeed. Hey! What if *I* keep the keys and take over the bookkeeping? That would stop the wife's frivolous spending."

"That's not wise; you're lousy with bookkeeping and money."

"But I'm *desperate* to get Yvette on track. I have to do something."

"It's worth a try. Bring your paperwork to me once a month. I'll help you do it free of charge for four months and we'll nip her spending."

"Thanks, pal," Luke imagined Yvette's distress. "I appreciate it."

"Where's Yvette? She usually brings us something to drink."

"She's in a hostile mood today. Wouldn't help me unload hay. I had to unload it myself; the cattle were bawling. She's so confrontational."

"Hey, why don't I drive us to Kalona for ice cream cones? We won't have to deal with a hostile woman and we'll be in air-conditioning."

"With our luck the waitress will be hostile, but I like the way you think, man." They rose and they ambled toward the SUV. "Are these new wheels?" Luke opened the passenger door.

"Yup. I got her last week," Alex stepped up into the driver's seat. "A new car every two years will cut repair bills. Come on. Get in."

"I should change clothes. You won't want a stinky farmer polluting your new-smelling car. Come on in and say hi to the wife while I change."

"That's what I like about you, Luke. You're considerate of others." He hesitated. "Will Yvette mind me coming in the house?"

"Nah," Luke strode around the front of the vehicle, jubilant he'd found a way to win and feel like a man again, "she won't bite your head off, if that's what you mean. It's me she's mad at."

In the house, Alex followed Luke to the kitchen and began to flirt with Yvette as Luke soaped up. "It's good to see you, Yvette," Alex shook her hand. "Did I forget how attractive you are, or do you get prettier as time goes by?"

Luke saw her blush and grin at him, her eyes all lighted up. "It's either your eyesight or your memory that's failing, Alex," she teased. "Or maybe your tongue gets so glib at soothing irate customers, that you dish it out to everyone you meet." Luke gritted his teeth and rinsed the soap off.

"But I meant it," Alex turned to Luke. "Isn't she good-looking?"

"Of course she is," Luke pulled the large brown towel on its roller and dried his face and hands. "That's why I married her." He turned to Yvette. "Do you have any pie, cake, cookies or ice cream to eat?"

"Sorry, we're out. You ate the last piece of pie last night and I *have* to do these apples before they spoil. There's plenty of applesauce," she motioned to the table full of quart jars and the dishpan full of applesauce behind her.

"We'll go to Kalona and grab a bite to eat then. It's too hot in here anyway. I'll go change clothes." He brushed past the refrigerator and purposely knocked a picture magnet with a snapshot of Ben, Yvette's dad, onto the floor.

"Will you pick up the boys when they're done catching chickens?"

"I don't know," he flung over his shoulder and glimpsed her replacing the magnet. "If I'm not back, you can get them. We're going in Alex's car."

He hurried to the bedroom and changed as fast as he could so Yvette would have a minimal amount of time to flirt.

When he came out, Yvette was handing a small dish to Alex.

"Do you want some, too, Luke?" she asked as he came into the kitchen.

"No. Let's go, Alex."

"Give me a minute to taste Yvette's applesauce." Alex took a bite. "You're right, it *is* worth it. She's a keeper," he winked at Yvette. I'm ready to go whenever you are, Luke." The men started for the door.

"I'll chore in an hour," Yvette said. "What about the boys?"

Luke stopped at the door and turned toward her. "Well, if they call and I'm not back yet, you'll have to stop milking and go get them."

"So you expect me to milk by myself, too?" her brows went up.

"You expected me to unload hay by myself, so why not?"

"Luke." There was no demand in her quiet voice, yet Luke couldn't look away. She said nothing, just met his eyes and held them.

He shifted. "I'll try to be back in an hour, hour and a half,"

"Thank-you. I appreciate that."

There was an awkward silence as the men went out the door and got in Alex's green sport utility vehicle. They started down the gravel road.

"Whew," Alex breathed. "What a powerful little woman. Janet is like a shrieking siren compared to her. What's the deal with the chores?"

Luke grinned. "It takes an hour or two for three people to chore. For one alone, it could take her 'til midnight. If the boys are done catching chickens soon enough, she'll have help—if they aren't too tired."

"Don't you help milk?" Alex turned onto a black top road.

"No, Yvette and the boys do the milking. I have other responsibilities."

"Like what?"

"I take care of the hogs and manage the farm. Sometimes I'm in the field or repairing tractors. Besides, I'm awful with cows and I hate milking. I'd prefer to get rid of them, but for now they're our main income."

"As your tax man I'm aware the dairy provides most of your living, but I didn't realize—Yvette told me they start choring at five and are usually done around seven. And that's when you and I eat out or play put-put golf. It looks like Yvette is the primary breadwinner and carries most of the workload. How long have you gotten by with sluffing the chores off on Yvette and the kids?"

"Whose side are you on, anyway? Yvette wanted to milk and the boys need to learn responsibility."

"Come on, Luke, I'm not stupid. We've been buds since first grade, remember? I'm on your side, and I'm telling it to you straight. I'd feel like a heel if I made Janet work as hard as you work Yvette. If you want a loving woman in bed at night, you can't treat her like a workhorse all day."

"Get off my case, Alex," Luke glared at him. "I don't tell you how to run your family so keep your nose out of mine."

"Okay," Alex held up a hand in surrender, "but don't say I didn't warn you. Say, why don't we pick the boys up after we eat?"

"That's out of the question. We said the boys could stay until the job is done. I promised Yvette I'd help chore so the boys could earn money."

"So what was all that about back there?"

"I was being a jerk," Luke admitted. "I keep wanting to get at Yvette, show her who's boss. I think I see a chance, so I grab it. The trouble is, she's so reasonable all the time, I end up looking like an irrational fool."

"You got that right," Alex slowed to a crawl to follow a buggy up the hill. "You did look silly. I don't understand, though, why you want to 'get at' her. She does everything a man could ask. The house is clean, she chores, she cooks and preserves food, she raises your children; what more do you want?"

"I don't know if I get it myself. I think part of it is I feel like a boy around her. She seems so in charge, she doesn't need me."

Alex passed the horse and buggy as they crested the hill. "It's pretty clear she needs you to help chore tonight."

"That wasn't the type of need I was talking about," Luke ground his teeth. Yvette undermines my authority. It's imperative for me to be in charge, but she doesn't let me. It's as if I've been hired to manage a company, but since someone else is taking my place, I'm left with taking their directions and doing the menial work those under me are supposed to do."

Luke waited while Alex pondered his words. "That makes sense," Alex nodded. "That's likely why I get upset at Janet. She doesn't take direction and makes decisions that are mine to make. If she takes my place, she won't need me anymore. You hit the nail on the head, Luke. I was hoping you'd tell me how to get my wife under control."

"You need to keep her from going to work. I heard sabotage works. Make her late often enough and she'll eventually get fired. Do stuff like mess with the engine so the car won't start, set all the clocks ten minutes slow, or pick a fight with her as she's leaving for work. The possibilities are endless."

"Sabotage." Alex grinned as the idea took hold. "I think you're on to something. Thanks, Buddy. Will controlling the finances be enough for you?"

"I'll take her to see our pastor, too. Val will straighten her out."

At the restaurant the men took their time eating and talking and got up to leave when the evening crowd started to appear. "Would you like to drive my new wheels?" Alex offered.

Luke drove up and down the streets of the small town before heading home, pointing out shops, the Kalona Historical Village, the Kalona Park, and the swimming pool. When he turned onto their road, Luke groaned, "Oh, no. I'm late. I should have been home an hour ago at the latest."

"Did you do it on purpose, or did you forget?"

"I forgot. Honest." Luke pressed a hand to his gut and hunched over the wheel. "I feel sick. I didn't mean to make her chore by herself."

"At the house you acted like you were going to. She'll assume you *meant* to be late. And frankly, I'd agree with her."

"You're supposed to help me feel better, not worse." Luke turned into the drive by the barn and drove around the circle to park near the house.

"I wouldn't be much of a friend if I let you hide your head in the sand or twist the truth to blame her. It would serve you right if Yvette—"

"Don't," Luke put his hand up in the stop gesture. "Would you mollify her while I change clothes?"

"Are you kidding?" Alex put his hands up and leaned away from Luke. "I won't touch this one. I have my own troubles."

Leaving the engine running, Luke got out and ran to the house, while Alex moved to the driver's seat and drove away.

After rushing to change clothes, Luke strode to the barn hoping Yvette wouldn't be upset with him. What would he tell her? If Alex didn't believe he'd forgotten, he doubted Yvette would. Now she'd think she had every reason to refuse him and she'd be impossible to control.

Who was he kidding? Life was out of control already. Maybe he'd come home on time if she'd take care of his sexual needs. Come to think of it, this whole thing was her fault. If she'd satisfy him in bed, submit like a wife should, and stop taking charge all the time and making him look like an idiot, he would have been home on time. She'd gotten what she deserved.

He heard the milker motor, and as he got closer, the rhythmic shhht, shhht of the pulsator. In the stable, he found the stalls empty and milkers hooked on their brackets. He spied Yvette in the feedway, pouring ground feed into one of the eight wooden grain boxes.

"What's the big idea of starting at *six-thirty*?" he glared at her. "You think you can sluff off because I'm not here?" *How long have you gotten by with sluffing the chores off on Yvette and the kids?* Alex's words replayed in his head and he rushed to silence them. "You've gone too far this time."

Chapter 14

Yvette started. She'd seen Alex's SUV turn in the drive, but hadn't heard Luke come into the barn. "You're late," she tried to sound upbeat instead of resentful. "Did you have a good time?" She watched as he fumbled to open the narrow wooden door separating the cow stable from the feedway and turned sideways to step through it. She glanced at the empty buckets in her hands and started to walk past him toward the feed bin at the far end of the alley.

Planting his feet apart in a commanding stance, elbows akimbo, he blocked her in the narrow aisle. "Why are you so late getting started?"

She blinked. "I'm not—"

"Don't lie to me!" he roared. "How *dare* you thumb your nose at me and start milking at *six-thirty*?"

"Luke, please move out of my way, so I can get feed," she tried to edge around him, but he shifted to block her.

He towered over her, his glaring eyes black with rage, his dark bushy brows drawn together. "You're supposed to start at *five*, not at six-thirty."

"I—" Yvette felt helpless to stop the storm she saw in his face.

"How many times do I have to tell you to get out here on time? This is why the cows are giving less milk!" he jabbed a finger at her. "You know it's extremely important to milk them at the same time morning and evening to keep up production! But of course," his purplish, bug-eyed face nearly touched hers, "you have to be bull-headed and do your own thing whenever you please! I am sick and tired of your continual rebellion! You're doing it just to spite me! I've put up with your defiance long enough! I'm taking you to see the pastor. I will not have this farm run downhill because of you!"

Stunned by his outrageous lies, Yvette stared at him.

He straightened, and she felt a mixture of relief that he was no longer yelling in her face and dread of what he'd do next as she tilted her head back to keep his glowering face in view. She wanted to step back, but didn't dare lest she stir him to greater rage. When the distance between them widened and she realized he had moved back, she drew a shaky breath.

"Don't you have anything to say for yourself?"

She opened her mouth to say something, but everything she wanted to say was so jumbled in her head, she couldn't think where to start.

"You're just doing this to ruin my chance to buy land, aren't you?" he stepped forward again and pointed at her.

The accusation was so ridiculous, she stared at him.

"Aren't you! Answer me!"

"When you calm down..." she finally found words, but they came out wobbly so she cleared her throat and tried again. "When you calm down," she repeated, pleased to note her firm, even tone, "and can speak rationally, I'll—"

"*Rationally!*" he raged. "I *have* been talking *rationally!* I will *not* let you order *me* around!" With a savage lunge, he seized her bare upper arms in a bruising grip. He shook her, making her head bob repeatedly forward and back like a rag doll. "You are *not* my boss," he gritted through clenched teeth. "*I* am in charge. *Do you understand?*" He administered another hefty shake, then released her, turned his back, and stomped to the open door of the feed bin.

Saying nothing, she inched back from him a step at a time, her eyes glued to him, one hand holding the buckets and the other rubbing her upper arm.

He glanced in the feed bin, then stalked toward her and stopped short. "Why are you staring at me as if I have horns growing out of my head? If you think that was scary, I'll give you something to be scared about. From here on, I expect you to act like a *Christian* wife and *do* what you're *told.* If you don't, you have *me* to deal with, *do you understand?*"

She nodded and took a step back, her sandaled heel grazing the Dutch door. She couldn't think. Her brain wouldn't function. She had to do something, but what? She became aware of the shhht shhht shhht of the pulsator above her head. *The milker motor is running. Cows. I need to milk the cows.*

"Don't just stand there! Get busy!"

A shrill noise blared beside her ear. She jumped. The phone just inside the door rang again. Dazed, she turned and lifted the receiver with a shaking hand. "Hello," she cleared her throat to steady her voice. "Hello," she repeated, then paused to listen. "Yeah, I'm okay; my voice is rusty." Pause. "Okay, Kyle. Someone will get you. Bye." She hung up the phone, hoping Luke wouldn't notice her hands and knees were shaking. She grasped the door frame to steady herself. "Th-the boys are done catching chickens. Shall I—"

"I'll get them," Luke interrupted, his voice normal, as if he hadn't just raged at her and shaken her. "I'll help start milking first." He headed toward the back shed, turning sideways to go through the narrow door between the feedway and the cow stable. "Are the cows chased out of the shed?"

"Don't—" she began, and stopped when he turned to glare at her.

"You *dare* order me about?" He stepped toward her, his eyes menacing.

"It's just," she shrugged, "those are milked."

He stopped and stared at her as if he didn't comprehend. "What?"

"Those in the shed are milked," she blinked to stop the prickling from turning into tears, and backed out the door, not sure what he would do next.

"Oh, they are *not*," he spat and strode to the shed.

She imagined him trying to plow through the shed and free-stall, which were full of milked black-and-white Holstein cows. She'd seen the whole thing numerous times. The cows closest to him would try to dash away from him, crowding and shoving into the others that hadn't seen him yet. They'd roll their eyes in desperation when they realized they were blocked between Luke and their stable mates, then try to bolt to the empty space behind Luke when he slapped their rumps, but their hooves would scrabble on the slick cement. Luke would whack the closest cow one more time before her feet would find purchase and she, along with the rest of the herd, would make a mad scrabbling dash past him, leaving as wide a berth as space allowed. Then he'd circle to the gate that separated the two lots, find it closed and the lot for waiting-to-be-milked cows nearly empty, and know she'd told the truth.

Her vivid mental picture stopped there. She couldn't picture what he'd do next, but sensed he'd come back and do something awful. She had to hurry and make a lot of progress before he came back and got really mad. She ran to the feed bin and scooped up feed with her buckets, rushed down the feedway aisle, spilled feed into every box, dropped the buckets beneath the phone, dashed to the cow stable and opened the door to let in the next-to-last batch of cows.

By the time Luke returned to the cow stable and slammed the door behind him, Yvette had the cows chained up and was leaning down and sideways to wash a cow's udder. She glanced around for an escape route, but there was none. She'd have to tough it out. She stood up tall.

"I bet you think I owe you an apology," he hooked the door behind him and turned toward her. "I'll take the blame for my share of the argument if you'll take the blame for yours. I shouldn't have jumped to conclusions, but you shouldn't have defied me, either. If you hadn't gotten into the habit of ignoring my orders, I wouldn't have any reason to think you had done it again. Furthermore, you could have told me you were nearly done milking."

She stared at him and tried to make sense of what she'd heard.

"Well? I'm waiting for your apology."

She found her voice. "I-I don't have anything to apologize for."

"Well, if you're going to act so hard-headed, I withdraw my apology. This misunderstanding was *your* fault. If you'd stop being so *domineering* like your *mother*, stuff like this wouldn't happen. When you start acting like a proper *Christian* wife instead of like some *feminist* imbecile, I can deal with you as a partner." He stomped through the cow stable and slammed out the door.

Yvette stared after him, tears stinging her eyes. *What a nightmare!*

Stunned, she moved to the head of the stall and lifted the milker down. Her hands shook as she put it on the cow, one teat-cup at a time. She moved on automatic to wash the udders of three more cows and put the remaining milkers on, then washed the next four. When that was done she couldn't think what to do next. She paused in front of the wooden shelf and frowned, but her brain refused to cooperate. She kept seeing Luke's angry snapping eyes, his dark bushy brows drawn together in condemnation, the tightness of his lips as hateful words spewed out. She felt an intense impulse to run away.

A slurping milker brought her back to the job at hand and she tended it, then remembered she needed to get feed and hurried to the feedway to fill the two buckets. She massaged her neck. *If Luke hadn't acted like an idiot, I wouldn't have forgotten. He always assumes the worst. He looked so mad I couldn't think how to tell him I had just emptied the stable so I could refill the five gallon feed buckets without being concerned a milker would wind up on the floor sucking up manure because I wasn't in the cow stable to tend it. I won't tell him I found out I can milk as fast as three people if I keep feed in the stable and hurry so I can keep the milkers going. He'd make me do it all the time.*

When she finished milking, she let out the last cow and carried an arm-load of milkers through the empty calf lot to the milk-house. In the distance she saw a car coming, kicking up a cloud of dust. *No one but Luke would drive like that.* Her heart picked up speed and started to pound. She ducked into the milk-house. *Oh, my!* she staggered to the washtub. *I'm afraid of my own husband!*

She set the milkers on their rests in the washtub, and took a few deep breaths to calm herself. Nausea churned in her stomach and her hands shook. What should she do if he came in the milk-house? She'd keep the bulk-tank between them. But what about being with him in the house? She didn't want to be in a room with him, let alone at the same table. Worse, what if he forced her into his bed? He said he expected her to do what she was told. She didn't know what he would do if she didn't obey him, but she knew she could *not* sleep with him. The degradation would be too distasteful, his demands too repulsive.

What about the children? Should she keep them from Luke? How could she protect Tanya? The girl would be terrified and have nightmares again if he raged in front of her. She had already returned to avoiding him. Kyle would hate Luke's behavior, but would be most able to keep his cool. And

Greg? Who knew how Greg would react. One day he challenged his dad's be-havior, and the next he copied it and blamed her.

Speaking of blame, was this her fault as Luke had said? Had she made him jump to conclusions by her non-submission? That didn't make sense; she always milked on time. Why did he make an issue of when she started milking? The cows had been *her* department before she met Luke. When had he become her critic? She thought back. Before they enlarged the herd she had milked at six o'clock. Luke had suggested she double the herd so they could increase his spending money, pay off his credit card debt, make double payments on the farm, and put big chunks in savings. She'd assented rather than continue their downhill slide and she'd had to start choring earlier to get to church and social functions on time. "Oh, I get it," she murmured. "The extra work is for *his* benefit. Since *he* wouldn't work so hard for me, he's afraid he'll lose spending money if he doesn't *force* me to chore early."

She shook her head. Solving that mystery didn't change anything. Luke blamed her and she had to decide what to do. Did she have any options other than to endure his rage? Yielding to his horrid demands, even once, was not an option. It would make everything worse in the long run. And she'd have to find a way to protect the children from their dad. Surely there was some way to motivate Luke to become a caring and reasonable man. There had to be; she just hadn't thought of it yet. She'd ask Delores; maybe she'd have suggestions.

Realizing she'd been staring, preoccupied, at the half-full glass ball that collected milk from the pipeline, she snickered at herself, flipped the pump switch and watched as the milk swooshed out the bottom of the ball. Hooking up the milkers for the rinse cycle, her thoughts returned to her plight. Maybe if she prolonged cleaning up until Luke was in bed, she'd avoid a confrontation. But the boys would be in bed, too, and she did want to talk to them. Kyle would have plenty to say about his first time catching chickens. She'd hurry with the cleaning up so she could talk to the boys. Thankfully, Tanya was staying at Jill's tonight. At least *she* was spared for tonight if Luke continued his tirade.

Halfway through the clean up she remembered she still had to feed the calves. Apparently no one—not even Luke—was going to help. She felt half-relieved; she and the boys dreaded Luke's appearances in the cow stable. His harsh impatience made both cows and humans nervous and accident prone. But she felt angry, too. Luke hadn't kept his word and she had to chore alone. She couldn't expect the boys to help after a grueling day of carrying chickens.

Finished with the clean-up, she took the hose and squirted warm water into four pails. She dumped a scoop of milk-replacer powder into each pail and reached to retrieve the wire whisk from its nail when she heard the milk house door open. Startled, she jerked. She turned and took a step toward the safety of the bulk-tank, her heart racing, her gut clenching.

"Oh, Kyle," tears pooled in her eyes. Angling her face away to hide her tears, she squatted and stirred the powder and water mixture with the whisk.

"Mom!" She heard the alarm in his voice. "What's going on?"

"I'm getting ready to feed the calves," she evaded with the truth.

"I can see that. What happened?" He squatted beside her and put an arm around her shoulders. "You're crying. I saw your face when I came in. You jumped and looked scared. You thought I was Dad, didn't you?"

"Yes," she rested her cheek against his chest and let the tears fall.

He rubbed her upper arm to comfort her. She flinched. He frowned and with both hands on her arms held her away from him. She shuffled back to hide her bruises if there were any, and Kyle lost his squatting balance and plopped backward onto the wet cement floor, bringing her down with him.

Yvette snickered through her tears, and pushed herself off his chest.

"It's not funny," Kyle protested, then began to laugh as he sat up. "Are you okay?" he got to his feet and helped Yvette up.

"I just have a wet seat," she couldn't stop giggling.

"What's so funny?" Kyle wiped the seat of his jeans.

"You were so grown up one minute," she dug a tissue from her pocket, "and then you were sprawled on the wet cement floor." She blew her nose.

"You were, too."

"Don't mind me," she stopped giggling with an effort and tried to divert him from questioning her. At thirteen, he was too young to shoulder adult problems. "I'm over-emotional and I like laughing better than crying."

"This is serious, Mom. Your arm hurts. What did he do?"

"He grabbed my arms," she put her hands on her arms where Luke's had been, "like this." She didn't tell him Luke had shaken her and her neck ached. Kyle would lose all respect for his father if he found out.

"Let me see." Kyle inspected her arm. "It's red. Why was he mad?"

She told him what happened.

"This doesn't make sense," Kyle paced to the door. "Dad came home late and got mad at you. He yelled at us to hurry up and get in the car, and then didn't say a word and drove home like a maniac. *He's got problems*. Well, let's feed the calves. I should have come out right away, but I was starving."

While they fed the calves, Kyle told her about his first day of catching chickens. They had removed old laying hens and would soon put in pullets. Since Kyle was tall, he'd had the job of pulling hens from the upper cages. He had scratches on his hands and arms from the cages and from being batted by flapping broken wing-feathers and clawing hens' feet and spurs. He talked of the young people he had worked with, and the snack of yeast doughnuts the employer had provided. Finished with the chores, they went in and washed up. Yvette relaxed as Kyle told more details of his day while she ate supper.

"It's quiet without Tanya here," Kyle said as Yvette stacked the plates. "Greg's reading instead of making her laugh. Where's Dad?"

"I don't know. Maybe in the hog stable. I'm tired. I'm going to bed."

"What if Dad gets mad about the dishes?"

"I can only do so much, Kyle. Dad will have to accept that and take responsibility for his own behavior. I've tried to be perfect so he won't get upset, but he gets upset anyway. I'm tired and need to take care of myself."

~   ~   ~

As Yvette turned to go into her studio bedroom, Kyle went down the hall to his room. Something about the evening bothered him, but he couldn't figure out what it was. His dad often got mad. But it was unusual for his mom to act so afraid. She was calm and level-headed, and he rarely saw her cry.

He tried to picture the event in his mind. Dad grabbing Mom's arms and yelling at her. Kyle couldn't remember his dad ever touching his mom in anger. Would that difference be enough to scare her? Maybe it was what Dad had said, or that Mom was innocent. But wasn't she usually on time? Dad was nitpicking about her going to the barn five or ten minutes after five o'clock."

Resolving to get to the bottom of the puzzle later, he stripped to his briefs, pulled on a T-shirt, and got into bed, leaving the lamp beside his bed on so he could read. He had just opened his book, when Greg came in.

"Did Mom tell you anything?" Greg whispered.

Kyle related what he knew. "I'm worried," he confided, keeping his voice low. "Something is *not* right. I can feel it."

"Me, too." Greg sat on the side of the bed next to Kyle's feet. "Do you think Mom told you everything?"

"I don't know. It feels like she left something out. Why don't—"

"Sshh!" Greg grabbed Kyle's arm. They heard a heavy, unhurried tread coming up the stairs. "That's *him*. What does *he* want up here?"

Kyle sat up in bed, making the springs creak.

"Sshh!" Greg hissed. "Snap off the light!"

Kyle reached over and pulled the chain. Grotesque shadows, caused by the light in the hall, splayed around the room. With bated breath they listened as their dad's footsteps stopped at their mom's room. He didn't knock. The door bumped the wall as he pushed it open.

"You owe me an apology," they heard him rumble. Wide-eyed, the brothers stared at each other. *She owed* him *an apology*? "You could have told me you were nearly done milking."

Greg stood up and franticly beckoned Kyle, who crept out of bed one slow move at a time, freezing each time the springs creaked.

"Hurry," Greg mouthed and yanked Kyle off the creaking bed.

They crept to the door and peered around the corner.

"Aren't you going to answer me?" Had Dad raised his voice? Kyle wondered. He could see the back of his dad's blue-and-white striped shirt as he stood just inside her room, the top half of his head hidden by the lintel, and his shoulders appearing to brush both sides of the narrow, old-fashioned doorway.

Kyle heard his mom's indistinct murmur, then Luke's loud and angry, "Why'd you bring that red lamp I gave you up here? It was never intended for this room. And where'd you get that red quilt with *my* pattern? You have no business buying such an expensive quilt for this *storage* room! Horrified, Kyle watched as his dad clenched his fists and stalked further into his mom's room.

Frightened, Kyle glanced at Greg and saw he, too, was alarmed. He dashed toward their mom's room, hearing Greg right behind him. Kyle rushed through the door and past Luke's bulk, his only thought to protect his mom, who was sitting fully dressed on a chair at her desk on the far side of the room. She stood as they dashed to her side, her face white, her eyes huge. She laid a hand on each son's shoulder as the boys pivoted to confront their father, whether to restrain or reassure them or herself, Kyle wasn't sure.

"—deceitful, conniving woman!" Kyle had missed part of his father's stinging accusation.

"I bought this lamp before you gave me the other one," Kyle thought he detected a quiver in his mom's voice, "and *I made* the quilt for this bed."

"Didn't you hear me say I wanted exclusive rights to that pattern?"

"The pattern is available at the store," Yvette's soft, respectful voice contrasted with Luke's harsh demanding one,

"Take that quilt off the bed and unplug that lamp," Luke glared at her.

"Luke," Yvette chided, "don't be ridiculous. Calm yourself."

"I *am* calm. I won't let *my wife* spend her time and *my money* deceitfully. Your job is to take care of the *family*, not to collect expensive stuff for yourself. This is selfish extravagance, like that patio, and I won't stand for it. Now *give me that quilt*," he stepped toward them, his narrowed eyes promising punishment if she did not comply.

Afraid Luke would close in on them, Kyle surged forward until he was a mere foot from his dad. "You better leave, Dad," he'd never heard his voice sound so much like Luke's when he reprimanded other people's kids.

Luke turned his narrow-eyed glare on him, and Kyle's heart started to hammer even faster. "Who do you think you are?" Luke shoved Kyle backward into Greg, who caught him, pushed him forward, and stepped up beside him.

"Why don't you pick on someone your own size, *Luke*," Greg, nearly a foot shorter than his father, taunted, restoring Kyle's flagging courage. "You aren't acting like a dad or a husband. Get out of here before we call the police." He moved forward a small step, crowding Luke, and pulling Kyle forward with him. When Luke turned his menacing glare onto Greg, fury welled up in Kyle and galvanized him forward until his chest pushed against his father's and he glared into Luke's eyes, which were slightly above his own.

Luke hooted, but retreated. "You'd *dare* call the cops on your dad?"

"You aren't my *dad* if you act like this," Greg snapped. "I'll choose someone else to be *my* dad—someone who's decent."

"Is that so," Luke's jaw muscles clenched.

Hearing a noise behind him, Kyle glanced over his shoulder and saw his mom step forward as if she planned to protect her sons.

"Sit down, Mom," Kyle put a hand on her arm. "We'll handle this."

"Better yet," Greg drawled, "call the police."

Keeping his eyes on Luke, Kyle heard her move to the phone.

"Oh, all right," Luke stepped back. "What babies. But I'm not finished dealing with this. I won't stand for being betrayed in *my own* house."

The boys followed Luke to the door and watched as he stomped down the stairs and slammed the stair door behind him. When they turned back into the room, Yvette was standing where she had been and staring toward the door.

"Mom?" Kyle wondered why she just stood there.

She didn't answer, but kept staring. Not sure what to do, he looked at Greg who raised his brows and shrugged.

"Mom." Greg shook her arm. "It's over. He's gone now."

She glanced at the boys. "Tell me it was a bad dream. Please. He—he didn't really—" she shook her head as if denying what she'd seen and heard. "I must have had a nightmare."

Kyle stepped to his mom's side and took her arm. "Why don't you sit down," he led her to the bed. He sat beside her, putting an arm around her shoulders. He saw Greg look at them, his brow furrowed. Then with a small nod, Greg joined them on the bed, putting an arm around his mom's waist.

"I'm sorry, boys," she said.

"It's not your fault," Greg jostled her. "Dad's a jerk."

"Keep your voice down, Greg; we don't want him to hear. It must be my fault. "Surely Luke wouldn't act like that otherwise. If I had just—just," she paused, "I don't know. If I had just—done something different."

"What should you have done?" Greg argued. "Given him your lamp or your quilt? He was absurd. Next he'll want the quilts off *our* beds, too."

"In the barn, I meant. I try to remember how it started, and I can't." She stared at the floor. "All I can remember is one minute he was making a big fuss and shaking his finger in my face, and the next he was shaking me."

"*Shaking* you!" Rage boiled up in Kyle and he vacillated between wanting to shake her for shielding Luke, and wanting to dash down the stairs and pound sense into his dad. Channeling his rage, he tightened his arm around Yvette's shoulders. "You said he *grabbed your arms*."

"I didn't mean to tell you that," she pushed at his hand, "it slipped out."

Kyle released her. "He *grabbed* your arms and *shook* you. "*That's* why your arms hurt."

"Okay, okay. Yes, that's what he did. Now you know it all."

"You better tell us the whole story," Greg tucked a strand of hair behind her ear. "Maybe telling what happened will help us figure out what to do. I doubt it's your fault."

She started with Alex's visit and Luke's promise to be home to help milk, then explained her solution for feeding the cows when milking alone and how she'd been nearly finished when Luke came out more than an hour late. "I was in the feedway, and Dad came through that small door from the cow stable. He was in a rage, and I was so surprised I couldn't think. If I had just said *something*, he wouldn't have gotten so mad. Then when he asked me to explain myself, the only thing I could think of was to tell him to calm down and be rational, and that really upset him. He said he *was* rational and shook me. I wondered if my neck was going to break, or if I'd get whiplash. My neck still hurts," she put a hand to the back of her neck to ease the ache.

"I don't see what you could have done differently," Kyle knelt behind her on the bed and massaged her neck and shoulders. "He came into the barn in a rage. That means he didn't *let* you explain anything. If you *had* been able to think what to say, he wouldn't have heard it or would have gotten madder."

"Kyle's right," Greg took his arm from around her waist and shifted away, leaving Kyle free to massage unhampered. "It was Dad's fault."

"They say it takes two to tango, so it must have been my fault, too. If I had kept my head together and explained, he would have stopped being so mad."

Greg took her hand. "Dad worked *himself* into a lather."

"Don't you see? I *want* it to be my fault. If it's my fault, I can *do* something to stop his rages." She began to cry. "I *hate* feeling so helpless."

"Oh, Mom," from behind, Kyle hugged her, wishing there was something he could do to reassure her and relieve her distress, "I'm sorry he shook you and threatened you, and I'm sorry you feel so helpless."

"He was so mad," Yvette sobbed. "He looked like he was going to hit me if I didn't give him the lamp and the quilt."

"I thought so, too," Greg got up and retrieved the box of tissues off Yvette's desk. "And Kyle did, too. That's why we ran to stop him."

"You're safe now, Mom," Kyle said, "don't cry."

Yvette shook her head. "He s-said h-he isn't finished deal-dealing with this," she stammered between sniffles. "He h-hates me."

Kyle looked at his brother, alarmed. Greg nodded and sat down next to his mom again. "We won't leave you alone with him, Mom. We won't let him hurt you. It'll be okay."

"I hope so," she began to shake and her teeth started to chatter.

"She's cold," Kyle said. "Pull up that quilt."

Greg loosened the quilt from the foot of the bed, and they wrapped it around her. Worried, but not knowing what to do or say, Kyle sat beside her and hugged her to provide more warmth. He questioned Greg with his eyes, but Greg just shrugged. They sat with her until the shaking subsided.

"I'm sorry, boys," Yvette said when her teeth stopped chattering. "You shouldn't have to see me like this. It's late. Let's go to bed and this won't look so bad in the morning."

"I'm going to call the police," Greg stood up.

"No, Greg," Yvette started to shake again, though not as violently. "He stopped now. If they came, they wouldn't do anything, and it would make Dad mad again. Don't stir up trouble."

"*Luke* is the one stirring up trouble," Greg picked up the phone. "He may have quit for now, but it's not over. You heard his threat. As soon as we aren't both with you, Mom, he'll start in on you again. You saw how he shoved Kyle out of the way. The only reason he backed down is because *both* Kyle and I were there crowding him. All he has to do is send Kyle *or* me off to do something, then he'll come after you again."

"God will take care of me," Kyle heard the quaver in her voice.

"I don't know how if Kyle and I aren't here."

"But what good will it do to call the police? They won't be here either. Don't you see; I unintentionally stirred things up; let's not stir them up more."

"Mom's right," Kyle repositioned his arms to provide more warmth and still her shivering. "Calling the police will just make Dad mad and he'll blame it on Mom. The police won't be here to protect her if he decides to-to make more trouble. It's up to you and me, Greg. We'll stay with her all the time."

"How?" Greg punched the talk button. "Tomorrow one of us has to grind feed, and who knows what *he'll* have the other do."

"If Dad tells us to go somewhere, we don't go unless we stay together and Mom goes with us. From now on, we're a threesome, and when Tanya comes home, we'll be a foursome. So when we grind feed tomorrow, we have to pretend we need Mom's help."

"*He* will get mad," Greg punched in two numbers.

"Greg," Kyle threw himself across the bed to grab the phone, but Greg held it out of reach, "don't make it worse. *Please* put the phone down until we've talked this out."

"What's to talk out?" Greg hit the off button. "We need help."

"Can we *try* sticking together?" Kyle sat up. "If he gets mad we'll tell him he can grind the feed himself, let us grind together, or we'll call the police."

"We can't hang around Mom forever; school starts in five or six weeks. *I* think we need help. How about calling Val or Grandma or Delores, Mom?"

"I couldn't," Yvette shook her head. "I just couldn't. It's too embarrassing. And Dad wouldn't listen to any of them anyway."

"What's there to be embarrassed about?" Greg put the phone back on its cradle. "*He's* the one who should be embarrassed."

"That may be true, but *I* picked him, and he's part of *our* family. Besides, Grandma and Delores would feel as upset and helpless as we do, and I can't deal with that right now. And Val would suspect I did something to upset Dad, or that I exaggerated or made it up. I read about stuff like this. No matter what I'd say, the pastor would blame me because he can't imagine Luke acting like that unless I provoked him. No, boys, we have to deal with this ourselves."

Chapter 15

The next morning Yvette kept an eye on Luke's closed bedroom door, hoping he'd stay asleep while the boys dressed as fast and quietly as they could. In the barn she glanced up in alarm at every sound. After she put the milker on Dinah, the cow flung out her hoof and smacked Yvette's thigh.

"Ouch!" she yelped, cradling the spot and leaning hard against the cow's flank to prevent more kicking.

"Are you okay?" Kyle rushed over to investigate.

"No," she grasped her knee and rocked back and forth trying to contain the pain. "She didn't kick at the milker, she aimed at *me*."

"What got into her?" he watched Yvette gingerly lift the smeared hem of her cutoff jeans to look at the injury. "She never kicks like that."

"Is everything all right over there?" Greg called from the feedway.

"Dinah left a big red imprint on Mom's thigh. There'll be a bruise."

"I'm not surprised. Didn't you notice the cows are nervous?"

"How can you tell from over there?" Kyle bent to peer at Greg through the space between the hayrack and the feed-trough.

"They jump back when I walk by, and they all must have lifted their tails and splattered up the cow-stable by now. It's gonna be a mess to clean up."

"Maybe there's a snake in the shed," Yvette gritted her teeth as she tested her weight on the injured leg. "Greg, do you have time to check?"

While Greg checked the shed, Yvette forced herself to bend and wash the udders of the next two cows in spite of the pain in her thigh. Hearing the back stable door open, she tensed and made herself squat down to peer under the cows. She saw bare ankles and Greg's flip flops on bare feet. She relaxed.

"Nothing," he stopped behind Yvette's pair of cows. "Nothing except you two, that is. You're jumpy, and I bet that's making the cows nervous. They're acting like they do when Luke comes out here."

"I wish you'd call him Dad," Yvette frowned.

"I won't claim a man like that to be my dad," Greg grabbed the two-foot hose off the wooden shelf and smacked the wall with it. "He's a wife beater at heart," he whacked the wall again.

"Hush and stop hitting the wall, or you'll get the cows more riled up. We all need to calm down. Let's pray together. How about going in the empty stall in the back where Dad can't see us if he comes in?" She led the way to the back, took their hands, and began to pray. "Dear God, we are scared. We don't know what to expect from Luke and fear the worst. Please help us be calm and at peace. And please stop Luke's nasty behavior. Show us how to handle this situation. Thank-you for hearing us, God, and for caring about us. Amen."

Wordlessly, they returned to their work, Greg to the feedway, and Yvette and Kyle to their sections of the cow stable. After they transferred the milkers to the next cows and let a new batch of cows in the stable, Yvette exclaimed, "I know! Let's sing a praise song. How about *Shout for Joy*, the Ninety-eighth Psalm? That'll remind us God is much bigger than Dad."

"Good idea," Kyle fastened the chain around a cow's neck and started to sing, "Shout for joy to the Lord, all the earth, burst into jubilant song w—"

"You all sound cheerful," Luke sneered from the doorway.

Yvette stopped singing the instant Luke spoke, and heard the boys do the same. Crouching next to the cow she had just washed, she waited.

"What happened?" Luke moved into the stable, the rubbers covering his sneakers soundless on the lime-covered concrete floor. "You think you got your way last night, and now you're on a winning streak? As I said, I won't put up with your defiance. God put me in charge of this family, and I *will* carry out my responsibilities. To help you learn to obey me, I made an appointment for all of us to talk to Val this afternoon. Greg, are you listening?"

"I'm here," Greg mumbled.

Yvette stood up and saw Greg had opened the narrow door from the feedway and stood at the shoulder of the end cow, a mutinous expression on his face. She glanced at the other end of the stable for Kyle, but couldn't locate him so she looked at Luke. With his muscular arms folded across his brawny chest, he leaned his behind against the wooden shelf and stretched out his long legs.

"Kyle, stand up and face me like a man," Luke ordered.

Yvette glanced over and saw dread on Kyle's face as he stood up.

"You boys stepped out of line last night, and I won't tolerate that. Threatening me is a foolish thing to do. Kyle," his piercing gaze fastened on his younger son, "I am confiscating all your art supplies for a month. Greg," he pinned Greg with his stare, "you are not allowed to talk to your friends for a month. You will stay with me during and after church. Is that clear?"

"Yes, sir," Greg muttered, looking at the floor. Probably to hide the resentment—maybe even hatred—in his eyes, Yvette guessed.

"Kyle," Luke barked, "look at me when I'm talking to you."

Kyle looked up, revealing tears welling up in his eyes.

"Don't you *dare* resort to that crying stuff," Luke spat. "Take your punishment like a *man,* not like a *sissy.* Art is for *sissies* anyway."

"Yvette," he clipped, and she jumped at the sound of her name. "You are not to sneak paper or pens to Kyle. Is that understood?"

"Yes, *Mussolini,*" she snapped, angered that he'd humiliate either of the boys after goading them to tears and venom. She gritted her teeth and decided she'd keep the letter of Luke's law but get Kyle canvass and paint, and send Greg to Clara's house to talk on the phone with his friends.

"I'm glad you recognize who's boss," he glared at her. "I'm changing things around here, starting today. Since you refuse to get in the harness with me, you force me to play hardball. I will take charge of the money from now on. I'll give you an allowance of *half* of what we budgeted to pay for groceries. You have to get permission to buy anything else. When you fulfill your wifely duties, I'll allow you more money. As the head of this house, I am responsible to God for what happens here, and I am stepping up to bat and shouldering my responsibility. You have to *ask me* before you go anywhere. I will keep all keys with me." He glanced from face to face, but no one responded. "We meet with the pastor at two. I want you all in the car at one-thirty. Is that understood?"

Yvette squared her shoulders. Never again would she allow him to chew them out in such a small space where escape was impossible. "We will go in a separate vehicle, or not at all. Take your pick."

"You dare defy me?" Luke narrowed his eyes and stepped toward her, but stopped at the dung-spattered gutter and placed his hand on the rump of the cow she had just washed. She let out the breath she was holding.

A movement caught her eye. Greg had surged toward them and was trying to squeeze between the end cow's belly and the wooden partition. Oh no! The cow was Iva, their biggest cow, who was notorious for refusing to get over and for pinning a person against the partition. Yvette wanted to tell Greg to go the other way, but didn't dare with only the gutter separating her from Luke. She cast about for a way to defuse Luke's anger and distract him from seeing Greg's movements. "You can call it defying if that makes you happy," she said. *Great choice of words, Yvette—if you want to goad him into a frenzy.*

Luke seemed distracted and looked in Kyle's direction, so she chanced a glance at Greg. She saw the back of his head, and then he disappeared from sight. She tensed. *Is he going to crawl under the cow?* Then she saw Iva's hind-quarters move away from the partition, and recalled Greg's technique for

133

making the cow get over. He'd wedge his rear under Iva's white belly, flex his thighs and push against the partition, and half lift, half shove her aside. In an instant Greg ducked under Luke's arm, crossed the gutter, and stood guard in front of her, and Kyle moved in and crowded Luke's elbow.

The milker slurped air, and Yvette bent to tend it while Luke chewed out the boys. Taking it off the cow, she straightened with the milker in hand. "You can yell and threaten, Luke, but we will *not* get in a vehicle with you."

Luke ignored her assertion. "Boys, stop interfering. *NOW!*"

They jumped, but did not move away.

"This argument is between your mom and me. Stay out of it! If you don't leave *now*, I'm going to thrash you both!"

"Go ahead and try," Greg urged. "You'll see what we're made of."

I have to stop him before he attacks the boys. "Luke, you scheduled a meeting with Val. Maybe Val will have ideas for a peaceable solution."

"Stay out of this, *Jezebel.* You caused enough trouble."

"Do you really want to destroy our family?" Yvette persisted. "It's one thing to play your king-of-the-mountain games, but another entirely for you to threaten us, and then punish us for protecting ourselves."

Luke blinked and relaxed his stance as her statement penetrated.

"Why don't you do your chores," she pressed when he didn't renew his attack, "and let us get these milkers off the cows? They're past done."

"*You* are the one destroying our family," Luke took a step back.

"No she's not," Greg said, "*you* are."

Luke's shoulders sagged. He turned away and rested his forearms on the Dutch door. "I'm trying to save our marriage," he sighed. "If you'd do as I say, instead of defying me, things would go much better."

"That's boloney," Greg stepped across the gutter. "If you'd shut up and do what *Mom* says, things would go better. *Mom* tries to make it work for *all* of us. You try to force everyone to jump through your idiotic hoops."

"When you marry and have children, Greg, you'll see I'm right."

I can't believe I feel sorry for him. He looks defeated.

"What a *jerk*!" Greg fumed after Luke had gone. "I'm *never* going to be like him. He's—"

"He's still your dad," Yvette wondered if reprimanding Greg when his dad *had* been a jerk was the right thing to do. "Watch your language."

"Well!" Kyle blew out a breath. "Let's finish and get out of here."

~   ~   ~

That afternoon they went in two vehicles to meet with the pastor. Delores had brought Tanya back from her sleepover with Jill, and Tanya opted to accompany them rather than stay at her grandmother's. Yvette sank down on the white leather couch in a Sunday School class room and Tanya plopped next to her, pressed herself against Yvette's bruised thigh and clung to her arm. Greg squeezed in on Yvette's other side, and Kyle sat beside Tanya, which brought a disdainful glance from Luke. As Luke settled into a stuffed chair, Yvette tried to decipher his expression. She thought she saw a mix of contempt and hurt or jealousy, but she couldn't be sure. Val chose a padded chair across from Luke.

Hot and sticky, her bruise aching with Tanya's every move, Yvette tuned out Luke's account of what had happened. Instead, she focused on Val's expression to discern whether he was buying Luke's tale. But Val's face stayed compassionate, yet reserved, and she couldn't tell what he thought.

Greg expressed his disgust with Luke. "I used to think *he* was right, and Mom was wrong. But when he was gone for two weeks and we managed that ice storm without him, I realized *he* is the problem."

Kyle seconded what Greg said, and Tanya refused to talk.

"The boys are right," Yvette began when it was her turn. "We all felt more relaxed and like a team when Luke was gone, even though we had to compensate for the power outage and handle Luke's responsibilities, too. Luke has always been difficult to live with, but recently he's been unendurable."

"*You're* the one who is difficult and unendurable," Luke countered.

"None of us want to be near him. He's criticizes, belittles, yells at us and orders us around. I've—"

"If you'd just *listen*," Luke interjected.

"For years I kept the house clean for him," Yvette went on, "and cooked and baked so we always had dessert to eat, but he still wasn't satisfied. When I realized I'd worn myself to a frazzle to satisfy him, I—"

"Oh, you did *not*," Luke scoffed. "Stop exaggerating."

"Luke," Val stepped in, "Yvette listened to you without interruption, please be as considerate. Let's hear her out."

"Well, she just goes on and on and says such lies."

Val looked at his watch. "You've been here forty minutes, and she just started talking. The boys didn't take much time, so that means you took most of half an hour. I'm sure Yvette could say you were going on and on. Now please, be respectful and listen. Yvette," he turned to her, "go ahead."

"Thank-you. Where was I? Oh yes, when I realized I'd worn myself out trying to please him and he still demanded more, I decided to stop baking pie so much and to be more relaxed about keeping the house spotless. At first I stopped cooking and left the house when he started griping and he stopped being so critical for awhile. But now he gets mad if I go to bed without doing the dishes—even if its past midnight. Yesterday—" she glanced down at Tanya and stopped. "I think the children should be spared from hearing this."

Greg jumped up and strode from the room, but Tanya clung to her mom. Tears prickled at the back of Yvette's eyes at the girl's fear and pain.

"Go with Kyle," Yvette encouraged. "You can play tic-tac-toe."

Kyle held out his hand to her and waited. Tanya put her hand in his, but hung back, turning to look at her mom as Kyle tugged her to the door.

When the children had gone and the door closed, Yvette continued. "Tanya didn't see Luke's recent behavior, and I don't want to increase her fear. She gets clingy when she senses Luke is upset. All of us walk on egg shells around him and the boys are so courageous when they step in to protect me. Luke acts like he's so angry he's going to physically attack us. We're—"

"As I said, she's a willful woman. She even refuses to *sleep* with me or make love. *She's* destroying our marriage."

"Yvette?" Val prompted, his expression grave. "That's a serious charge. What do you have to say for yourself?

She sighed and looked at her clasped hands. What were the chances Val hadn't decided against her already? One in ninety-nine? But she had to try. She squared her shoulders. "I moved upstairs three months ago. Luke has used me sexually all these years, and I don't want to be degraded anymore."

"I wasn't *using* you," Luke uncrossed his legs and stretched them out until his sneaker nudged Yvette's sandal and she shifted away from him. "You were enjoying it, too, so *you* must have been using *me*."

"He decided what we did in the bedroom. It was degrading. He orders me around all day, and then expects to use me at night. That's not marriage; it's prostitution. I won't be party to such a mockery, such a—" she searched for the word she wanted, "—a *perversion* of marriage."

"I get the picture. Yvette, may I talk to Luke alone a few minutes?"

Wondering what Val wanted to say to Luke, Yvette joined her children in the outer room. She frowned as she pondered the meeting and watched Tanya and Kyle play tic-tac-toe. Val had asked Luke to listen, but that didn't mean he sided with her. He acted like her refusal to sleep with Luke was worse than Luke's behaviors. What if he and Luke were planning a punishment for her?

"What's happening?" Greg whispered.

She jumped. She hadn't heard him approach. "Val wanted to talk with Dad alone—I have no idea what about." She wasn't going to pass her fears to her children. "Hopefully, this means things will be better."

"What if it doesn't help?"

"I don't know." She turned away from Kyle and Tanya's game and crossed the room to the window, turning her thin gold wedding band around and around on her finger. Greg followed her. She studied the tombstones in the cemetery beyond the churchyard. "All we can do now is pray."

Chapter 16

The following Sunday, Yvette dressed with care, taking time to apply makeup to cover the shadows under her eyes. She studied herself in the mirror wondering if anyone could tell she was wearing makeup. At church she tried her best to act normal, to look bright-eyed and hide her distress. She joked with other choir members before church, but when they got up to sing, she lip-synced through the second song as she fought to keep from crying.

After she filed out of the sanctuary with the choir, Delores pulled her aside and led her into an empty office. "What's going on?" she hissed after she closed the door. "You look awful and you didn't sing the second song!"

"What do you mean?" Yvette smoothed her hair from the crown of her head to the curled-under ends at her shoulders. "Is my hair a mess?"

"Don't play dumb with me. Luke's getting worse, isn't he?"

Yvette nodded, lowering her lids to hide the moisture that welled up, unbidden. Lately she teared up over every little thing. It was embarrassing.

"Are you going to let him get by with it by not talking about it? That's what he wants. Your silence gives him more power."

"We went to Val for counseling on Tuesday," with a fingertip Yvette smoothed away the tears under her eyes, thankful she had waterproof mascara.

"I told Steve about the doctrinal heresy in one-way submission, and he set up Bible study sessions with Val. They've been meeting weekly to study the book, *Beyond Sex Roles.* They'll discuss it with the elders when they're done."

"Would Val listen to a lay person?"

"Steve's an elder, remember? He and Val respect each other and work together a lot. Has counseling with Val brought improvement?"

"I don't know; we only had one session. Luke hasn't apologized, but neither did he enforce his threats." Yvette told her about the two incidents in the barn and the one in her room upstairs, that she became conscious of constantly being afraid of her husband, how the boys had stood up to him to protect her, and that Tanya clung to her and avoided Luke even though she hadn't witnessed those incidents but had heard Luke and the boys express their views to Val.

"I'd be afraid, too. And he's the man who vowed to love and *cherish* you." Delores studied her friend's face. "But that's not everything, is it? Let me guess. You have physical symptoms: can't sleep at night, indigestion, palpitations, chest pains, and headaches?"

"And I cry over everything. How did you know?"

"You don't normally use makeup, your face is strained and you seem on edge. My sister, Joyce, looked and acted like that, too. She developed stress symptoms and the doctor told her they aren't likely to stop unless the stressor is dealt with or she goes on medication. What do you plan to do?"

"I'm hoping Val will help Luke see reason. They scheduled two more sessions, one with Luke, then one with both Luke and me. I'm too tired to think straight. What shall I do?"

"Try calling DVIP—the Domestic Violence Intervention Program. That's the women's shelter. I got 'Advocate' training from them, remember? But you'd get better help from someone with more experience."

"But I don't want to get Luke in trouble, and I don't want to leave the farm. What would I do for an income? It's *my* inheritance, not Luke's."

"I wasn't suggesting you leave the farm. There may be a way to make Luke leave. He did shake you. Do you have bruises?"

Yvette pulled up her sleeve, displaying the finger-marks on her triceps.

"And you're afraid of him, too. You could charge him with assault and get a no-contact order. If it's okay with you, I'll come over tomorrow and take pictures of those bruises just in case you need the documentation."

"I don't want to get him in trouble. Our marriage won't stand a chance if I make him madder. I just want him to stop being nasty."

"He's not likely to stop unless someone makes him. I suggest you call the DVIP and then decide what to do. Think about it, okay?"

"I'll think about it. Bring your camera over tomorrow. I'll call you when Luke goes to the field. You can park at Mom's to be on the safe side. Bring Jill, so things'll look innocent if Luke pays a surprise visit to the house."

~   ~   ~

The next morning, in the continuous effort to avert a tirade from Luke, Yvette and the boys rushed through chores and breakfast preparation. Yvette kept her senses on full alert, lest Luke suddenly appear and pounce on them for a mistake they'd made. When breakfast was ready, Yvette leaned on the door jam and peered into the living room to gauge Luke's mood. He seemed absorbed in a sports magazine. She hesitated, then murmured, "Breakfast is ready."

She sat as close to Tanya at the foot of the table and as far away from Luke as she could and saw Greg, too, crowded close to Kyle as he had all week, rather than sit across from his dad. When Luke sat down, he acted as if all was normal and the rest of his family wasn't huddled together at the other end of the table. Yvette saw the resentment on Greg's face and the distaste on Kyle's as Luke exclaimed about the beautiful day and asked Greg to pass the jam. She glanced at Tanya and saw the girl's big round eyes riveted on her dad's face.

Yvette whispered in Tanya's ear, "Don't look at him."

Tanya turned to her mom, and Yvette saw fear ebb from her eyes.

A foot nudged Yvette's knee under the table. When she looked up, Kyle pointed at his buttered toast and nodded toward Luke's end of the table. She passed the strawberry jam and watched Kyle spread it on his toast. Greg elbowed Kyle and pointed at his own toast, and Kyle passed the jam. After Greg finished with it, Yvette passed it to Tanya along with the pitcher of milk.

When Luke poured cereal into a bowl, Yvette abandoned her half-eaten fried egg and jumped up to get coffee for him and fix his lunch. *Maybe this time he'll stay in the field until the children and I are in bed. But even if he does come in, at least I don't have to traipse across the field with his dinner and stand there waiting for him to empty his plate while he chews me out.*

After she finished preparing his lunch and water jug, she washed the dishes, wishing he'd hurry and go out. But he took his time, nursing his second cup of coffee while he told the boys to make sure both south grain bins were empty and to move the telescoping spout to pour into those bins. "The spout's at the north end, so you'll have to push it together to get it past the middle. If one of you holds it up where it sags, it'll be less likely to jam."

When silence fell over the group at the table, Yvette looked over her shoulder and saw Luke pour more coffee in his cup, appearing satisfied with himself. Meanwhile, Greg looked mutinous as he stirred his cereal, Kyle watched his finger go round and round the inner circle of his cup handle, and Tanya leaned close to Kyle.

"Greg," Luke set the hot coffee pot on the table and Yvette jerked to move it to the hot pad, but stopped herself before Luke could notice and chew her out, "bring two wagons to the field and haul oats to the bin. Kyle, you can stick thistles in the wooded pasture. Make sure you get the tap roots out."

Yvette glanced at Luke. Was it coincidence he assigned the hated chore to Kyle? Why not to both boys? Kyle wouldn't have stood up to his dad alone. But if Luke silenced Kyle, Greg was no match for his dad. Yvette clenched her jaw as anger swept through her. *Two can play divide and conquer. When Delores leaves,* I'll *help Kyle, and get Greg to help between loads, too.*

When Luke finished his third cup of coffee and strode out, she waited until he had driven the combine into the narrowed section of lane which led to the back fields before she called to tell Delores the coast was clear. As soon as Delores arrived with Jill in tow, Yvette urged the boys to follow Luke's orders; she'd be safe as long as Luke stayed in the field and she had company.

After the boys went out, the women sent the girls to play on the patio, and Yvette tried not to fidget while Delores took pictures of her bruises. As Delores put the camera away, Yvette started pacing. "I should start a project so Luke will assume I've been working, but I can't think what to do."

Delores sat in the armchair by the phone. "You have enough to handle with all the emotional work on your plate. Take the morning off. But I wouldn't mind some work to keep my hands busy while we talk on the phone. Do you have any green beans stashed in the refrigerator? Buttons to sew on?"

"Green beans. What a great idea," Yvette rushed to the refrigerator, glad for something concrete and non-scary on which to focus.

When she had gathered the beans and supplies for Delores, she picked up the cordless and called the shelter while Delores stemmed green beans and listened on the wall phone. Yvette paced from kitchen to dining room to living room and back as she told her story to Fay, the woman who answered the phone.

"Shaking you is physical abuse," Fay said. "If you call the police, you'd deal with the Johnson County Sheriff's Department, since you live in the country. They aren't likely to intervene unless there's physical evidence. If they do intervene, your husband would go to jail, and the court would probably order him to go through a program for men who batter."

"He left bruises," Yvette paced to the dining room door and listened for a tractor, but heard nothing. "This is the first time he went that far."

"So he's escalating his power and control and getting more dangerous. Besides physical abuse, he's using intimidation and threatening to use economic abuse and isolation to keep you and the children under his control."

"Economic abuse," Yvette repeated. "What's that?"

"That's when a man limits his spouse's spending or use of resources; in your case, the car and money. Some men put their partner on an allowance or make her ask for money, and others say the partner can freely use the credit cards and checkbook, but severely criticize her choice of purchases or punish her so she is afraid to buy anything without his approval."

"*I* handle the finances according to the budget we agreed on," Yvette frowned, remembering all the times Luke had asked her for money. "The budget was my idea to limit his spending, so we'd have enough for necessities, our bills and his credit card debts. Does that mean *I'm* controlling?"

"Luke used excessive spending to limit your access to money and you negotiated a more equitable deal," Delores snipped the stem and tail off a green bean, and picked up the next one. "He manipulated the finances by making large purchases, so *your* funds are limited. He bought a canoe and that quilt you pieced, eats out often, and makes you set aside lots of money to buy more land, but you and the kids spend almost nothing. You daren't even buy a pie."

"That was our deal. Luke said he'd stick to the budget if I put money in savings every month to buy land and machinery and allot him a big slice of spending money. I had to double the dairy herd to keep my end of the bargain. Luke complains when he runs out of spending money and tries to get me to give him the little I shave off the budget for the children and myself."

"So he's abusing you economically by doing the lion's share of the spending and abusing you emotionally *and* economically by carping that he doesn't have your spending money, too," Fay said.

"Are you sure?" Yvette frowned and stopped to look out the living room window in time to see Tanya hand a plate to Jill through the arch on the rock wall. "Luke says I control *him*. He says I'm a killjoy because I limit how much he can eat out, treat his buddies, and have fun."

"Abusive men often reverse or twist the truth," Fay explained. "If he can convince you you're at fault, he can gain control of you without expending much effort. But if he keeps the keys from you, it will be difficult for you and the children to get to safety—especially since you live in the country."

"That didn't occur to me," thinking she'd heard a tractor, Yvette moved to the dining room, looked out the window, and listened hard.

"Has he limited your access to friends or family otherwise?"

"What? Oh, in a way," not hearing a tractor after all, she turned from the window and paced to the kitchen. "He doesn't want me to talk to my mom more than once a month and he accompanies me when I visit her. I manage to sneak a visit sometimes, but if Luke finds out he gets upset."

"What about your other friends? It's common for victims of abuse to have very few friends. It's a strategy the abusive man uses to make it easier to convince his partner his lies are the truth. The fewer people his partner talks to, the less likely anyone will contradict his statements."

"He doesn't complain when I spend time with Delores."

"When I phone your house," Delores reached forward and sliced a handful of stemmed green beans into a large stainless steel bowl, "Luke answers and tries to discourage me from talking to you. He says you're busy."

Yvette touched the soil of her three African violets on the dining room window sill to see if they needed water. "I always thought *you* were in a hurry, so I tried to keep it short. You mean all this time it's been *Luke*, not you?"

"Yeah. He's using isolation to control you. Right, Fay?"

"Right. It's a subtle way to isolate you from others, Yvette."

"Is that what he's doing when he tells me Delores is a feminist?"

"Yes," Fay and Delores said.

Yvette sat at the dining room table. "Before I met Luke, I used to have lots of friends. After we married, he said horrid things about them. They started being too busy to talk to me, and eventually I stopped calling them. Luke drove them away, didn't he? This makes me sick. How can I stop him?"

"Unless someone holds him accountable, he's likely to become more abusive," Fay said. "Men who abuse believe they have the *right* to control their partners. We call it entitlement. They believe they have rights women don't have, and are entitled to have their way, to be served by their women, and to dictate their partner's behavior."

"That sounds like Luke. He thinks the Bible teaches a wife to willingly do what he says no matter what he does or how he treats her."

"Some men use the Bible, God, or the church to justify their behavior, and others claim special rights because they make the money or because they are the man of the house."

"So *that's* why Luke's friend, Alex, does the same to his wife, even though he doesn't go to church. Luke says it's a universal principle and if women would just submit, they'd have happy marriages."

"I doubt that," Fay said dryly. "Men who choose to control their spouses, are more likely to increase their demands if their partners are yielding. At first the men may appear satisfied, but in time they raise the bar and demand more. And sometimes they totally change the rules."

Yvette sighed. "I feel stupid for having married him."

"It's not your fault. Before you married, he showed you his loving side. He didn't say 'When we get married, I'm going to scream in your face and shake you like a rag doll if you don't milk the cows as I say.'"

"You're right, he didn't. So what shall I do now?"

"I won't advise you. My advice may be wrong for your situation and bring disastrous consequences. You know your husband better than anyone and can trust your gut instincts. *You* are the one who knows your husband's body language and expressions. You recognize his signal that he is about to get angry or violent. That's why you're so scared now. For some men it's the lift of an eyebrow or 'the look,' the tightening of a jaw muscle, the way they drive the car when they come home, the way they close a door, or even how they walk."

"You're right; I can tell when he's upset part of the time. Other times it comes out of the blue when I think everything is okay. But I still don't know what to do. Can you give suggestions?" *Why did they tell me Luke is abusive if they won't tell me what to do about it?* "If I know what I'm doing wrong, I could change my approach and build a good marriage."

"You aren't doing anything wrong. *He* needs to stop abusing you. The action most likely to save your marriage is to hold him accountable."

"What about counseling?" Yvette blurted out and began pleating the lace edge of the blue-flowered tablecloth.

"Couples counseling is dangerous for an abused woman," Fay said. If you don't say much, the counselor will pressure you into giving up the precious little ground you have left, and your marriage will become more painful than it is now. But if you voice your distress, your husband is likely to get upset or violent after the session is done. I recommend individual counseling."

"We went to our pastor, and he asked to see my husband alone. Luke doesn't dare do much while the boys are here. What else can I do?"

"Keep clothes, money, spare keys, and important papers packed so you and the children can get to safety in a hurry. When a partner is threatening or violent, women are often too upset to think clearly. Have a plan of where you will go and how you will get there, and an alternate plan as well. You can talk about your situation with a neighbor and plan a signal to alert her to call 911."

"What kind of signal?" Yvette picked a dot of lint off the tablecloth.

"Some have used a lamp in the window, left a light on, or taped a poster to the window so the neighbor will know help is needed."

"But what about what he did to her?" Delores put her knife among the bean clippings in the cake pan on her lap. "He shouldn't be allowed to get by with that. I took pictures of her bruises. Is there anything else we can do?"

"As long as your friend doesn't want to get her husband in trouble, the best you can do is lend a listening ear and be as available as you can."

"What if Yvette calls the police and he goes to jail?"

"Everything would be out of her hands. He'd be in jail until he appears before a judge. If the court finds him guilty, he would have to spend a few days in jail if he didn't already, pay a fine and court costs, attend a class for men who batter their wives, and pay the fees for taking the class."

"That would make him really mad," as Yvette turned sideways in her chair her gaze fell on the Renoir print Luke had chosen for the one bare dining room wall. Every time she looked at the two young girls at the piano, she hurt all over again. She usually avoided looking at it. Not only had Luke refused to listen to her protest that the green and white print didn't belong in a blue dining room, he had also refused to allow her to buy a used piano so she and Kyle, who'd been ten at the time, could take piano lessons.

Actually, she had paid seventy dollars for the piano, but when she asked Luke to haul it home, he at first consented, but on the way to pick it up he ordered her to ask for her money back. When she refused, saying she planned to put the piano in the empty space under the print in the dining room, he went to the seller's door himself, and told the thin elderly woman Yvette's house was so full of junk she had no room for a piano, and that Yvette was too embarrassed to admit her mistake. The woman returned the cash to Luke, who pocketed it.

On the way home, Yvette told him the house was *not* full of junk and she didn't like being maligned. "You wouldn't do what I told you," he said, "and the woman wouldn't return the money to *me* without an explanation."

"Okay," Yvette held out her hand for the money, "you got your way, please give me my money so I can buy something else."

"No!" he snapped. "I worked to get it back; it's mine now."

"Luke! I scrimped to save that and it's all the spending money I have!"

"You should have gotten my approval before you bought it."

"It was a *garage* sale! Be reasonable, Luke. How could I have gotten your approval? Furthermore, you buy things without *my* approval."

"How *dare* you question me?" he slammed the steering wheel with his palm and pulled the truck onto the shoulder. His eyes bulged and his fists clenched as he vented his fury on her. "God gave *me* authority, not you. I don't *have* to ask for your approval about *anything*. *I* am the master of the house and I won't tolerate you questioning my decisions. Is that clear?"

She nodded shakily.

"I'm glad we got that straight," he pulled the pickup back on the road. "God was smart when he put men in charge. Buying a piano; how stupid! When would you play it, and where would you get money for lessons?"

She didn't answer, afraid he'd turn his wrath on her again. The rest of the ride home, he kept shaking his head, snorting, and commenting about the stupidity of women in general and of her in particular. She defended herself in her head and determined someday she and Kyle would take piano lessons.

Yvette's gaze circled the room as she surfaced to the present and tried to remember what they'd been talking about. Oh, yes, about Luke getting angry if she reported him. Fay was saying, "…to consider how much damage he is doing to you and the children, and how dangerous he may become if you don't report him. Do you want your boys to become abusive like their father or your girls to become abusive or choose abusive mates?"

"What if I report it and the police question him but do nothing?" Yvette asked. "He'd be furious and things would get much worse. He'd think he's in the right and can get by with anything short of murdering me."

"On the other hand," Delores put in, "if you don't report him, he'll get worse, and so will your stress symptoms. How much are you willing to take before you ask for help?"

"Both reporting and keeping silent are risky," Fay said. "Only you can decide which is the safest option, Yvette, and what risks you dare take."

After they hung up, Yvette asked, "What should I do, Delores?"

"Report him," Delores put on the earring she'd taken off. "If you do something to stop his abuse, Luke has a better chance of becoming a loving husband. Call the sheriff's department and ask how they'd handle your situation."

Yvette paced to the window. "Would you call? I'm too nervous. Luke could come in any time. Ask if it's worth reporting and how they'd respond."

While Delores called the sheriff, Yvette stepped outside to determine Luke's whereabouts. She heard a tractor laboring up the lane and ran into the shop to look out the window and see who was coming in. Seeing Greg driving the tractor pulling a wagon-load of oats, she dashed out to meet him.

"Where's Dad?" she asked when he had stopped the tractor.

"Combining in the northwest field. I'll warn you if he comes in," he reached for the key. "I better unload and get out there or he'll investigate."

"Thanks," Yvette mouthed as the tractor started up.

As she reentered the house, Delores hung up the phone.

"The deputy wanted to talk to you," Delores said, "but I told him you're afraid of upsetting your husband and making matters worse. He wanted to know if you had injured Luke, too. I said you hadn't. He said the bruises are physical injury and if you report it, they will arrest him. You can have them come out here, or go to their office to document the bruises, whichever you think is safest. I told him we'd talk about it and decide what to do."

"But if I report him, they'd put him in jail and he'd have a criminal record. Luke would be terribly upset with me when he gets out."

"Oh, the deputy said you could get a 'no contact' order against him that would allow him to run the farm, but not get near you or the children."

"How long would that last and would Luke respect a court order? And then there are all the court costs and fees. Luke would get really upset when money that's earmarked for more farm ground ends up going for fines and fees."

"But you can't let him get away with abusing you, either."

"You're right. I have to do something, but what? Reporting him to the police isn't the answer. I'm sure there's a solution to this, there has to be. We haven't thought of it yet. Let's pray about it, and maybe inspiration will hit."

They prayed together and discussed possible options, but Yvette felt too uneasy to act on any of them. "There isn't going to be a perfect solution," Delores picked up the pan of beans and resumed cutting the ends off. "Luke is going to get mad no matter what you do, whether you report him or not. You need to make a decision based on what is best for you and the children, instead of on what will keep Luke happy."

At that moment Kyle burst in the door. "Dad's coming in on the tractor with Greg," he panted. "They're almost at the hog stable, and they don't have a wagon to unload."

Fear shot through Yvette and she sprang to her feet, her heart pounding. "Oh no!" she circled the table to the window, but Luke hadn't come into view, yet. "You have to leave, Delores. I can't chance him finding you here."

"Go out the back door to Grandma's house and call for Jill from there," Kyle opened the back door. "If he has to go to town for a part, he'll see your car if you don't leave right away."

"Here, Yvette," Delores thrust the large bowl of cut up beans into Yvette's arms, "take these and wash them. Shall I send Tanya over?"

"Yes, please," Yvette took the beans and watched Delores scuttle out the back door.

"Dad's rushing up the walk, and Greg's almost running to keep up," Kyle announced from the window. "Hurry, take the beans to the kitchen. I'll keep him busy so he won't look out the window and see Delores or Jill. If Tanya sees or hears Dad when she comes in, she'll keep quiet."

Yvette ran water on the beans as Luke came in the door.

"Why aren't you out sticking thistles?" Luke frowned at Kyle.

"The thistles are going to seed and should be burned. I thought I could get Tanya to pull the cart around for me so I can pile them on it."

"She can move the cart for both you and Greg," his heavy tread rattled the dishes as he strode past the china cupboard toward the bedroom. He came out, counting the cash in his billfold. "I have to go to Kalona to get an alternator for the combine. Where's the checkbook?"

"In my workroom," Yvette dried her hands on a kitchen towel. "I'll get it," she glanced at Luke to gauge how fast to hustle. He didn't seem upset or rushed, so she chose a fast walk, hoping that would give Delores time to drive away before Luke headed to town and saw her car in front of Clara's house.

"Move it!" he barked. "I don't have all day."

She blew out an exasperated breath and sprinted to her room, then took as long as she dared when she got there.

After Luke left and Tanya and the boys went to stick thistles, Yvette returned to the kitchen. She still didn't have a clue what to do about Luke. She prayed and waited as she washed the green beans and put them in quart jars, but no solution came to mind. Feeling lonely and vulnerable, she put the jars of beans in the refrigerator, grabbed a pair of leather gloves and a spade, and headed for the pasture to help with the thistles. "Dear God," she prayed, "if you don't give me direction, I guess I'll muddle through and avoid him as much as I can while I wait for Your insight."

Chapter 17

By Wednesday evening, two days later, Yvette still hadn't come up with a solution that felt right to her. She sighed as she pulled out her chair to sit at the supper table with the children. If two days of mulling over information she'd heard in those phone calls didn't bring any ideas to light, she didn't know what would. To make matters worse, the boys had relaxed their vigilant attitude and apparently gone back to normal yesterday. She guessed Luke's jolly-good-fellow act had lulled them to a sense of safety.

What am I supposed to do? She tuned out Kyle and Tanya's chatter as they waited for Greg to finish washing up. *Remind them Luke hasn't apologized or revoked their punishments? Which is worse? Living in fear all the time or being broad-sided again when Luke renews his attack? I know from experience it isn't if, it's when he attacks. Unless he'll focus the brunt of his aggression on* me *instead of on me and* the boys.

"Greg, stop looking at yourself in the mirror," Kyle said. "I'm starving and you're wasting our time. Anyway, I thought you wanted to go to the youth shindig at church tonight."

Greg came to the table, looking embarrassed Yvette thought. "Your character and how you treat others is more important than your looks," she said as he pulled out his chair and sat down, "Tanya, would you say grace?"

As they linked hands, and bowed their heads, they heard a knock.

"I'll get it," Kyle bounded up when they'd finished saying grace, and dashed to the door. Yvette didn't have to strain to hear Alex's booming bass voice, although his superficial charm seemed more subdued than usual.

After Alex came into the kitchen and they had exchanged pleasantries, Yvette sensed Alex wanted to talk to Luke and sent Greg to the field with the pickup to fetch his dad. Meanwhile, she set a place for Alex across from Luke's spot, offered him cheese, carrots, and garden-fresh broccoli, and shared Kyle's and Tanya's achievements with him until Luke came in.

Luke clumped to the kitchen door, a gray-brown dust covering him from head to foot. It clung to his eyelashes and bushy eyebrows, and made him look like a gray-haired man. It mingled with sweat to become streaked grime on his face and his old white cotton dress shirt. "What's up?" Luke asked.

"Hey Dad," Kyle said, "why'd you come in so dirty? Did you open the cab windows to let the dust in?"

"The air conditioning quit, so I opened the windows for ventilation. It's a hot, dusty job when the cab isn't enclosed. I'll wash up. I stink."

"You look like a coal miner," Yvette placed the kettle on the table.

"He's not black enough for that," Alex dipped a broccoli flower into the ranch dressing as Luke headed for the bathroom.

"I should have taken a picture," Kyle helped himself to more carrots. "It would be fun to try to get that effect with paints."

"What would you call it?" Greg rinsed his hands in the washroom.

"How about 'After the Harvest'?" Alex suggested.

"I'd make him look worn out," Kyle stared into space. "His shoulders would sag, his eyelids would droop half shut, and he'd be taking a short step to show he's so tired he can hardly drag one foot in front of the other."

Greg came to the table and sat between Alex and Kyle. Conversation flagged until Luke returned to the kitchen, clean and in fresh clothes. "What brings you here?" Luke pulled out his chair and sat down.

"Plenty," Alex replied. "The wife and I had a big argument that night after I was here. She called the cops and had me put in jail, then got a no-contact order against me and won't let me see my own kid or step foot in my own house. I didn't even *do* anything to her, and she called the cops. She makes me so mad I want to strangle her."

Luke hitched his chair forward. "It's just like a woman to turn against her husband and send him to jail."

"*She* ought to go to jail," Alex chomped off the end of his carrot. She's been nothing but trouble for the last five years. I think she's going crazy. I ought to have her committed to the psych ward."

"She has been hostile without reason lately, hasn't she?" Luke gulped half his glass of water. "What's for supper?"

"Chili," Greg pulled on the hot pad bringing the large kettle with it.

"Chili!" Luke leaned across Yvette to grab two slices of cheese. "It's too hot for chili. Why not make something cold like salami sandwiches?"

"You had that for lunch. I figured you wouldn't want cold bread soup with red raspberries again, either. The weather has cooled down some, and I made strawberry shortcake in the microwave for dessert. Tanya, please pass the cheese and relish plate to Kyle."

"What's cold bread soup?" Alex ladled a dipper of chili into his bowl.

"It's broken up bread in cold milk," Yvette explained. "We add fruit and sugar. I serve that in the hot summertime to keep the kitchen from getting hot, and because it's simple to fix and a relief to eat something cold."

"What about cherry or raspberry cobbler like my mom used to make?" Luke accepted the kettle Alex pushed toward him.

"That has to be done in the oven and heats up the kitchen. Besides, I thought you wanted something with meat in it."

"There's protein in the milk and you could serve bologna with it."

"I'll try that tomorrow night. I'm sorry, Alex. It sounds like you've been having an awful time." Yvette filled Tanya's glass with milk and passed the pitcher to Kyle.

"Yeah. She got this no-contact order against me and sent me a letter saying she won't drop the order until I finish a class for wife beaters." Copying Luke, he tore his slice of cheese into pieces and dropped them into his chili. "She called it the *Batterer's Education Program*," he enunciated mockingly. "I saw my lawyer today to find out if she can keep me from my property and if she can force me to take that class."

"What did the lawyer say?" Luke asked.

"He said going to the class right away would likely work in my favor in court, and I could go home sooner. It shows I'm willing to be cooperative or some such drivel. I think our legal system stinks. If a woman takes advantage of the system and presses false charges, there's nothing the man can do. He's considered guilty and is forced to leave his home and property, pay fines, pay for these classes, and if he doesn't do it on his own, the court will force him to or put him in jail and make him take the class there. How can I defend myself when the deck is stacked in her favor? Since when is a man not in charge of his own house anymore?"

"How long is the program?" Yvette pushed the basket of saltines across the table toward Alex. "Help yourself to the crackers."

"Sixteen weeks in Johnson county," he took a handful and passed the basket to Luke. "When I complained about that, they told me it's twenty-four weeks in other districts."

"Sixteen weeks is not real long," Yvette said.

"It is if you can't go home and see your family," Alex crushed the crackers between his palms and dropped them into his soup. "Where am I supposed to live? In a motel room or an apartment?" he stirred the crackers and cheese into his chili. "Sixteen weeks is a long time to sleep on somebody's couch or in an expensive motel room." He took a bite of soup. "Umm. You're a good cook, Yvette. I wish *my* wife knew how to make a decent pot of chili."

"Sixteen weeks in a motel or wherever is better than spending that time in jail," Yvette tried to keep her tone friendly rather than sharp. Something didn't ring true about Alex's story. When Greg and Kyle were young, she had been in Alex and Janet's home, and had felt uncomfortable when Alex had barked orders at Janet. He'd made scathing comments about how she cut the lettuce and salted the food, and told her she set the table wrong, undercooked the potatoes, and overcooked the roast beef. Janet had said nothing, but had looked distressed. Yvette suspected if Alex felt free to verbally attack his wife in front of guests, he would likely do more than that in private.

"That's beside the point," Alex retorted. "I'm being forced to spend sixteen weeks away from home when I'm innocent of any wrongdoing."

Yvette wanted to say 'I doubt that,' but decided to hold her tongue. If she wasn't careful, Luke would cut her down.

Alex's story gave her plenty to think about while she dug out an extra pillow, sheet and blanket for Alex to sleep on the couch, and later while she prepared for bed. Even though Luke had done more than give her a tongue lashing, she didn't want to press charges. Besides, it was a waste of money to pay all the legal fees and fines. If she lost in court, Luke would never let her forget it. And it wouldn't help their marriage if she won; a class for batterers wasn't likely to change Luke's mind, since he hadn't hit her. He'd just find other ways of being nasty—like taking the keys and controlling the money as he had threatened.

She prayed for guidance and wisdom. A perfect solution niggled at the edges of her mind, but she couldn't grab onto it. "Oh God," she prayed, "make it clear when the time is right. Show me what You want me to do."

Go talk to your mom. She hadn't heard a voice, but she sensed the idea came from God in answer to her prayer.

~   ~   ~

The next morning after breakfast, Luke went to Kalona to buy feed supplement for the cows, and the boys and Tanya went to stick thistles in the orchard. Yvette hurried to her mom's house, hoping to catch her before she left for the day and before Luke came back. She paused to admire the window boxes of deep red geraniums that lined the walk then knocked on the door.

At Clara's "Come in," Yvette stepped inside, noting the sunroom was bare of plants. Clara sat on a rocking chair in the living room, a Bible in her lap.

"Oh, I'm sorry," Yvette backed up a step. "I should have called."

"I'm finished reading. Come in and sit down," Clara motioned to the blue couch with pink flowers. "You caught me praying for you and your family situation. I take it things are worse and Luke is out in the field?"

Yvette sat on the couch and hugged the pillow to her stomach to still her jitters. "He went to town and Alex went with him; Alex slept on the couch last night." She told her mother Alex's story, and what Fay from the women's shelter, the sheriff, and Delores had said. "I can't go on like this," she concluded, "but I don't know what to do."

"Fay is right," Clara rocked slowly, thoughtfully. "Luke won't stop unless someone makes him stop. That's what it's taking to stop Alex."

"You think I should press charges against Luke?"

Clara pursed her lips as she studied the blue mountain print on the wall. "You may not have to go that far. From what Alex told you, Luke probably thinks he'd go to jail and would be kicked off the farm and away from his family if you report him. That should give you leverage."

"What are you getting at?"

"Because of what Alex said, Luke probably thinks you have the law to back you up, and that he could be in trouble for what he did. I'm guessing you can demand about anything. What do you want, Yvette?"

"I want him to be a loving, cherishing husband like he promised."

"What will it take to get that?"

"According to Fay at the shelter, I need to hold him accountable."

"What about that class Alex has to attend? Let's call them and ask if their program would help Luke or if they can recommend something else."

"I wouldn't know who to call," Yvette hugged the pillow tighter.

"Call the women's shelter. They'd know who to contact."

The woman who answered the phone at the shelter, directed Yvette to the Department of Correctional Services. After calling that number and connecting with Pat, the woman who coordinated the Batterer's Education Program, Yvette explained the situation and asked if the program would help Luke.

"That's up to him. Each person chooses his or her behavior," Pat said. "We teach the men that violent behaviors or controlling ones like intimidation are a choice, not a foregone conclusion, and encourage them to choose to be respectful and fair. The facilitators work hard to hold the men accountable for what they have done, and to challenge their thinking. Some men decide to change, and others don't. From what you've said, I think the program would be beneficial for your husband, but *he* will have to make the arrangements with me if he chooses to participate."

"His main concern is his Christian beliefs on submission," Yvette wound the phone cord around her finger. "How would that be handled?"

"Our facilitators are prepared to discuss and challenge his religious views as they affect his relationship with you and your children. We come from the standpoint that a man chooses to be controlling and uses whatever is at hand

151

to support his view. In your husband's case, he uses God and the Bible to support his view, figuring who can argue against God? He would be challenged, but what he does with that will be up to him."

After hanging up, Yvette relayed the information to Clara. "I thought the class would just be for men who hit their wives, but she said it includes threatening and other nasty behaviors, too. Luke needs that class."

"So if his sessions with Val don't bring about change, tell him he has to go to that class, or you will report him to the police and get a no-contact order."

"Hmm. That might work. But what if he gets upset by what he hears in class? He'd come home and be awful to the children and me, or he'd choose more subtle ways to control me and his abuse would be harder to recognize. I have a tough time with that as it is. I'd be stuck with being miserable, and wouldn't have a way to make him stop it—short of divorce or separation. And that's practically unheard of in our Mennonite churches. I read in one of the church papers that according to a study in 1998, only four percent of Mennonites have *ever* divorced. The figure is probably higher by now, but not by much."

"Have you considered separating?"

"Of course not. I vowed to stay with him for better or worse, and I meant it. Besides, I want a *loving* husband, not none at all."

"But what if that's the only way to get him to stop his nasty behavior? It would let him know you're serious. Remember that couple from Florida your sisters were talking about? They separated and now they're back together."

"In their case the husband had an affair and refused to stop seeing the woman. Paula, who goes to my church, was in a situation like mine. She hoped her husband would stop abusing her if she and the children left him. He didn't change, and five years later they're still separated and he blames it all on her."

"What does your pastor say about that?"

"There's not much he can do. Some of the older members disapprove of her having left him. They say she should forgive him and go back to her husband, and that it's damaging to the children to be separated from their father. I heard her talking about it to someone in the bathroom a few weeks ago."

"It's so sad people criticize when they don't know what they're talking about," Clara sighed. "Forgiveness won't solve this type of situation. I've seen you forgive and reconcile with Luke again and again, even though he keeps betraying your trust. Now you realize he has no intention of respecting you and he's only sorry you aren't under his thumb. Your trust has been destroyed by Luke, himself. To reconcile with him when he has no intention of giving up his power tactics would be foolish. If Paula's situation is like yours, separating from her husband was the best thing she could do. At least she and the children don't have to endure his nastiness every day. It's an option worth considering."

"Mom! I thought you're against divorce and separation."

"I am. But I'm against women and children being mistreated even more. As I think and pray about your situation, it's becoming clear to me that Luke mistreats you because it's getting him what he wants—power and control. The more you submit and turn the other cheek, the more he abuses you. He seems to think because you are Mennonite and Mennonites don't divorce, he can treat you as badly as he wants. And he's right. He has no reason to stop abusing you as long as there are no consequences. That should not be. The Mennonite Church should hold husbands to a higher standard than the law does. If the church won't step in, *you* have to hold him accountable."

"But what about the consequences of holding him accountable?"

"Then again, how would you feel if Tanya's husband yelled at her and criticized and ordered her around like Luke does you?"

"I'd hate it. She is so sensitive and sweet. It would destroy her."

"And I hate what Luke is doing to *you*. He's destroying you, too. I hurt and hurt for you and am helpless to make Luke shape up. If you don't stand up to him, Tanya is more likely to endure abuse from her husband, and the boys are more likely to abuse their families. Is that what you want?"

"No!"

"Then tell him you won't put up with it anymore. If he knows you are willing to report him and make him leave the farm, he may reconsider."

"I don't want to separate!" she wailed and her stomach lurched. She hugged the pillow tighter to stop the twitching and lowered her voice. "I want a loving relationship with Luke."

"You have to be realistic, Yvette. You've wanted that before you married, yet most of the time Luke is anything but loving. Maybe reporting him or suggesting separation or even divorce is the way. I know you hate power plays, but that's the only thing you haven't tried. Think of it as *tough love*. Because you love him you won't allow him to debase you. But be prepared to stand firm if he doesn't stop abusing you, even if it leads to divorce. If you back down, he won't take you seriously."

"Divorce," Yvette mused, "I never dreamt I'd hear you suggest it. But you're right, splitting up is the one option I haven't tried. And that may be what it takes to motivate him to change. Still, that's a big step and I doubt I'd ever feel right about it. Can you imagine? I'd have to buy out Luke's half of the farm and all the machinery and livestock, too. We'd have to decide how much the children will see Luke, and I don't know if they'd feel safe without me there as a buffer. Tanya would be traumatized, who knows how Greg would react, and Kyle would get moody. I can't do that to the children. Besides, I don't have money to buy Luke out, and if I got a loan from the bank we'd drown in interest payments and lose the farm."

"Not necessarily. One of the women who hired me as mid-wife told me about her sister who got a divorce. She didn't have to pay him his half until the youngest child was eighteen or left home. How old is Tanya?"

"Seven," she relaxed her hold on the pillow, relieved the twitching had subsided.

"You'd have eleven years to whittle down your current loan and save money to pay him off. After you pay him what you save up, I could probably cover the rest of what you owe. Come on, let's go to the table, and I'll help you figure an estimate." Clara got paper, pens, and calculator, and they sat at the kitchen table and wrote down estimates of everything Yvette and Luke owned.

After adding up the figures, Yvette sat back and sighed. "It's not as bad as I thought, but I'd be deep in debt."

"God will provide a way. If Luke doesn't shape up, I'd rather see you in debt than constantly mistreated. He's sucking the life out of you."

"Do you think I could handle farming on my own?"

Clara doodled on the margin of their page of figures. "Considering that Ben was spending most of his time building our church and you did most of the farming the year you met Luke, I think you could. Especially if the boys help."

"This goes against everything I've ever been taught about marriage. Christian radio says, 'For better or for worse, marriage is for keeps.' I'd feel like such a failure and I'd be a marked woman at church, like Paula. The people who respect me today would look down their noses at me. And who knows if anyone would buy my quilts."

"*Luke* is the failure," Clara dropped her pen, "not you. Can you live with *half* your food budget and be a prisoner in your own home? Will you allow Luke to isolate Greg from his friends and stop Kyle from drawing just because they protected you? Are you going to let him scare Tanya all the time? Is she being permanently damaged because of Luke? And will you prostitute yourself for Luke every time you need more money?"

Yvette felt something drain out of her. She felt discouraged. And so tired. *No matter what I do, it won't be the right thing or good enough.* "No," she sighed, "I can't do that either. It looks like I have try to stop him if he starts enforcing his penalties."

"Even if he doesn't enforce the things he threatened, he has to be held accountable for what he did. Next time he could do much worse."

"Next time?" her stomach lurched again. She clamped her arms over her middle.

"Are you okay?"

154

"I just have a nervous stomach. It'll quit in a minute."

"How long has this been going on?"

"About a week," Yvette shrugged to ease her mother's worry.

"Listen to your body, Yvette," Clara leaned forward. "It's telling you he's getting worse and you have to do something to stop him."

"I *know* he's getting worse. But how much of it is my own fault? He wasn't that bad until I started standing up to him. Maybe he wouldn't get so upset and I wouldn't end up a nervous wreck if I'd do what he says."

"He was getting worse *long* before you stood up to him. You didn't do anything to deserve being shaken, scolded or put down. Come on, Yvette, don't turn everything around and say it's your own fault. You know it isn't."

"How do you know that? *Luke* thinks it's my fault."

"Have you forgotten your dad and your grandpa managed this farm? Neither I, nor Ben's mom worked as hard as you do. It's only a matter of time before Luke gets mad at you for getting sick or *being unable* to do everything he demands. He's an explosion looking for a place to happen, and it has nothing to do with what you do or don't do. If he'd expend more effort loving you instead of controlling you, he'd have a happy wife and a willing bed partner."

"Wow," Yvette gibed, "I bet you're glad to get that off your chest."

"Don't make fun of me," Clara narrowed her eyes in mock seriousness. "I wanted to get that off my chest for a long time and finally got the chance. Ben always told me to stay out of it, but I can't bear to see you turned into a spiritless work horse. You used to be so vibrant, so spunky and full of life, and Luke sucked it all out of you."

"I'm not dead yet," Yvette deadpanned.

"At least you still have your sense of humor, but it seldom comes out. You'd get your spunk back if you made Luke attend that batterers group."

"If he went, he'd feel I had the upper hand and do all kinds of nasty things to put me in my place again."

"Why don't you use your leverage to make him leave the farm until he finishes the sixteen weeks with that group? Make him counsel with your pastor, too. If he is truly sorry and shapes up, he can court you to regain your trust. If he doesn't, you can insist on living separate and file for a no contact order if he tries to come back. That may force him to take responsibility for his behavior. And you could give him as much time as you like before you file for divorce."

"That sounds like a sensible solution. It would be a relief to get him off the farm and not have to scramble so he won't gripe at us, chew us out, make fun of us, or call us names. He'd have a chance to change his behavior and build good relationships with the children, too."

"The timing couldn't be more perfect," Clara pushed back her chair and stood up. "Luke and Alex can rent a place together and split the cost. Would you like some peppermint tea? It's fresh from the garden."

"I shouldn't stay; Luke could come home any time now. But you go ahead," she paused while Clara put tea leaves in the kettle and turned the gas burner on, then resumed the conversation. "I think you may be right; the timing is perfect. With Alex in the same boat, Luke could cut his housing expenses in half. But what about the children? Should I allow him to see them?"

"Until he finishes the class, none of them should *have* to see him or talk to him on the phone. After that, he could see them in counseling sessions, and then if they are willing, you could arrange to have him see more of them."

"What a sensible solution, Mom. You are so wise, you scare me." She rose and hugged her mother. "I better go home before Luke comes back."

Chapter 18

Luke climbed to the haymow on Saturday morning, while Yvette and the boys were milking, to see how many layers of last year's bales of straw were left. He'd left Alex sleeping on the couch, since Alex had difficulty sleeping at night. Now that he'd finished combining oats, he'd have the boys move the old straw bales to the side of the mow so this year's bales could be stacked on the bottom and the old straw wouldn't be buried under the new crop.

He decided to check if they'd have room for another cutting of hay in the double section on the west side. He climbed the ladder and stepped on top of the bales. *Finally! The boys finally took the bales off in horizontal layers like I've been telling them. Now it'll be easy to figure how much more the mow can hold.* Calculating the distance to the eaves, he guessed half a cutting could go on this side, then he'd switch the hay fork to the track that went to the east mow.

As his gaze swept the mow, the cracks of light coming in around the door to the south caught his eye. He moved toward the door to see what progress his neighbors were making. As he unhooked the latch and swung the door open, the cool morning breeze wafted in, caressing his face and rippling his shirt. He eased himself down on the bale of hay and dangled his feet outside.

He'd enjoyed harvesting oats all week. But the three breakdowns with the combine and enduring Alex's ranting had been frustrating. Alex had gone with him on the combine Thursday and Friday, and had talked nonstop of how Janet had ruined him and all his troubles were *her* fault. When Luke brought up his frustrations with Yvette, Alex always turned the subject back to Janet.

I'll never be in Alex's shoes. Not if I can avoid it. I won't go to jail, sleep on someone's couch, be kept from my family, or go to that wife beater's group. And I certainly won't pay to do those things and hire a lawyer, too.

Fear zinged through him. He suspected Yvette could report him for shaking her. Somehow, he'd have to keep her focus elsewhere, while he fought to win this war. There wouldn't *be* a war if she would get in her submissive place. No matter what Val said, this whole thing was her fault.

He shook his head. It was crazy how everyone blamed him. *She* had taken over his rightful place. *She* had usurped authority over him. Now, after making every effort to right his marriage, it still wasn't right. And she had turned the boys against him! The appointments with Val hadn't helped. He had hoped Val would persuade Yvette she needed to change, or would tell him how to be a more effective leader. Instead Val had shown him from the Bible how God intended marriage to be a union of equals, both in authority, responsibility, and servanthood. Val had emphasized that God wanted the pair to be a unit, utilizing the perspectives and desires of *both* spouses, not just the husband's.

After Luke's initial protest, Val had requested Luke hear him out and take a week to consider what Val had to say before discounting it. Feeling pressured to appear reasonable, Luke had agreed to think about it and to delay taking charge of the finances and enforcing the punishments on Greg and Kyle. But he had waited long enough. Today he'd take action.

That decision made, he focused on the checkered landscape which was dotted with farmhouses and barns. From his vantage point in the haymow he could see for miles. Rectangular fields of golden oats—some standing, some harvested, some sporting shocks of grain—fields of green and gold corn or beans, and green fields of hay or pasture all failed to give him satisfaction. He wondered if the men on those farms felt emasculated, too, or if they ruled their families. One by one, he considered each neighbor's relationship to his wife, and one by one deduced the husband was in charge. *Yvette's the problem. I'll have to teach her to ask me for direction and obey my leadership.*

His stomach growled and he quickly finished in the haymow and went in for breakfast. Alex came out to the washroom as Luke soaped up.

"Did you sleep okay?" Luke put on a concerned tone he didn't feel.

"Better. I need to go back to work so I don't think about her."

After breakfast, Alex left to go to his office, Yvette and Tanya went to weed the garden, and Luke and the boys went to move bales of old straw.

"After we're done moving straw bales," Luke said, "I'll go out and rake the straw. It should be dry enough. You boys can start moving old hay from the east mow to that covered walk-through. Stack them to the top, but make sure you leave a path on one side." When neither boy responded as they carried bales of yellow straw to their new location, Luke pressed, "Did you hear?"

"Of course we heard," Greg snapped.

"What's wrong with you anyway? You don't have any business talking to me like that. You are supposed to obey and respect your parents."

"*Mom* is my parent, not you," Greg's dark brown eyes looked black as Luke caught their angry glare. "You forfeited the right to my respect."

"Just what do you mean by that?" Luke dropped his bale and stared at his eldest son. He saw Kyle stack his straw bale and turn to look at Greg, too.

"I don't have to explain anything. You know what you did. Kyle and I made up our minds; the two of us are sticking together. We'll come out here as long as we can keep an eye on you. But if you think you can get us out of the way so you can attack Mom, think again. If Mom comes out and helps stack bales, we'll come out here. If not, we won't. It's that simple."

Feeling as if he'd been punched in the mid-section, Luke sank down onto the nearest bale. "I owe you boys an apology," he took off his bill cap, ran his hand through his hair, and resettled the cap on his head. "I was wrong to behave as I did, and I won't do it again. You have my word."

"For whatever that's worth," Greg jeered.

"I'm not stupid. You heard what happened to Alex. Do you think I want to get a police record or go to jail? I'm not going to hurt either you or your mother. We may have problems, but I'll find other ways to solve them."

The boys studied him, saying nothing. Luke waited, looking from one to the other, but they stared back. *What shall I do now? They seem to be waiting for something. Maybe they don't realize I apologized.*

"Can you forgive me?" Luke broke the silence.

"We forgive you," Kyle said, "but we're not sure we can trust you."

"Then you haven't forgiven me," Luke shot back.

"Whatever," Greg shrugged.

"Look," Luke stood up, "please give me a chance. You're right, I do want to talk to Mom alone. You can make sure she has the intercom nearby so she can call you if she wants your support. Is that a deal?"

"If Mom feels okay with that and you apologize to her," Greg said.

By the time they'd finished eating dinner and Yvette stood up to clear the dishes off the table, Luke had mentally tried and discarded various apologies until he found one that wasn't too demeaning but would satisfy the boys. "I'm sorry if my actions were inappropriate last week," he said watching his thumb make trails in the sweat on his water glass. "Please forgive me. I will *never* do *anything* that would warrant reporting me to the police. I'm not that stupid."

No one spoke for a long awkward moment and Yvette continued to clear the table. He wasn't sure what to do next. Had his apology worked?

Tanya broke the silence. "Can I go to Grandma's and help her snap green beans, Mom? She said if I help she'd let me eat fresh apricots."

"Sure," Yvette sounded amused, "you can help her. Make sure you don't eat too many beans or apricots so you don't get an upset tummy."

Tanya pushed her chair back and rushed out of the house.

Luke saw the boys exchange glances. Greg opened his mouth, but Kyle spoke first. "Mom, Dad wants us to move hay and straw out of the mow. Do you want to help us, or stay in the house?"

"I'd rather help you," Yvette started running water in the sink, "but I have so much work to do. I better stay in and get my work done."

"Do you want us to help you?" Kyle asked, and Luke guessed Kyle hadn't bought his apology, but was leaving the choice to his mother.

Luke spoke up before Yvette answered. "I want to talk with you after I start the boys in the mow," he couldn't bring himself to say her name. "We can take the barn intercom up to the haymow so you can call them if you want."

"I guess that's alright," she kept her back to the room.

Luke watched her a moment, looking for signs of insubordination, but found none. Satisfied, he went to move the intercom and start the boys in the haymow, then returned to the house to confront his wife. When he didn't find her in the kitchen, but saw the open stair door, he decided to check upstairs. As he mounted the bottom step, he felt like turning and going out to the field. What if she made one of her condescending remarks and he couldn't stop himself from hitting her? The boys would never forgive him.

Luke took a deep breath. He *had* wanted to hit her that night. If the boys hadn't forced him out of her room, he may have yielded to the impulse. But since they intervened, he'd never know for sure. He wondered if she could still report him for shaking her. Probably not, he decided. Besides, shaking her wasn't really abuse. But he'd make sure it didn't happen again no matter how desperate he felt. The risk was too great. Alex's troubles made that clear. He'd get what he wanted another way. Squaring his shoulders, he climbed the stairs. He found Yvette in her room bent over her sewing machine, a box fan blowing at her bare legs, while her damp bangs drooped on her forehead. How like her to make him endure this hot room! It had to be as hot as the attic!

When she saw him, she started, rose and moved to the side of her desk. Ducking his head to avoid hitting the lintel, he stepped into the room and perched on the corner of her dresser, the one that had been in his bedroom. He glanced around the room, noting the dingy-white walls needed fresh paint.

"Garden caught up?" he tried to sound conversational.

She shrugged.

"Look, this isn't easy for me," he began again. "I'm trying to make our marriage work. I know you don't believe me right now, but I do love you. Honest." He saw her shoulders relax a degree, and pressed on. I want to be united with you in purpose, in effort, in love, in every way a man and wife can be united. Don't you want that, too?"

"I did once."

"What does that mean?" he reined in his temper.

"When we married, I thought we'd become a unit. I worked toward that end until I found out you didn't want to be a unit, you wanted to make me into an extension of you. You wanted to use me and my labor to make a larger Luke. At the same time, you started to wipe Yvette off the face of the earth. I refuse to be a nobody so you can double or triple your somebodyness."

Luke wanted to throw words back at her, but took a deep breath to calm himself. "What do you think it takes to make a unit?"

"The couple becomes an 'us.' They discuss and decide things together. No one orders the other around. They request and don't demand. Both further their talents and encourage each other. Lovemaking pleases both spouses, not just one. The resulting harmony is from both getting their way, not from one playing dictator while the other sacrifices even her dignity."

"But you've taken charge of the money and made me sacrifice my dignity. How is that working together or making decisions together?"

"As I recall, we talked it over and agreed to try this so we could reach our goals. When it worked, we kept it going."

"Well, it hasn't been working. I'm constantly embarrassed because of the lack of funds. I can't even treat my friends to dinner."

"Let's refigure our budget, then. We could put less in savings."

"I don't want to put less in savings. I'm tired of this budget crap, and constantly having to get your permission to spend money."

"But it wasn't me giving permission. You asked that so much be set aside to buy more land or a new tractor, and I figured the budget around that as well as other necessities. You gave it your stamp of approval."

"Of *course* you'd *say* that. From now on, things will change around here. Either you let me handle the money, or you triple my share."

"We'd only save fifty dollars a month. Don't you want more land?"

"Don't cut savings; cut the grocery spending."

"If I do that, we won't have anything left for food."

"Then take out the amount you use for extra spending."

"I see what you're after, Luke. Your allotment is three times what I shave off the food budget so the children and I have spending money. It's not fair to take away our tiny amount so you can spend more."

"What about those books on your bookshelf?"

Yvette glanced at the walnut five-shelf bookcase. "I bought most of those before we married. Buying a book occasionally is *not* frivolous spending. Even if it was, you shouldn't do all the frivolous spending for the whole family."

"That patio is worse than frivolous."

161

"Not to me. Besides, I saved for it for years and most of it was free."

"Of *course* it was free if you don't count your labor. You never did scrub the ceilings and walls and clean out the closets and cupboards this spring, did you? And it's all because you spent so much time on that patio."

She took a deep breath and blew the air out through her mouth. "Stop it, Luke. Stop trying to pick a fight."

"As I said, triple my allowance, and it can't come out of savings."

"That's impossible."

He reveled in the surging sense of power that welled up in him at her protest. "Well then, we'll go to plan B. *I'll* decide where the money goes."

"What happened to deciding things together?"

"That was your idea, not mine. From here on, we are going to be a unit. It's up to you how hard you make this on yourself. You can choose to support my decisions, or you can fight me tooth and nail. Either way, what I say goes. *I* am the head of this farm. As I stated before, I will allow you *half* of the current food budget to keep us fed. Anything else you want, you'll have to get permission from me. *And*," he dug in his pocket and one by one pulled out four rings of keys, and slipped the rings over his forefinger, "*I* will decide when and where the vehicles are to be used."

"Is that what Val advised?"

Hearing her unruffled response, he felt the winning edge whoosh out of him. Although she appeared to bend to his will, it wasn't enough. He grappled to regain his feeling of manliness. "No, it's not. He's wrong, and I won't listen to such heresy. The Bible clearly states the husband is the head of his home, and the wife is to submit to him in *everything*."

"I won't live like you described, Luke," she straightened to her full height and squared her shoulders. "I thought it over, and decided to wait and see how you choose to respond to Val. From what you just said we are at odds, and unless you decide to change, we always will be. You've vowed before God to love and *cherish* me till one of us dies. You haven't kept those vows, and have broken them again and again. I want you to leave, Luke. Maybe when we're apart for awhile, you'll rethink your beliefs and your behavior."

"What are you saying?" he hissed through clenched teeth. He pushed away from the dresser and stood tall, hoping to intimidate her.

"I want a separation." Her quiet dignity galled and scared him. "I want you to leave the farm. My mom lives here and it is my inheritance."

"How *dare* you tell me to leave my home?" he shouted, covering the distance between them in one stride. "This is *my* farm," he glared down at her and screamed in her face so she would know how furious she had made him, "*I* paid for it, and I will *not* let you take it away from me. What utter *gall*, to think you can kick me off *my farm*. I'll call the cops on *you* for threatening me."

When he saw Yvette stayed erect and composed and studied him with curious detachment, he knew his show of anger hadn't had the desired effect, and suspected she was waiting for him to hit her so she could call the police. For two seconds he weighed his options of turning up the volume, punishing her, or appealing to her sympathetic nature. Not wanting to risk jail time, he chose and implemented the latter.

"I can't believe you said that. How could you even *think* of asking me to leave my farm?" he backed from her a few inches and put on the saddest, most reproachful eyes he could muster. "You *know* how I love farming. It's my *life*, my *dream*," he dipped his knees and swept his arms down and wide in an all-encompassing motion to demonstrate the depth of his longing. She appeared unmoved, so he added the children. "And how can you raise the kids all alone? They need their *dad* to teach them and spend time with them every day." She raised her brows and snickered, so he abandoned that line of reasoning. "*Please* don't break up our family. Don't be so hard-hearted and selfish. Think about my needs for a change. If you split us up, you'll never live it down."

When her expression didn't soften, he stopped. He fidgeted as she studied him, starting at his face, wandering down to his feet and back up.

"Stop looking at me like that," he shifted his weight to one foot.

"Like what?"

"Like I'm a bug or something."

"A roach or a pinching June bug?" she tilted her head. "Or maybe a snake," amusement crinkled her eyes and turned up the corners of her mouth.

"It's not funny," he spat.

"You're right; it's not," she sobered. "You've already made your viewpoint about marriage clear, and have resisted any teaching otherwise. As I said, unless you change your mind, we are incompatible. I refuse to be a part of the abusive marriage you described. Why don't you attend that men's group with Alex and room together somewhere? If you change your mind after you've finished the group, we might have something of substance on which to build a marital relationship. If not, divorce would be the best option. Neither I nor our children want to endure any more of your rages or your lord-it-over attitude."

"I will stay here," he copied her demeanor. "This is *my* farm, too."

"Then I'll report you to the police and show them the bruises you left on my arms. They'll put you in jail and give you a 'no contact' order."

He considered arguing about that, but knew she had heard Alex's story, too. *Blast her bruises! Now my only option is to try to keep her from ruining me.* "And if I leave, what do you have in mind?"

"I checked into that Batterer's Education Program Alex mentioned. If you go there for sixteen weekly sessions, and get counseling from Val once a week during that time, I'll consider a reconciliation."

"You'll *consider* a reconciliation!" he shouted. "That's no deal. It's an insult. No reasonable man would accept such an offer."

"I *am* being reasonable. The children and I refuse to tolerate the tyrant you've become. If you aren't willing to be a loving husband and father, we won't live with you. It's not healthy for any of us."

"Who will do the farming?"

"I will. I was farming anyway before I met you."

He snorted. "When will you find the time?"

"I'll cut back in the house. You can take half our savings, the pickup, and your tools. Leave my tools and the tools that were Dad's here."

"How am I supposed to pay for that group and the motel?"

"Your half of the savings should cover it, and you can get a job."

Not willing to admit defeat, he tried another ploy. "I don't have to march to your orders. Why should I jump through your hoops? Anytime I don't do as you say, you'll threaten to call the police or divorce me. I don't want to live with that over my head. *I'll* file for divorce. Then you'll buy my half of the farm, and will end up over your head in debt. Is that what you want?"

"You're right, it would be a setback. But perhaps we should divorce. That way, you'd have money to buy a farm of your own, maybe one of those huge farms in Canada or Montana where you can drive tractor all day. You'd be free to marry a woman who embraces your notion of marital roles."

Luke hadn't expected her to take up his suggestion; he'd thought she would back off on her demands. Maybe she wasn't just talking to win her point, but actually meant what she said. He'd have to take time to think this through. "Do I have a few days to make up my mind?"

"Why don't you talk it over with Val? If you don't act nasty and don't take charge of our money and vehicles as you threatened, I'll give you until Thursday to make up your mind. Maybe Alex will show you how to get into that men's group. If you get on it right away, you can probably attend together."

"Why can't I stay here while I take the class?"

"The children and I need space to heal."

"That sounds like a made up excuse."

"Those are your choices, take it or leave it."

He took a deep breath. Maybe if he sounded amicable now, he could get her to change her mind later. "Okay. I'll think about it." He turned and left her hot room. Surely he could make her change her mind. Surely, he could.

Chapter 19

Tanya sat at the dining room table playing with her Barbie, Skipper, and Kelly dolls. The Ken doll lay face-down at her elbow, while the three girl dolls whispered together and cast glances in his direction. Mom had gone up to the attic to get a suitcase, and told Tanya to go play and stop hanging around her all the time. Tanya could hear Dad opening and closing drawers in his bedroom. *He seems strange*, she frowned at the bedroom door. *But he doesn't sound mad. Maybe it's because he's leaving today.*

Yesterday before chores, Mom and Dad had told her and the boys to sit in the living room. Mom hadn't minded that Tanya sat real close to her that time. Dad sat on the recliner and said nothing. Mom told them Dad was going to live somewhere else for awhile, and he would be leaving tomorrow—today now. He was going to go to a men's group. Tanya didn't know what that meant; she hadn't dared ask.

Greg had asked how long Dad would live somewhere else, and Mom said at least four months. Four days seemed like a long time to Tanya; four months felt like forever. She felt sorry for her dad; he looked so sad.

Kyle had asked who was going to farm. Mom said she would, and all of them would help her. *Will I have to drive tractor?* Tanya shivered; the thought was so scary. Maybe she'd have to milk the cows now so Mom could drive the tractor in the field during chore time like Dad sometimes did. She shuddered. Those cows were huge.

She heard Mom coming down the stairs and looked up in time to see her set a big green suitcase on the floor in the doorway to Dad's bedroom, and then walk past her to go to the kitchen. Dad came out to pick up the suitcase, and took it into his bedroom where Tanya couldn't see him anymore. Tanya wanted to go to the kitchen to see what Mom was doing, but Mom was acting weird, too, and she was afraid Mom would tell her to go play.

She wished Kyle would sit with her, but Greg and Kyle were in the shop. She didn't know what they were doing, but she had heard Mom tell them to pull out all the tools that had Grandpa's name on them. Did that mean they were to put Grandpa's tools on the wagon and pull the wagon out of the shop?

After she'd played with her dolls awhile, Dad came out of his room carrying one of the ugly brown lamps from his bedroom and the beat up green suitcase Mom had brought down. Maybe if she didn't look at him, he wouldn't yell or look mad at her. She looked down at her dolls, and listened to his feet cross the floor from his room to the front door. He didn't stomp as loud as usual, and when the door closed behind him, she suddenly wasn't scared of him anymore. She scooted off her chair and went to the window to watch. He put the lamp and suitcase in the front seat of the pickup, then went to the shop.

When he came out of the shop, he had two long boards. He opened the tailgate, and leaned the boards against the tailgate, then went back in the shop. Tanya ran to the washroom window to see better. The next time he came out, he was pushing a big and tall red square thing and started pushing it up the boards.

"What's that?" Tanya asked.

Mom came to the window and leaned forward to see under the window-shade. Tanya sniffed the sweet smell that meant her mom had recently showered. Tanya loved that smell and had asked if she could use Mom's shower gel, and Mom had said to wait until she was older. "That's Dad's tool-chest," Mom answered. "He got a job working at the tractor repair place he had worked at before he started farming, and he has to take his own tools."

"Where is he going?"

"Remember I told you he's going to live elsewhere for awhile?"

Tanya nodded, watching her dad kick the tool-chest when it didn't go up the boards, then go back into the shop. "Where is he going to live?"

"Alex and Dad will live in a motel in Coralville for awhile. They found one with a kitchenette that lets them pay by the month."

"Why is he leaving?"

"I'll explain later when Greg and Kyle are here, too. Right now I need to pack dishes for him. Now go play. Please." Her mom hurried to the kitchen.

When her dad didn't come out of the shop for awhile, Tanya wondered back into the dining room and scooted onto her chair. She turned Barbie's, Skipper's, and Kelly's legs so they could sit down to eat. Pretending to feed them spoonfuls of their meal, she made chewing noises.

"Yum, that was good," she said for Kelly, wiping her own mouth.

She picked Ken up and stood him in front of the other dolls. "Why aren't you out there stacking bales on the drag?" she yelled for Ken. "I told you an hour ago I was going out to bale straw and here you are, sitting around doing nothing! Now get out there! If you think you can make me work in the hot sun by myself all day just because I'm leaving, you can think again."

"Luke," Tanya changed to a quiet voice, "be reasonable. We were in the hot sun sticking thistles. You knew that. And after being out there with no breeze we needed to cool down before we went out again."

"When do I get to cool down?" she snapped for Ken.

"Any time now," she said with a straight face, then snickered. She pushed the dolls to the end of the table and went to the washroom window again.

Dad's tool chest was on the back of the pickup and he was coming with long, fast steps to the house. He looked upset. She scurried to the living room to be out of sight when he came in. She started for the couch, then remembered *that man* had been sleeping there all week and she didn't want to touch anything he had touched. Even though he never talked to her, she didn't like him. He was big and loud like Dad, and she felt afraid of him even though she'd never seen him act nasty. She chose the stuffed chair in the wide doorway. If she faced backward, she could hide while she peeked into the dining room.

Dad shoved the door open, slammed it behind him, and stomped into the kitchen. "What's the big idea?" Tanya could see the side of his face beyond the kitchen door. His face was red and he looked mad. "Why'd you empty my savings account? I called the bank to transfer savings to the checking account, and it's not there. What did you do with my money?"

"That's *our* money," Mom said in her firm voice. "I used *half* of it to open my own checking and savings accounts."

"I never said you could take that money!" Dad yelled. "You have no business dipping into money earmarked for investing in the farm."

"Half of it is mine. Since you said you want money to spend, I figured I'd move my half out of the way so you know how much you have." *Mom sounds different. Not mad, just different.*

"Jezebel!" *What's a Jezebel? It must be really bad.* "You force me to leave my farm, and then take my money, too."

"The farm is my inheritance, so it's more than half mine."

"This is utterly disgusting! You deliberately planned this, didn't you? You're a scheming, man-hating, emasculating *feminist*, and it's no wonder we've had such a miserable marriage! I don't know why I married you." Tanya wanted to hide her face, but she couldn't stop watching. Was Dad going to hit Mom? She wanted Kyle, but didn't know where he was. She stuck her thumb in her mouth, but she had given that up years ago and it felt strange. She picked at the nail with her front tooth, then bit it.

"I don't know why you did, either, unless it was to get the farm."

"How was I to know your *good-little-Christian* front was an act?"

"I'd think you'd be in a hurry to get away from somebody as awful as me." Did Dad's nasty words really not bother her?

"You bet I am. Where are the boys?"

"I don't know. Weren't they in the shop with you?"

Dad didn't answer, but stomped to the front door. Tanya ducked down, and when he yelled out the door for the boys to come in, she scrambled off the chair and hid beside it so he wouldn't see her when he turned around. She sat there waiting, until she heard the door click shut, then moved forward on her hands and knees to peek around the bottom of the chair and make sure it was safe to get on the chair again. Dad wasn't at the door, so she crawled on the chair, and looked over the back.

They were in the dining room, and she saw Mom hold the handle of a big bag with shiny red cars on it. She offered it to Dad. "Here are dishes and tableware I don't need. You can shop for pots and pans at Goodwill."

"Give me good dishes," he brushed the bag away, "not *cast-off* junk."

"We need those, and I don't want to split up our sets. With your attitude, I'd never see them again. Are you sure you don't want these? There are three plates that didn't break from that blue set you liked so well." Tanya heard the door squeak as Kyle and Greg came in the wash room, although she could tell they were trying to be quiet.

"Oh, all right," he grabbed the bag out of Mom's hand. "Are you sure this is what you want?" he looked and sounded nasty. "You want to humiliate your husband in the eyes of the *whole* community? After I leave, there's no changing it. I won't be your puppet, coming and going at your command."

"If you're humiliated, you did it to yourself."

"And when will I be *allowed* to see the children again?"

"After you finish the Batterer's Education Program—*if* they want to."

"I suppose you're planning to turn them completely against me."

"I don't have to. You did that all by yourself. Change your attitude and learn something from that group. I won't force the children to see you."

"Where are the boys? Did they come in yet? Greg? Kyle?"

"We're here," Greg answered as they stood in the washroom doorway.

He turned his back to Tanya and faced the boys. All was quiet for a long time, and she didn't know what was going on.

"I'll miss you boys," his voice sounded strange, and it took Tanya a moment to realize he was crying. She didn't remember hearing or seeing Dad cry before, not even at Grandpa's funeral. He hugged them, one at a time. Greg didn't hug him back. Kyle put one arm around him, but looked around the room as if he didn't like it. He saw Tanya and smiled at her. She shook her head frantically. *"Don't tell Dad I'm here,"* she mouthed.

"What you're doing to me and the children isn't right," Dad turned to Mom, wiping his eyes.

"That may be so. But it's the only way I can see that has a *chance* of salvaging this marriage, if there's anything left to salvage."

"How can you say that?" he sounded strange, sad maybe. He turned and Tanya dropped out of sight. She heard him walk to the door and open it. She waited until she heard it close before she peeked to see if he had gone. Greg and Kyle watched him from the dining room window, and Mom joined them, putting her hands on their shoulders.

Tanya scrambled off the chair, ran to the living room window, and ducked behind the window shade to watch. She saw Dad put the bag with red shiny cars in the cab of the pickup, then go to the pickup bed and push at the tool-chest. It didn't move. He got in the cab and closed the door. She saw him looking down and knew he was turning the key. The pickup rolled out the drive and turned onto the road and out of sight.

Tanya stared down the empty road for a minute. When he didn't come back, she went to the stuffed chair and sat down. She blinked very fast, but the tears came anyway. He hadn't looked toward the house—not even once. If he had looked, she would have waved good-bye to him. He hadn't said good-bye to her, either. She pulled her shirt up to her face so they wouldn't hear her cry.

"Where's Tanya?" she heard Mom ask.

"In the living room," Kyle said.

Tanya heard a footstep on the patch of linoleum by the front door, then felt a touch on her shoulder. "Tanya?" Mom said. "Why are you in the dark?"

She didn't answer and kept her face in her shirt.

"Move over so I can sit beside you," Mom squeezed in next to her and rocked her until her tears stopped. "Do you want to talk about it?"

Tanya shook her head. Mom's arm felt so good.

"It's okay if you don't want to talk right now. We'll talk about it later. Greg, Kyle, come in here, please. I need to talk to all of you."

Tanya put her shirt down as her brothers shuffled into the room.

"This is going to be a tough time for all of us. The hardest part may be that we feel mixed up. One part of me is relieved Dad left and we don't have to be afraid of him now. Another part is sad and scared. One part wants him to come back, and another part never wants to see him again. I expect all of you have feelings like that. It could make us grouchy. Let's try to be patient and kind, and pray for each other—and Dad. He's going through a rough time, too."

"He didn't tell me good-bye," Tanya tried to keep from crying.

"No, he didn't," Mom gave her an extra squeeze. "I'm so sorry. This makes the whole thing even harder for you."

"I thought you didn't want him to, Tanya," Kyle said. "If I knew you wanted to tell him good-bye, I would have—"

"He didn't re-member me," her voice broke as the tears came again.

"So you feel he doesn't love you or think you're important," Mom rubbed Tanya's back.

Tanya nodded.

"In his own way, Dad loves all of us. He just doesn't know how to show it very well. I asked him to leave and get counseling so he'll stop yelling and being grouchy with us so much of the time, and be able to show how much he loves us instead. I'm sorry he didn't remember you, Tanya. Would you like to call him and talk to him on the phone? I have his number."

Tanya shook her head. Dad still hadn't remembered her; calling him wouldn't change that.

"Kyle, Greg, that goes for you, too. If you want to talk to Dad—I'll tape his phone number above the phone. You'd better talk to him when I'm around, though, so I can help if you feel too uncomfortable. Okay?"

Nobody answered.

"It's going to be just us for awhile. Grandma will probably help some-times, but it will be up to us to get the work done and help each other deal with our situation. I'm going to be very busy, but if any of you need to talk to me, or whatever, I'm here for you. Each of you is more important than this farm."

"I don't want him to come back," Kyle said.

"Me either," Greg seconded.

Tanya nodded, glad her brothers had said the very thing she felt.

"Would you feel like that if he changed and started acting like Steve?" Mom asked. "What if he was kind and never yelled or made nasty comments?"

Greg snorted. "He's too bull-headed. He won't change."

"Don't forget God's working on him, too," Mom said, "let's not give up hope yet. Dad can be nice when he decides to be."

"Haven't you noticed, Mom? When he *acts* nice, it's just another tactic to get his way."

"Greg! Don't talk like that."

"It's true. I've been watching and listening, and I even copied him for awhile. If he acts like Steve, it's because he wants you to let him come back. Set up hoops for him to jump through and see if he goes back to his nasty ways."

"You have a point," Mom said. "But *you* changed, and Dad can, too."

Chapter 20

Yvette entered the dates Lucy had calved and been bred into their laptop computer, then copied her due date onto the barn calendar. "So we should stop milking her October 14th," she said aloud as she wrote *dry Lucy* on the matching square. "That's a little over a month from now! I've *got* to devote more time to dairy records." She stopped for a bite of chicken-fried rice. She'd been falling asleep over bookkeeping after supper, and was trying to catch up during her half hour lunch break. Did she dare take an *hour* for lunch? *I have to try it.*

A knock at the door interrupted her. Ruth and William Yoder, a retired couple from church, greeted her with friendly smiles. With their tall, big-boned frames and oval faces, they could have passed for brother and sister. Ruth was one of the few women at church who still wore a white, net veiling and a dress. Often sporting a twinkle in his blue eyes, William seemed to be the fun-loving type. Yvette invited them in and led them to the living room, wondering why this couple she barely knew had come to call.

Yvette waited until they sat on the couch, then perched on the edge of the stuffed rocking chair. After pleasantries about the weather, Ruth cleared her throat. "Luke hasn't been at church lately, and we wanted to tell him we miss him. Sunday School isn't the same without his thoughtful comments."

"You see," William ran his huge hand over his shiny bald head," when I was his age, I got fed up with church and quit going for several years. If someone had made a friendly overture, I may have gone back sooner."

Wishing they'd leave, but wanting neither to explain nor be rude to this caring couple, Yvette aimed for graciousness. "I'll tell him you stopped by."

"I'd rather talk to him," William said. "When will he be home?"

"I'm not sure."

"You have a nice house," Ruth ventured, looking around. "Your plants look so healthy. I suppose Luke grew up here? I don't remember his folks."

"No, this farm belonged to my parents, Ben and Clara Kinsinger. Luke's folks lived closer to Iowa City. They moved to Illinois ten years ago. Did both of you grow up around here?"

That sidetracked William for awhile, but he soon came back to Luke. "I suppose Luke will be back this afternoon or evening sometime?"

Yvette hesitated. She couldn't lie, but she could avoid telling him Luke wasn't coming back for several months. "I don't know when to expect him." *That's the truth.* She stood up, hoping they'd follow suit and leave.

"I don't want to pry," William rose, "but I'm concerned about his spiritual welfare. Could you tell us why he hasn't been at church?"

Please, not that question. If she evaded it, they'd stop in again. Maybe they'd be satisfied with the partial truth. "He's attending church in Coralville."

"But why?"

Apparently she couldn't avoid the issue. Yvette drew a deep breath. "I asked him to attend another church for awhile."

They stared at her, openmouthed. William found his voice first. "*You told him to go to another church?* I've never *heard* of anything so outrageous," he slowly lowered himself to the couch. "You better explain."

Yvette ran her finger across the laptop touch pad. *If I don't tell them, they'll assume* I'm *at fault.* "It's hard to talk about," she gripped the back of her office chair for support. "Luke's been abusive; I'm afraid of him, and so is Tanya. The boys shouldn't have to be home all the time to protect us. So I asked him to leave and get help to deal with his issues."

"That's ridiculous," William blurted out. "Luke's one of the kindest men I know. He'd never abuse his family."

"There's another side to Luke," Yvette outlined what had happened.

"You must be exaggerating," William frowned. "I can't imagine Luke acting like that. I was on his crew when we went to Georgia, and was impressed by his effective, yet considerate leadership. He's one of the most respected men in the community, and a story like that could ruin his reputation."

"I'm not exaggerating. If anything, I'm *understating* his behavior."

"Then you provoked him. Luke wouldn't act like that otherwise."

"Even if he was awful," Ruth spoke up, "couldn't you forgive him? We all behave in sinful ways at times, and need the forgiveness of others."

"I've been forgiving him for years, but forgiveness isn't the solution when the person never repents and isn't sorry. He's been getting nastier every year, partly because he hasn't had to suffer any consequences for his behavior. Luke needs to be held accountable so he *chooses* to stop abusing."

"'Perfect love casts out fear'," Ruth said. "If you had perfect love, you wouldn't be afraid of him. I'll pray that you develop a deeper love for Luke."

"I appreciate that, but isn't it reasonable to be afraid of a dog that growls and bites you, or a bear that mauls you? I don't know what that passage is referring to, but I doubt it's verbal or physical assault."

"Well, we aren't here to take sides," William said. "But don't you think asking him to leave and stop attending his church was going too far?"

"I could have reported him to the police. Then he'd go to jail, owe fines and court costs, and be forced to stay away from me and the children. Would you like to see pictures of the bruises he made on my arms?"

"No, no," William shook his head, "that's not necessary. But making a man leave his home seems extreme to me. Are you getting a divorce?"

"No. I'm hoping Luke will take a look at his behavior and decide to stop it and be loving instead. But if he doesn't choose to change, I can't let him keep abusing me and the children. It isn't healthy for any of us."

"Splitting up the family isn't healthy," Ruth said. "Children need their dad. Luke's getting upset once or twice is *not* enough to make him move out."

"He got upset much more than twice," Yvette said dryly.

"Even if he shook you every day," William's steel-blue gaze held hers, "that's not good enough cause to split up the family. You married for better or for worse, and should honor your vows before God and man. I realize splitting up families is encouraged in today's culture, but it's not biblical. As Christians, we're to live by *God's* standards. Is Val aware you made Luke leave?"

"Yes."

William frowned. "I'll speak to him about taking disciplinary action."

"Look, I have a farm to run," Yvette went to the door and opened it.

William and Ruth rose, and with a last critical look around, sauntered to the door. "I hope you don't expect the church to get your crops in," William said when they stepped onto the porch. "That would be the same as condoning what you did. You'd be wise to apologize to Luke and stop provoking him."

Yvette shut the door and locked it. *What a nightmare!* She sank onto her chair in front of the roll-top desk. Picking up the barn calendar, she tried to focus on what she'd written, but couldn't because it was shaking.

That visit cast a pall on the rest of the day, and Yvette made annoying mistakes as her thoughts kept returning to what Ruth and William had said. She entered Marian's information in Marjorie's file, burned her dinner because she got sidetracked reading about abuse in a book from Delores, which also made her late gathering the eggs so there were a lot of broken ones, which made straw stick to the goo or dried egg yolk on the other eggs in the nest.

~   ~   ~

Kyle sat on the school bus fighting sleep. *I'm almost home; I have to stay awake so I won't miss my stop.* His eyelids drooped, reminding him how tired he was and how little sleep he'd been getting lately. Was he wrong to keep his sleepless nights a secret from Mom? He didn't want to worry her, and didn't know what she could do about it. But it would be a relief to tell somebody.

Saturday he'd almost fallen asleep while driving tractor. And when he did sleep he had bad dreams—dreams of being upset because Dad, with a suitcase in his hand, was walking away and laughing at him. In one of the dreams Dad had sneered, "I never wanted you anyway." After a dream like that, he couldn't go back to sleep, and worried it was how Dad actually felt.

Why couldn't Dad be like Steve? And why did Greg choose to be a bully? Was life ever going to get better? Would he ever get to paint on a weekday again? Would he *ever* stop being tired?

The bus stopped at Lester's; Kyle scooted forward on his seat to put on his backpack. When he stood up for his stop, Greg brushed by and smacked him on the back of the head. "Ouch!" he said under his breath so neither Greg nor the driver would hear.

Things weren't much better in the house. "I hate to take your free time," Mom said when he entered the kitchen, "but I just realized we're out of potatoes. Have a quick snack and change your clothes, then we'll all dig a row of potatoes before chore time. You, too, Tanya," she tousled Tanya's hair. "Grandma said she'd help. Kyle, you get the cart, Greg get both potato forks, and Tanya and I will get buckets. We can talk in the garden."

To escape being hassled by Greg, Kyle wolfed down a graham cracker, scrambled into chore clothes and rushed outside. When he arrived in the potato patch with the cart, Grandma was already there.

"How are things going?" Clara squatted to pull a weed. "I mean since Dad isn't here."

"Terrible. Greg's a jerk, especially to Tanya, and is almost failing school. Mom works hard all day long. Tanya's pitching in more, but complains about having to work work work, and I just work and work, too."

"You look tired. Are you getting enough sleep?"

"I can't sleep at night. Don't tell Mom; I don't want her to worry."

"You can't sleep at all?" her brows furrowed.

"I eventually go to sleep, but I wake up and can't go back to sleep."

"What do you think about when you can't sleep?"

"Dad. I think about him living in that motel room. I feel sorry for him, but think he deserved it too."

"You miss him."

"No," he shook his head. "How could I miss him jerking us around?"

"No matter what he does, you still love him." Her tender eyes and soft voice made him want to cry. "And you're scared of what will happen next."

He nodded, afraid if he said anything he'd start crying.

"Would it help if you talked to him on the phone?"

"It might," he croaked.

"I'll talk to your mom about it. Here come the rest. I'll dig the first shift," she called. She took the potato forks from Greg and handed one to Kyle.

"Where do I start?" Kyle frowned.

"A foot from where the dried stems come out of the ground," his mom said. "Don't start too close to the plant or you'll slice into the potatoes."

"What a dingbat," Greg jeered. "Even a retard would know that."

"Greg, stop it." Mom sounded tired, Kyle thought. "We all feel over-worked and scared, but we can still choose to be kind."

"That's easy for you to say; you got what you wanted."

"What do you mean?" Mom bent to pick up the potatoes Grandma dug up. Tanya squatted to help her.

"It's your fault Dad got so mad. You never wanted to do what he said and you planned all along to drive him away, didn't you?"

"Don't be ridiculous, Greg," Kyle dug up a big fat potato. "Surely you remember all the times Mom urged us to do what Dad wanted so he wouldn't be upset. If anything, *Dad* acted like he wanted to drive *Mom* out."

"Dad's behavior drove all of us away from him," Mom blinked rapidly and Kyle realized she was trying not to cry. "When you act nasty, nobody will want to be around you, either. You're hurting yourself with behavior like that."

"Hey," Kyle said, "I ought to take pictures of us digging potatoes. It would make an interesting painting. Norman Rockwell took lots of pictures from various angles to help get his paintings just right. Can I get my camera?"

"Yes," his mom said, "if you hurry. Run and come right back."

He ran hard and raced back. "Wait, Tanya," he panted. "Balance that bucket on the edge of the cart and wait 'til I'm ready. When I give the signal, dump the potatoes in the cart real slow." He took more snapshots, making sure he got some with large potatoes on the ground and someone picking them up.

"Come on, Kyle," Greg glared at him, "you're just trying to get out of work. What if we all got our cameras and snapped a bunch of pictures?"

"Well," Kyle grinned at Greg, "I snapped enough for everybody."

"Actually," Mom leaned on the potato fork, "not all families have a big garden like this. And someday we may look back with fondness on our family times of digging potatoes, planting and weeding."

"Greg, you sound like you're having a rough time," Grandma's caring tone brought tears to Kyle's eyes. "Is there anything I can do to help?"

"There's nothing you can do," Greg burst out. "Dad's gone, and that's that. Mom drove him away and there's nothing anyone can do."

"What would you like to have happen?" Grandma asked.

"I want Dad to come home. Mom could call him and apologize."

"What did you think I should apologize about, Greg?"

"For not being submissive. That's what made him so mad."

"I think he got mad because I was *too* submissive. I tried very hard to do what he wanted and he kept finding more things to get upset about. Have you noticed how messy my room is upstairs? That's the real me. Maybe I shouldn't tell you all that, but you deserve an explanation."

"Is Dad going to come back?" Tanya asked.

"I don't know. If he keeps being mad and blaming me, I can't let him come home. But if he says he's sorry for what he's done, I have to decide if he means it and will be kind. Does this mean you all want to talk to Dad? Kyle?"

Kyle frowned. "Not if he's going to be nasty.

"Tanya? Do you want to talk to Dad on the phone?"

"No," she bounced her curls.

"I want to talk to him," Greg announced, "in person."

"Luke called me last week," Grandma began. "He's sorry he's been horrid to you all, and says he'd get what he deserves if you never forgive him. He misses you and hopes someone will call him so he can tell you he's sorry. He said I could tell you when I thought you were ready to hear it."

"Who did he want to talk to?" Greg asked.

"All of you. Between the challenges he's getting from the men's group and the pastor, he's rethinking the beliefs he thought he got from the Bible."

"I'm going to call him," Greg stomped his potato fork into the ground and started for the house.

"Greg," Yvette called after him. "wait until after the chores are done."

By the time they stopped digging potatoes and went out to chore, Kyle's doubts dwindled. He fed and checked the sows, who were due to farrow in a month, and was reminded of Dad, who usually had that chore. He hurried to the house and tried calling Dad, but there was no answer.

After they milked the cows and fed the calves, Kyle rushed through the cleanup. He sprayed the buckets with a single pass of the water hose, then placed them upside-down on the double bars that served as a bucket-rack.

"Mom, the buckets still have milk in them," Tanya tattled.

"Do it right, Kyle," Yvette dumped a scoop of powdered soap into the pipeline washtub. "I don't want the calves to get sick and die."

"I want to be *done*," he hissed as he jerked the buckets down again.

"You in a hurry to talk to Dad?"

"I guess," he mumbled, not wanting to hurt Mom's feelings.

"Why don't you help Greg throw down hay to the heifers? Tanya and I will finish here. Then you can both call Dad. We'll race and see who gets in the house first, the girls or the boys. Be sure you do it right, though," she called before the door slammed shut behind him.

Kyle shimmied up the ladder to the hay mow, nearly missing a rung in his haste. Scrambling up the hay-bale steps, he panted as he neared the peak.

"What are you doing up here?" Greg scowled.

"I came up to help. We're supposed to try to beat Mom and Tanya to the house. How many bales do you have to throw down yet?"

"Two, plus this one. You can do that one," Greg pointed to the other side of the mow and tossed the sections of his bale down the hayrack.

Kyle dashed toward the bale, sunk to his knee in a crack between four bales and nearly fell down. He pulled out of the hole and continued toward the bale, taking long strides to step squarely on the center of each bale. He tore one twine off, and dumped the bale down the rack as he jerked the other twine off.

"Hey," Greg objected. "you're supposed to spread it out so they don't crowd and hurt each other."

"I don't care," Kyle half slid down the bale-steps. "Grandma said Dad's sorry and I want to call him. Maybe he wants to come back."

"I don't know that I want him back if he's going to be wimpy."

They rushed to the house, and slammed into the washroom.

"We beat you," Tanya crowed, taking off her coat.

"So what, Twerp," Greg pulled her bangs. "We were working."

"Greg," Yvette washed her hands, "you will wash the dishes tonight. Name-calling and hair-pulling are unacceptable. Tell Tanya you're sorry."

"Sorry, Brat," he threw over his shoulder as he hung up his coat.

Yvette reached for the roller-towel, "Would you like to miss supper?"

"Now *that* would be abuse. You can't starve your laborer."

"Greg, cut it out," Kyle snapped as he soaped his hands. "Apologize and stop ruining our chances of talking to Dad tonight."

Startled, Greg flicked a glance at Kyle, then opened his mouth.

"Don't even think of it," Kyle warned before Greg could say a word. "I'm in the mood to knock your teeth out." *Wow! It felt good to say that!*

"Boys!" Yvette scolded. "What is going on with you? Greg apologize decently or you won't get supper, and Kyle, stop that violent talk."

"Sorry," Greg mumbled.

"What was that?" Mom prompted.

"Sorry!" Greg blared.

"Can we call Dad now?" Kyle rinsed the soap off his hands, hoping Greg's attitude hadn't ruined their chances of calling Dad.

"Do you expect me to reward poor conduct? *If* you all behave, you can call him after supper and cleanup."

~   ~   ~

Scowling, Luke stormed out of the Department of Corrections building, jerked open his pickup door, threw himself onto the seat, and slammed the door. Drumming his fingers on the steering wheel, he waited until Alex hoisted himself onto the passenger seat before he vented his anger. "Those facilitators are man-haters! I can see why what's-her-name would claim men are privileged, but that man is a blasted turncoat. I never dreamt he'd feed us such a line." He turned the key, and tore out of the parking lot. "This is only our fourth week of this ridiculous group; how on earth are we to endure twelve more? The other men in the group are *wife beaters*, for goodness sake, I don't belong here. Those facilitators make me so mad; they say *I* used economic abuse and intimidation, but *she* has the right to protect herself. Don't *I* have the right to protect *myself?* I want to quit this group and get a divorce. The wife can pay me my half and I'll buy a farm in Canada."

"What will happen to your kids if you move to Canada?"

"They don't want me around anyway. They liked it better when I was in Georgia. It's time I take care of myself and do what *I* want for a change. I don't need to hear those facilitators preach more of that garbage."

"I thought their statements were far-out, too," Alex grabbed for the dash as Luke went around a curve too fast, "but aren't you over-reacting?"

"No. I'm fed up. I'm done jumping through Yvette's hoops."

"If you don't finish the sixteen weeks, Yvette said she'd report you to the police. Besides, my attorney says Janet probably won't have to pay me my half of the house until Jody turns eighteen, and I have to pay child support, too. Divorce looks rotten financially. In your case, you'd have to wait until Tanya is eighteen before you get anything from the farm. You'd be stuck as a mechanic for years, and you'd have to pay child support out of that."

"I'll just disappear, then," Luke hated how the conversation was going and said the first thing to pop into his head to get Alex to stop.

"Not if you want to get your half of the farm. I bet you can't buy a farm in Canada with no money down. You'd end up being the hired hand."

"What do you advise? That I eat dirt like the wimps in that group?"

"Look, you're fortunate to have choices. Janet doesn't give me any; she's already filed for divorce and I can't do anything about it because of that *stupid no contact* order. You have options. If you wait to file for divorce until Tanya is almost eighteen, Yvette will have to buy you out right away and you won't have to pay child support."

"That's eleven years! I can't suck up to Yvette that long," Luke braked hard for a stop sign. "That's a prison sentence."

"You'd get to farm and wouldn't have to be a mechanic. Just stay away from Yvette, shut your mouth when you're around her, and have fun. "Say," Alex sat up, "I heard about a man who played his cards right. He got his settlement right away, and doesn't pay child support."

"How'd he accomplish that?" Luke perked up.

"He took the kids with him, so *she* had to pay child support and couldn't keep the house. They sold the house and he got his half at once."

"I don't want the kids around all the time."

"Get the kids to take care of the house and themselves so you can do your own thing. You can live wherever you want, get child support checks from Yvette, and have a tax write off. You'd be on easy street."

"Yeah, right. *She* has Kyle and Tanya tied to her apron strings and Greg told me if we split up he's staying with Mom. They won't live with me."

"They will if you win them over. Just finish this class, suck up to your wife so she'll let you move home, and do fun stuff with the kids. Take them out for ice cream cones, give them gifts, tell them they don't have to work—anything to get them to like you better than her."

"I don't have time to do all that."

"Sure you do. Take them swimming or to the park, and let them do what they want while you flirt with the most attractive women there. Afterward, treat the kids to ice cream. It's easy, and it would be the perfect revenge."

"What do you mean by revenge? I'd be giving Yvette the easy part while I take on more responsibility. That's the stuff I've refused to do."

"How do you think she'd feel if you took the kids away from her and she only got to see them every other weekend? On top of that, she'd have to pay you a settlement plus child support. She could lose the farm."

"I'd hate dealing with the kids every day, and it wouldn't be good for them. I admit she's a better parent than I am. Why don't you try it?"

"I think I will. I bet Janet will stop divorce proceedings if I suck up to her. If she won't stay home for Jody and me, she can pay *me* to do the job."

Luke grabbed the chance for payback. "That's one of the points on the violence wheel—using the children to harass her. Don't you care about Jody?"

"It's *Janet* who doesn't care about Jody. All *she* wants is a career."

"Why can't she have a career? You do."

"*Her* job is to take care of us; *mine* is to bring in the money."

"What if Janet disagrees?" As they waited for the light to change, Luke turned his head so Alex couldn't see his grin. Baiting him was *fun.*

Alex thumped his leg. "Then she's a *feminist pig.*"

179

"This isn't about her not having a career. It's about you thinking you have the right to call the shots because you're the man. It's *male privilege*."

"Whose side are you on anyway?"

Suddenly Luke realized the viewpoint he'd been pretending to hold was the correct one. He *liked* Janet and Jody and would feel bad if Alex hurt them. "Yours. But shoving Janet against the wall and pinning her there while you scream in her face is *not* doing nothing like you told the group. You deserved to have her call the police. She'd be smart to *never* trust you."

"Who are you to talk?" Alex glared. "You shook Yvette and told the facilitators you didn't do controlling stuff. I'll bet you were screaming in her face, too. She should have reported you and not given you the easy way out."

"She deserved it," Luke turned into the motel parking lot and pulled up to their door. "But you're right," he cut the engine. "If I don't change my act, Yvette won't take me back and I'll lose the farm."

~   ~   ~

At the farm, the family sat at the table and Kyle peeked at Tanya as she said grace. When Tanya finished, Mom pushed the pot of soup on its hot-pad toward Greg. He lifted the lid and looked inside. "Mushroom soup!" he frowned. "We had that last night. Can't you make anything else?"

"That's enough, Greg," Mom took two slices of kohlrabi and passed the plate. "Why don't you cook instead of relaxing before supper?"

"I'm tired of this. We haven't had dessert for months—ever since Dad left. This soup and meat and potatoes stuff is getting really old."

Kyle snorted. "You complain and exaggerate like Dad; he's only been gone five weeks."

"Greg, I said that's enough," Mom warned.

"No, it's not enough," Greg ladled three dippers of soup into his bowl. "I told you to make a cake last week, and we still don't have any."

"Who died and left you boss?" Mom raised her brows. "If you want it, make it. I have to catch up on bookkeeping."

"I don't know how to make a cake."

"It's time you learn. Choose a recipe from the file. You don't get to call Dad until you have the cake in the oven and the dishes washed."

"That's Tanya's job."

"You earned it by pulling her hair and calling her names, remember? Kyle, would you clear off the table and wipe it after we're done eating so I can bring the laptop out here and be on hand to give Greg directions?"

"Can I go play, Mom?" Tanya asked.

"After you finish eating."

"The *baby* gets to *play*," Greg screwed up his face.

"Behave yourself, Greg," Kyle said, "or we won't get to call Dad at all. Can I paint while Greg mixes the cake and washes dishes, Mom? I'd like to try those new oil paints you got me after Dad left. If I sell a painting, maybe Dad will let me paint more."

"If you set up out here, I don't see why not."

Kyle cleared and wiped the table, then got his painting supplies. As he spread newspaper under his table easel, he watched as Tanya helped Greg select a chocolate cake from the recipe file and broke eggs into the bowl for him.

"That's enough," Greg slapped her hand when she opened the flour canister. If you help any more I can't say I baked my own birthday cake."

"Your birthday!" Mom set the laptop and a report of the cows' monthly test results on the table. "I'm sorry, Greg. This week has been so hectic, I forgot. We'll have a little birthday party for you after the cake comes out of the oven. Tanya look in that first bottom drawer and see if we have candles."

Kyle squeezed a blob of red paint onto his palette and began to dab at it with a paint brush. "You're sweet sixteen now, Greg, and old enough to date. Maybe you'll impress Kathy if you bake her a cake."

"Oh, shut up. I'm no sissy."

"What if you don't get married?" using his full paintbrush Kyle tried various strokes on the canvass. "Will you think you're too manly to wash your own dishes and cook for yourself?"

"I'm going to get married." Greg stopped to glare at his brother.

"Who would marry you if you keep acting like a jerk?"

"Greg," Mom looked up, "if you don't get busy, you won't have time to call Dad. Tomorrow's a school day, so bedtime's in an hour and a half."

After Greg put his cake in the oven and finished washing dishes, Kyle sat in the armchair and dialed. Greg took the cordless and looked out the front door. "Dad," Kyle blurted when he heard Luke's hello. "It's me and Greg."

"It's so good to hear your voices," Kyle thought Dad sounded choked up. "How have you been? How are Mom and Tanya?"

"We're all okay," the butterflies in Kyle's stomach subsided. "We dug potatoes today. Grandma helped."

"Are the crops in?"

"Mom finished combining beans Monday. I stayed home from school three days this week to chop silage and fill the silo with late maturing corn."

"Why didn't Greg help?"

"His grades aren't too good."

"I was afraid that would happen. Look, Greg, I'm learning how to be a better father and husband. I'll be home soon. Hang in there and do the best you can. Try to get those grades up. Isn't basketball sign-up in a week or two?"

"What good will it do me? They don't want short players. I'm sixteen. I'll never be tall enough to get on a college team, let alone the NBA."

"That's right, today's your birthday. Happy Birthday, Greg! I hope you had a special day. Don't worry about your height. I didn't have my growth spurt until I was sixteen and a half. You could still end up taller than I am. Meanwhile, get your grades up and practice shooting baskets."

"When?" Greg sneered. "I have to do *your* work all the time."

"Things will settle down this winter. You'll see. Life will be better when I come home. Don't give up just because we're going through a rough spot. Keep practicing and doing your best. This, too, will pass."

"Right," Greg scoffed. "Having a wimpy dad makes things worse."

"We'll see. When I come back, you can play basketball with the guys when there's no practice at school, and Kyle can take art classes. This class I'm taking has challenged me to be respectful and supportive to my family."

"When are you coming home?" Kyle asked.

"I don't know. Mom and I need to work things out. I've neglected you boys, too, and I want to make it up to you. I should have played basketball with you, Greg, and taken an interest in your art, Kyle. Instead I was selfish and a bad example. I'm so sorry. Can you forgive me?

"Sure, Dad," Kyle said, "no problem."

"Thank-you, Kyle," Dad's voice choked up again. "Your forgiveness means a lot to me. It's late. I should let you go to bed."

"Will you come to church tomorrow?" Kyle cringed when church came out as a squeak.

"I've been going to church in Coralville. I'd love to see you, but Mom needs time to heal. When she's ready, I'll attend our church again."

"You didn't need to be so easy on him," Greg said as they hung up.

"What was I supposed to do, yell at him so he'd never come back?"

"You could delay forgiving him. He should pay for what he did."

"It's five after eight," Mom appeared in the kitchen door. "You have forty-five minutes until bedtime. I suggest you get to it, rather than stand there arguing. Tanya and I are making icing. Would either of you like to join us?"

"No, thanks," Kyle dashed past Greg toward the living room. "I get the recliner!" he yelled. Greg took off after him, grabbing his arm and trying to squeeze past him onto the recliner. Kyle wrenched his arm loose and threw himself on the recliner seconds before Greg plopped half on top of him and grabbed the remote control.

Chapter 21

"**I** don't know which one I like better, Yvette," Delores called, as she and Clara waited at the twin-sized quilt-in-frame in Yvette's room two months later. "Both the burgundy quilt-top on your bed and this pink one are beautiful."

Yvette brought a chair from Kyle's room and placed it opposite Delores at the side of the quilt. "I had fun playing with the color variations. I hoped to have these feather plume border designs quilted before you came so we could unroll a few more inches and wouldn't get in each other's way."

"I like doing feather plumes," Clara tucked a strand of hair behind her ear. "And since we started with a coffee cake break, I can't complain."

Delores chuckled as she threaded her needle. "Maybe we should *treat* our workers every morning. Look how fast we're moving now."

"Socializing motivates," Clara worked a knot through the top layer.

Enjoying the camaraderie, Yvette picked up the threaded needle she'd stuck in the quilt and began to quilt where she'd left off. Using her thimble, she drove the needle up and down through the layers until she had four tiny stitches on the needle, then pulled it through. Down and up four times, then pull; down and up four times, pull, the monotony of the task freed her mind to think. She half listened to their chatter as her mind went back to her confusion about Luke. Had he really changed? Why did she feel incapable of embracing the new Luke? Should she force herself to take him back? Or should she follow her gut and avoid him? At an impasse with herself, she decided to wait until Delores and Clara seemed ready to talk about serious things.

"Why are you so quiet, Yvette?" Clara finally asked. "We've been chattering away, and you haven't said a word since you sat down."

"How are the meetings with Luke, you and the kids going?" Delores asked. "Is Val a good counselor? Has Luke pressured you to take him back? Did he excuse himself? Say 'I know I was a jerk, but'?"

"No. He asks the boys to tell him every awful thing he did to them. He listens and says 'that was emotional abuse' or 'I was using male privilege.' Then he apologizes, saying he's sorry he hurt them and betrayed their trust, and he'll make every effort to choose better behaviors in the future."

"That sounds genuine," Clara used her needle to knot a tail of thread.

"It may be genuine for now," Delores said, "but it's impossible to know if he will permanently stop his abusive behavior. Has he apologized to *you*?"

"In a general way; not for specific things. He thanked me for making him face himself. He hoped I could forgive him."

"What about Tanya?" Clara asked. "Has he made any effort with her and does she still avoid him? She's an astute young girl."

"She stays close to me, but doesn't hang onto my arm. She watches him as if she isn't sure he's trustworthy. He mostly focuses on the boys."

"How does he behave toward you?" Delores asked. "Oh, no, my thread knotted. And I was being so careful." She picked at the knot with her needle.

"Here," Yvette leaned over the quilt, "let me try. I'm good with knots." She worked the knot a few seconds. "There, it's gone."

"I don't have much patience for knots," Delores confessed.

"When your life is as knotty as mine, you develop patience. That's probably why I'm confused. I'm so used to dealing with knots, I don't know what's reasonable. After finding out I was responding to Luke the wrong way, I'm not sure how to treat him now. Should I give him the benefit of the doubt and welcome him with open arms, or do I need to keep on being the loving-but-firm spouse? And at what point am I crossing the line into unforgiveness?"

"As long as your attitude is to stop the abuse, not to get even, you aren't crossing the line," Clara said.

"Clara's right. There are verses in both the Old and New Testaments about how God hates oppression. Jesus, Himself, came to free the oppressed. One of the books I read says we each are to follow His example and do what we can to free others and ourselves from oppression."

"Well, thanks," Yvette blinked back tears. "That means so much to me. Sometimes I feel like the Wicked Witch of Kalona. Except for you two, I don't have support from the community, and feel more isolated than I did when Luke was here. If he had hit me, maybe folks would think I did the right thing. One couple came to visit Luke and ended up telling me if Luke shook me every day that wouldn't be a good enough reason to split up the family."

"You don't have to listen to them. They don't have a clue what Luke is like, and probably think you should stay together even if he's beating you."

"He *was* beating her," Clara extended her arms to start quilting another line. "He was beating her with his words and with the power he had over her.

She's been black and blue on the inside, but nobody can see that. *I* heard how he talked to her, and *I* hurt for her."

"You're absolutely right," Delores squeezed Yvette's hand on top of the quilt. "People need to know that just because a woman doesn't have bruises on the outside, doesn't mean he's not beating her. Wife beaters need to be held accountable. The way you are dealing with this, Yvette, is a positive example to every man and woman, and I, for one, applaud you."

"Thanks. I needed to hear that. Even the boys have been—difficult. Greg blames me, and Kyle was the one who was so desperate to talk to Luke."

"That's likely why he started with them," Delores returned to quilting. "Once they're in his pocket, *they'll* pressure you for him."

"I sensed that, too," Yvette sighed. "That's why I feel so confused and scared—and pressured, too. When we go to church, nobody says anything, but I read it in some of their faces. I didn't avoid separation and divorce at all costs, so I'm to blame. The boys pressure me to reconcile with Luke. They've been starving for his attention all their lives; he's giving it now, and they want more."

"How is Luke treating you?" Delores asked.

"He's been respectful; no put-downs or power-plays. He asked that we go out as a family after each counseling session, and I consented. But he invited me out for a date tonight, and I didn't answer him yet. What do you think?"

"It seems to me," Clara began slowly, "you have to spend time with him to find out if he has truly changed. He may be putting on an act. Luke can be a charming talker, but talking is not doing."

Yvette wrinkled up her nose. "I was afraid you'd say that."

"I don't think you should make yourself spend time alone with him if you aren't ready for it, though," Delores said. "Give yourself time to heal. Let him see the result of what he sowed. If you make restitution easy, he'll return to his old ways. Maybe you should start with group outings, first."

"We did. As a family we went trail walking twice, ice skating at the Coral Ridge Rink once, to the Art Museum and to the Hoover Library Museum. Tonight he wants to take me to the Lone Star Steakhouse in Coralville."

"That sounds innocent enough," Delores said. "But you're right to pay attention to your intuition. What does it say?"

"I'm not sure. I think it might be that I can't believe the old Luke is gone forever and this stranger will take his place. I don't know what to expect from him. The change seems too good to be true."

"Your intuition says he's charming you into taking him back," Delores jarred the quilt frame as she straightened, causing Yvette to prick her finger. "Then, when you have no way to make him leave, he'll get nasty again. He knows you won't leave because of your contract with Clara."

"Is my intuition right?" Yvette dug a tissue from her pocket and dabbed at the blood beading from her finger.

"I have no way of knowing," Clara drove her needle up and down through the quilt, "but you'd best beware."

"Apparently Val doesn't think so. He's asked me several times what's holding me back. He pointed out Luke has apologized, has changed his beliefs about marital roles, and wants to make it up to me. I feel pressured to reconcile with Luke. I'm considering quitting counseling."

"That's not a bad idea," Delores threaded her needle. "I like Val, but he doesn't know much about abusive men. The success rate for rehabilitation is only fifty percent if even that, so your instincts are on target, Yvette. Abusers often con people into believing they have changed. At the women's shelter they recommend you make him prove himself *at least* nine months to a year before you take him back. Besides, it's easy for him to put on his best behavior now, since he doesn't have the daily irritations of family life to test his patience."

"That gives me an idea," Yvette giggled. "For the next family outing, he can help us milk cows. He never did handle that well."

"Good plan. You need to see him in action," Delores said. "Go horse-back riding or bowling. Pick activities he's not comfortable with."

"What about going to Chicago? Luke asked Tanya what she wants to do. She wants to go to that American Girl doll store in Chicago. Luke suggested we go for a weekend, but I'm concerned about the sleeping arrangements. A weekend feels like too much, at too close quarters, too soon."

"Another way to look at it," Clara said, "is that a trip to Chicago may be just what you need to see him in action. When Ben and I went, we commuted by train from our motel to the bus station and from there to the museums. The trains didn't run as often as we assumed they would, and we almost gave up on finding the place to get the bus special we'd heard about. We rushed from one clerk to the other, waiting in line after line to get our bus passes. Ben, my easy-going Ben, lost his patience until I reminded him the trip was about being together, not about getting to as many places as possible. Chicago is the perfect testing ground for Luke's act."

"But if I spend much time with Luke, he could sweep me off my feet. I don't want to take him back just because he charms his way into my emotions or relieves our workload. I want it to be a well thought-out decision. *After* I decide he's safe and reasonable, *then* he can win me emotionally, but not before."

"You both make good points," Delores said. "This reminds me of the boy I dated before I met Steve. My mom said I could only date him in a group. It was good advice. I saw how he treated my girlfriend and the waitress, and decided I wanted a better husband than that."

"You think the family would provide enough protection?"

"Why not? You won't likely go through the museums five abreast. Just latch onto Kyle or Tanya, or even Greg so Luke can't make it a twosome."

"I suppose you're right," Yvette sighed, dreading the trip. "But I'll need someone to do our chores. Would you and Steve chore for us, Delores?"

"Sure. I'll ask Steve, but I think he'll consent to it."

"I need to know soon. Luke wants to discuss the trip tonight. And thanks—both of you. You've helped clear the confusion and I don't feel like I'm blindly riding the waves in a storm anymore."

"We're glad to help," Clara slipped an arm around Yvette's shoulders.

Delores squeezed her hand. "Keep listening to your gut instincts. If you spend time with him, don't be quick to give him the benefit of the doubt."

They stopped for dinner, then went on to talk about other things, like the perfect weather and the fact that, like most farmers, Yvette had finished harvesting corn and beans. Now she could quilt and catch up with bookkeeping. Clara planned to reduce her time working for families so she could help Yvette at least one day a week, and Delores volunteered more hours at the women's shelter during the greenhouse's slack season.

Her confidants left an hour before the children were due home from school. Yvette left a message accepting Luke's invitation to eat out, then baked an angel food cake for the children.

~   ~   ~

That night she met Luke at the Lone Star, a restaurant featuring country western food, music, and décor that included a rustic wood floor. He had suggested the place, hoping they'd get to see the serving staff dance in the aisles.

"We timed it perfectly," Luke opened his menu. "They do line dances when there's a crowd. How's it going on the farm?"

"Okay," she wished she hadn't agreed to the date. "Got the pullets into the hen house and took six steers to market."

"Did you keep any year-old hens?"

"I culled out fifty to keep, butchered twenty-five, and sold the rest."

"I'm thankful I can trust my wife's judgment. I used to act like I couldn't, because I wanted you to feel stupid. But *I* was the stupid one."

Yvette bunched her napkin in her lap. *What am I supposed to say? Yeah, you were the stupid one? or No, I was the stupid one? or I wouldn't call it stupid exactly?* "I don't know what to say."

"Then don't say anything. I was the schmuck. You were wise to make me take the Batterer's Education Program. Mark and Donna, the facilitators, challenged me to examine my beliefs. Who says I'm not a *man* unless I make you do what you don't want to do? I thought I was doing it because God said

187

I'm to be in charge, but Val straightened me out on that, too. I'm to lead in *serving*, not in demanding. It's hard to be as concerned about others as I am about myself, but I'm learning. You're not talking much. What's up?"

"I was listening."

"No, really. I want to know what you're thinking. Ever since we started the counseling you haven't said much. What's going on in your head?"

"Could we order first? The waitress will come any time for our order, and I haven't even looked at the menu."

"You're right. I meet a pretty woman at a restaurant and forget to eat."

His flattery was wearing thin, but she kept that to herself. If she told him she wasn't impressed, he'd try to win her favor another way.

They ordered, and Yvette told the waitress to bill hers separately.

"Why did you do that?" Luke frowned when the waitress had gone. "You're not giving me a chance to make it up to you."

"I'm here," she controlled her irritation. "Shall I leave?"

"You know I didn't mean that. This will be harder than I imagined. I hoped you'd see I've really changed and you'd let me make it up to you for the next seventeen years. One year for each year of our marriage."

"And after that?" not wanting to look at him, she gazed around the room, noting the square posts spaced at intervals between the booths.

"I don't know," he retrieved a peanut shell someone had missed from behind the dessert advertisement and pushed it around on the table with his fore-finger. "After that, maybe I'd feel more on equal terms with you."

"What does that mean?" she watched him move the peanut shell.

"That did sound bad, didn't it?" he flashed her a sheepish grin. "I meant right now I feel I should do things your way to make it up to you."

"I don't expect that, and I certainly didn't ask for it," she snapped, then blushed, afraid her retort revealed too much. She hoped he wouldn't guess she was trying hard to resist his charming smile. She had forgotten how good-looking and endearing he was when he smiled in that self-effacing way. For months all she'd seen was his ugly nastiness.

"I said that's how I *feel*. I'm sorry for all the times I griped at you and didn't respect you. I'm especially sorry for the time I shook you and then scared you and the children. I know I don't deserve your trust, but I still want it."

"That makes sense, but maybe you need to look at this from my view-point. For seventeen years you treat me nice for awhile, then you chew me out or put me down during the day, and use me at night. Now you say you're a changed man, and I'm supposed to believe you're totally different after a month of hearing you go on and on about how sorry you are. You don't pressure me in so many words, but by your actions you're still trying to *make* me forgive you and trust you. I don't think you've changed as much as you say you have. And you still gripe at me for the decisions I make."

His eyes widened. "When did I gripe at you?"

"You frown when I pay for my meal and complain that I don't let you pick me up," she blurted, then regretted divulging that information.

He stopped pushing the peanut shell and stared at her. "You know," he bit his lip, "I hate to admit it, but you're absolutely right. The facilitator warned it will take awhile to get it right, and now I see what he means. I'm sorry. I'll try to do better. Could we—I'd like to plan our trip to Chicago if that's okay. It's my fault we didn't get a vacation this summer, and I hoped a weekend in Chicago would make up for it. Oh good, here's the appetizer you ordered," he leaned back as the waitress set a huge batter-dipped onion, cut open to resemble a rose, on the table. "Smells good. Is this just for you or to share?"

"Do I look like a pig?" she laughed, pulling off a three-pronged section. "Dig in," she broke off a spear. "Mmm, scrumptious. It's spicy; you'll love it."

"That's the first time I heard you laugh with me in ages," he watched her face. "I used to get jealous when you laughed with Delores or your mom. But it was my own fault. I was like a bucket of ice-cold water on your spirit."

She dipped her head in acknowledgment. "That's a good description. Go ahead, have some," she pushed the plate toward him, wishing he would stop reminding her of his abusive behaviors. Didn't he hear her say his constant apologies and references to how he used to be felt like pressure to her?

He pulled off a section of onion. "I used to excuse my actions by telling myself you weren't any fun. Now I suspect if I stop acting like Mussolini, as you called me once, you could become the laughing carefree spirit you were before I married you. What a dimwit I've been."

"You know," she waited until his eyes met hers, "if you keep bashing yourself as much as you used to bash me, you'll fine-tune those bashing skills."

"You have a good point. But this time I'm laughing at my arrogant self and discovering more reasons to quit being such a dictator."

"Well, in that case, please continue with the verbal self-clobbering."

"I didn't mean—" he stopped. "You know very well what I meant. What a wicked sense of humor you have."

"Look," Yvette cocked her head toward the walkway behind him, "they're gathering in the aisles to dance."

They watched the uniformed men and women line dance between the tables. Neither of them knew the country-western number, but they enjoyed watching the coordinated dancing.

"Anyway," Yvette began when the song ended and the staff returned to their tasks, "do you want to go to Chicago? Where will we sleep?"

189

"We'll get two adjoining rooms, and sleep boys in one room, girls in the other. You and Tanya can come to our room any time you choose."

"I was afraid you'd insist we all stay in the same room." She changed the subject. "How's Alex doing? Is the class influencing him to change?"

"He *sounds* like he's changing, but it might not be the real thing."

"Why do you say that?" She wished he'd quit hedging.

"If I tell you, you'll end up with another reason to not trust me."

"Not telling will give me reason to not trust you, too. I'll imagine you're plotting all sorts of evil. If you tell me, it will narrow it down to one."

"Good point. Don't forget, *Alex* said he'd do it. Not me. He talked about playing his cards right and making Janet believe he has changed. When she lets him move home, he'll win Jody over, until Jody prefers him to her mother. Then he'll leave and take Jody with him."

"Why take Jody away from Janet? He doesn't want to care for Jody."

"So he won't have to pay child support or wait for his settlement."

So they had *talked about their options, and Luke decided returning home was the better plan. Be very cautious, Yvette.* "That's ridiculous. He'll have to support her if she's living with him or not."

"He's mad at Janet for pursuing a career, and he wants revenge."

A second flag went up. "Is his plan working?" with an effort she tried to sound nonchalant and curious instead of suspicious.

"Not yet. Janet filed for divorce and won't talk to him. He says he feels terrible about it because he loves her and is so sorry."

"Sorry for what?" she snorted. "For getting kicked out?"

"Sorry for mistreating her. He says he's been a heel. He started going to church with me. By the way, do you mind if I attend our church again?"

"Suit yourself," she shrugged, glad he hadn't noticed her suspicion. "But I'll sit with the choir and go to that Bible study class I like."

"Will you ever sit with me in church again?"

"Who knows?" she shut her mouth lest she disclose anything revealing. But when her stomach knotted up she realized Luke often used her silence to get his way, too. He'd talk as if her inner resistance wasn't there, as if how he wanted things was how they actually were, and she'd feel too pressured by his seeming goodwill and embarrassed by her own presumed pettiness to resist him. She wouldn't let him snowball her this time. "Maybe you should sit with the children so you can charm them away from me," she suggested.

"See," he rolled his eyes, "I shouldn't have told you."

"Are intending to charm the children away from me?"

"Absolutely not. Children need both parents."

Chapter 22

Greg raced Kyle to the house after they finished the evening chores, white puff-clouds coming from his mouth with each breath as he fought to pass Kyle.

"I beat!" Kyle crashed against the door and fumbled to open it.

"No fair," Greg plowed into Kyle and tried to shove him aside, "you have longer legs and I slipped on ice."

"That's never stopped you from winning before," Kyle dashed into the house and Greg lunged after him, grabbing at his arm and the back of his coat.

"Wait for me," Tanya wailed, but Greg ignored her. *I have to beat Kyle.* Ever since they'd contacted Dad again and Dad spent hours looking at Kyle's drawings and paintings, checked the internet for art schools, and suggested how Kyle could sell his work, Kyle had gotten a big head. Now he'd bested Greg in a race. The whole state of affairs had become intolerable.

As Kyle plowed ahead, pulling Greg up the two steps and into the washroom with him, Greg tried to brace his feet on each stair, but to no avail. He was pulled into the washroom and ended up with Kyle's coat in his hands. Dropping the coat on the floor, he kicked off his boots, unzipped his own coat and shrugged it off then slammed sideways against Kyle as he splashed water on his face at the sink. Kyle dried his hands and face and dashed through a corner of the kitchen and into the dining room before Greg could catch up with him.

Greg charged through the other door directly into the dining room, overturned a dining chair as he shot past, and swept into the living room one step ahead of Kyle. "I beat," he panted, "I got to the living room first."

"Who cares? I want to see if Dad brought our Christmas presents while we were choring. Take off your boots, Tanya," Kyle rushed toward her to stop her from tracking across the powder blue dining room carpet.

Greg surveyed the gifts wrapped in green, red, and blue paper under the lighted tree. "The presents are here, but where is Dad?"

"Don't you remember?" Kyle called from the washroom where he was kneeling on the floor taking off Tanya's boots. "On the way home from ice skating at the pond yesterday he told us he'd drop off our gifts while we're out choring, then take some gifts to Val and his family. He said if it weren't for Val's encouragement, he wouldn't have stuck with the Batterer's Education Program and our family wouldn't be reuniting."

"Oh, yeah," Greg looked at the name on the biggest present, a tall flat one standing on end between the tree and the wall. Kyle. It felt like a canvass. "I barely heard; I was cleaning the sticky marshmallow off my ice skates."

Kyle returned and hovered in the doorway. "Those s'mores makings Dad brought yesterday were a hit with the kids. Dad can be fun if he wants to. I used to wonder why Mom married him, but now I suspect he was fun like that when they were dating."

Greg didn't reply as he hunted for the label on the second largest gift. Kyle again. Another canvas. As far as he was concerned, Dad had been fun before Mom kicked him out. He'd enjoyed those times when Dad made fun of Kyle and when he'd explained a man's role was to take charge of his wife. He missed those sessions. Now when he made fun of Kyle, Dad told him to respect and encourage others.

"I *knew* he brought presents," Tanya dashed into the room and dropped to her knees in front of the tree, her eyes shining with excitement.

She'll probably get all kinds of expensive presents just like Kyle, Greg looked for the tag on the third large flat present. Maybe this one would be the cutout of Michael Jordan he'd asked for. *Kyle again*. Three *packages for Kyle. Dad must think he has me in his pocket, but he has to make it up to those two.*

"I wonder what he got me," Tanya picked up a large box wrapped in red and white striped paper. "Snap on the light so I can read the tag."

"Dad said to leave them alone," Kyle lingered in the doorway.

"He won't care if we look to see who they're for," Greg countered.

"Wait till Mom comes in," Kyle insisted. "We'll ask her."

"Don't be a goody-goody," Greg strode to the light switch and snapped it on. "He brought them early so we could look at them."

"This one's for me," Tanya set it aside. "Here are two huge ones for Kyle, and a big one for me. This one says *To my darling Yvette; all my love, Luke.* I can't move it."

"Aren't there any for me?" Greg asked.

"Here's one to Greg from Mom. Oh, here's one. It's so flat I almost didn't see it. The card says 'To Greg; from Dad.'" She handed it to him. "What do you think it is?"

One tiny present. He shook it next to his ear. "I can't hear a thing."

"Come on, you two," Kyle urged. "That's enough. Dad's been real good to us; let's not make him so mad he won't come home."

"He was *teasing* when he told us not to touch them. He *wants* to come home; it's Mom who won't let him. I bet he got American Girl stuff for Tanya when we were in Chicago, and those huge flat packages are canvasses for you, Kyle. I can't figure out what he got me. It's too tall to be a basketball card."

"Maybe it's something from one of the gift shops. Did you see anything that size at the Aquarium or the Planetarium? He wouldn't have gotten you something from the Art Institute or the American Girl Place." Greg hated the pity he heard in Kyle's voice.

"Here comes Mom," Tanya put the gifts back as the door opened.

Yvette slipped off her boots and padded to the living room. "Looks like having Dad gone has its benefits. You never had a Christmas with so many presents in your entire lives. I bet they're expensive ones, too."

"What do you think is in here?" Greg shook his flat present next to his mom's ear. "I can't figure out what it is."

"Well," she turned the package over as if pondering the question, "since it's all wrapped up, I'd guess," she grinned at him, "it's a secret."

He yanked the present from her hand, "You're no help at all."

"Okay, you've seen the presents, now let's get to work. Dad's coming in an hour and we have to eat and get the house in order before he gets here. No opening presents until things are picked up and dishes are done." She headed for the washroom. "Whoever knocked this chair over can pick it up." They trailed her to the washroom, Kyle righting the fallen chair on the way.

"Why don't you let Dad move back?" Greg jammed his coat over a hook. "He hasn't yelled at anybody since you kicked him out, not even once."

"Yeah," Kyle set his boots on the boot mat. "He took us to Chicago and made sure we all got to do something we liked. We even went out of our way so Greg could see that Chicagoland Sports Hall of Fame in Des Plaines. He listens to us and plays with us, but you won't let him come home. I want to see Dad *every* day, not just on Sundays. Even Tanya thinks that, don't you, Tanya?"

Tanya nodded. "Dad's not mean anymore. I wish he'd live here."

Yvette dried her hands and face and sighed as she went to the kitchen. "I understand how you feel," she took a stack of plates from the cupboard and set them next to the crock pot. "Unfortunately, it's not that easy. If I let him come home too early, he could go back to mistreating us. He'd be more likely to stop short of doing anything physical, so it would be impossible to make him leave. But I will consider what you've said, and see if Dad and I can resolve some of our disagreements. Don't get your hopes up, though."

"Thanks, Mom," Tanya squeezed her mom around the waist.

After supper, they washed the dishes and straightened the house, then retired to the living room to wait for Luke. Greg sat on the recliner and watched Tanya wriggle onto the stuffed chair, holding a Barbie doll. He saw Kyle's hand hover over the light switch until Yvette turned on the CD player. The overhead light went off, then Yvette and Kyle sat on the couch. "Behold, I show you a mystery," a man's voice sang as Greg gazed at the red, blue, green and yellow lights that blinked on and off, on and off.

"The tree is so beautiful," Tanya turned Barbie to look at the tree.

"What did you children decide to get Dad for Christmas?"

"The three of us decided to get him one of those florescent camping lanterns," Kyle began, "but-but..." he trailed off.

"The *artist* didn't have his share of the money," Greg snickered

"We were hoping it will be on sale after Christmas," Kyle said.

"Or the price may go up," Yvette sighed. "Well, it's too late to worry about that now. Hey, I have an idea, but I need your help. Here he comes," she added as headlights flashed across the wall. "Come here," she motioned them to come close. They scurried to her side and listened as she whispered her plan.

"Great idea," Kyle enthused.

"It's dumb," Greg scoffed, "it won't prove anything."

"Tanya?" Yvette prompted. "Hurry, he's coming up the walk."

Tanya frowned. "What if it hurts his feelings?"

"That's the point," Kyle hissed. "We want to see if he'll get mad."

"Well, okay," she acquiesced as Luke knocked on the front door.

"You'll work things out with him if he passes the test?" Kyle asked.

"I'll try," Yvette held out her hand, palm down.

"Put 'em here," Kyle placed his hand on hers and Tanya added hers. Greg hesitated, then with a shrug put his on top. "Go team!" Kyle cheered as they pulled back their hands.

In the living room later that night, Greg watched Kyle and Tanya fiddle with their gifts. Tanya played with Felicity, the American Girl doll Luke had given her. She hung the two doll dresses from Yvette in the wardrobe Luke had given, and put her in her new brass bed, then read her a bedtime story.

"You better wash her dishes and clear the table," Kyle teased, sitting Indian style on the floor as he arranged the new tubes of paint in the walnut-stained wooden box, both of which he'd gotten from Luke, "so they'll be ready for her to eat breakfast tomorrow morning."

"Yeah," Greg selected a basketball card from those he had spread around him on the couch and slipped it into the album on his lap, "you don't want her to get food poisoning."

"I already washed her tea things," Tanya turned a page. "At least she's prettier than those basketball cards Dad gave you."

"But my cards will be worth a lot of money."

"So," Tanya tossed her head, "you can't *do* anything with them but *look* at them. At least I can *play* with Felicity."

"Felicity-Prissity. What a stupid name. Only a dork would comb Miss Priss's hair and change her clothes all day. *I* got the good stuff. *I* get to go with Dad to see the Chicago Bulls," he waved the tickets in her face. "I'll have Dad to myself one whole day."

"Don't listen to the braggart," Kyle advised Tanya, getting up to stack the smaller canvasses on top of the larger ones. "Dad loves us just as much. He said he'd do special stuff with each of us, remember? He's planning a day of checking out the local art galleries with me. If you tell Dad what you'd like to do, he'll plan a day with you, too."

"Don't expect him to play with dolls."

"Stop it, Greg," Kyle warned.

"I was just teasing. She should be able to take a joke."

"Maybe so, but that wasn't a joke and she still won't want to be around you. You owe her an apology."

"All right, have it your way. Sorry, Tanya," he squinted his eyes and stretched his lips wide in a sarcastic smile. He felt a pang of guilt when he saw Tanya's face crumple as she caressed Felicity's hair and tucked the covers tightly around the doll, but he shrugged it off. "Are you satisfied, Kyle?"

"Sure. As you can tell, she's falling all over herself to shower you with affection. She's had a hard time dealing with Dad's nastiness, she doesn't need you to make it worse." Kyle lowered himself to the floor next to his box of oil paints. "Dad passed the test, didn't he?" he hugged his knees.

"I told you he's changed. I don't see why you thought he'd pout or get mad just because he didn't get a present from us. He didn't get mad in Chicago, not even when Tanya had to go to the bathroom and made us miss the train."

"I know. But Mom's still afraid he'll get nasty again. If he stays like this, I can stop watching how Steve Webster handles things."

"Even I can copy him now. He's no wimp. When we missed that train he said, 'Let's check out that sporting store we passed on the way over here.' Steve would have been wimpy and asked Delores what she wanted to do."

"Now that you mention it, that's why Mom's not sure. What would he have done if Mom didn't want to go to the sporting store?"

"Now you're nit picking," Greg rolled his eyes.

"Mom needs to know what he will do when things don't happen as he expects or when she disagrees with him. That's why our test was important."

"I think we hurt his feelings," Tanya arranged the dishes on Felicity's table. "He looked sad and disappointed."

"But he smiled when I told him we nearly had enough to buy his gift," Kyle said. "Do you think Mom will let him move home now?"

"She might let him stay tonight," Greg inserted another basketball card in his album. "That's probably what they're talking about in the kitchen."

"It'll take longer than that for them to work things out," Kyle said. "Remember that couple who separated? Mom told me it took them two years to get back together. And Gail's parents—remember the girl from church whose parents separated? She's a year older than me. They've been separated five years. Gail wishes her dad would shape up, but he's talking divorce."

What if Mom and Dad divorce? Greg couldn't stand the thought and put as much conviction into his voice as he could muster. "Mom and Dad won't get divorced. But I hope it won't take them two years to get back together. I'll be eighteen by then."

"And I'll be nearly sixteen. I hope he moves home in January, just in time for my birthday. That would be the best present ever."

"It's almost time for bed," Yvette came into the living room. "Dad has to leave soon. Why don't you all come out for hot chocolate before he goes?"

"When are we going to see him again?" Kyle closed and fastened the lid on his walnut paint box.

"Maybe Sunday, if you children want to drive to Illinois with him to see Grandma and Grandpa Miller and the cousins, that is."

"Aren't you going?" Greg set his card album on the couch.

"Not this year. I want to spend time with my mom and take it easy. That'll give you children time with Dad. Besides, someone has to stay home and chore. What do you think, Tanya? Do you want to go?"

"If Kyle goes, I'll go," she clambered to her feet.

"Kyle?"

"Of course I'm going. I haven't seen my cousins since New Year's."

"I wouldn't miss it," Greg said when she glanced at him. "I'll sit in the front with Dad so Kyle and Tanya can play baby games in the back seat."

"Come on," Yvette beckoned, "before your hot chocolate scorches."

"Did you and Dad work out your differences?" Greg asked as they headed for the kitchen. "Is he going to move home soon?"

"You'll have to wait and see like the rest of us," Yvette said.

Chapter 23

Luke tiptoed into the cow stable at five-thirty, well before sunrise. He stole behind Yvette, who had taken the cow calendar out of the cabinet over the wooden shelf and was turning pages and counting weeks.

"Don't forget to feed the heifers hay, Kyle," she said, "and spread it out this time so they don't hurt each other trying to get to it."

"What are you looking for?" Luke kept his voice just above a whisper.

"Luke!" she whirled around. "What brings *you* out here so early?"

"I wanted to be here when you tell the kids," he focused on her lips, wishing he could kiss her. "I wanted to be with my family. Alex is no piece of cake to live with."

"What's wrong with Alex?" she looked concerned.

"Janet refused to talk to him, Jody wouldn't see him during Christmas vacation, and school resumes today. He acts like a raging lunatic."

"You left him like that?" she looked at the calendar.

"He came home drunk last night, and passed out. He stinks, and I don't want to be around him. Maybe if I'm not there to pick up the pieces for him, he'll pull himself out of his irresponsible mode. What are you looking for? What can I do to help?"

"I'm checking to see if we have any cows due to calve, dry up, or get bred anytime soon. For a minute I thought I recorded the dates wrong."

"What do you want me to do?"

She looked up, her brows raised. "I'm glad to have another pair of hands; it was four below out here this morning. Something's wrong with the heating element in the watering tank between the cow and calf lots; the water in the tank is frozen solid. Somebody will have to start a fire under the tank and check the rest of the waterers. Would you rather do that, or keep two milkers going? Greg went to check the waterer in the shed to make sure that one's working. He's supposed to run the two milkers on the north end. I decided to have him work in the cow stable so he won't get a chance to pick on Tanya and will hopefully develop better character."

"That sounds like a good solution. With your creative thinking and wisdom, hopefully we can repair the damage I did to him and stop his tendency to nastiness," he looked at the cows with milkers on. All four had large, well-rounded udders. "You're milking the ones at this end, I presume?"

"Yes. Both cows get lank-looking udders when they're done."

"I'll milk the cows. That will give me a chance to talk to Greg."

Her finger stopped on one of the calendar squares. "Ramona is due to calve any day now. You or Greg can put straw in the back stall and we'll bring her in after we're done milking. We should chase three heifers over, too. They're due to calve in four to six weeks."

"I can help with that," he watched her put the calendar in the cupboard, close the door and hook it. "By the way, do I get a kiss?"

"Give me time. That was our agreement, remember?"

"I know," he sighed. "But it's hard to wait when I love you so."

Greg came in as she went out to check the other waterers, and Luke drew him into conversation, sharing what he had learned from Val and from the Batterer's Education Program about respecting women. "All that stuff was news to me," he made a wry face. "I felt mad at the facilitators at first. But after I understood my behavior *caused* Mom and you children to distance yourselves from me, I started paying attention to what the facilitators were saying. All this time I thought I was building our marriage by making Mom submit to me, but I was actually destroying it and driving her and you kids away."

"You mean you're going to be a wimp now?"

"No, I'm committed to being a man of real strength. Using others and cutting them down doesn't make us men. But being respectful and kind and building people up is the purest evidence of strength. Val had me learn a quote from Francis de Sales that says it very well: 'Nothing is so strong as gentleness; nothing so gentle as real strength.'"

"And you believe that garbage?"

"It's not garbage; my children *want* to be with me now, and I influence them in a positive way instead of provoking them to avoid me. Kind and caring conduct is more powerful than I realized. What man wants his wife to refuse to sleep with him? Yet *I* drove her away. And you're driving Tanya away. You could be the big brother she admires, but that won't happen if you keep cutting her down and teasing her." Greg hung his head and appeared thoughtful, and Luke hoped he'd made a positive impression. "I want you to apologize to

Tanya, and make it up to her. You need to build trust with Tanya and Kyle, and treat your family in a way that pleases God."

The milker made a slurping noise, and Luke hurried to tend it. After they had transferred the milkers to the next four cows, let out the cows they'd finished milking, and let in and prepped the new batch, Greg rushed to the bucket of warm water on the wooden shelf and immersed his hands in it. "Ah, that feels good! My hands get so cold and that makes the rest of me cold."

Luke joined him and warmed his hands in the bucket, too.

"I don't get it," Greg reopened the conversation. "How is a man to be the leader in his home if he has to do all this gentleness stuff?"

"Val and I talked about that," Luke took the towel off it's nail and dried his hands. "I didn't believe what he said at first, either, but the more I think about it, I can see he's right. The husband leads by *serving* his wife and family and through his example. Look at the way Jesus led. He taught by example and showed compassion for people. If he had demanded, no one would have chosen to follow Him. A man becomes a leader when people *want* to follow. Otherwise, he's a dictator, not a leader."

"That's stupid. What's the point in being married if a man can't get what he wants? I don't need a marriage like that."

"If you always insist on having your way—even at the expense of your wife and children—why would a woman want to be married to you?"

Greg ran his hand back and forth in the water, making wavelets. "I didn't think of that."

"I hadn't either. Now I realize what's most important is for my wife to *want* to stay with me and care about me enough to spend time with me and consider what I want, too. That won't happen unless I treat her right. If you want a woman to care about you, practice respecting your siblings."

When Yvette came back, Luke and Greg were on the last batch of cows, and the stable was quiet and calm. Luke was glad she hadn't seen him get upset and yell at Greg for letting a cow crowd into an already full stall. "What was I supposed to do?" Greg had retorted. "Take a flying leap and land on her head? Practice what you preach. Instead of yelling, go to the feedway and smack her nose. She'll back out and find the empty stall. Don't make a federal case of it." Abashed, Luke shut up and followed Greg's directions.

"Everything's so quiet," Yvette ignored Luke and walked the length of the stable, her eyes scanning each cow. She stopped behind the last pair of cows where Greg crouched to tend a milker. "Any problems?"

"None we couldn't fix," Luke grinned and followed her to the back of the stable, hoping she'd look at him. "Greg is a good teacher. He taught me everything you've taught him. Just stay calm, and the little hitches will stay little. If I had learned that years ago, we'd have been spared piles of grief."

"How'd he do, Greg? Did he keep up his end?" She kept her gaze on Greg. Feeling like a rejected, love-sick school boy, Luke resisted the urge to sulk or snap at her. *I produced that distrust in her*, he reminded himself.

"He did okay," Greg took the milker off, hung it on its bracket, and turned her way. "When he comes home to stay, he can help with the milking every day, and you can stay in the house when I don't have basketball practice. We've been working you too hard."

"Is that so? What if I want to come out and milk?"

"Then maybe we'll have to take turns," Luke said, "and whoever stays in the house can catch up on sleep or cook the next meal."

~ ~ ~

After chores, Luke sat at the table and looked from face to face. A sense of love and connection washed through him. *Why was I such a pigheaded ogre when I could have had this?* He caught Yvette's eye. "Shall I tell them?"

"You can if you want to," she set the platter of fried eggs in front of him. He took two and passed the platter across the table to Greg.

"Tell us what?" Kyle asked.

"How about if we both tell them?" The toast popped up and Luke took a piece and tossed the other slices to Greg, Kyle, and onto Yvette's plate.

"Fine. I'll start." She cleared her throat. "As you know, Dad and I have been discussing our family situation and trying to figure out how we can work as a team. We've decided to try some changes."

"The changes we talked about in the barn?" Greg buttered his toast.

"That's some of them. We'll talk about those later. Luke," she rested a hand on Luke's shoulder, "do you want to take it from here?"

"Sure," he squeezed the hand on his shoulder. "Mom and I hashed out a lot of our differences. Mom has decided we've arrived at enough workable solutions that I can move home."

"When?" three voices chorused.

"Today. I have my things with me, and I'm here to stay."

He enjoyed the shocked silence before Tanya slipped off her chair and rushed to hug him. "I'm so glad," she choked out.

He kept an eye on the boys while he returned Tanya's hug. They stopped mid-motion and watched; Greg's spoon paused in the bottom of the grape jelly jar, and Kyle's knife hovered over his half-buttered toast.

"So what are the other changes?" Kyle asked after Tanya had hugged her mom and returned to her chair and Yvette seated herself.

"You want to start?" Luke turned questioning eyes on Yvette.

"Dad will help with the milking," Yvette scooped the last egg off the platter. "We want to make a rotation schedule for milking so each of us gets a break now and then. We'll keep expecting you children help straighten up the house, and I'll teach you more cooking, baking, and cleaning skills, so I can bring in an income by piecing quilts."

"What about your job, Dad?" Kyle asked. "Where's your toolbox?"

"I'll keep my job until it's time to work in the fields again. That way we'll have additional money to set aside for another parcel of land."

"Greg, would you pass the jelly?"

"Sure, Mom," he slid the jar across the table.

"If you behave yourself, Greg," Luke mopped his plate with his toast, "and stop picking on Tanya and Kyle, you can play basketball with your buddies one evening a week in addition to practicing and playing with the school team. There's no reason basketball has to be all work and no play."

"Super!" he dipped his toast into the yellow yolk and took a bite.

"That's *if* you behave," Luke reminded. "And Kyle, we gave you those painting supplies at Christmas for a reason. We've arranged with Steve and Delores to have you paint a mural of the Swiss Alps on their bedroom wall, *if* they like your version of the Alps on canvas. They will pay you one hundred dollars plus the cost of paints for the job. Please pass the cereal, Greg."

"One hundred dollars!" Kyle squeaked. He cleared his voice. "They'll pay me one hundred dollars? I can't believe it! I'll actually get paid for my art"

"There's one thing Dad and I have not agreed on," Yvette swallowed and laid her toast on her plate. "He thinks we shouldn't tell you this, but I think you deserve to know what's going on, so I am taking the responsibility to tell you this one." She paused. Luke looked up in time to see her meet each of the children's eyes. "These changes are on a *trial* basis. Dad promised if he chews us out, belittles, nitpicks, or scares us, he will leave again. We'll try it for three months then decide if this is working. If it's not, we'll change the arrangement for the next three months until we find what works for our family."

"You mean you two might split up after all?" Kyle asked.

"That's possible. If Dad chooses to behave in ways that are damaging to the family, I can't let him stay. He understands that."

No one spoke and Luke looked from child to child. Greg mopped up his plate, while Kyle stared at the gold milk pitcher with the black Iowa Hawkeye logo, and Tanya pushed the remaining half of her egg around on her plate. Luke poured Total into his cereal bowl, aware of thick tension as three pairs of eyes watched him fold down the inner lining and close the box.

Kyle scraped his chair back and his lip curled as he glared at Luke. It reminded Luke of the night in Yvette's room when he'd been so mad he'd wanted to hit her. Suddenly his chair felt too hard and he shifted to ease the discomfort. *Is this how the family feels when I get mad at them? Especially when they did nothing to deserve it?*

"Would you like cereal?" Yvette asked Kyle. Luke wondered if she was unaware of the tension.

"Blast the stinking cereal!" Kyle sprang to his feet, sending his spoon flying across the table.

"What got into you?" Greg held his last bite of bread next to his mouth.

"What do you mean 'what got into me?'" Kyle clenched his fists. "This whole thing is a rip-off. You don't intend to stay, do you?" he glowered at Luke. "You'll just stay until you find something better. Maybe a woman with more money or a bigger farm."

"Kyle!" Yvette protested, shocked.

"Why let him come back at all if he refuses to *commit* to his family?" He didn't take his eyes off Luke. "All my life I wanted you to like me as I am, but you kept putting me down. Then after Mom made you leave and get help you started behaving like a *real* dad. Now that I finally got my wish, you're planning to leave. It's not right. When—"

"Kyle, you owe Dad an apology," Yvette interrupted. "He *did* commit to being a loving dad and husband to this family. *I'm* the one who wants a trial period. *I* need to know we're safe and won't be stuck in a nasty situation. Since you children wanted Dad to come home, but I still feel uneasy, I decided a trial period takes your needs into account while addressing my fears. Dad and I both are trying to make this work, but it will take time."

Kyle stared at his mom, then relaxed his fists. "Oh," he dropped onto his chair, deflated. "I thought..." his voice trailed off.

"It's okay, Kyle," Luke said, relieved to be released from that glare. "If I were in your shoes, I'd be upset, too. Although I didn't want you to know, I think Mom did the right thing to tell you I'm on trial here. You boys need to know how hard it is to rebuild trust once you've torn it down, so you'll think twice before you treat your family like I treated all of you. Anyhow, as Mom said to me, you'll see soon enough things still aren't quite right between Mom and me. Don't get after Mom for that. Her distrust is the consequence of my behavior. You can't force trust when you've destroyed it."

202

Chapter 24

Luke floored the accelerator and barreled down the hill of the chip-sealed oil road toward Old Man's Creek, the speedometer hitting eighty as the pickup jounced through the square-framed, truss bridge. Excitement coursed through him. After years of scrimping and saving, his dream was coming true. He couldn't wait to tell Yvette. No more forcing himself to fix tractors—at home or in the mechanic shop. No more milking cows twice a day, seven days a week. And no more doing the self-talk he'd learned at the Batterer's Education Program. After holding himself in check all these months, he'd finally get what he wanted. And maybe, just maybe, Yvette would trust him enough to sleep with him again. *Finally,* there was a light at the end of his tunnel.

When he reached the straight stretch of road, he noted the patches of snow lingering in the fields and hoped the ground would still be frozen enough to spread manure on Saturday. He had today and tomorrow to convince Yvette, and Friday he'd consult the banker.

In the house, he started across the dining room, then realized he hadn't taken off his shoes. *Oh well,* he shrugged, then stopped short. *I can't expect Yvette to care about me if I don't respect her.* He backtracked to the washroom.

"Yvette," Luke called up the stairs when he had taken off his shoes.

"What's up?" her voice floated down to him.

He bounded up the stairs three steps at a time, and dashed around the banister. "Guess what I heard today," he burst into her room. Tanya watched him. "Ray Hansen is selling his five hundred acre farm."

"Don't get too close to the quilt; your jeans are greasy," Yvette pushed the needle through with her thimble. "So who's Ray Hansen?"

He perched on the edge of the dresser several feet from the quilt. "He's seventy, lives east of here, and wants to quit farming. He'll sell two hundred acres if that will produce a buyer this spring."

"What's his rush? That's nice, Tanya," she studied the embroidery Tanya held up. "Now thread your needle with yellow floss, and I'll show you how to make French knots for those dots in the center of the flowers."

"It's out of the Amish community and it's reasonably priced."

She stuck her needle into the quilt and looked up. "You've wanted a huge crop farm all these years and we've been saving toward that end, but do you think we have enough to swing it in addition to paying for this farm?"

"We can scrape the down payment together somehow. With what we have in savings, and if we cull out the worst of the cows and take a load of hogs to market, we should have enough to make the down payment for two hundred acres. We'll make so much money you won't have to milk cows anymore."

"You said we'd use the proceeds from the hogs to roof the barn."

"The barn's not that bad; it can wait another year."

"That's what you said last year. I looked at it last week. We *can't* put it off; the timbers are rotting at one spot. We don't need the extra expense of replacing beams."

"So we'll ask your mom for a loan to cover the down payment."

"I don't know, Luke. It doesn't feel right."

"Come on, Yvette. We have the down payment, interest is lower than it's been in years, and the land will pay for itself. So let's do it."

"Have you figured the yearly interest and investigated how much that farm produces? Does it have good soil? Making a living as a farmer is *not* a foregone conclusion, especially if we start with just ten percent down. If that farm doesn't pay for itself we'll have to make payments with the income from the home place. Then we won't be able to pay Mom. Social Security isn't enough for her to live on, and people often can't pay much for her midwifery."

"Oh, come on. This is our big chance. You wouldn't have to milk cows morning and evening or clean the eggs and take them to market. You could piece quilts all day. If it doesn't pay for itself, we'll sell it."

"If it won't pay for itself, we'd end up deeper in debt."

"Mom," Tanya held up her needle and yellow thread for Yvette to see, "I can't get the thread into the needle."

"Did you cut it at an angle so it makes a sharp point?"

"I forgot," the girl reached for the scissors.

Luke frowned. "You shouldn't let her interrupt."

Yvette raised her brows. "She's important, too; cut her some slack. About that farm—I need a few days to run figures. We don't have cows to cull out or steers to sell, but maybe I can think of a way to make it work."

"Sell the dairy herd." He knew it was a stupid suggestion, but hadn't one of the facilitators in the men's group told them to brainstorm for ideas?

"I like milking cows and we'd be without an income until harvest."

"Sell this farm. It'll bring top dollar since it's in Amish country."

"That's out of the question. This is my home and Mom's as well. It's been in my family for generations and I want to pass it to our children if they want it. That's been *my* dream. Please, Luke, let's keep saving a few years. There'll be more land when we're financially ready."

A wave of frustration swept over him. He opened his mouth to yell, "You're going to let someone snatch my dream right from under my nose?" but stopped himself. He fought to tamp down his anger. "I thought you'd jump at the chance," he substituted, keeping his voice calm with an effort.

"Luke, I *want* to help you realize your dream, but this sounds too risky. Our machinery is old and you'd want newer and bigger machines to handle the increased acres. We're paying for this farm, plus setting money aside so you can have your dream of more land. Things are looking good for us, and I don't want to sabotage that by jumping prematurely."

"Promise me you'll at least think about it," he pressed.

"I'll said I'd run some figures and think about it. I'd feel better if we had more for a down payment. Why don't we both compile figures and compare notes? Maybe we've saved more than I realized."

~   ~   ~

That night after the children were in bed, Luke mounted the stairs to talk with Yvette. *If I spend time with her, maybe she'll relent and help me buy that land.* The thought flitted through his head. "That is not why I'm talking to her," he whispered through gritted teeth. "I am *not* manipulating her." But he suspected that was false. "Okay, I won't mention the land."

"Mind if I sit and talk with you while you quilt?" he entered her room. "Some things aren't appropriate to talk about when Tanya is present."

"Sounds serious. Have a chair," she motioned to the straight-backed chair at the quilt beside her. "What's up?"

"I came up to talk about you. It seems you haven't gained much in the trust department. I don't understand. I feel I'm doing my best and it's not good enough. Can you tell me what's going on in your head?"

"Well," she drove the needle up and down through a purple flower petal on her quilt, "maybe a hypothetical story will help. Suppose someone you trust and who is close to you betrayed you? What if Alex, your trusted friend, overcharged us by three hundred dollars for doing our taxes? What would it take for you to trust him? What if he overcharged you an additional fifty dollars each year, but you didn't realize it until he had been doing it for fifteen years and the price was very steep? Would you hire him to do your taxes again? Would you be his friend? What would he have to do to regain your trust?"

"When you put it that way, it's an eye-opener. First of all, he'd have to pay back the money he overcharged. Then he'd have to demonstrate he had something in place to keep from overcharging again—maybe hang a statement of his fees on the wall—and a sincere apology, of course. I'm trying to do those things, but it's harder since we aren't dealing in money. It'll take me years to pay back what I stole from you, and some of it, like lost sleep, I can never repay. How can I show you I won't fall into those behaviors again? Should we redo the dining room, get a piano, and set aside money for piano lessons? Or maybe you want to redo this room. We could adjust the budget so you and the children have more to spend."

"I have paint and stencils for this room, and if we put less in the land and machinery fund we'll have to save longer before we can afford more land."

"Then how can I earn your trust and make up for my behavior?"

"There isn't a shortcut, Luke. As you stay considerate and respectful, my trust will grow. You handled our conflict this afternoon fairly well, but I need to know it's not an effort to get your way. When I'm sure this is the real thing, I'll feel safe enough to let you get close."

"I thought I had proved I was safe."

"You *have* kept yourself in control and behaved like a loving husband, but it's easy to act different for three months. It doesn't mean you've changed. So far you've given in on every issue. I don't know how you'll act when you want something badly. Unless you want to count earlier today, that is."

"I *do* want something very badly."

"What?"

"I'd like a satisfactory sex life. I know you prefer to sleep alone, but we can still be lovers. That's all I'll say about it; I won't pressure you."

"I appreciate that. But what will you be like after you reach your goal? Will you treat me as if I'm of no consequence again?"

"I hope not. You won't get that question answered 'til you try me."

"On the other hand, do you want a body or the whole person? At this point, you'd just get a body and that would slow the healing process."

"Would counseling help?"

"Not if the counselor pressures me to hurry up, and asks questions like 'What is holding you back?' as if that's abnormal."

"You've been a good teacher for me, Yvette, a very good teacher. If I hadn't been so bull-headed, I would have learned from you years ago."

~   ~   ~

In early April two weeks later, Luke stopped in the farrowing house to check the pregnant sows after he'd finished milking the cows and left Greg to clean up. He reached through the gate to tug on the pink teat of the nearest sow.

Milk beaded from her nipple and dripped to the floor. "So your milk is finally coming in and you're ready to have your pigs, girl. Think you can wait another day? I don't have time to put you all in farrowing crates this morning, but I'll do it first thing after work. And, no, I will *not* ask Yvette to do it. She has enough on her hands."

He exited the farrowing house and latched the door. Last April he'd dumped the responsibility of his farrowing sows on Yvette and the children. He shook his head. How could he have been such a moron? He hadn't had a clue how draining it was to milk cows at five o'clock morning and evening, seven days a week. No wonder she'd been angry with him. And after all his carping and stupid behavior, he'd had the audacity to expect her to eagerly fall into bed with him when he came home. He snorted at his idiocy as he grasped the top bar of the gate and vaulted into the outdoor lot to check the sows' feeder.

I was a big jerk. And now, when she has a legitimate reason for saying we can't buy that farm, I grumbled to myself how unfair she's being. "'Yvette shouldn't always get her way,'" he mocked his logic as he lifted the lid on the big round feeder and looked inside. "'Isn't she supposed to make me happy? How can I keep treating her as an equal if she doesn't reciprocate? I endured a whole year of no love-making, and now she expects me to give up my dream of farming a big spread. She's depriving me of too much.'"

"You agreed it's too risky," his conscience had reminded him. "You saw the numbers; you'd wear yourself out making payments on both places."

"But," he'd defended himself, "if it weren't for her, I'd have secured a loan at the bank."

"If it weren't for her, you wouldn't be farming at all."

He'd talked to Val about it, and Val had encouraged him to respect Yvette's input. "You're fortunate," he added. "So many wives say no to a proposition for some intuitive reason they can't explain. At least you have solid figures to consider. Besides, this isn't a case of you *never* buying more land or of Yvette being selfish. She has scrimped and sacrificed for years so you can have your dream. When is she going to get *her* fair share?"

Shamed by Val's reminders, Luke resolved to question his thinking when he felt dissatisfied with Yvette. He remembered an activity they'd done in the men's group. Each of the men had written a complaint about their partner and shared it with the group. He had claimed Yvette controlled their sex life. The group questioned him to discover if his perspective was accurate, and found that until recently she had done what he wanted.

"You mean she's been your personal prostitute for years?" one man asked. Remembering Yvette's similar statement, Luke had turned red. "A good lover tries to please his partner," the man told him.

He flushed, remembering how uncouth he'd felt. It hadn't occurred to him to aim to please Yvette—except when he wanted something from her.

How am I supposed to know when my reasoning is skewed? He sighed as he strode toward the house and breakfast. He'd have to ask someone to evaluate his thinking until he learned to be honest with himself. Who should he ask? Val? He shook his head. He'd rather attend the men's group on occasion and ask the facilitators. He wanted to look good to Val from here on out.

On the drive to work Luke resumed his train of thought. Why, oh why had he reverted to his old patterns of thinking? When he'd completed the Batterer's Education Program, he'd been so sure he'd never fall into his old habits. But once again he'd blamed Yvette even though she'd been his best financial asset. After all, he'd still be a full time mechanic if it weren't for her. She'd saved him from financial ruin and it was through her efforts they'd saved so much. From here on, anytime he blamed Yvette he'd question his thoughts.

But Ray Hansen came into the mechanic shop again during his lunch break with an offer Luke couldn't refuse. By three o'clock, he was home and hunting for Yvette. He found her on the patio, pushing a wheelbarrow of mulch.

"There you are!" he exclaimed. "I looked all over the house for you."

"What's up? You're home early. Aren't you supposed to be at work?" she parked the wheelbarrow and picked up a spade.

"I took the afternoon off," he tried to keep the excitement out of his voice and sound matter of fact. "Ray Hansen came in again and offered to sell me *one* hundred acres. I told him I'd take it, and went to the bank to arrange a loan. They want twenty percent down if we live there, and twenty-five percent if we just farm it."

"So we'd have to come up with even more than we figured before." With her gloved finger she wrote calculations in the mulch. At the rate we're saving, it'll take at least three years to save that much, and that doesn't include updated machinery."

"We have most of it and could borrow the rest from your mom," he crossed his fingers behind his back, wishing he didn't feel like a kid asking for a bicycle. *Is this how marriage should be, or is Yvette controlling me?*

"The bank makes the down payment that high, so farmers will be able to make the payments instead of defaulting. Getting a loan elsewhere will make it harder to meet our obligations. Low as interest is, we'd still be overextended even if we had the whole down payment. Did you tell the banker we're still paying on this farm?"

"No. This farm shouldn't have anything to do with it."

"Well, it does. If anything happened to Mom, we'd need a loan from the bank at a higher rate of interest so my sisters could get their inheritance."

"What about your share? That should lower our principle."

"Don't you remember? My folks sold the farm to us for a third less than they would have on the market. The lower price *is* my share."

"But I *told* Ray I'd buy it!" he burst out. Seeing Yvette jerk back and her eyes go wide, he quieted himself. "I can't go back on my word. I'd never live it down. The guys will talk about me behind my back and say I'm hen-pecked. Come on. Please."

"Tell them the bank won't give you a good enough deal," she'd relaxed some, but looked wary as she stabbed the shovel into the ground.

He hated to see fear in her eyes, but he had to protect his reputation too. He took a deep breath. "If I go back on my word," he succeeded in achieving a slower, less pushy tone, "no one will want to do business with me."

Yvette dropped a shovelful of mulch at the base of a bush and went for the next shovelful. "Hmm, that could be a problem." She dropped a few more shovelfuls around the bush. "What about renting?" She seemed more relaxed.

"I want to buy, not rent."

"Think about it. If we rent, we'd increase our acreage without risking our farm. We'd make more money and you'd get your dream at the same time. Eventually we could buy land and newer and bigger equipment."

"Yes, but I don't like it," he twisted a budding twig off the tree.

"It would be a step in the right direction. You'd be showing good faith. Maybe you could rent the two hundred acres, or the full five hundred."

"Hey, I like the way you think," he threw the twig down. "Give me that shovel. You shouldn't do all the work while I stand here."

"I'm ready to up-end the wheelbarrow on the next bush."

"I'll dump it," he grabbed the handles, "you can rake it into place."

"It's so balmy out here," she leaned on the shovel. "Oh, look, the bulbs are sending up shoots. I wonder what color they're going to be."

"Hopefully, deep red. What are those bushes with purple flowers?"

"Rhododendrons. Say, since you're home, could you help me take two of those heavy storm windows off so we can air out the house?"

"It'll turn cold again," he said as they headed for the house.

"I know. That's why I only want two off for now. I'll go in and unlatch the one in the washroom and one in the living room for you." She ran ahead of him to open the door as he carried the storm windows out to a side room of the wood-house for storage. They selected the green-painted screens that fit those two windows, hung them, then sat on the porch swing.

"I'd like to put in combination storm windows," Luke started the swing moving, "if you think our finances can handle that. Something tells me you've been muscling those storm windows for years. They're too heavy for you."

"I've managed. Though I will admit you do it in half the time."

"What do you say? Shall we update those storms this year?"

"Let's get a quote first. I'd hate to not have enough to rent that land or get the tractor we need. But it would be nice to just slide the window up. Thank-you for helping me take the storms off, and thank-you for the thoughtful suggestion, Luke," she leaned over to give him a hug and a kiss on the cheek.

He turned his head and met her lips with his, then caught himself and pulled back. "I'm sorry," he studied her face, "I didn't mean to take liberties you aren't ready to give."

"It's okay. After all, I started it."

"Are you sure?"

"I'm sure," she stretched up and touched her lips to his.

He savored her lips, then deepened the kiss and encircled her shoulders with one arm. When she snuggled into his embrace, he pulled her closer. At the end of his endurance, he broke off the kiss.

"What's wrong?"

He wanted to kick himself for the confusion on her face. "It's been so long and I'm afraid I can't keep myself under control. I want to respect your wishes, but you feel so right in my arms and I don't want to stop. I want to tell you how much I love you, but words aren't enough. Would you—would you let me show you?"

She studied his face, then nodded and pressed against him.

He pulled back. "Are you sure? I don't want to rush you."

"I'm sure."

Chapter 25

Yvette turned the black dirt in her rock wall garden with her trowel, then sliced into it repeatedly until all the chunks were gone. What a month they'd had. Ray Hansen had refused to rent his land; he wanted to sell it so he'd have the capital to build a retirement house for his wife and himself. After weeks of applying for a loan at various banks and lending institutions, Luke hadn't found a deal she felt free to sign. Nor had he heard of farm ground for rent. With April nearly over and the weather just right, farmers were already in the fields. Time was running out, and he desperately wanted to step into his dream this year. Much as she wanted to give him his heart's desire, all her instincts screamed, "This deal's too risky."

Every day, several times a day since he quit his mechanic job, Luke had asked if she'd please reconsider, and each time she'd told him she couldn't. She dreaded running into him, and yesterday had ducked into the wood-house when she spied him heading toward the house. When she'd heard him call her name before the door shut behind him, she decided to sneak out to the wooded pasture and look for morel mushrooms while she dreamt up a solution to their dilemma. *The walk produced nothing*, she sighed and bent to pick up several trailing burgundy geraniums, then glimpsed Luke nudging the porch swing aside as he came toward the patio. *Oh no, here he comes again.*

"Aren't the trees beautiful with those red buds on them?" she avoided looking at him as he approached. "Spring has always been my favorite season. Did you see those tulips over there?" she pointed toward Tanya's play corner. "They turned out to be my favorite shade of deep red. I couldn't have picked a better shade myself."

"What are those groups of purple flowers?"

"Grape hyacinths."

"You created a beautiful place, Yvette. You're a gifted woman."

"What brings you out here?" she laid each plant on its side on the freshly turned soil, spacing them evenly.

"I need to buy a few things in Iowa City. I was hoping to go to the bank and get a loan written up. Are you sure you won't change your mind?"

"Please, Luke, stop nagging," she scooped a hole with her trowel and planted a geranium. "Let's keep saving money and praying about it, and maybe a better deal will show up this fall. That's not so long to wait."

"It is when I've been waiting for twenty years."

"You haven't waited twenty years," she stabbed the trowel into the dirt and turned to face him. He'd dressed up in khaki slacks and a blue polo shirt, which surprised her. He preferred jeans. "You've been farming—living your dream. Granted, it's not as big as you want—yet. If you jump at it before we have enough, you'll lose the whole dream and have to start over from nothing."

"So you say, but I've seen farmers start up on less than we have and make it," he brushed a few grains of dirt off a jutting flagstone shelf.

"They also scrimp and live hand to mouth for years. And you aren't looking at the ones who try it and don't make it. Furthermore, I don't know any of them who risk losing the farm that's been in the family for generations."

"I don't know why your folks didn't just *give* you the farm."

"Because they needed the money and wanted to be fair to my sisters. Anyway, they sold it to me way below market value at a super low interest rate. Because of the good deal they gave me, we're way ahead of most farmers our age. Why don't you try thankfulness for a change, and set yourself to working toward your goal, rather than expecting others to *give* it to you? At the rate we're going, in seven years we'll have this farm paid for and enough for a down payment. If you keep your job at the shop, we can do both in three years, *and* buy a bigger tractor. We have it really good, Luke. Please, don't blow it, and please stop whining and begging." She turned to plant another geranium.

"Look, Yvette, I got counseling and went to that class like you wanted. I've changed how I behave and bent over backward for you. But what's in it for me? Again and again I have to wait and wait to get what I want. I had to wait four whole months after I moved back before you'd be my lover again. I admit you helped me start farming, but this farm is only a fraction of my dream. If I have to wait twenty years for each hundred acres, I'll never own five hundred acres. You continually hold me back. If we're to be a team, I need you to let up on your controls. I'm not the only controlling person in this family; you've been doing it, too. And right now, you're obviously the one in control."

She firmed the dirt around the plant. "Don't I have the right to control *myself?* I haven't said you can't buy that parcel; I've said I won't put my half of our savings toward it or put my signature on it. There are a lot of things I'd like to get with that money, but instead I'm choosing to help you reach your dreams. I don't see how you can call that controlling."

"You're making decisions that block me. We should decide things together, but you're deciding for both of us, and that is controlling."

"Be reasonable, Luke. If I did as you want, I'd be going against everything I think and feel. I'd be dishonoring myself, and I can't do that."

"So you make me dishonor myself."

"That's not what I'm doing. I haven't told you an absolute no; I've asked you to wait and save a few more years. I'm *honoring* your request as best as I know how. Why isn't that good enough for you?"

"Because," he rested an oxford-clad foot on a low jutting flagstone, "I'm tired of being held back. Your standard answer to me is 'wait.' Well, I'm done waiting. I'm tired of you always telling me my dreams are out of reach."

"What are you saying, Luke?" she furrowed her brows in concern.

"Look, Yvette, for twenty years you kept telling me 'wait.' As long as I'm tied to you, that's the way it will be. My change in behavior is working for you and the kids, but it doesn't get me what *I* want. I've tried it your way, but it's not working for me. I can't go back to the old way; that doesn't work for any of us. As I see it, there's only one option left. That's splitting up."

"Splitting up?" she noticed a weed between the flagstones. Was it a thistle or a dandelion? She frowned at it. "What do you mean, splitting up?"

"I mean I want a divorce."

"What?" her head jerked up. "You're joking."

"I'm serious. I've thought about this a long time. I thought when we became lovers again, it would be okay, but it's not. Even there, you slow me down. I need the freedom to barrel ahead and not constantly ask my partner if what I want to do is acceptable."

"I'd think you'd want to be acceptable to whoever your partner is. And what happened to 'making it up to me' for the next seventeen years? What about all the years I put up with you barreling ahead and using me? Aren't you at least going to discuss it first? Try to work something out, like I did for you?"

"I'm sorry, Yvette. You've given me the benefit of the doubt, you've put up with so much, and you've helped me start farming. But you don't have the capacity to dream big and I can't live like this anymore. If I stay tied to you, I'll always be stuck with a tiny farm operation. Even if you agree to purchase that one-hundred acres, we'd deal with this issue again and again."

"Not if you'd run the figures yourself, instead of asking the impossible. Once we've saved the whole down payment and have this place paid off, the income from the two places will stack up faster, and it would only be a few years until we'd have enough to put a down payment on the next hundred."

"Land prices are going up faster than we can save money."

"Paying huge chunks of interest won't help you get there faster. What has this been to you? A business deal with sex and children thrown in on the side? Your business partner isn't as advantageous to you as she once was, so you'll discard her and get another partner?"

"No. It's not like that at all. I thought I explained. I used to hold you back, but now you're doing it to me."

"If I'm *holding you back,* I'm doing it to save my children, my mom, myself, and even you from financial ruin."

"I don't see it that way. Our trial period is over. We've had more than three months to decide if this will work, and I've decided it won't. I need the freedom to get ahead without you constantly hindering me. If I have a wife, she must support me, back me up, one hundred percent."

"How will divorce get you ahead?" She picked up a handful of dirt and watched it sift through her fingers. "You'll have to give up this farm."

"If I have the settlement from this farm and don't have you to obstruct my progress, I can buy two hundred acres, maybe more," he planted both feet on the ground, and folded his arms across his chest.

"How will you get the bank to give you a loan?"

"Alex loaned me money for the down payment and will co-sign."

"Alex. Why am I not surprised? What about the vow you made before God to be committed to this family?"

"I'm still committed to my family. You and I can still have whatever relationship you care to offer, and I will always be there for the children. We'll just be technically divorced so we can both pursue our dreams."

"That's hogwash," she squared her shoulders and looked him in the eye. "This isn't about you following your dreams; it's about controlling everything in our relationship. You still think when we disagree, *I* should be the one yield, no matter what I think or feel. You may not yell at me and put me down anymore, Luke, but you're still insisting on the right to dictate my life. You're just using different tactics. I was right not to trust you, wasn't I? I should have listened to my instincts and not let you come back. But you won the children over first, so they'd pressure me. When I finally set aside my gut instincts and decided to *trust* you, you pull *this.* Does that mean you plan to take the children away from me, too?"

"No! I didn't intend to hurt you," he nudged at a pebble on the flagstone floor with his shoe. "I tried to make it work. Really, I did."

"Sure. That's why you're divorcing over something so ridiculously minor. A difference of three years—perhaps only six months. Tell me, how will you feel if I lose this place because of what you're doing?"

"You won't lose it. Your Mom won't let that happen."

"So you'll put both Mom and me in the poor house so you can have your dreams. You aren't anywhere close to the man I thought I married, Luke. If this is who you are, don't let the door catch your heel on the way out." She returned to planting flowers. "You better see a lawyer while you're in town."

"I have an appointment with a lawyer at two," he admitted.

"And how soon are you moving out?"

"When the sale is final," he looked away. "In a month or so."

"And when will you tell the children?"

"Whenever you like."

"Don't you dare try to shift that responsibility onto me!" she glared at him. "You can tell them yourself."

After Luke left for Iowa City, Yvette sank onto the porch, cradled her head in her hands and stared at the flagstones at her feet. She couldn't bear to sit on the swing. It brought back memories of that night she and Luke had sat there and kissed until she'd gone crazy with wanting him. She forced her thoughts to the issue at hand. Was she controlling? She frowned. She didn't think so, but what if Luke was right? Was she too cautious? Other people bought farms, and some of them made it. But what about those who failed? Had they gambled even though their figures hadn't added up? Or had their calculations suggested success? Had she skewed the figures to keep Luke from having his dream?

Confused, she shook her head. She needed to talk to someone who'd stop the confusion. Delores would know. She got up to phone Delores, who listened to her story. "Is Luke right? Am I controlling?"

"Why don't you turn it around?" Delores suggested. "If you wanted to buy something real expensive for the farm—a new milking parlor, for example. What if you'd been saving to modernize your dairy, and you heard of a good deal, but Luke said you couldn't afford it yet? Would he be controlling?"

"It would depend on whether he's right or just making it up."

"Are you making it up?"

"No. I figured it several different ways and can't make it work unless we have bumper crops and high grain prices the first five years."

"So your conclusion is…"

"I'm not controlling."

"I think you're right, Yvette. The problem is in how Luke framed the question. He should have told you the farm is for sale and asked if you think you've saved enough yet, and if that is property you want to buy. From there you'd discuss it and come to a mutual decision. But he didn't frame it that way. Instead, he had an expectation that amounted to a demand. When you didn't comply, he equated that to controlling him."

"He's filing for divorce today. Even if it isn't my fault, Luke thinks it is. Maybe if I support that farm purchase, he'll stop the divorce proceedings."

"Is that how you want to live? Anytime Luke wants his way, you have to yield or he'll accuse you of controlling him and file for divorce?"

"No, it's not. But this seems stupid. Surely, it can't be all his fault. After all, they say it takes two to tango."

"Actually, it takes two to make the marriage work, but only one to destroy it. Marriage is like a team of horses pulling a wagon. God is the driver, the One who gives direction. But if one of the horses gets the notion to go his own way, he rears and bucks or jerks his teammate this way and that over hazardous terrain at perilous speeds. Owners are concerned about the safety of the partner horse that's being jerked around and kicked, and do their best to stop the rogue horse from doing damage. Perhaps Luke's decision to divorce is God's way of 'selling' the kicking, runaway horse and saving you from harm. I'm sorry it came to this, Yvette. You've been the steady one of the team and did what you could to encourage him to follow the Driver's direction. Going against your intuition and reason will make your marriage worse, not better."

"So you think I should stand my ground?"

"Definitely."

That afternoon Luke met the children when they got off the bus, and without explanation to Yvette, drove off with them in the car. Yvette watched from the dining room window as Tanya reluctantly got in the front seat with Luke, and the boys sat in the back. Yvette guessed he was taking them out for ice cream while he told them he had filed for divorce.

She was in the washroom pulling on her boots when they returned home and headed directly to their rooms to change. Hurrying to the barn, she didn't talk to any of the children until Kyle came out to the milk-house where she was scrubbing the inside of the bulk tank.

"Where's Tanya?" she glanced toward the door.

"She went to look for baby kittens," he stood just inside the door, watching her scrub the milk spatters off the huge rectangular lid she had propped open. "She thinks Midnight had hers since she isn't fat anymore."

"Where'd she look?" Yvette propped open the top on the other end of the tank, blocking him from view, and scrubbed the inside of the lid.

"In the wood-house. She thought she heard mewing."

She leaned into the tank to scrub the underside of the non-lid section with her long-handled brush. "Where'd Dad take you? Out for ice cream?" her voice sounded strange in the tank, almost an echo, yet muffled, too.

"He took us to see the farm he's buying, then we went to get ice cream cones at Dane's Dairy in Iowa City," he moved into her view on the other side

216

of the milk-house and leaned against the old-fashioned refrigerator. Tanya and I decided to share a banana split instead."

"What did he tell you?" she leaned over the edge and began scrubbing the tank's inner side wall.

He curled his lip in disgust. "He filed for divorce. This whole thing is stupid. Things were going good until you chose to be contrary. Why can't you just sign the papers and let him have his farm?"

Shocked, Yvette straightened and hit her head on the stainless steel bulk tank lid, jarring a small round stainless lid off, which bonged several times on the steel bulk tank, crashed like a cymbal on the cement floor, then sang as it swirled round and round, faster and faster, until it settled flat on the floor. "Is that what he told you?" she asked when the noise had finally stopped and she had picked up the lid and laid it on the midsection of the tank.

"You're doing the same thing to him that he used to do to me. And all this time I thought you were the agreeable one, and Dad was difficult. He'd just like to have his dream. Is that too much to ask?"

"There's more to consider, Kyle. Do you know *why* I won't sign?"

"Did you even look at the place, Mom? It has a nice house and a swimming pool. There's a sun-room with a skylight that would make a perfect art studio, and we can add a basketball hoop to the tennis court."

"And what would happen to Grandma?"

"Oh, I forgot about her. I guess she'd find a place of her own."

"We, Dad and I both, made an agreement with Grandma that she could live here until she dies, and we'd be next door to take care of her if she needs help. This is her home and my home, too. We love it. My Grandpa bought this place, built this barn, and cleared the land. You're the fourth generation to live here. Selling this farm is not an option. If we try to buy a second place before we've saved enough, we couldn't make enough money to meet our obligations. We'd have to give the bank payments first priority and Grandma wouldn't get paid. Our contract with her needs to be our first consideration."

"Yeah, he said that's what you thought, but that there'd be plenty of money, and the new farm would pay for itself."

"I ran the figures on that. We'd have to have bumper crops the first five years to squeak by. I can't gamble that way. It's more likely we'd take the income from this farm to pay for that one, and Dad would get angry because there wouldn't be any spending money for him."

"Dad said we'd be rich on that farm. Who's right?"

"Maybe the question is who do you *want* to believe? If you want to know who is right, ask your math teacher to help you figure it out. He shouldn't be biased one way or the other. Or better yet, ask Greg. He's good at math."

"I don't want to figure it out; I hate math. I just think it would be nice to not have to work so hard. I'm tired of milking cows, gathering eggs, and grinding feed. It'd be nice to live like other kids and have a dog and a couple of cats, and that's it. Maybe we'd have a gerbil or a horse, too, but no livestock."

"You think if I'd agree to sell this place and buy that one Dad would change his mind about the divorce?"

"I'm sure he would."

"He told me he wouldn't. From what he said, I gather the only way he'd stay married is if I go along with anything he wants, no matter what I think or how wise it is. He wants total control, Kyle, and I can't give him that."

"Dad's not like that anymore. You're making a mountain out of a molehill. Just stop being a scaredy-cat and sign the papers."

"Since signing those papers goes against my gut feelings and my better judgment, I can't do it. I'm sorry to disappoint you. I hope Dad's bluffing about divorce, but if he isn't you'll have to think about where you want to live."

"I want to live with Dad."

Her face contorted in pain, and she turned away from him.

"I mean, you're—you're still my mom and I want to see you often, but at the new farm I'll have more time to draw and paint and goof off. Besides, Dad is a real dad now, and I don't want to give him up. I want to do things with him I never got to do before. Try to understand."

"I understand," her voice wobbled in spite of her attempt to keep it steady. As the tears seeped from under her eyelids, she kept scrubbing what was already clean so she could keep her face hidden. She had to get control of herself. She'd expected Greg to go with Luke, but not Kyle. If Kyle chose to live with Luke, Tanya would, too. *Had Luke planned this all along? Surely not. Surely he couldn't be that despicable. When had Kyle turned self-centered? Had his good behavior been aimed at winning Luke's attention? Maybe—*

"Mom," Kyle interrupted her train of thought, "say something. Are you okay?" he leaned into the tank next to her and tried to turn her head.

"Stop it, Kyle," she averted her face so he couldn't see her tears. "Of course I'm okay. I'm as okay as anyone would be who finds out her husband is divorcing her and her son wants to go with him, all in the same day. Go. Go muck out the cow stable. I want to be alone for awhile."

"But, Mom—"

"I said *go*," she spat through clenched teeth. She waited until she heard the door slam shut before she straightened from leaning over the bulk tank and escaped, sobbing, to the utility room at the back of the milk-house.

Chapter 26

Clara stepped out her front door and stopped to enjoy her perennial flower garden. Those groups of rich pink and blue hyacinths had been worth the money, and so had those deep red tulips next to her house.

She stooped to pull a dandelion from her flower garden. It broke off. *Luke's faults are like this dandelion. He didn't eradicate the root, so it grew and is reproducing again.* She sighed. *If only he'd dug the whole root of self-entitlement out and replaced it with honor and high esteem for Yvette, the faults wouldn't have stood a chance and flowers of harmony would have taken root.*

Perhaps he'd change his mind. When Yvette told her yesterday about Luke's decision to divorce, she'd asked Yvette if it was okay for her, Clara, to try to talk sense into him. "You can try," Yvette had sighed, "but I doubt it will do any good. He's convinced himself if he doesn't get his way, I'm controlling him. He's turned everything he learned backward to suit himself. I'm done fighting for this marriage, Mom. I'm tired. I can't do it anymore. I sacrificed so he could have his dream. But I won't go back on my word to you and sacrifice this farm for him, too. Our marriage is dead. As Delores once said, getting a divorce will make the paperwork consistent with what already is."

Clara sighed again. Maybe talking to Luke wouldn't help, but she had to try. Yvette and the children deserved better than this. Hopefully, confronting him in front of his family would goad him into feeling accountable. What would she say? She wanted to tell him to shape up, but suspected that wouldn't help. "Oh Lord God," she prayed, "please put Your words in my mouth. Make them effective and cause Luke to reconsider. But most of all, do Your will."

Strengthened, she stepped onto the gray-blue L-shaped porch. Two cats, a white and a tabby, streaked around the corner and darted back and forth in front of her feet, mewing up at her. She shortened her stride to avoid stepping on them. At the front door, she knocked and bent to pet the cats as she waited.

Tanya, who was holding a doll with long braided hair, opened the door. "Hi, Grandma. I like your flowered dress. Are you going somewhere?"

"Yes, I am," she twinkled at her granddaughter, "and I just got there. Want me to braid your hair so it matches your doll's?"

"Yeah, I'd like that."

"Tell the rest of the family to meet in the living room, and then get your brush. I'm calling a family meeting; I'll braid your hair afterward."

When they were gathered—Clara on the couch between Kyle and Yvette, Luke stretched out on the recliner, Greg in the stuffed chair, and Tanya on the floor playing with her doll—Clara started in. "Are you sure you want a divorce, Luke? Did you talk it over with your pastor or anyone? I thought you wanted your marriage to work and the family to stay together."

"You didn't tell us the meeting was about divorce," Greg scooted forward in his chair. "Do I have to stay and listen to this?"

"It concerns all of us," Yvette said. "If we keep things in the open where all of us can join in the discussion, we'll have fewer misunderstandings."

With a groan, Greg flopped back in his chair and picked up a book off the end table between his and Luke's chairs.

"I did want to stay together," Luke shrugged and looked Clara in the eye, "but it takes two to make it work. I've been doing my part, but Yvette isn't doing hers. One thing I've picked up from the batterer's group is that I don't need to control Yvette. All I have to do is decide if I am willing to live with the choices she makes. If I'm not, divorce is the best option."

"I thought you believe marriage is until one of you dies."

He looked away. "I did believe that, but I'm sick of living like a wimp. I'm tired of her telling me I have to wait for I want, or that I can't have it. I hate milking cows. And I'm tired of having a wife who won't keep the house clean. If I have to do housework, I may as well have my own house. I want to do things my way without someone telling me to do it differently all the time."

Clara scooted forward. "Yvette has worked hard to help you attain your dreams. Why are you jerking the rug out from under her now?"

Luke pursed his lips thoughtfully. "Because she's trying to control me," he said at last, "and I won't tolerate that."

"So you've made it into an either-or situation. Either you're in control, or Yvette is. There are no other alternatives."

"The other alternatives didn't work," he pushed the recliner's back to a horizontal position. "I can't find land to rent and I've been poor long enough."

"How will you support yourself until harvest?"

"I can work at the mechanic shop," he picked up the remote control and ran his thumb up and down the keypad.

"Yvette tells me if you keep working at the mechanic shop a year or two while you wait, you'd have enough for a down payment, be able to afford both farms, and have farm income all year. I think you're unreasonable to jump the gun and then blame it on Yvette when she doesn't agree with your change of plans. The breakup of your family is one hundred percent your fault."

"I can live with that; I have broad shoulders," he flicked on the TV.

Yvette is right; he has *twisted everything around.* "Would you please turn off the TV?" Clara sat back. "We don't need distractions."

"What's left to say?" Luke punched the off button. "I've made up my mind. She'll get the divorce papers in a few days."

"Did you think about the children?" Clara glanced around at their faces. Kyle stared at his bare foot as he rubbed it back and forth on the variegated brown, black, and white carpet, while Greg studied the cover of his book and thumbed its pages, and Tanya put a tiny teacup to her doll's mouth. Luke, whose face was in profile, appeared to have settled down for a nap. "Who will they live with and where will they go to school?"

"I want to live with Dad," Kyle glanced at his mom and grandma, then focused on his dad, "and stay in the same school. A classmate stayed in our school after he moved, and I could, too. Greg could drive us; he's sixteen now."

"Greg, where do you want to live?" Clara swallowed hard.

"With Dad," he opened his book. "I won't have chores there."

"What about you, Tanya?" Yvette clenched her hands in her lap.

"She's too young to know what's best," Luke roused to object. "She should stay with the boys to reduce the impact of the breakup on the children."

"It doesn't hurt to let her say what she wants," Yvette said. "Maybe the children should stay together. Then again, is that good for Tanya?"

"You don't trust me to take care of her?" Luke glared at Yvette.

"You haven't proven yourself trustworthy," Yvette hugged her middle. "You've only acted like a parent for the past four months. I've been here for them all their lives, and now you want to lure them away with promises of a life of ease? That's not parenting. You've convinced me your parenting was just an act. If your real concern is getting out of paying child support, surely we can work out something that's better for the children than living apart from me."

"But I won't have much time to paint when I'm here," Kyle leaned forward to look past Clara at his mom, "unless I paint while you chore."

What had happened to their caring son and grandson? Clara mused as she studied Kyle. Was this a teenage thing, or Luke's influence? Did Kyle's desire for Luke's affection warrant such a radical change?

She looked at Yvette and caught her furtively wiping her eye. Seeing her daughter's pain, Clara blinked back tears. Maybe Tanya had retained her reason. "Tanya," Clara leaned forward until her face was level with Tanya's, "where do you want to live?"

Tanya rocked her doll. "With both Mom and Dad." She looked at Clara. "I want to play at your house and be with Kyle, too."

"See," Luke exulted, the glint of victory in his eyes as they met Clara's, "I told Yvette it's important to keep the kids together. When the sale is final, they can move their stuff to my place."

"I don't think so," Yvette's dark brown eyes flashed. "They'll need furniture, clothes, and their personal stuff while they're here, too. You can buy furniture, and we'll decide the rest after we figure out the details."

"What do you mean?" he frowned. "Their things belong with them."

"They will be here, too," Yvette ran her palm over the arm cover and smoothed out the wrinkles. "You made the decision to divorce, and that will put me deep in debt. I don't need a bigger financial burden; you can bear the cost of your own decision."

He shrugged. "If you say so. What do you think, kids?" He turned to look at Greg. "Shall we look for new furniture tomorrow after school?"

"Yes!" Greg plopped his book on the end table. "Let's—"

"Not so fast," Yvette interrupted, her jaw set. "You saw them after school today. I want to see the children after school, too."

Luke stared at her a long moment. "You're right," he subsided back into the upright recliner. "We'll go in a day or two."

"What about my painting supplies?" Kyle leaned forward to talk to his mom. "Can I take them to Dad's?"

"Of course. Dad can buy you another easel and canvasses, and you can carry the paint supplies in that wooden box you got for Christmas."

"This just isn't right," Clara shook her head, feeling ineffectual and helpless. "It's all wrong. Won't you change your mind, Luke? You admitted the breakup will impact the children. Is this the legacy you want to leave Greg, Kyle and Tanya?"

"It won't all be negative. Getting away from their controlling mother will be one benefit, and not working all the time will be another."

"How can you say such outrageous things!" Clara jumped to her feet. "And in front of the children, too! Yvette has taught your children responsibility and balance. They have leisure and time to pursue their dreams. You're the one who blocked them. I suggest you get counsel and think again."

"I've decided and there's nothing to discuss," he clicked on the TV.

Clara shook her finger at him. "You will regret this decision for the rest of your life. Come, Tanya," she extended a hand to her granddaughter. "I'll braid your hair if you still want me to."

Chapter 27

Kyle hunched over his cereal bowl and avoided looking at his mom as she peeled potatoes for Sunday dinner. Ever since he'd announced he wanted to live with Dad, he'd felt guilty for the hurt and sadness in her eyes. But he couldn't change his decision. He'd wanted a *real* dad all his life, and now that he had one, he *wouldn't* give him up. He wished he could ease her distress, but couldn't think how, so he avoided her.

Somebody poked him in the ribs.

Startled, he looked in time to see Greg's finger jab his ribs again.

"Stop it!" he glared at Greg.

"Pay attention and pass the salt," Greg scowled. "I asked you to pass it three times, and Tanya asked for the milk."

"Oh," Kyle passed the milk and salt. Scooping the last bite from his bowl, he gulped it down then scraped his chair back and headed for the stairs. If he hurried he'd have a minute alone with Dad to ask to sit with him in church.

As Kyle reached the stairs, Luke exited his bedroom in his navy suit and tie, the scent of cologne swirling in his wake as he strode to the front door.

"Aren't you going to church with us?" Kyle frowned.

"No, I'm going to church in Coralville."

"Can I go with you?"

"You children will go to church with Mom so you can see your friends. Besides, you aren't dressed yet, and I have to leave now to get there on time."

Kyle watched Luke stride to the pickup. "It's not fair," he muttered as Luke drove out of sight. "Is this the thanks I get for choosing to live with Dad?"

That afternoon wasn't any better and Luke still hadn't come home after the chores were done. Kyle rebounded for Greg in the barn driveway. "Why is Dad staying away so much?" Kyle tossed the basketball to Greg. "Do you think he changed his mind and doesn't want us to live with him after all?"

"Of course he wants us," Greg did a jump shot. "You heard him. He has stuff to do. Yesterday he helped us choose and order furniture. He even got you more paints and an expensive easel. Today he had more details to handle."

"Doesn't it bother you he won't play basketball with you?"

"Why should it? I'd rather play with my friends. When we move we won't have chores and he'll let me practice with them every day. Mom and Dad should have divorced long ago; I don't know how he put up with her so long. She kept us all from having fun; I'm done with her and this farm."

"Greg! How can you say that after all she's done for us?"

"She's been making us wash dishes and do our own laundry. That's *women's* work."

"Is milking cows women's work, too? Don't you feel guilty for leaving Mom to chore by herself?"

"No, I don't. I'm not the one who decided to milk cows and raise pigs and chickens. Mom can hire help. It's time I get to live like a kid."

"Don't expect *me* to wash your clothes and cook your meals," Kyle hurled the ball up into the haymow and stalked out of the barn.

~   ~   ~

A week limped by, and Yvette fell into bed exhausted, but sleepless, every night. Greg refused to help with the chores; he practiced basketball and did his homework. Kyle helped milk and fed the hogs and chickens, but avoided Yvette or spoke to her in monosyllables. Luke slept and ate alone, but left home after breakfast and didn't return until supper. Yvette spent the week hauling manure, castrating piglets, washing dishes, and cleaning the house.

Tanya troubled her mother most of all. When she wasn't in school, she played in the living room. Once, when Yvette peeked in on her, she caught Tanya staring into space. Yvette asked if something was bothering her. "I'm just thinking," Tanya had replied. Not knowing what to do, Yvette had gone to Clara for advice. "Give her time," Clara had said, "she'll come around."

Not satisfied with that answer, Yvette watched her daughter and looked for a chance to connect with her. If only Tanya would hang around like she used to, Yvette could help her deal with the strangeness of this family breakup. At least Luke had made his awful announcement *after* Tanya's birthday party. That thought gave Yvette an idea. Maybe if she started planning next year's birthday party, she'd break through that barrier of silence.

"Tanya," Yvette sat beside the girl in the living room. Tanya looked up from her book. "What kind of party do you want next year?"

"The whole class begs to get invited to a haymow party, but we can't have one because the kids who don't get invited would get mad at Jill and me. Anyway, I don't want to talk about a party. I want to read."

"Well, okay." Feeling awkward, Yvette stood up. "Why don't you go to Grandma's to read? I have to get field work done while the weather holds, and I don't want you here alone where Greg can hassle you."

"Okay," Tanya rolled her eyes as she got up. "Anything *else*?"

"No." *Stop the sarcasm*, Yvette wanted to say, but restrained herself.

Feeling overworked, isolated, and lonely in her own home, Yvette went to the washroom, got her kerchief, and looked in the mirror while she tied it behind her head. *Can anyone see the grief and sadness on my face?* She couldn't tell, since she never studied her own expressions.

Luke came in from outside, and she quickly turned into the kitchen, pretending an interest in the towels in the corner so he couldn't see her face.

"When are you going to wash my pants? This is my last pair."

"Are you trying to start a fight?" Yvette kept her tone mild.

"No. I'm asking for clean pants. I'd think you'd fall all over yourself to please your husband so he'd change his mind about the divorce."

"You said nothing I do will change your mind. Besides, I've been hauling manure and castrating pigs, so I think you can wash your own pants."

"Nobody said you had to do those things. If you take care of the house, I'll do the fieldwork until I move."

Reward him with his favorite job after he'd skipped the nasty ones? Never. "When will that be?" she opened the refrigerator, keeping her back to him. *I should take something to the field to eat, but what?*

"The closing is May seventeenth. I'll move on the eighteenth."

"Maybe Roy will let you plant early. Did you buy machinery yet?"

"Of course. What did you think I've been doing?" he stepped behind her. "You don't have to be like this, you know. We can still be friends."

She tensed as his arms circled her waist and pulled her against him.

"Take your hands off me, Luke."

"I'm still your husband; I can touch you if I want."

"Let go of me or I *will* call the police."

He let her go. "Come on, Yvette, we could be good friends now. We don't have to be enemies just because we're getting a divorce."

"Friendship is based on trust, Luke. When you show me you're trustworthy over a long period of time, I *might* consider being your friend."

"Have it your way. Will you wash my clothes?"

"No."

~   ~   ~

Tanya reached out for her mom's arm, but the instant before her hand touched it, her mom became a misty form that turned into a shapeless rain cloud, and her hand closed over nothingness. Lightning flashed and thunder crashed in

225

her face. She put her hands over her ears and tried to run away, but her legs wouldn't move. Thrashing from side to side, she tried to hit and kick it away, but it turned into a monster putting a hood over her head. She thrashed harder and her hand hit something cold and solid. She screamed and woke up, conscious of a thrumming in her head and footsteps running into her room.

"Did you have a bad dream?" her mom's voice came out groggy and rusty as she leaned over the bed and felt Tanya's forehead.

Tanya didn't answer. All she could do was curl up and cry.

Her mom turned on the bedside light. "I'll snuggle with you," she slid into the bed as Tanya scooted over. Tanya felt an arm go under her head, then she was cradled against her mom's side. She held herself tense for a minute, then relaxed. "Want to tell me about your dream?"

"I reached out to hold your hand and you went away. Then it thundered and I got scared. Is God mad at me because I'm going to live with Dad?"

"I don't think so. God understands and loves you very much."

"Are *you* mad at me for wanting to go with Dad?"

"No, I'm not mad at you. I'm sad, though. I'll miss you."

"You often look mad, and you don't talk to me like you used to."

"I'm sorry, Tanya. I *am* mad about the situation. I feel helpless and scared, too. But I'm not mad at *you*. How do you feel about things?"

"Scared, I guess, and sad, too. Will I ever get to see you again?"

"I should hope so. You'll probably be with me on the weekends. I wish you could be here all the time, but I'm not mad at you and it's not your fault. I understand you want to be with Kyle and with Dad, too."

"Dad said I'll have my own room, and he'll get me a playhouse with a stove and refrigerator and wash machine. We looked at one when we went shopping on Saturday, and he said he'd get it for me after we move. It had an upstairs with a bed and a night-stand, and hooks to hang clothes on."

"Super. You'll have a playhouse at Dad's and a patio one here."

"He said I could invite Jill over to play in my playhouse after school. Can I have Jill come here to play on the weekends, too?"

"Probably. But we'll need to keep weekends as our special time. The book I'm reading says it's important for me to have less work when you're here, so I'll have more time with you children."

"You mean you'd play house with me?" Tanya snuggled closer.

"Or we could play games, bake cake and cookies together, or go on walks. Sometimes I'll be with all you children, and sometimes with each of you separately. Would you like that?"

"Uh," Tanya heard but couldn't answer because she was half asleep.

Chapter 28

May eighteenth, the day Luke had decided he and the children would move to his dream farm, the day that would forever be etched like a spill of battery acid in Yvette's mind, arrived all too soon. Yvette vowed to herself she would not cry when the children got on the school bus that morning, but she hugged each of them as they went out the door.

"Mom!" Greg said, "I'm too old for that."

"I'm not. And you'll always be my son." *Life won't ever be the same.*

"You'll be okay," Kyle pecked her cheek.

"But this may be the last time I'll see you off to school."

Tanya exchanged a hug with her mom. "You've grown so tall; I can rest my chin on your head. You better go; the bus will be here soon."

"I wish I could be two people and stay with you, too."

"Wouldn't that be nice? Dad will pick you up at school and bring you here to get your things. I hear the bus. Give me one more squeeze and a kiss." Yvette watched her dash across the patio, then waved as the bus drove off. Tanya pressed her face to the window and waved back.

Wanting to be alone, she grabbed a handful of tissues, and went to the basement to get an egg bucket. The hens wouldn't care if she cried. As she opened the door to the hen house, their noisy cackling quieted. Two hundred seventy brown hens looked at her, the closest ones tilting their heads. "Bach?" the hen at her feet broke the silence, then several others repeated the inquiring, "Bach? Bach?" their heads tilted in jerks by increasing degrees one way then the other. More hens joined in, and the house resumed its previous uproar as the hens returned to eating, laying eggs, and foraging.

Yvette stepped to the first nest and felt under the hen. Two at a time, she put four eggs in her dull red, covered-wire bucket. The next hen glared at her and pecked her hand. That was enough to incite tears to fall. She set the egg bucket on the straw-strewn floor and let the tears flow. Her babies. Did she have to let them go? Was there any way to stop him from taking them? She dug the wad of tissues from her pocket and peeled off the outer one.

Her lawyer had said if Greg and Kyle chose to live with Luke, there was nothing she could do, unless she could prove Luke was an unfit parent. The pictures of her bruises would only be evidence of Luke's abuse of *her*. She could fight for Tanya, but the court would be slow to separate siblings. Since Luke had been harsh with the children, her best bet was to let him taste single parenting, and let the children experience life without their nurturing mom.

How long would it take? A month? Half a year? Years? She sobbed and soaked tissue after tissue. How could she go on without her children? She had given them birth and been the major parent in their lives. And now he had snatched them away. Of all the betrayals of their marriage, this one surpassed them all. He had vowed to love and cherish her, but disdained and abused her instead. But that seemed insignificant compared to taking the children from her. She couldn't grieve for him and the loss of their marriage—she hadn't had a marriage worth grieving for years—she could only grieve for her children.

A hen pecked her boot. Shooing it away, she blew her nose and resumed gathering the eggs. Then the cold hard truth hit her. She had given Luke a chance, the benefit of the doubt, and he had *chosen* to use that chance to hurt her to the max. Why had she sent him to the Batterer's Education Program and taken him back? Why, oh why, hadn't she divorced him when the children wanted nothing to do with him? In her anguish she hugged herself and rocked back and forth. Her legs felt weak; her knees as if they would buckle. She looked for a place to sit down, but the floor, the chicken feeders, the roosts, were filthy with bird droppings. Why did her church pressure couples to stay married, even when a husband repeatedly chose to abuse his wife? Didn't they care about the destruction to his wife and children? *If only* she hadn't given him that final chance. If only he had chosen to be strong, decent and nurturing.

Feeling numb, she took the bucket, three-quarters full of eggs, into the cool unfinished basement, then went upstairs to pack Tanya's clothes, dolls and books. All was quiet in Luke's bedroom, so she assumed he had gone out. But hearing his footsteps on the stairs, she realized she had been mistaken.

"Do we have any empty boxes?" he entered Tanya's room.

She averted her tear-blotched face. "In the attic." Her voice sounded dull and flat to her own ears. "We have plenty of plastic bags."

"I wish you wouldn't take this so hard. You know it's for the best."

She wanted to shriek, "*No, it's* not! *Taking children from their loving mother is* not *for the best.* Choosing *to be a loving and respectful man is.*"

228

He left the room, and she heard him go up the attic steps. She stood on a chair, and felt on the ledge above the door till she found the old-fashioned, flag-shaped key, then locked herself in Tanya's room.

~   ~   ~

Luke brought the children home after school, and they trooped into the kitchen for their snack of popovers, a treat the children loved, but Luke hated.

"Isn't there anything for me to eat?" Luke asked.

"Yeah," Yvette spooned creamy tapioca pudding into one, "popovers."

She sent the boys upstairs with bags, and followed to help them pack. Greg packed all his books, cassettes, CDs, and playthings. Kyle sat on his bed, looking around his room in bewilderment. "What shall I take, Mom?"

"Take what you'll want this week. You can get more things on the weekend. Do you need my help, or shall I look in on Tanya?"

"Go help Tanya; I'll be okay."

Yvette found Tanya sitting cross-legged on the floor in front of her bookshelf. "Where are all my books?"

"I packed them in those bags to go to your dad's house," she pointed to the bags on the floor. "They'll be like old friends, so you won't feel lonely."

"I don't want them at Dad's house. If I take them there, you'll never read to me again," tears trickled down her cheeks.

"Oh, Tanya," Yvette knelt on the floor and pulled her daughter into her arms. "You can leave them here. Why don't you choose one for each night you'll be there? Then every week you can bring those back and get others."

Tanya nodded and wiped her tears with the back of her hand.

When they had finished packing, Yvette helped them carry their bags to the new, blue, extended cab pickup Luke had purchased and to the family car, which Yvette had conceded he could take since he'd have the children with him.

"Well," Luke brushed his hands together as if getting the dust off, "we're ready to go. Greg, you drive the car."

Greg rushed to the car and sat in the driver's seat, while Kyle and Tanya stood next to the pickup bed and looked at Yvette.

"I'd like to say good-bye to the children," Yvette tried to sound matter of fact and keep the grief out of her voice and off her face.

"Hurry up," Luke planted his feet and crossed his arms over his chest.

"You didn't pack anything to eat. Why don't you go to the basement and help yourself to canned goods and frozen meat and vegetables?"

He kept his pose for an extended moment, then uncrossed his arms, and sauntered toward the house as if he had all the time in the world.

When he had gone inside, Yvette stepped forward and hugged Tanya. "I'll miss you," aware of Tanya's silence, she squeezed her eyes shut to hold back the tears. When she had herself under control, she looked up at Kyle and offered her free arm. "Are you too old for a hug?"

He glanced at Greg, then stepped into Yvette's embrace.

"You two look out for each other like you do here, okay? Do your best at school, and don't forget everything I've taught you."

Kyle pulled away. "We aren't going to Timbuktu, Mom."

"But I won't see you for three days," she forced herself to let go of Tanya before the girl pushed her away. Apparently, Luke had painted a glowing picture of their lives without her, and even Kyle and Tanya felt excitement, not sadness or dread, at going to their new home and leaving their mom and their old home behind. Much as it hurt, she couldn't pour cold water on their anticipation. She should say good-bye to Greg, but he'd likely rebuff her, too.

She approached the car and knocked on the driver's window.

Greg rolled the window down, but kept his hand on the window crank.

Suddenly she didn't know what to say that wouldn't incite contempt. I love you? I'll miss you? Hardly. Behave yourself? Drive safely? Be nice to Tanya? Ditto. How about starting from his viewpoint? Bingo.

"I know you're looking forward to your new living arrangement. But if you ever want to talk or need help, call me."

"Is that all?"

"Yes," she stepped back as he rolled the window up. *He'll get too hot with the window up. Let him go, Yvette. He's old enough to care for himself.*

She went back to Tanya and Kyle, who had gotten into the pickup, but left the door open. "Don't be afraid to call," she said.

"We won't," Kyle looked straight ahead.

"Are you okay, Tanya?" Yvette met her eyes. "You're so quiet."

"I'm wondering what my room will be like. Dad helped me pick out a dresser and bunk bed so my friends will have a place to sleepover."

"What color is your furniture?"

"It's maple," Kyle said. "I chose a red bunk bed, one of those metal tube ones, with a full-sized bed on the bottom so I can have friends over."

"I know what you mean. Did you pack your easel?"

"Dad got me a deluxe one to set in the sun room."

"I'm glad he's letting you paint. Did you say good-bye to Grandma?"

Kyle wiped dust off the dash, "We did that last night."

Hearing a door slam, she looked up. Luke was striding toward the truck with plastic grocery bags in each hand. "Do you want to get here by bus on Friday, have Greg drive you here, or shall I pick you up after chores?"

"Pick us up after chores," Kyle reached for the door handle, "so there won't be a problem if Greg goes out with his friends."

230

That hurt, but she masked her pain. She'd hoped he would want to come back on the bus—as soon as he could on Friday.

Luke dropped the bags in the pickup bed and got behind the wheel.

"Good-bye," Yvette stepped back so Kyle could close the door.

"Bye Mom," Tanya waved as they started off.

Yvette waved back and tried to smile, but her lips felt stiff. She hoped Kyle would wave too, but he turned toward his dad and appeared too busy to notice her waving at them. Greg gunned the car engine and followed the pickup.

Feeling discarded and desolate, Yvette checked her watch. *Four-thirty.* Not sure what to do, she stood in the middle of the drive. She didn't want to go in that empty house just yet. If she went to the brood-sow shed she'd think about the time she and the children had taken care of the farrowing sows and their piglets. If she went to the garden she'd remember the times Tanya had helped her pick beans, corn and kohlrabi, and when the boys had helped her plant sweet potatoes and weed the garden. The only place that wouldn't bring bittersweet memories was in the upper level above the garage and shop.

She went into the shop and up the stairs, pushed the trapdoor up, and surveyed the space they used for storage. Free of memories, the place became her haven. She could live here until the weather got too hot. She'd get a small refrigerator and use the camp stove and an air mattress. Then she remembered: Luke had taken all the camping gear.

Spying a nail keg left there by her grandpa, who had been a carpenter, she upended it and sat on it. To her left, two chewed up wooden sawhorses, one stacked on the other, stood beside three slabs of plywood that leaned against the unfinished sloped ceiling. *One of those would make a nice table.* To her right, bare bed springs and a black metal headboard and footboard leaned against the wall next to the window. *If I put the bed together, and put a slab of plywood on the springs, I'll have a rustic apartment out here.* Her eyelids drooped.

A scratching noise woke her. She checked her watch. Four fifty-five. She'd dash in, change into chore clothes, and grab a bite to eat on the way to the barn. If she kept her brain blank and pretended her children had been a fantasy, she'd be okay. Only the animals and her surroundings were real. Keeping her mind focused on her task, she dressed, then hurried to the milk-house.

With the system she had stumbled upon the day Luke had come home and shaken her, milking alone and feeding all the animals only took an extra hour. Late that night she sat on the couch to eat her supper of leftovers, then zoned out watching TV. She fell asleep in the middle of the first movie.

~   ~   ~

Yvette woke, disoriented, not sure why a light shone in her face and the TV was on. She sat up, turned off the TV, and forced her heavy lids open so she

231

could check the clock. Five o'clock. Time to get the boys up. Then reality smashed her in the midsection. "No," she whispered, shaking her head. "No." Tears started streaming down her cheeks. "My God, please, no!" she wailed. "Don't let him do this to me. Please. Don't let him take my children away! Do you hear me? Where are you, God?" She listened to the stillness, but heard nothing. Feeling forsaken, helpless, and betrayed by Luke, her children, and God, Himself, she got up and went to the barn.

Like an empty, pain-wracked shell, she muddled through the day in a daze. She ran the Rototiller up and down the weedy garden, then realized she'd tilled up the peas she'd planted two days before Luke announced he was filing for divorce. Oh well, she wouldn't have time to shell peas this year, anyway.

She sat on the grass strip between the two plots, sorting through the packets of vegetable seeds in her seed box and dithering over how much sweet corn to plant. Since she suspected the children would choose to live with her, but they were now with Luke, she had no idea how much to plant. She finally decided to plant as usual. If she had sweet corn left over, she could plant little or none next year. She dragged her hoe through the dirt to form a deep furrow.

Clara came out as she started the second row. "Everything's quiet, so they must have left. I'm sorry I wasn't here; I had a baby to deliver yesterday and didn't get home until this morning. Are you holding up okay?"

Yvette leaned on her hoe. "I'm making it so far, but I dread tonight."

"I never dreamt Luke would take the children. They annoyed him."

Tears pooled in Yvette's eyes, and she dug a tissue from her pocket. "My eyes feel hollow and dry from crying, but they tear up any time I think of the children. Please tell me this is a bad dream and I'll wake up in a few hours and get the children up and send them off to school."

"I wish I could," tears welling up in her own eyes, Clara hugged her daughter until Yvette had cried herself out. "Come have supper with me," she accepted the tissue Yvette offered. "It's important for you to be with friends, to reach out for support. Why don't you take time to see Delores tomorrow?"

"I have so much work to do. I should have planted sweet corn and squash two weeks ago, and I don't have tomatoes out yet."

"You're planting in plenty of time and I'll help you today. Don't fret about the children. Kyle will come to his senses; it's you he's been close to."

"I can't blame him; boys need a male role model. The problem is, I don't want him to copy Luke. If only I'd made sure he had lots of opportunities to be around Steve Webster, maybe he wouldn't have chased after Luke."

"What about that mural? If you follow through with that, Kyle could have the pleasure of being paid for his art, and spend time with Steve, too."

"Thanks for the reminder, Mom. You're a Godsend."

Chapter 29

Yvette turned into the drive and parked her second hand, blue Kia in the garage. After rattling around in her empty house, choring by herself, and crying frequently all week, she'd picked up the children from Luke's. Although she'd endured four weeks of the new arrangement, the pain was still constant and fresh. Her whole being rebelled at the injustice of only being allowed to teach and guide them eight days out of thirty. She yearned for them when they were gone, and when they came for the weekend, she couldn't fully enjoy them because their time would be so short and swift. Every Sunday night after they'd gone to Luke's, the silence from their absence was deafening. Tears hovered on the surface now, ready to spill out with minimal provocation.

Every Saturday Yvette had taken them to the Webster's, so Kyle could paint the mural and spend time with Steve. Greg had grudgingly gone along and hung out with Ryan, the Webster's eldest son, and Tanya had reveled in play-time with Jill. Yvette forced herself to take the children to church, knowing she was sacrificing precious hours she wanted to spend alone with them.

"It's good to be home," Kyle reached for the door handle. "I feel like I've been gone forever. The first thing I'm going to do is paint a picture of Tanya on one of those scroll-arm benches on the patio. I tried and tried to draw or paint something at Dad's, but nothing turns out right. It's annoying. Yet I finished painting that mural for Delores and Steve without any trouble."

"At least *you* get to draw and paint as much as you want," Greg threw open his door. "Dad says I can't get a job or a hoop unless I keep the kitchen clean. He always gripes about something. If it's not about a mess I made, it's about a spot of dirt on the floor. He didn't keep his promises to me, but expects me to be his cleaning service. Well, I *refuse* to be his slave."

"Does that mean you're going to sit around and do nothing all day?" Yvette got out of the car. "That sounds boring to me."

"He plays Nintendo most of the day," Kyle got out and slammed his car door, "and expects me to cook for him and clean up after him."

"So there's trouble in paradise," she followed the boys to the house and Tanya trailed after them. "Greg, what have you done to your pants? They look like you washed them in hot water and they shrank. I can see your hairy legs."

"He's getting his growth spurt," Kyle held the door open for her and rolled his eyes. "Dad's broke and can't pay us an allowance right now, and my pants don't fit him, so we have to go shopping for pants this weekend. Ummm, smells like barbeque something. What's for supper?"

What is Luke doing with the child support I paid him? If Luke won't buy clothes for them, I'll have to—in addition to paying child support. "Baked corn, barbeque chicken, and scalloped potatoes. We'll see if any of Kyle's outgrown jeans fit you, Greg. If not, we'll check the secondhand stores."

"You aren't *that* poor, Mom," Greg dropped his bag on the floor.

"I'll be very poor after the divorce," she put Tanya's bag on the table.

"Then sell cows or pigs or something."

"I have to put all the money I can scrape together into paying off debt." She couldn't tell them she may have to sell the farm. Not yet. Perhaps the settlement wouldn't be as large as she had estimated, or she could think of a way to increase her income so she could make the payments. "You're a math whiz; sit down and figure it out yourself. We'll have to make do the best we can."

"Great, now I'm stuck with no way to get cash," Greg sighed.

"Has he finished planting and started working at the shop again?"

"He started last week," Kyle flipped through the pile of mail.

"I suppose that means you don't have any food in the house and he won't get paid until next week," Yvette guessed. "You can take food from here when he comes to pick you up on Sunday. There's frozen beef, pork, and chicken that we butchered last fall, and I canned and froze plenty of fruit and vegetables last summer."

"We can't use anything but the canned stuff since we don't have a refrigerator," Greg grabbed for the sports magazine buried under the pile of mail.

She raised her brows. "I thought Dad got furniture for the house," She hurried to the kitchen and checked the chicken and potatoes in the oven, then returned to the dining room. For the first time she noticed Tanya stood inside the front door, cradling her doll in her arms. "Let's play a game," Yvette suggested, hoping to help Tanya loosen up. "How about charades?"

"I don't want to," Tanya hugged her doll tighter and backed a step.

"We won't play then," Yvette said. "Why don't you boys go upstairs or play basketball in the barn, so Tanya and I can have a girl chat?"

With a whoop, Greg dashed for the stairs.

"Are you okay, Tanya?" Kyle lingered behind and squatted down in front of her. "She's been quiet all week, and won't talk to me."

"She'll be okay," Yvette put an arm around Tanya's shoulders. The girl stayed tense for a minute, then relaxed and leaned into her mom. Seeing this, Kyle turned to go upstairs.

"They say divorce is hardest on the children," Yvette said after a long silence. "It really hurts, doesn't it?" When the girl didn't respond, she softened her voice. "Do you want to be at Dad's more, or here more?" With a forefinger she tilted up Tanya's chin. "You've been so quiet. Is everything okay?"

"It's okay," Tanya turned her face away.

"Are you glad to be here, or would you rather not have come?"

"I wish I didn't have to go back."

Maybe Tanya will live with me after all. Hope zinged through Yvette, followed by alarm. "Why? Is someone mistreating you?"

"I don't have anything to do and there's no one to play with. Kyle's busy drawing and painting, and Dad can't afford the doll house. His credit card is maxed out and he needs to buy a refrigerator first. What's maxed out?"

Won't he ever learn? "It means they won't let him buy anything else with his credit card until he pays for part of what he owes on the card."

"Well it's not fair," Tanya raised her head. "He got Nintendo games for Greg and art stuff for Kyle, but nothing for me."

Odd. Nintendo, which Luke was opposed to, but no basketball hoop. "You can take more books and things from here. Is Greg treating you okay?"

"Yeah. He played house with me and made peanut butter and jelly sandwiches for a tea party."

"I'm glad he's treating you well. Come. Let's get supper on the table. It's just us tonight, but I invited Grandma for tomorrow."

When they all sat at the supper table and had said grace, Yvette took a piece of chicken and passed the platter to Greg. "Tanya says you played house with her, Greg. Hearing that eases my mind; I appreciate you playing with her. Are you aware she doesn't want to go back because she has nothing to do?"

"I've been painting a picture for Dad," Kyle heaped scalloped potatoes on his plate. "He's different than he was when he moved home."

"Wise up, Kyle," Greg bit into a chicken leg, "that was a fluke. Dad's always going to be a self-centered grouch with a stack of complaints. Hey, this chicken is great, Mom. Kyle's isn't very good."

"We'll cook together while you're here; practice makes perfect," Yvette put down her chicken thigh. She'd had trouble eating ever since Luke told her he wanted a divorce. Food tasted bad and she had a constant knot in her stomach. She'd lost weight; her face looked gaunt, and her clothes hung on her.

"I'd like that," Greg said. "Being at Dad's has taught me a lot."

"Like what?" Kyle challenged.

"Like knowing how to cook is important, and managing money like Mom does, instead of impulse buying, gets you what you *really* want. Mom, after living at Dad's I've learned to value what we had with you. I know I've been a jerk, but I'd like to live with you if it's not too late to change my mind."

Hope and caution bubbled up from her mid-section. "Have you thought this through? You'll be expected to work hard here. There won't be time for Nintendo. You can practice basketball, possibly with your friends on occasion, but you won't have day after day to do whatever you please."

"I'd rather work here than goof off at Dad's. I feel the same as Tanya; I don't want to go back. Dad hasn't kept his promises and is a grouch. "

"Before you make up your mind, I want you to think about this. I won't put up with you playing your parents against each other. I'd be glad to have you move back. But perhaps you'd like to live one week at Dad's and the next week here, or spend half a week at Dad's and the other half here."

"No. I don't want to live at Dad's and I'm not game playing. *This* is where I want to live. I'm willing to do my share of work and respect all of you."

"Can I move back, too, Mom?" Tanya asked.

"I'd love to have you here, Tanya, but I want you to think about this. Remember why you wanted to live with your dad?"

"She wanted to be with me," Kyle looked down at the table. "Actually, I've been thinking some of the same things, but I'm not sure I'm ready to give up on Dad yet. If I wait a little longer, maybe he'll be a decent Dad again."

"Don't hold your breath," Greg reached for his glass. "Where's the milk? I've been thirsty for milk from home all week."

"It's in the refrigerator," Yvette jumped up to get it. "I'm sorry, I forgot." She filled Greg's and Tanya's glasses and passed the pitcher to Kyle.

"Dad will probably be more of a dad to us if he only sees us one or two days a week," Greg said. "Maybe he'll be glad to see us instead of gripe at us."

"That's possible," Yvette conceded. "I'm sorry he hasn't been what you hoped. But I want each of you to think it over carefully before you decide. Have you talked to Dad and given him a chance to correct things?"

"We never have to remind you of your promises," Greg said,

"I'd feel better about you moving here if I know you tried to work it out with your dad, first." *Furthermore, he'll make a fit if all of you move home.*

Chapter 30

Luke parked his new pickup in the garage, picked up his lunch cooler, and dragged his feet to the house. He couldn't remember being so tired in his life, and this was Monday. How he'd keep working twelve hours a day all week he had no idea, but he had to, to pay his bills. Money was tight now, but when Yvette paid the settlement, he'd be on easy street, while she struggled to make ends meet. Then she'd be sorry she'd been controlling.

He stepped into the entrance-sunroom, and knew from the odor Kyle had been using oil paints. Rags, brushes, and tubes of paint littered the table next to the easel. He shuffled into the kitchen and surveyed the mess. The table and counters were cluttered with dirty dishes as they had been when he left for work. Only now a pink puddle settled in the low spot on the white vinyl floor in front of the sink, and pink trails ran down the white cabinet fronts next to the new refrigerator he'd had delivered on the weekend. *Greg must have spilled lemonade. Neither Kyle nor Tanya would leave a mess like that.* He stacked plates to make room for his lunch box, then went to look for the children.

A strung-out pile of towels littered the floor in the unfurnished dining room, and another flattened pile of dark laundry covered half the couch and spilled onto the chocolate-colored living room carpet. Shirtless, Greg slouched at the far end of the couch, his thumbs punching the Nintendo controller, one bare leg squashing the laundry on the couch, and the other bare foot on the floor.

"Get your foot off the clean clothes," Luke snapped the ball of Greg's foot. "You haven't lifted a finger around here ever since we moved in."

"Yes, I did," Greg moved his foot to the floor, "I mowed the lawn."

"Which didn't need doing half as bad as the kitchen does. The least you could do is clean up that puddle of pink lemonade you spilled on the floor."

"I was *hot* and *tired*, and there's no other way to cool down, since you won't let us run the air-conditioning. If you don't like it, you can lump it."

Luke gave up trying to control his temper. "No, I won't lump it! You will do your share around here! You aren't so big I can't thrash you."

"That really scares me," Greg jabbed the controller buttons.

In an instant, Luke covered the distance between them and snatched the controller out of his hands. "Get up *now* and wash the dishes!"

"I don't owe you anything until you keep your word," Greg bolted upright on the couch. "You promised me an allowance, a basketball court, time to practice with my friends, water in the swimming pool, and no chores, but you haven't delivered on *any* of them. You got me here under false pretenses so I could *slave* for you the way Mom did. Well, I *won't* do it."

Fear shot through Luke. *If he moves to Yvette's I'll lose child support and won't get a settlement for years. And the community will vindicate Yvette and consider* me *guilty and a failure.* Luke sank into the recliner. "Come on, Greg, be reasonable. I'm working twelve-hour days, six days a week to pay our debts and so I can buy enough land to *make* it as a crop farmer. I didn't realize setting up would cost so much. I can't work long days and come home and clean up after you children, too. Please, kick in your share. Things will be much better once your mother buys my half of the farm."

"I *did* my share," Greg set his jaw, his eyes defiant.

"Kyle cooked and cleaned last week and painted for Steve and Delores, too," Luke said. "He *made* money with his painting; I won't assign him your work. And Tanya's been keeping the bedrooms in order. I expect you to do your share. Where are Kyle and Tanya?"

"In the basement."

"I'm cooking supper. If you want to eat, you'll wash dishes and clean up your pink mess." Luke forced himself to his feet and trudged to the kitchen.

"If you're going to be that way, I'll move to Mom's," Greg called after him. "*She* lets me play basketball and have friends over." Luke noticed Greg took his time getting off the couch and sauntering to the kitchen.

"I might have known Mom's behind this," Luke opened a package of hamburger. "If she'd have supported my leadership, I'd be farming two hundred acres instead of in this financial mess. And now she's teaching you to be lazy."

"Mom didn't make this mess," Greg opened the top drawer and closed it, "*you* did. We were doing fine until you insisted you *had* to have this farm. And now you *have* to buy more land. When are you going to control your *greed* and stop blaming Mom? Now she may have to sell the farm because you—"

"Did *she* tell you that?" Luke flattened a chunk of burger between his palms. "*She* chose to lose the farm when she didn't support me."

"*She* didn't tell me anything; I figured it out myself. Why couldn't you work with *her*?" Greg opened the middle drawer and closed it. "You'd do better if you'd sell this farm and go back to Mom. If you don't, you'll have to work overtime at a job you hate just to pay for your mistake. What a *loser.*"

"Things will improve after the divorce is settled and the crops are sold," Luke defended with a confidence he didn't feel. If Greg had done the math and concluded it wouldn't work, maybe Yvette *had* been right and he'd always struggle to survive. He wished he had waited until he had more money before he bought the farm, but he wouldn't admit that to Greg.

"*If* we have a harvest," Greg sneered. "You keep saying how dumb Mom is, but *you're* the dumb one. Where are the dishcloths, anyway?"

"In the laundry, where else? If you think Mom's so great, why don't you go live with her?" Luke retorted and instantly regretted it.

"That's exactly what I'm going to do," Greg threw over his shoulder as he headed into the living room. "You say you're a man of *integrity* who keeps his word, but you *still* haven't put up the basketball hoop you promised me. And now you've gone back to criticizing everything I do."

"Wait, Greg," Luke hated his begging tone, but he felt desperate and helpless. "Give me one more month. Please. And try to understand. I need a *minimum* of three hundred acres to *scrape* by as a crop farmer. That's why I wanted this farm; it has enough acres to make a decent living."

"But *you* don't have the money to buy it," Greg returned to the kitchen sink, "unless you ruin Mom and make her and Grandma and us children give up the farm that's been in our family for generations."

"Mom told you that bunch of drivel to get you to side with her." Luke dropped the last hamburger patty in the pan and went to wash his hands.

"I told you *I* figured it out. I got farming figures from Lester and told Kyle and Tanya my conclusions. They decided to move to Mom's, too."

"What! You can't do that to me!" Luke shouted. "You *chose* to live here! I went into debt to buy a new truck and new beds and dressers for all of you. I've slaved so you can have anything you want. Is it too much to ask that you clean up after yourselves? I tell you, *I'm* the reasonable one, and your mother's the slave driver! You'll be sorry you moved back with that *Jezebel.*"

"She's not Jezebel!" Greg screamed. "Don't *ever* call her that again!"

"I'm sorry," Luke dried his hands. "I shouldn't have said that. You made that up about Kyle and Tanya just to make me lose my cool, didn't you? Call them for supper. They probably plan to stay here."

"After they heard you yell and talk about Mom like that?" Greg opened the basement door. "Get real."

Luke noted Tanya hovered close behind Kyle as they came into the kitchen. *My goose is cooked. She'll never stay here now.* He studied them. *Unless—unless I can win their sympathy.*

"Sit down for supper," he invited as he got a gallon of ice cream from the freezer compartment and brought it to the table. "Greg, let the dishes go for now. We can start with ice cream while the hamburgers fry. Did you notice the refrigerator I bought while you were gone this weekend? Now we can cook normal meals." He got out blue granite camping plates and cups and plastic spoons rather than risk alienating one of the children by asking them to work.

They sat in silence while he piled their bowls with ice cream and considered how to begin. He'd play down their decision to leave, overstate the rest, and be his most friendly self so they'd feel guilty for hurting him. He'd use that old salesman trick and get Kyle to answer yes to everything; Kyle would agree to stay and then persuade Tanya. With a plan like that, he couldn't lose.

"Greg tells me you're considering living with Mom, Kyle," he began. "Before you decide, could I share some points for you to consider?"

"Uh, sure Dad," Kyle looked down at his ice cream bowl, while Greg eyed Luke, and Tanya glanced at him then looked away. *So far, so good.*

"Remember that day Grandma came over? Each of you promised you'd live with me." He wanted to emphasize *promise*, but knew that would tip them off, so he skimmed over the word hoping they wouldn't notice the lie. "On the basis of what you said, I borrowed money from Alex to buy machinery and make the down payment on this farm, and to buy new furniture for each of you. I maxed out my credit card, too, knowing I'll have the money as soon as Mom pays me for my half of our farm. If even one of you moves back with her, I'll lose this farm and the money I paid on it. I'd be poor for years. You want your old dad to have a decent place to live, don't you, Kyle?"

"Well," Kyle gulped, "yeah."

"You want to keep the furniture you picked out, don't you?"

"I guess so."

He patted Kyle's shoulder. "Wouldn't it be a nuisance to move all your stuff back to your old room and put your clothes in that beat up old dresser?"

"Not really. I didn't bring that much here." Kyle swallowed and looked Luke in the eye. "We already decided to move back to Mom's tonight after supper. I hope you don't lose this farm and will have a decent place to live. You can take my bed and dresser back to the store. I can sleep on the floor when I spend the night here. Tanya—well all of us—really miss Mom."

Luke wanted to yell, but knew that would be counter-productive. He sighed, trying to sound as heartbroken as he could. "I-I hoped we could forge a close father-son bond."

"I hoped for that, too, Dad. But maybe we still can when we visit."

Feeling thwarted, but unwilling to admit defeat, Luke got up to check the hamburgers while he considered his next move. It would be pointless to appeal to Tanya. That left one option. He'd call Yvette and convince her to pressure the children to stay with him and pitch in and keep his house in order.

After supper, Luke retreated to his bedroom to phone Yvette. He shucked off his grease-stained clothes and dropped them in the clothes basket, then sprawled belly-down across his king-sized bed and on top of Yvette's blue dahlia quilt that he'd bought at the Mennonite Relief Sale. Plucking the cordless off the night-stand, he punched in Yvette's number.

"How's it going?" he feigned friendliness.

"It's going."

"Still mad at me?" he fished for a way to get her to be friendly.

"Who said I was?"

"I'm not stupid, even though I act like it at times," he chuckled, hoping she'd think he was being friendly, not starting an argument.

"Neither am I. What do you want, Luke?"

He rolled onto his back and decided to try a different tact. Ask how the weekend had gone? No, that would remind her she only had weekends with the children. Talk about Kyle's art? He wouldn't have a clue what to say. Maybe if he eased into the subject, she'd be receptive.

"I had that coming. Look, Yvette, I don't blame you for not liking me. I just want to keep communication open for the sake of our children." *There, that sounded good. She should warm up any minute.* "If we work together, we can keep them from using the divorce to manipulate us."

"What do you have in mind?" she didn't sound warmer, but she'd asked the crucial question.

"I've been talking with other single parents, and they say it's important for parents to have the same rules in both houses." He paused, hoping she'd respond so he'd have an idea how to proceed. She said nothing.

He positioned a pillow under his head and turned the friendliness up a notch as if her lack of response had been encouraging. "Greg is manipulating both of us, and if we join forces we can out-smart him. What do you think?" he held his breath hoping his ploy had worked.

"I'd have to hear what you have in mind before I commit to anything." Did she sound a fraction warmer, or was it wishful thinking? He studied the neutral-colored drapes, but they didn't give him inspiration.

"If both of us require him to work before he gets to goof off, he won't be able to pit one against the other. He needs to do his share."

"So what are you saying? What exactly do you want me to change?"

What a dense woman! Do I have to spell it out for her? How can I get her to cooperate without telling her the children want to live with her? Knowing her, she hopes they will so she can keep the settlement and get child support until Tanya is grown. She'd love it if I lose my farm. Well, she won't get them if I can get her to help me. "I'm saying Greg needs to be more responsible."

"But I can't make him work at your house."

"So you're going to play dumb!" he punched his pillow. "You aren't *capable* of cooperating, and expect things to go *your* way all the time! And now you're trying to influence the children to move back with you!"

"Luke, stop it! If you don't cool down and talk in a reasonable tone of voice, I'll hang up the phone. I *do* expect Greg to be responsible here, so I don't have a clue what you're after. You've been talking in circles and still haven't spelled out what you want."

"I said I want us to agree on the rules we have for the children so they can't manipulate us. If we don't work together, they'll have both of us trying to outdo each other to keep them from moving to the other's place."

"I get it. They must have told you they want to move here."

"Well," he evaded, "Greg threatened to leave when I said he couldn't eat if he didn't work." *It's the truth, just not the whole truth.*

"Greg is quite aware he'll have to work harder here than he does there."

He cast about for another angle. He *had* to win this battle; his whole future depended on it. He had it! Basketball! "Then it's basketball that's the problem," he crooked his knee and rested his ankle on top of it. "You've been encouraging him in his fanciful daydream of playing in the NBA. We both know that's not going to happen, so why indulge him? It's time he explores realistic careers. Neither of us should allow him to play basketball so much."

"My views don't coincide with yours, Luke. He's only a sophomore and should be allowed to enjoy his high school years. He could save us money if he got a scholarship. He's really good, and if he's allowed to practice I think he could play professionally. Go to his games and see for yourself. By the way, did you notice he's been shooting up? He could end up taller than you."

"I don't care if he *is* good enough for the NBA. That's not a lifetime career, and he'll be out of work or disabled by the time he's thirty. He needs to learn real life responsibility."

"It's obvious we differ on how to handle Greg's dreams for the future, so there's no point arguing about it," she sounded calm. "From what Greg said, you stopped being the type of person they want to be around, Luke."

He paused, not ready to concede defeat, but not sure how to turn the tide in his favor. "Look, I'm offering to work with you if you work with me. The very least you could do is tell them to stay with me. If those kids move in with you, they'll be back here before the month is out, and then we won't have any idea where we stand financially."

"We talked about that, too, and—"

"Oh, yes," he mocked, rolling onto his side and slamming his fist on the bed. He didn't want to hear his argument was doomed. "You have such a *good* relationship with the kids, you don't have to listen to *me*. Well, get this, woman. Your marriage failed because you *insisted* on having *your way*. Just keep it up and everything you put your hand to will fail, too."

"I have to consider the children and be true to myself. I incorporated your point of view as much as I could. If you'd be less critical, more n—"

"Sure, blame it all on me. It's always *my* fault!"

"Stop interrupting, Luke. As I was saying, if you'd let up and—"

"You're too easy going!" he bolted upright on the bed. "You baby Greg and let him be a dreamer instead of making him face the real world. You did the same with Kyle, and now he thinks he can be an artist."

"For *ten* years I worked in support of your dream, and you have the *nerve* to say that? Are you the *only* one who is allowed to pursue your dream? As I was saying—and don't interrupt me this time or I *will* hang up. If you'd consider the children's points of view, they'd be more likely to—"

"Of *course*," he couldn't bear to listen to her, "*you* know *everything*."

He heard a click.

"Are you there?"

Silence.

"She hung up on me. What a *shrew!*" he flopped back onto the bed.

A door slammed. He heard voices outside and strained to hear what the children were saying. Another door slammed. His eyes widened when the car started, its headlights filtering through the drapes. He sprang off the bed, tore out of his room, down the stairs, through the house, and out the front door.

Red taillights winked at him in the distance.

~   ~   ~

Yvette plodded toward the house, untied the knot of her red kerchief at the nape of her neck, took it off and fanned herself with it. The heat seemed hotter after Luke's phone call. Would the pain of living apart from her children never end? Did Luke have to make it worse by continuing his abuse over the phone? Could she have handled that call better? After this she'd tell him she was too busy to talk. That would keep him from chewing her out and make him deal with his own problems.

Clara, carrying a yellow, covered-wire basket half full of brown eggs, saw her coming and waited for her in front of the shop.

"It's too hot," Yvette said as she came alongside her mother. "Thanks for gathering the eggs; you don't have to do that, you know."

"I plan to clean them, too. I wish I could do more. As hard as it is on me when the children are gone, the pain must be excruciating to you."

"It is. Things we did together every day, I now do alone. The place is desolate. So silent. My eyes are raw from crying. Most of the time I can't think how to pray. And when I do pray, my chest hurts so bad I'm afraid the stress will cause a heart attack. When will this nightmare end? I knew I'd have an empty nest someday, but not this early. Not all three leaving at the same time. The children aren't ready to live without me, Tanya especially."

"Isn't there anything you can do?"

"Not as long as the boys want to live with Luke. My lawyer says judges are loathe to separate siblings and tend to set up custody based on what children fourteen and up want. Tanya and the boys *say* they want to move back, and I gather from Luke's phone call tonight Greg is giving him trouble. But I daren't allow myself to get my hopes up."

"We'll keep praying. Maybe the boys are coming to their senses."

"I've been praying as much as I can, but time is running out. Our court date is August second. That's a month and a half from now."

"They can change their minds after the divorce is final. Have faith. You raised them to be decent, to discern what is right. They'll figure it out."

"Not if they prefer freedom from responsibility."

"Take heart, Yvette. The boys chose to move with Luke because they thought he'd keep showering them with attention. If they're talking of moving here, things aren't as they expected. I doubt they'll put up with Luke returning to his old ways—especially with your example of drawing the line at abuse.

"But waiting is so hard. I need an odd chore to keep my mind busy," Yvette studied the yard, looking for an idea. "I know. I'll change the oil in your car. It's been years since I changed oil; it will take all my concentration."

"Are you sure you're up to it? You aren't a teenager anymore."

"You can hand me the tools I need. I used to get nauseous if I had to sit up to get something and scoot back under the car too often. Go get your car. I'll get the car ramps and my tool box, and move my car out of the garage."

When Clara returned with her car and had driven the front tires up the ramps, Yvette scooted under the car. "Now where is that plug?" she mused. "It's dark under here. There's the oil pan—oh, here's the plug. Could you hand me that socket wrench set?"

Clara pushed the set in it's black case under the car.

Yvette selected a socket at random and fitted it on the nut. "Oh good, I picked the right one the first time. Fancy that. Now if Luke didn't put the nut on too tight, we're in business." She snapped the handle onto the socket and pulled. "The nut is too tight," she grunted. "Where is that pipe Dad told me to use for leverage? I hope Luke didn't throw it away."

"There's a pipe in the tool box," Clara handed it under the car. "Before I forget, has Luke said anything about a settlement?"

Yvette took the pipe and focused on her mom who squatted down to look under the car. "He wants me to pay him for half the farm, machinery and livestock right away. Margie Bender, the one who is president of the quilting committee, offered me an interest-free loan for the whole settlement. But even with an interest-free loan, I'll barely make it. I'll have to get a job on the side and may have to sell the farm. Keeping it is painful if none of the children want to live here and farm. It feels so desolate. I suppose I'll try to keep the farm running as long as you're alive and until I know for sure none of the children want it, but I see little reason to live like a pauper for the rest of my life."

"You only owe him for a third of the farm, since a third of it is your inheritance. Don't forget you paid for some of the cows and machinery before you married. And if the children move back, the settlement should be delayed until Tanya turns eighteen. According to the figures we did together, you'll be able to make it if you don't have to pay two loans at the same time."

"In all the heartbreak, I forgot about those details," she slipped the pipe over the wrench handle and pulled on it. "No wonder Luke sounded desperate tonight. If the children move here, he could lose his farm and have to wait ten years to buy another one. The trouble is, he'll be impossible to deal with if he loses his favorite toy, so I'll likely pay him two-thirds of what's in savings so he can keep his farm. There," she said as the nut loosened. "Now send me that black oil-pan."

Clara pushed the pan under the car. "Delay paying anything as long as you can to give the children time to move back. *When* they do move back, you should only make a partial payment to Luke *if* he signs a paper stating you don't owe him the rest of the settlement until Tanya turns eighteen. And don't pay him one cent until he agrees a third of the farm is your inheritance and you don't owe him anything for that portion."

"Smart," Yvette positioned the oil pan under the nut. "The only way Luke gets an immediate partial settlement is if, and only if, he reduces the total to what is fair. Otherwise, he'll have to wait until we go to court and that may cost him his farm," she unscrewed the stopper. "But until the children move back, and Luke and the judge consent to reduce and delay the settlement, I still have to be ready for the worst."

As oil poured into the pan, a car turned in the drive.

"Here comes the answer to our prayers," Clara sounded jubilant.

"Please don't toy with me, Mom," Yvette scooted from under Clara's car. "I hurt enough."

"See for yourself."

Yvette sat up. It *was* them. Her heart beat a rapid tattoo.

The car stopped in front of her, a door opened, and Tanya tumbled out, dashed toward Yvette and fell into her arms.

"Oh, Mommy, it's *so good* to be home."

"What brings you here?" Yvette's voice wobbled and tears leaked from her eyes as she smelled the sweet Barbie shampoo scent in her daughter's hair.

"We're home to stay," Greg said. "Dad was a complete jerk tonight; he hasn't changed and he hasn't kept his promises. We'd rather help you on the farm than be strung along with promises he never intends to keep."

Yvette struggled to her feet and hugged all three children at once. "I'm glad you came back. So glad. But are you sure this is what you want? Are you *sure* you won't run back to Dad when you get tired of working, or if he ends up doing the things he promised after all?"

"We're *sure*," Kyle and Greg chorused, pulling back from the hug.

"There will be loads of work here," Kyle explained, "but you are fair and will work as hard as we do. And you won't make promises you can't keep. Anyhow, Tanya needs her mom."

"You won't yell at us or treat us like slaves," Greg added. "And you'll teach us how to be decent young men. I don't want to be like Dad."

"Neither do I," Kyle said.

"You don't have to be like he is now," Yvette kissed Tanya's forehead, "but I'd like you to be like he was those months after he finished the Batterer's Education Program. Even if he was pretending, he was behaving like a loving husband and father."

"Your mom is forgiving and wise," Clara laid a hand on the shoulders of both boys. "If you remember what your dad was like then, you will always have an example to follow."

"What's wrong with Grandma's car?" Kyle flicked an ant off the hood.

"Nothing. I'm changing the oil. It's overdue."

Greg picked up the new oil filter. "Changing oil will be my job. Dad taught me how."

"Can I help?" Tanya begged. "Greg's nice to me now."

"That sounds like a good plan," Yvette patted the girl's shoulder. "While Greg and Tanya finish changing the oil, Grandma and I will clean and grade the eggs, which haven't been done all week, and Kyle can have his choice of making fresh iced garden tea for all of us, or helping us with the eggs. Oh, I'm *so glad* to have you all home again," she felt for her mom's hand and squeezed it.

Resources

Christian:

Alsdurf, James & Phyllis Alsdurf. *Battered into Submission, The Tragedy of Wife Abuse In the Christian Home.* InterVarsity Press, Downers Grove, IL, 1989

Bilezikian, Gilbert. *Beyond Sex Roles, What the Bible Says About a Woman's Place in Church and Family,* second edition. Baker Books, Grand Rapids, MI, 1985

Fortune, Marie M. *Keeping the Faith, Guidance for Christian Women Facing Abuse.* HarperSanFrancisco/HarperCollins, NY, 1987

Hegstrom, Paul. *Angry Men and the Women Who Love Them, Breaking the Cycle of Physical and Emotional Abuse.* Beacon Hill Press, Kansas City, MO, 1999

Kroeger, Catherine Clark & James R Beck, editors. *Women, Abuse, and the Bible, How Scripture Can Be Used to Hurt or Heal.* Baker Books, Grand Rapids, MI, 1996

Kroeger, Catherine Clark & Nancy Nason-Clark. *No Place for Abuse, Biblical & Practical Resources to Counteract Domestic Violence.* InterVarsity Press, Downer's Grove, IL, 2001

Rinck, Dr. Margaret J. *Christian Men Who Hate Women, Healing Hurting Relationships* Pyranee Books, Zondervan, Grand Rapids, MI 1990

Smith, Conrad. *Best Friends. (Why just be married when you can be Best Friends?)* Navpress, Colorado Springs, CO, 1989, second printing 1991.

Secular:

Bancroft, Lundy. *When Dad Hurts Mom, Helping Your Children Heal the Wounds of Witnessing Abuse.* Berkley Books, New York, 2004

Ibid, *Why Does He Do That? Inside the Minds of Angry and Controlling Men.* G.P. Putnam's Sons, New York, 2002

Evans, Patricia. *The Verbally Abusive Relationship, How to Recognize it and How to Respond.* Bob Adams, Inc. Holbrook, MA, 1992